Twelve *military heroes.*
Twelve *indomitable heroines.*
One **UNIFORMLY HOT!** *miniseries.*

Don't miss Harlequin Blaze's first 12-book
continuity series, featuring irresistible soldiers
from all branches of the armed forces.

Watch for:

LETTERS FROM HOME by Rhonda Nelson
(Army Rangers—June 2009)

THE SOLDIER by Rhonda Nelson
(Special Forces—July 2009)

STORM WATCH by Jill Shalvis
(National Guard—August 2009)

HER LAST LINE OF DEFENSE by Marie Donovan
(Green Berets—September 2009)

RIPPED! by Jennifer LaBrecque
(Paratrooper—October 2009)

SEALED AND DELIVERED by Jill Monroe
(Navy SEALs—November 2009)

CHRISTMAS MALE by Cara Summers
(Military Police—December 2009)

Uniformly Hot!
The Few. The Proud. The Sexy as Hell.

Blaze™

Dear Reader,

I was so very excited to be asked to be part of the UNIFORMLY HOT! miniseries, because, quite frankly, what could be sexier than a strong, capable hero's hero?

Then I realized that although I had a family friend who was a former SEAL, I didn't really know much about that part of the military. I began an amazing journey learning not just what it takes to become a SEAL, but also about the career-long training and the commitment these men make. I really stand in awe of these men, but also the women and families that support them along the way. All I can do is say thank you for your sacrifices.

I had a lot of fun learning about BUDs and SQT and of course downloading pictures of SEALs in action off the Internet—that kind of research could go on for days! I did take a few liberties in the name of fiction, but I hope *SEALed and Delivered* lives up to the awesome reality.

I love to hear from readers. You can visit me on the Web at www.jillmonroebooks.com or www.authortalk.tv.

All my best,

Jill

Jill Monroe

SEALED AND DELIVERED

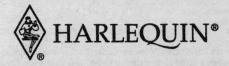

HARLEQUIN®

TORONTO • NEW YORK • LONDON
AMSTERDAM • PARIS • SYDNEY • HAMBURG
STOCKHOLM • ATHENS • TOKYO • MILAN • MADRID
PRAGUE • WARSAW • BUDAPEST • AUCKLAND

Recycling programs
for this product may
not exist in your area.

ISBN-13: 978-0-373-79509-3

SEALED AND DELIVERED

ABOUT THE AUTHOR

Jill Monroe makes her home in Oklahoma with her family. When not writing, she spends way too much time on the Internet completing "research" or updating her blog. Even when writing, she's thinking of ways to avoid cooking.

Books by Jill Monroe

HARLEQUIN BLAZE
245—SHARE THE DARKNESS
304—HITTING THE MARK
362—TALL, DARK AND FILTHY RICH
378—PRIMAL INSTINCTS

HARLEQUIN TEMPTATION
1003—NEVER NAUGHTY ENOUGH

Don't miss any of our special offers. Write to us at the following address for information on our newest releases.

Harlequin Reader Service
U.S.: 3010 Walden Ave., P.O. Box 1325, Buffalo, NY 14269
Canadian: P.O. Box 609, Fort Erie, Ont. L2A 5X3

Thanks again to Pink, my amazing daughters and all my family for their support.

To Gena Showalter—may everyone have a friend as good!

Thanks to Kassia Krozser, who's been with me from the beginning—some day I promise to put in a serial comma, and you'll know that's for you.

For technical help, I often turned to HelenKay Dimon and James Miyazawa—thanks so much to the pair of you.

Alison Kent, Betty Sanders, Donnell Epperson, Sheila Fields, Stephanie Feagan and Wendy Duren all allowed me to bounce an idea off them, and I appreciate it so much.

Many thanks to both Kathryn Lye and Deidre Knight.

Prologue

NEW CITY. NEW LIFE. New bookstore.

Same old, same old, in the self-help section.

Hailey Sutherland ran her fingers along the familiar titles; most of these books she already owned.

Maybe the Problem IS Your Sex Life.

Owned it. And yeah, the problem probably *was* her sex life, in that she always picked complete jerks to have it with.

Make Love Happen to You.

Yeah, as if women hadn't been trying to make *that* reality for centuries. Besides, the book was mainly a bunch of self-esteem exercises. She and her self-esteem had come to an understanding some time ago. They loathed one another.

Becoming the Woman You Are Meant to Be.

"Come to mama," Hailey whispered as she pulled this new book from off the high shelf. She thumbed through the glossy pages. Personality quizzes, wish-list management sheets, projection tips… With a sigh, Hailey returned the book to the shelf. She'd done it all before.

Yet, here she was again in the bookstore looking for the answer. Her cell phone rang just as she was returning the book to the shelf.

"Hailey, you won't believe it. I've just booked a wedding shower in the Tea Room," gushed her sister, Rachel. She'd always been the enthusiastic one.

"I don't believe it," Hailey deadpanned.

"Well, believe it, and I'm going to need you to stop at the paint store on the way back home."

"So you finally decided on a color?"

"Papaya Whip."

"Sounds yummy."

"I think it's as close to the original color as we're going to get," she said with a heavy sigh. Her sister's search for *the exact same shade* that highlighted the Tea Room's ornate wooden scrollwork since the 1920s had been mercenary. Just like Hailey, Rachel had returned to The Sutherland a few months ago to take away control of their family bed & breakfast from the management company they'd hired after their parents' death five years ago.

Management company, what a joke. They'd mainly managed to run the place into obscurity and out of cash. But Hailey and Rachel were determined to change that. The B&B had kept generations of Sutherlands off the streets and employed, and it wasn't going down on their watch.

"With only two weeks, it'll have to do," her sister continued.

Hailey almost dropped the phone. "Did you say two weeks? As in, we're hosting a wedding shower in the Tea Room in two weeks?" Her stomach began to hurt.

"I had to take the booking," Rachel defended without sounding defensive. "You know how much we need the cash." Enthusiastic and practical…that was her baby sis.

With fewer and fewer reservations, her sister's now exhausted savings caught them up on the pile of unpaid bills the management company had left them with. Hailey's "rainy day" was to cover the soon-to-be established marketing plan that would return The Sutherland to San Diego's preeminent social spot.

At one point the Tea Room in The Sutherland had been *the place* for showers and parties in this area of California. It seemed a lot more doable three months ago. "Okay, but two weeks? We've never hosted anything like that before."

Rachel groaned into the phone. "Come on. You've been engaged three times."

"True, but all I had to do was show up for those parties."

"I'm sure something rubbed off. We can do it, Hailey. Look how easy everything has gone so far. We were both between jobs at the same time so we could come back and take advantage of that nice little loophole that let us drop the management company as if it's hot."

"You're still doing the song-lyric thing," Hailey teased. After gradation, Rachel had grabbed her guitar and drove herself to Nashville to try and make it as a songwriter. Song titles often made it into her everyday conversation.

Rachel ignored her and went on. "It's as if fate wants us to revitalize The Sutherland."

Fate and a lot of hard work.

"Okay, paint store it is," Hailey agreed and she closed her cell phone. She turned on her heel, nearly running into a large cardboard display. Overhead, a flashy red banner hung from the ceiling proclaiming, Don't Wait On Fate—Jump-Start Your Life Today!

Fate.

Strange, her sister had just mentioned the word and here she was almost being attacked by it. The display was talking her language. Jump-start life—sounded like self-help to her. Although what awaited her inside the cardboard display was not a book, but rather a deck of cards. Fate Delivery Cards. Somehow those cards managed to make their way onto the counter and into her bag with a colorful and very detail-oriented book on ceramic tile—the real reason for her trip to the store.

And since she was in the mood, she'd chalk her purchase up to fate, rather than poor impulse control.

1

Two Weeks Later

NOT EVEN THE SOUND of footsteps echoed in the Naval Special Warfare Center as Lieutenant Commander Nathanial "Nate" Peterson led his trainees through the corridor. Each exercise had grown steadily more dangerous, and even though they'd gone over every aspect in the classroom, actuality always heightened the senses. Made the tension more acute.

"Where's the party?" a trainee called laughingly from the back. "I hear you always know."

Nate's shoulders straightened. Strange thing about tension...some soldiers rose to the challenge, some men snapped and some, well, some of them bellowed smart-ass remarks to their superior.

"You're never going to live that reputation down." Riley laughed quietly beside him. Their steps slowed as they approached the locker area where the men would change into their wetsuits.

Nate shot a disgusted look at the man he'd known since their BUD/S training class. True, Nate had earned a reputation as a man who liked to play hard but he worked just as hard. Harder, actually. And yes, he always knew where the party was. But there was something all SEALs understood, and that was to keep priorities in order.

Something that smartass hadn't yet realized. Some men knew and understood from the beginning when to turn *it* off and on. Others needed that knowledge worked into their thick heads. Like the Ensign behind him. As it had been for Nate a few years back.

Nate stopped, and turned to stare at the man who'd called the question, not needing to see the man to know who he was. Harper treaded toward a familiarity he hadn't yet earned. "Maybe a party isn't what you should be concerned about, Ensign Harper. Your swim time is slipping."

The younger man's back stiffened, and the other trainees hustled quickly into the locker room.

"So's your conditioning," Nate added. This next minute would be crucial. How Harper handled the criticism would prove to Nate if that man had what it took to earn his Trident. SEALs took evaluation and adapted and made themselves better.

The Ensign swallowed. "I've passed."

Eight years ago Nate *was* this guy, with his BUD/S, Hell Week and Jump School behind him. All that stood in the way between the Ensign and the Trident that turned a man into a SEAL was The Finishing School or the official name—SEAL Qualifications Training, here on Coronado. With the end prize in sight, that was something a man could get cocky about. But that cockiness *would* be a downfall…no question about it.

Although surely *that* had been long gone in Nate by the time he'd hit SQT. Some hardass instructor had ensured it. A man lost his swagger when he was wet, cold and covered in sand. Lost the arrogance, because his life, and that of his Team, depended on professionalism not ego.

Now it was his turn to make sure these men thought only of focus and discipline, and each other, not themselves.

Unfortunately.

"*Minimum* standards are forty-two pushups in two minutes. You content with the minimum?" Nate asked.

Something stony and strong-willed flared inside the other man's eyes. *Good.* "No sir," he answered, with nothing but determination in his voice.

No sir was right. Harper might just be the best man to come out of this class.

"Suit up," Nate ordered and turned, not waiting for a response. Their next drill was in an hour.

Once the candidates were out of earshot, Riley glanced at him. "How do you keep a straight face during that?"

Nate let his guard down a little and smiled. "By counting the hours until I'm out of here," Nate told him as they continued down the hall, just the two of them. "Besides, if I'm not on the Teams, I'm damn well going to make sure my replacement can do the job."

"Still doing the physical therapy?" Riley asked.

Nate shrugged. Three months ago, he'd been injured while rescuing a pirated freighter with rigged explosives. Now another man had his spot on his Team. While Nate was teaching. The muscles of his right leg cramped, and he breathed through his nose. *Control.*

But as soon as he was healthy, goodbye settling for being an instructor, goodbye Coronado Island, goodbye San Diego.

"If it's any consolation, I've heard good things about the training you're providing. I guarantee your fresh-off-deployment perspective will save a life."

He knew what Riley was trying to do, and appreciated the effort but men didn't join the SEALs for a pat on the back. Most of the stuff he and his fellow SEALs had done was so covert the files wouldn't be opened until he was long gone. Little would ever make the history books.

But Nate's friend did point out a reality. In another year, these men might be beside him down range. Most of these men he'd be happy to serve next to as SEALs... but they weren't there yet. He might not like instructing, but he'd make damn sure the new guys wouldn't hold a Team back. They'd be ready on day one. "So is there a party?" Riley asked hopefully.

"After this exercise, I'm on my way to pick up the beer," he said, with a wink.

"Hoo yah."

"WHOO HOO! NAKED!"

The echoes of laughter flowed from the newly-re-painted Tea Room into the modernized kitchen. Hailey glanced at her sister Rachel and smiled. "Those are the sounds of a good party."

"I have to hand it to you, Hailey. You did a great job with this wedding shower."

"As you've pointed out, I've had three. Glad something useful came out of those relationships." With a flourish, Hailey topped the last of the mousse with chocolate shavings. "Of course you can't really go wrong with chocolate and champagne."

"Or naked beefcake."

"I don't think The Sutherland is quite ready for that." Hailey lifted the tray and scooted backwards, pushing the door out into the Tea Room with her backside.

"The chocolate's here!" called Amy Bradford, the bride to be. Although they'd been friends since school, they'd lost track of each other. Reuniting with old pals was another positive she could attribute to returning home.

"Wait," said a redhead, who Hailey had learned was the maid of honor. "The girls and I chipped in and bought you something to wear on your wedding night." The other guests met this announcement with everything from giggles to a few oohhs. In a flourish, she presented to the bride a large paper-wrapped box tied with a bright yellow bow.

"Five bucks says that box is empty," Rachel whispered.

Hailey glanced at the dozen or so women. Despite their pastel sundresses, these ladies looked like they were up for a little mischief. Hailey shook her head. "Not taking that bet."

Careful not to rip the ribbon, the bride did indeed open an empty box to the laughter of the group. With the last present now revealed, Hailey and her sister moved forward to serve the desserts. The rest of the guests made room on the table for the treat their little B&B had always been known for in decades past.

Amy glanced up toward Hailey. "I can't tell you how excited I am that you have reopened The Sutherland. When I was seven and a flower girl, my aunt had her shower here."

"Amy's had her heart set on this place ever since," the maid of honor added. "I couldn't believe my luck when I found out you just happened to have a free weekend."

The two sisters looked at one another. Yeah, they had plenty of free weekends. But it was nice to keep up the illusion of exclusivity.

"It was fate," Amy said with the kind of beaming smile only a woman about to be married could get away with.

Had Hailey ever worn such an expression at any of *her* wedding showers? She doubted it.

"And the Tea Room looks just as beautiful as I remember," Amy continued.

"Tell your friends," Hailey encouraged, ever the businesswoman, and ready to tear her thoughts away from her failed engagements.

After serving the ladies, and refreshing their tea, Hailey and Rachel began to discreetly clear away the wrapping paper. "I can't tell you how relieved I am," Rachel said quietly. This was the first real test of their hosting skills. While The Sutherland had been in their family for generations, and they'd performed their fair share of serving, their mother had always been the hostess.

Just to make sure the place shined, the last coat of paint to the Tea Room had gone up sometime around two that morning. Now looking around the beautiful banquet hall, Hailey experienced a swell of pride to see her home restored to as close as the sisters could remember it. The cypress wainscoting she was never allowed to touch gleamed. Prisms of light reflected around the room from the newly washed crystals hanging from the chandelier. The cornice molding gleamed with its new coat of papaya whip.

She just hoped no one looked under the crisp linens because the tables were a disaster. The management team apparently held an aversion to coasters. After hearing the delight of their new guests, the memory of all their hard work faded away. Grandpa Sutherland would be proud.

"This dessert is to die for," one of the ladies exclaimed.

Hailey winked at her sister.

"What's next?" asked another guest.

The smile faded from her sister's face.

The bridal party had already played Groom Trivia, Wedding Night Surprise, opened the presents and consumed dozens of champagne soaked strawberries. Hailey had heard so many off-color wedding night jokes, she could probably start a stand-up routine. "What's next?" her sister mouthed.

After being awake for nearly twenty-four hours, Hailey had hoped it was a nap.

The bride had mentioned something about fate, and ding ding ding, that little word triggered a memory in her sleep deprived and work fogged brain of a bookstore purchase not so long ago. So far fate had worked on their side, maybe they should keep it rolling. "Our *last* game will be ready as soon as we've cleared," Hailey told them demurely, then turned to race up the stairs two at a time to her bedroom. If her grandma had seen her run through the hallway like that...

Four months ago, the funding for her junior assistant curator position at the Dallas Museum of Art ran out, leaving her jobless. Back in San Diego, she'd reclaimed the bookshelf-lined room that had been hers. The corner room with a small window to the ocean had been her refuge from the oh-so-embarrassing job of working in her family's B&B when she was growing up.

While her friends were hitting the sandy beaches,

she'd been learning the secrets to making spider web Grenache, or worse, taking care of the guests' laundry. She smiled at the memory of her teen angst. What she wouldn't give now to sit beside the large stove and talk to her mother as she made the delicious meals for their guests, or hear her grandma's lessons of how a real lady crossed her legs at the ankle.

A time when she didn't have to worry about bills. Hailey wouldn't lose the battle for The Sutherland before she'd really had a chance to implement her ideas. Growing up in a work of art, like The Sutherland, with so much history, it was no wonder she'd been drawn to preserving and showcasing the past. Now she was saving something infinitely more personal…her family's legacy. Though she had work to do on the first step— save this wedding shower. She scanned the various self-help titles that now filled her bookshelf, looking for the bright red packaging. There they were—the Fate Delivery cards.

She peeled off the plastic wrapping as she raced down the hallway, stuffing the cellophane wrapper into her apron. Hailey plastered on a serene expression reminiscent of their mother as she returned to the Tea Room where Rachel finished the last of the clean-up. Their guests were talking quietly, looking over the various gifts the bride had received.

Needing to set some kind of mood here, Hailey flipped the switch cutting off the light provided by the chandeliers. The natural sunlight filled the room with its warm tones.

"Okay, ladies, the time is now," she said, her voice low and laced with dramatic flourish. An instant hush fell over the room. Hey, they were into it. Maybe Hailey had finally found the silver lining of taking that acting class in college, which sadly had led her to Fiancé Failure Number One.

"Amy is about to embark on a new journey that fate has ordained. Now it's our turn to see what's destined for the rest of us." Hailey fanned the cards in her hand. "Pick your fate, but don't look at it."

Each guest in the circle took a card, holding it to her chest, giggling to one another about taking peeks. Hailey held out the deck to Amy.

"Maybe I shouldn't take a card," the soon-to-be-bride said.

"Oh, take a card, Amy," said the maid of honor with a quick nudge. "It's just a game."

With a good-humored smile, Amy slid a card from the deck and placed it face down on her lap.

Hailey returned the unused cards back in the card-board box they came in and set them aside. "Now ladies, the bride will choose who goes first," she instructed, making the rules up as she went. "You will show your card to the rest of the group, then look at it yourself. Some of the fates are silly and fun, but others are true life-changing destinies."

She hoped.

Maybe.

Hailey backed away to the wall where her sister watched. "Fate had ordained?" Rachel whispered to her. "I've forgetten how dramatic you can be."

"If it works, it works. Did you catch my emphasis on the word *last,* when I talked about this game?"

"Here's hoping they did," Rachel said, hiding a yawn with her hand.

"Tori, you go first," Amy said, clearly fired up to get this game going.

Tori turned her card to show to the rest of the group. A few groans followed.

"Oh, you have an easy one," one of the ladies called out.

Tori twirled the card around and read aloud. "Kick off your shoes and run into the wind." Then she glanced at her friends, raising a brow. "Speak for yourself on that being easy. Once I get these heels off, they're not going back on."

"No, you can't get out of it," Amy insisted, now fully involved in the game. "The beach is right outside this window."

Floor to ceiling windows dominated one side of the Tea Room. Shrouded in beautiful lace, the curtains allowed natural sunlight to filter into the room. But sweep them aside, and the Italian tiled terrace beckoned, as did the beach. The perfect place to kick off shoes and run.

"I'll handle this," Hailey said as she pushed off the wall and walked to the curtains that hid the glass door to the terrace. After draping the heavy material in the ornate holdbacks, she unlocked the doors so the women could step outside.

"Oh, this is beautiful," several of the guests murmured as they stepped out onto the terrace, their heels clacking on the original tile some Sutherland relative had installed. She and Rachel hadn't done much to this area but clean up the landscaping, although her sister had big plans to add tables and chairs, and serve brunch accompanied by an ocean breeze. There were other ways for the B&B to earn money besides guests in the rooms.

"Tori, just because it's pretty out here doesn't mean

we've forgotten why we've come. You've got some running to do."

With a sigh, Tori reached down and slid the straps off her heels, and carefully tucked her shoes to the side. "Here I go!" she called out.

Hailey had to join in the laughter as Tori took off down the beach in her sundress, the wind blowing in her hair. She turned to run backwards, raising her hands in the air like a winning marathon winner.

"Oh, no. Tori, look out."

But Tori was too far away to hear Amy's warning call, and Tori jogged right into the very solid chest of a man enjoying the beach with his dog. Now off balance, Tori began to slide to the sand until the man dropped his Frisbee and caught her. He steadied her against his body.

Amy's warnings turned to laughter as Tori glanced up to her savior's face. Then smiled. Slowly. The man didn't let go.

"Get his name," one of the guests called.

"And his number," Amy added.

"I tell you, she meets men in the weirdest ways," said the maid of honor. "Amy, choose who should go next."

Amy glanced over at Tori, who was now tilting her head and brushing sand off the man's arm. "Should we wait for her?"

"No, that's going to take awhile. Look at him, he's a goner."

With a nod, Amy agreed. "Then you should go."

Just as the maid of honor was about to reveal her card, her cell phone rang. Looking down at the display she frowned. "Amy, I'm sorry, I have to take this." The maid of honor thrust the card toward Hailey and quickly made her way back inside the Tea Room.

"Oh, but—" Hailey stammered.

"Show it, Hailey," Amy said.

Hailey glanced across the veranda to the Tea Room. It didn't appear as if the maid of honor was coming back any time soon. Well, Hailey had bought these cards for a reason. Maybe now it was time to do something for herself. With a sigh, she turned the card toward her guests.

To a lot of laughter.

"Oh, that's hilarious."

"That could be really good or really bad."

With some alarm, Hailey quickly turned the card over and read, "Kiss the first man you see."

No. NO. And hell no. Getting away from men was the second reason she'd come home. Hailey wasn't about to actually throw herself at one. And, as far as she was concerned, certainly nothing good ever came from kissing.

Some of the women were already moving toward the end of the terrace to search the sandy beach for available men, their skirts twirling in the breeze. "I see a few contenders way down the beach," one said, smiling.

"Just think, five minutes earlier and it would be *you* in the arms of that guy instead of Tori," said another.

Tori was welcome to him. To all men.

A strange whooshing sounded over their heads. Hailey's skirt practically lifted to her chin thanks to a strong, very out-of-place gust of air. Okay, not completely out of place. Shielding her eyes with one hand, and trying to hold strands of her carefully constructed chignon in place, Hailey looked up to spot the now familiar helicopter hovering over the ocean.

The Navy SEALs were back.

Hailey suppressed a groan. The SEALs had been conducting their training nearby on a semi-regular basis ever since she'd returned to Coronado. But Saturday afternoons had always been blissfully free of the noise and the wind. Why now during their first formal event?

The door of the helicopter's cabin slid open sharply and some kind of rope was thrown out, the end suspended just a few feet above the water.

"What's going on?" asked a guest.

"Would anyone like more tea?" Hailey tried, but no one was paying her any attention. Everyone's focus was on the chopper.

At the cabin's entrance, a man emerged, clad in a skintight black wetsuit. Hell, she might as well look, too. She squinted, but Hailey was too far away to make out features. Besides, she was paying too much attention to the fact that he was solid, lean muscle. She swallowed as he caught and pulled the rope toward him, wrapping it around his wrists and hands while securing it with his long legs. Hailey gasped as he flung himself over the side of the helicopter, strength evident in his every move. Her mouth went dry as he slid down the rope, heading for the rough, churning water. When he reached the end of the rope, he dove into the ocean, leaving little splash.

"Did you see that?" one of the women asked, her voice hushed.

How could she not?

After a moment he resurfaced, and the breath she'd been holding finally released.

"I'd think that would qualify as the first man you see,

Hailey," Rachel said, not able to suppress the laughter from her voice.

"Hope you have a nice bikini to wear to swim out there to meet him," the bride said, joining in the fun. "But look."

With reluctance, Hailey took her gaze off the man easily treading in the ocean to find even more men scrambling out of the helicopter.

Great. This was just great. The last thing she wanted to do was kiss a man, and fate had sent them literally falling out of the sky.

2

"WHICH ONE ARE YOU GOING to choose?" Rachel asked, her voice filled with laughter. Gleeful, encouraging-of-others to torment her sister kind of laughter. Now Hailey didn't feel so bad about the "haircut" she'd given Rachel at the age of four.

"Five, six, seven," Amy counted as each man propelled himself onto the rope. "And they keep coming. So would the first one technically be the first one out of the helicopter?"

"I have a self-help book that would be perfect to cure you of that sarcasm. It means you're hiding a lot of pain," Hailey whispered to her sister.

"Nah," Rachel said with a growing smile.

"No, I think it would be the first one she'd reach," said another guest.

"Well, that could depend on which direction she swam, giving her a choice."

These ladies were applying the same kind of arguments and logic one would use when discussing String Theory or macroeconomics. It was just a guy.

"So which one?" Amy asked.

Curious eyes now gazed her way.

None of them.

Thankfully, the whooshing sounds from the helicopter drew their guests' attention away from her.

"Oh, they're leaving," one of the ladies said, clearly disappointed.

"Just the helicopter. The guys are still in the water. Look."

Sure enough eight men waded in the water. Sometimes they would point, or go under the waves for a moment, but basically stayed in the same general location, performing what looked like drills.

"Now that can't feel good. The water is cold this time of year. Why would they be out there?" asked one of the women, frowning.

The bride leaned forward. "One word—training. Those are Navy SEALs."

"SEALs?"

The sisters nodded in confirmation. They'd witnessed this little scenario play out with several of their female tourists. First the confusion, then the excitement followed by the gawking.

"Why didn't you say so before?" Two of the women rushed to the railing to get a closer look, their heels clacking against the tile. *Yeah, it was pretty much downhill from here.*

"I didn't realize you could see them from the B&B."

"All up and down this area. They train right on Coronado," Hailey told them.

One woman, who Hailey thought might be the guest book attendant, pulled out her camera phone and snapped a picture.

"What's going on?" Tori asked. She'd left her new

friend, slipping a note inside her purse as she rejoined the group.

Amy looped her arm through Tori's and led her to where she could see the beach. She pointed out toward the water. "Hailey's fate is to kiss one of them."

"Lucky her," Tori said, turning appreciative eyes out to the ocean.

Amy propped her hand on her hip. "Didn't you just have a bit of luck yourself? Was that a phone number I saw you squirreling away?"

A slight flush touched Tori's cheeks. "I have a date Friday night."

"Tori, you're the only person I know who could snag a date at a wedding shower."

This *had* to be good for business. Following clean up, and a nap, Hailey would be buying more sets of cards. After she ducked out on fulfilling the dictates of the card thrusted upon her, that is.

Amy put an arm around Hailey's shoulder. "I see you backing away. Don't think we forgot about you, kiddo. You still have a Fate waiting for you."

When had the bride become so menacing? Maybe Hailey wouldn't be buying those additional decks after all.

"Come on, ladies, you know I'm not swimming out there," she told them, with a touch of fun firmness that said she understood she was in on the joke.

"Maybe you won't have to," Tori said, pointing at the ocean. Two of the men had broken away from the group and were now swimming straight for The Sutherland. Straight toward her.

Hailey's eyes widened as she realized one of them wasn't swimming, and appeared to be unconscious. She sucked in a breath, then watched in amazement as the swimmer rolled the other onto his back, then secured the inert man to his side. With strong sure strokes, he headed for shore. Swimming from that distance would have been exhausting, but pulling the weight of another full-grown man must have been almost impossible. She scanned the beach for some kind of boat. Maybe she could meet them half way.

Kicking off her heels, she lifted her skirt and flew down the tiled stairs of the terrace to the sand below.

"Looks like she found her kissing candidate." Whistles and catcalls from the shower guests followed Hailey onto the beach.

"Call 9-1-1," she hollered and she raced toward the man, kicking up sand behind her.

"What?" The ladies' teasing turned into murmurs of concern.

The swimmer was now standing waist deep in the water. She'd never seen anything like him. Clad shoulder to foot in a dark, skintight wetsuit, he emerged from the ocean. The powerful muscles of his thighs flowed with strength. His suit outlined every solid ripple of the lean lines of his shoulders and arms. He reminded her of Colossus, the powerful X-Man who transformed into solid, dark steel. Her second fiancé sold a ton of those comic books in his store, and witnessing someone with such a show of strength in aid of another, she understood Colossus' appeal.

The SEAL's burden still hadn't moved, and her breath shallowed in panic. The cool water of the Pacific splashed at her ankles as she raced to meet them.

"Stay back," he warned.

"Let me help," she offered, seeing the fatigue lining his face. "I'm stronger than I look."

At five feet two inches, she must look pretty scrawny to this big man. With a reluctant nod from him, she looped the injured man's arm around her shoulder, taking only a little of the weight. Colossus still managed the bulk of the load. "My friends are calling for help. 9-1-1," she added.

"I've already radioed for the helicopter."

"From in the water?" she asked, feeling almost instantly silly. Seeing the men up close in their wetsuits or rash guards or whatever they called that tight-fitting dive garb, there was no question they were military. Of course they had some kind of waterproof device. "I know CPR."

Colossus shook his head as they eased the man to the sand and positioned him on his back. "He's breathing. He hit his head and blacked out. I made sure he didn't take in any water."

"Oh," she said, sitting back on her heels, her breath coming out in little pants. Okay, well. Colossus seemed to have everything in hand. What was the protocol in a situation like this? Offer him some mousse as they waited for rescue? It didn't matter. He wasn't paying her any attention, instead checking on his fallen comrade, counting out his pulse against his watch and lifting the man's eyelids.

Water ran crazy paths down his forehead and cheeks, but he never brushed it away, utterly focused on the task at hand.

"Is there anything I can do?" she asked, wanting to help.

The man simply shook his head. He didn't seem to

mind the cold she knew he must be feeling. His breathing was heavy, but he hadn't handed over responsibility for the other soldier to her so he could take a break. His words had been confident, and his actions seemed to back him up. Unlike Fiancé Failure Number Three who never wasted an opportunity to offer an "expert" opinion, but was only adept at giving completely useless advice.

After a few minutes, the man beside her signaled to his crew still in the water. With a few waves of the hand, that Hailey was sure meant something, they continued on with whatever it was they were doing.

Now, after taking care of everything and everyone else, the SEAL lowered himself to the sand and stretched out his long legs. She tried to avert her eyes, she really did, but that dark wetsuit he wore like a second skin left nothing to the imagination. Actually, both her imagination and reality were enjoying a great show. He finally slicked the water from his face, then glanced her way. His eyes widened as if he was seeing her for the first time.

"Than—"

"Uhh," the man between them stirred, reaching toward his head. A trickle of blood mixed with the water from the ocean was beginning to trail down his temple.

"Don't touch."

"Try not to touch," she said, injecting calm into her voice.

They spoke at the same time. Only his words sounded more like an order.

The injured man blinked a few times against the sun, then his gaze settled on her. "What kind of salvation is this?" He slowly rubbed the saltwater from his eyes. "An angel, and my head hurts like a bi—"

"That's enough, Ensign Ortiz," Colossus said, authority lining every word.

The Ensign's gaze cut toward Colossus. "What happened?" he asked.

Yeah, she was curious about that, too.

"Head."

Okay, not helpful.

The man on the sand squeezed his eyes tight for a moment, took a deep breath and then with a force of will she'd never seen in another person, pushed himself up to a sitting position. "I'm ready."

It didn't fully sink in that the Ensign, who was unconscious only seconds before, had every intention of going back into the water. And that Colossus was going to let him. "But you can't," she said, scrambling to her feet. Colossus had already smoothly stood, his tall frame blocking the sun from her eyes.

"It's his job," Colossus told her.

With another show of will, the Ensign shoved to his feet. He barely remained upright, then gathered his balance steadily. "Ready," he repeated.

"Look this way," Colossus ordered. He examined the Ensign's eyes, his face relaxing a tick. "Knots on your head?" he asked.

The younger man felt along his scalp, shaking his head no.

Colossus angled his head toward the water. "Okay."

With a look of relief, the other man began to walk to the ocean.

"But he's bleeding," she protested.

"The saltwater will take care of his wound," Colossus stated, seemingly unconcerned.

She glanced back toward The Sutherland. "I have some anti-bacterial foam—"

Colossus's lips moved as if he was trying to suppress a smile. "He's trained to fight with worse."

She swallowed. Of course he was.

"I can't believe what he's doing," she said, watching the Ensign as he made a smooth dive into the waves, and swam toward the other men still treading water. "Maybe we should have waited until the paramedics arrived." Yet with every stroke he seemed to gain more strength.

"I've had combat medical training. I checked for signs of concussion. He's fine."

These men lived in a different world, far away from the corresponding bridal ribbons, chocolate shavings and the waterproof bandages she would have suggested next.

She turned away from the swimming soldier to face Colossus, and that's when her gaze collided with the steel gray of his. Her breath hitched. Sure she'd noticed the strength of his body outlined so perfectly in his wetsuit, his air of authority and control as he'd handled the situation with the injured soldier, but this man's eyes were something else. Something inviting and very, very sexy.

A cool breeze from off the ocean fanned her face, her bare arms. Although she tried to fight back a shiver, her nipples tightened. She hoped he'd think her bodily reaction was due to the weather and not the hot, suddenly carnal thoughts popping into her mind about him. Like running her fingers along his arm to feel the solidity of his muscles. To lick that drop of saltwater off his cheek. Or discover just how one gets a wetsuit off a man. Zipper? Scissors? Who knew?

No. No. And hell no. These thoughts were ending right here. She was not in the market for a fling. Or a boyfriend. Boyfriends tended to become fiancés in her world. This would make Fiancé Failure Number Four. And that she was finding someone attractive that she didn't normally go for meant nothing. In fact, her virtually nonexistent male filtering system had probably just widened the search parameters.

Then Hailey realized they'd both been standing facing one another far longer than necessary. A pause, a tension sprang up between them, and hung heavily in the air. His gray eyes narrowed, something deep in those depths flared. Her lips parted, and she acknowledged her urge to lean into him, get closer. His gaze flickered to her lips, then returned to her face.

And what that brief glance at her mouth did to her.

Go. Now was the time for him to leave. To turn around and head back to the ocean.

"I'm glad your friend is going to be okay." The words rushed out of her. Okay, so she wasn't actually ready to let him go. "That was pretty impressive what you did."

He shrugged, obviously uncomfortable with that tiny bit of praise.

"I liked the way you rushed to help." Not that she'd done much, but it was nice to hear.

She should be uttering a quick goodbye, and get back to her guests. But her gaze settled on his lips and a rush of warmth blasted through her.

You're supposed to kiss him.

That heat became a fire. What would his lips feel like? Did she dare? With the fate card in mind, Hailey gave herself permission to do what she really wanted to do all along. She followed that push to be closer, and found herself tilting slightly forward. His hands raised, and—

The sounds of giggles had her taking a quick step back. Hailey looked away from Colossus to see Amy, Tori and her sister carrying their shoes and casually making their way towards her and the Navy SEAL.

"Oh, Hailey. That is definitely 'first man you see' material," Tori teased.

In addition to the cards, this would be the last time they served champagne at any wedding showers.

"I've been keeping my eye on you, and you haven't fulfilled your fate yet," Amy said with faux sternness as she handed Hailey the card.

Hailey's gaze went to her sister who only shrugged and flashed her a smile. Why had she even bothered looking at Rachel for help? She was obviously getting a kick out of this.

Colossus was retreating, clearly confused by the conversation, happy not to get involved. "Thanks again for your assistance." He was all business now.

Hailey would just have to ignore that disappointment she felt at the loss of heat between them. Well, from his side. She was still very, very hot.

"Wait, you can't go." Amy's voice lifted higher on each syllable.

"Right," Tori said, lifting up her nearly empty champagne glass. "Hailey hasn't kissed you yet."

Colossus paused. He glanced her way. "You Hailey?" he asked, interest in his eyes.

Did she hear a hopeful tone in his voice? Dear God she hoped so. Hailey surveyed the ladies all eyeing her Navy SEAL. Amy lifted a brow, but her lips twisted in a smile.

They didn't think she was going to do it.

They weren't egging her on because they thought it was funny or were trying to encourage her. They were goading her because it would be even funnier when she *didn't* kiss him. Well, now. She was having none of that. Hailey hadn't read a dozen self-help books on visualizing the goal and actualizing, for nothing.

Goal = Navy SEAL's lips.

Now for the actualization part.

Hailey straightened her shoulders, determinedly took the two steps to reach the man's side and tugged on his shoulder until he fully faced her. Surprise widened his eyes, but that was the last thing she saw as she closed hers, stood on tiptoe and pulled him down to meet her mouth.

For a moment, he stood still, his lips warm, firm and unmoving beneath hers.

One. Two. Three seconds and she was done. Fate fulfilled.

But apparently fate wasn't done with her yet, because her Navy SEAL had just gripped her hips and crushed her to his chest. The water from his wetsuit seeped to her breasts, making her shiver, but she didn't care because his lips weren't unmoving anymore. They were opening and drawing a sweet response from hers. His tongue traced the seam of her mouth, and a deep longing flowed inside her.

He smelled of the sea and ocean air, and tasted of salt and delicious man. Hailey wanted nothing more than to keep kissing him as she sunk her fingers into his short hair, still wet from the swim. And just when she settled into the kiss, his hands began to roam.

Hailey's heart raced, her legs weakened and she

could think of nothing better than to keep doing what she was doing.

So that's why she pushed herself away.

That shove was an effort, but she took a step back, and their gaze collided. His face was tight, and desire burned in his eyes. Desire burning for her. She sucked in a breath, but walked away. If she kept looking at the clear hunger in his confused eyes, she'd be right back in his arms. Instead, she stopped at the three stunned ladies staring at her. Hailey gave them a breezy smile. "Done."

The sand sifted between her toes as she ambled slowly back to The Sutherland where the rest of the guests waited for her on the terrace. She swore she felt Colossus's gaze on her back as she walked away from him, but that was ridiculous.

"Wait, Hailey," she heard her sister call, but she kept on walking.

After grabbing her shoes, she ascended the steps. She was greeted by a mixture of uncertainty from the guests. And in herself. Her self-imposed male isolation hadn't done much by way of inoculating her from their sweet temptation.

The maid of honor was only then leaving the Tea Room with cell phone still in hand. "What'd I miss?"

Hailey's fist tightened around the Fate Delivery Card for a moment before she thrust it at the woman whose fate she'd just fulfilled. "Here's your card."

NAVY SEAL TRAINING HAD prepared Nathaniel Peterson for a lot of things. But after Hell Week, Phase Two, SQT and two deployments he shouldn't have been caught off guard when a beautiful woman kissed him.

And he'd stood there like an idiot when she'd walked off. The hottest, most unexpected kiss of his life, and he failed to follow up. He deserved to watch her walk away, but oh, how he would remember the sweet taste of her mouth and curves of her body pressed to him.

"I can't believe she did that?" said one of the women.

They traded incredulous glances between themselves then began to laugh.

Stop standing there like an idiot.

"Okay, well, bye," said the one woman with a bunch of mismatched ribbons in her hair. She caught the arm of the woman who'd called him "first man you see material" and the two of them followed along the same path his kisser had fled.

The last lady eyed him up and down. Then, with a nod to herself, she whispered, "Her name's Hailey. She works at The Sutherland." With a point at the large Victorian, she took off, following the others.

A slow smile spread across his face. How could he not appreciate it when the locals provided much needed intel? Or the way Hailey's skirt cupped her ass as she climbed the stairs away from the beach. With a shake of his head, he turned and sprang into action, hitting the waves and swimming back to his trainees.

They continued to tread water; this long and cold endurance exercise would prepare them for the water insertions they'd practice next. From the tight looks on his men's faces, they were fighting grins. And losing.

"That looked real dangerous."

"We were considering whether or not you needed backup."

Yeah, yeah yeah. He probably deserved the razzing. But should he end it? Instructing was still so new to him. Training was exhausting, stressful work, and handling a few cracks from another SEAL was a low price to pay for pushing them as hard as he did. Besides, he'd already played hardass once today.

"She need mouth-to-mouth?"

Low price to pay to a point. "Shut it, before I drown you."

The water grew choppy, which signaled the helicopter's return. The men were then forced to handle their communication by hand signals. It was just as well. Nate had a few hand signals in mind that weren't Navy regulated.

A rope ladder descended from their transport above, and Nate supervised as each man made his way safely out of the water. He gripped the rung, and hauled himself out of the water, his knee aching with the effort. He gritted his teeth and began to ascend the ladder. It was no secret to the men he trained he'd rather be out with his Team than in San Diego, but orders were orders, and he had enough discipline to admit that until he was fully healed, he'd be more of a hindrance than a help.

It still didn't make him wish for something different.

Nor did it stop him from glancing once more at the beach. Commander Nate Peterson knew three things: he was in for a longer stretch in San Diego than he'd planned, his need for the woman who'd kissed him hadn't lessened, and he *would* see her again. He'd make sure of it.

3

"YOU KNOW HE STOOD there even after you left. He watched you."

Hailey put down the dishtowel she'd been using to dry the pretty yellow-flowered china that Sutherlands had served delicious meals on for generations. Gripping the delicate plate between her fingers, she stared at her sister. "No, he didn't."

"I think he was waiting to see if you'd turn around or something," Rachel said as she wiped suds off a saucer.

"I'm going to swat you with this towel if you don't stop talking about it," she warned.

Rachel lifted her hands out of the soapy water in surrender. "Fine, don't believe me. I was just wondering if you wanted to rinse off or something since that was the most intense eye-screw—or do you prefer eye-loving since you're such a romantic—I've ever seen."

He'd watched her? Something warm and tingly shimmied down her back, and she blinked. What was that? Some kind of shiver of desire? Nope, not going to acknowledge it. Didn't happen. What shiver of desire? She should never have dissed fate.

"And then with the other girls laughing, it had to have been weird for him," her sister continued.

Nope, Hailey would ignore that twinge of guilt. He was a Navy SEAL, he could handle it. "I thought we were going to drop this subject," she said, pulling the newly rinsed saucer out of the water.

"I remember you suggesting it," Rachel said, grinning. "Who knows, he might sort of…show up. Or maybe you could stroll up and down the beach in case Mother Nature starts raining men again."

Hailey wouldn't even respond to that little bit of insanity.

But she'd lived with the woman beside her almost her whole life, and knew when her sister wasn't going to let something drop. She placed the newly dried china saucer in the cabinet above her head and faced Rachel. "Why are you pushing this? You know my track record. The last thing I need to be is within shouting distance of a man."

The playful look on her sister's face faded. "Maybe you need a little hair of the dog?"

"Like cures like? Use a man to get over a man?" Hailey shook her head. "No, thank you. I'm pretty sure that rationale is what got me engaged time number three."

Rachel reached over and squeezed Hailey's hand. "I hate seeing you this moody, Hailey. For a minute there, out on the beach, I saw the feisty, never-turn-down-a-dare Hailey. I miss her."

If she were being honest, Hailey would admit she missed her old self, too. But something wasn't right in her life. And hadn't been for a while. "Yeah, well, the old Hailey made great work of her life so far. Four years of college, a degree in Art Adminstration under my belt and where do I find myself? At a complete dead stop in my career and right back at the family business. Art's to be experienced. I should be out there working to bring the best collections to the people. Managing field trips and docents. Helping teachers present the arts in their classrooms."

"Maybe this is where you're meant to be," her sister said gently.

Hailey released a heavy sigh. "Even if I gave that some credence, which I don't, there's still the issue of my three failed engagements. And let's not forget, you were the first person to tell me how bad my taste is in men. So, no, we may miss old Hailey, but at the age of twenty-seven, I'm here to find myself and nothing is going to stop me no matter how great a kisser the man is."

Or how solid his chest.

Or strong his legs.

A little shiver fluttered through her stomach.

Rachel's lips twisted in a not-so-great effort at hiding another grin. "Did you say find yourself? Now you sound like crazy Aunt June. What happened to her?"

"I think she moved in with her sister. We called her cool Aunt June until then," she reminded her sister dryly.

Her sister propped a hand on her hip. "See? There's the old Hailey I missed."

"You missed sarcasm? Now shoo—the new Hailey has a lot of work to do. I want to finish these dishes, take a nap and tackle that new self-help book." And work on never thinking of that man and his dangerous kisses again.

"Okay, okay," Rachel said, sinking her hands into the soapy water.

They worked together in silence cleaning the last of the china. The very modern stainless steel commercial dishwasher took care of the rest of the party utensils and serving dishes, but the Sutherland china was always washed by hand.

"This kind of reminds me of mom," Hailey said.

"I was thinking the same thing. How many times did we talk about boys, and dates with our hands in this sink?"

"Lots." She smiled at the happy memory.

"So, he was a good kisser?" Rachel asked.

God save her, yes. "Stop," she said in exasperation, then swatted her sister with the towel anyway.

AFTER A CHECKING ON the Ensign and a quick debrief, Nate Peterson headed to the weight room. He worked to mask the usually slight limp to his leg, more pronounced after the arduous training swim and carrying the injured man's weight up onto the beach.

He willed the pain away.

He'd dealt with worse. Fought with worse. Soon, the wicked scar wrapping around his thigh would be the only evidence he'd ever been hurt. His leg injury might prevent him from running, but it couldn't stop him from strength training. Nothing would stop him from returning to SEAL condition and taking his rightful place in The Teams when he was called.

Nate may have been looking for an escape from his old man, but fate had looked out for him that day when he was in the Navy recruiter's office at the age of eighteen.

He wasn't half way through basic when Nate realized he'd found a home. The Navy provided rules and discipline, something he'd never experienced growing up. His father may have laughed, but Nate actually excelled when there was a level of expectation. He wasn't a benchmark kind of guy. If there was a challenge, Nate didn't just want to meet it, he wanted to surpass it.

With the SEALs being the most highly regarded and trained of all the Special Forces, Nate knew that Trident would one day be his. He wouldn't let something like an injury prevent him from doing what he was supposed to do.

He adjusted the weight for the reps to work his upper body. Almost every base he'd been assigned housed a weight room. Different locales, different climates, different languages…this room with its benches, mirrors and weights, was like coming home. Working out was as much a part of his normal routine as shaving or eating. Only the physical therapy exercises were new. The movements, which would return the tone and flexibility to his muscles, he kept to himself and performed away from the eyes of others.

Nate controlled his breathing as he lifted and lowered his arms. Muscle memory took over, and his mind began to wander. To telling eyes, and soft warm lips.

What the hell had that been on the beach? With familiar discipline, he'd kept his thoughts squarely on his tasks and his men. But now…now he allowed himself to remember. And think of her. Of the flowery scent of her mixed with the ocean breeze. Or the way she felt, soft and warm against him.

His thoughts quickly turned to another kind of workout all together. Finding the zipper on the back of her dress, and drawing it down. Sliding those slender, tantalizing straps off the smooth skin of her shoulders, and letting her clothes fall to the sand at their feet.

Why had she kissed him?

Who the hell cared?

Nate heard footsteps in the hallway. His few moments alone were almost over.

"It looked to me like she just pulled him over and kissed him."

Yeah, that's exactly how it happened.

"He didn't handle the attack so well," another trainee said as they entered the weight room.

The hell he hadn't.

"If she'd had a knife stuffed in her purse, he'd have been a goner."

She didn't have a purse. Just a thin, thin dress.

"Maybe it's new Navy protocol." The three men laughed. At his expense. He knew they were only blowing off steam. SQT was just as mentally demanding as Hell Week was physically demanding. But he'd lose their respect if he didn't call them on it. He realized now he'd made a mistake out there in the water.

Nate lowered the weight and it clanged. Three gazes whipped his way. Followed quickly by three alarmed faces. He met each man eye to eye. His message was clear.

"We didn't know you were here, Instructor."

"Obviously," he replied.

The three stood together, uneasy, but not letting one man take the heat. Whatever Nate had to dish out at them they'd take together. The Teams would do well with soldiers such as these. Like him, they'd had a tough afternoon in the water, and he was impressed by their drive to hit the weight room instead of their bunks.

One day he might be fighting alongside them. They'd learned what he needed them to know.

"It's always preferable to make nice with the locals,"

he told them honestly, then turned, letting these guys off the hook. Yeah, he was a SEAL, "instructor" didn't sit well with him.

Relieved releases of breath made him smile as he left the room. He liked the men he was teaching; he just didn't want to be teaching them. Nate knew he could better serve the Navy and do what he was meant to do *out* of the classroom. He rubbed at the muscles above his knee. Soon. He'd be out of here soon.

Besides, none of them had the sexiest woman in San Diego wrap her warm body against them and plant the kind of hot kisses a man usually thought about on long, arduous hikes out in the dessert. In fact, with their training, the men hadn't talked to the fairer sex in awhile. However, *he* wasn't in training. Nothing was holding him back.

Being laid up in Southern California hadn't been his idea, but like any tactical move, he planned to take advantage of it. He had the whole night ahead of him, and it was no secret SEALs worked best when the sun went down. And he knew just where to find her. Hailey of the Sutherland Hotel.

She was a woman worth missing a party for.

Hoo ya.

HAILEY COULDN'T NAP LONG. Luckily, her sister's work on their Web site had yielded a booking for the evening, and she needed to be up and ready to help them check in. Like most B&Bs, the Sutherland served a delicious breakfast, but it had become a tradition to serve a light spinach and basil quiche in the afternoon for guests weary from travel and reluctant to fend for food in a strange city. Just one of the small touches that built a hotel's reputation. Something the management company hadn't understood.

The guest doorbell rang. The poor thing still sounded rusty. Wiping her hands on the apron protecting her clothes from the food prep, she quickly made her way to the door. Opening it wide, she almost wanted to slam it shut as quickly as she could.

It was *him*. The SEAL she'd kissed on the beach a few hours ago. Well, of course it was him. She'd just stood there in the kitchen dissing fate and fate obviously didn't like it. Her payback was a gorgeous man at her doorstep while she looked horrible. Then the nerves kicked in and her heart turned all fluttery.

"I don't normally walk around wearing this," she managed, thinking it might work to draw his attention away from the blue and white checked bib-style apron monstrosity. The baby doll blue dyed bias tape was even fraying around the edges.

Yet if someone were keeping track of the absolute stupidest things to tell a man, that would probably make the Top Ten. Why hadn't he said anything?

His eyes crinkled in the corners, he almost smiled, and it was almost a little too much. Whatever. He hadn't been invited; anyway, it was his own fault he saw her with her hair lazily knotted on the top of her head with a pencil she'd found in the kitchen. It's just, why did he have to look so good?

Fate.

His hair, thick with water the last time she saw him, hadn't revealed its true color brown, with a few strands turned copper, probably from his days under the California sun. But those gray eyes of his, the color of steel were the same, and they burned into her right now.

Yeah…it was still there. That heat, that unyielding attraction that lay between them even before she kissed him, only grew now. Now that he was here in her home looking big and sexy and so, so kissable.

She didn't need to worry about the stupid apron, apparently he was thinking about that kiss they'd shared, too. The intensity of his eyes as they met hers told her what was on his mind. Her skin heated, and she felt a flush in her cheeks. His gaze dropped to her lips and she found herself holding her breath.

Her sister charged through the door that led to the laundry, singing a Prince song. Rachel fumbled awkwardly to a stop when she saw them both. "Oh, my God, you're the…you know, the SEAL."

"I am," he said with a nod. Hailey wished she could read his expression. Right now it was agonizingly neutral.

Her sister had never been subtle. Today she was perfecting her art of embarrassingly stating the obvious.

"But you can call me Nate rather than the SEAL."

Rachel laughed. "Kind of sounds like you should be balancing something on the end of your nose."

Hailey felt sick to her stomach.

"I'm just kidding. Come in, come in," invited Rachel. "Not sure why Hailey still has you outside," she said, flashing her sister a confused look as she rushed to the door. "Welcome to The Sutherland. I'm Rachel, and of course you already know who Hailey is and how she tastes. Can I get you a mojito?"

"A what?" he asked.

Man, he had one sexy voice, Hailey thought. He may have only spoken a few words to her, but that rich baritone was hard to forget. And she'd be strangling her sister later.

"A mojito. Rum, lime, sugar and mint. I'm trying out some recipes. Nothing?" she asked as she ushered him inside and shut the door.

The SEAL shook his head. Actually, to Hailey he *gained* points by not knowing what the drink was. The three of them stood in the foyer, looking at one another. No one said a thing. If she'd thought her apron remark had been awkward...

"Oh, my gosh," Rachel exclaimed, her voice overly bright. "Would you look at the time? It's like, wow, late. Gotta run."

And being extremely obvious in the process. Actually, Hailey wanted her sister and Nate out of here. Okay, not really.

Since Nate was staring at her, Hailey forced herself not to roll her eyes at her sister's comment. Although Hailey had a feeling this man didn't miss much. Rachel had always accused her of becoming like The Terminator when it came to men. She'd automatically run through a list of options and choose which would best annihilate a man's sense of wanting to stay single.

A woman didn't get asked for her hand in marriage without knowing a few things.

With the emo guys, it was music. The brainy type always had a sweet spot for all things techno and gadgety. Her experience didn't run along military lines, but...

She flashed him a small smile. "If you don't mind, I need to finish up a few things in the kitchen. You do like homemade chocolate chip cookies, right?"

He swallowed.

Got him in one.

Hailey suppressed a groan. It could have been so simple: hear what he had to say, turn down anything if he offered, then send him on his way. Male isolation back in full force. But no, she had to let her curiosity take over, and try to find out his weakness.

Back to the bookstore tomorrow. Surely there was something new on impulse control.

And anyway, the fact that he fell so easily to a little cookie manipulation wasn't even sporting. Most men loved anything they didn't have to cook. This man was probably used to that dried powdery stuff you added water to for a meal. Fun on a Girl Scout backyard campout in the third grade, but it'd probably lost its appeal sometime around adulthood.

"I may have some leftover lasagna, too. Actually you'd be doing me a favor by eating it. Leftovers never taste the same to me, and with all the fresh ingredients in the sauce, it would be a shame to leave it wrapped up in the refrigerator." She may have heard him groan.

He silently followed her down the side corridor to the kitchen.

"This is some contrast from the lobby," he said.

She nodded, noting the modern appliances and bright efficient lighting. They'd maintained the Victorian feel of the lobby and foyer that reflected The Sutherland's origin. It still needed a bit more TLC, but she was pretty sure her mother would be pleased. "We take the breakfast part seriously here at The Sutherland B&B, so we needed a good working kitchen. Was that a yes to the lasagna?"

He nodded, and she dished out a healthy serving and

graced the side of the plate with buttered garlic bread. "This was my grandmother's recipe," she said, and she handed him a fork and napkin embroidered with an S.

His eyes closed in appreciation at the first bite. *Thank you grandma.* A man with a full stomach was always easier to deal with. He attacked his food like she assumed he handled life, with focus and determination. He ate while she gathered the ingredients for the cookies. With the former men in her life she would have felt obligated to keep up some kind of running conversation. And despite the fact that her thoughts drifted to that kiss he'd ramped up the heat on more than she cared to admit, she was sticking to her no-men plan, and giving herself a break.

It didn't matter that this guy had an amazing body as evidenced by his skintight wetsuit.

Nope, it wasn't important that he had the most firm, kissable lips she'd ever seen.

And the fact that he had heroic tendencies to throw on top of all that other good stuff, just to ensure she went a little weak in the knees, meant nothing. Hailey was all about self-improvement, and home improvement, if she counted The Sutherland. Men didn't factor into either one of those goals. In fact, men usually interfered with a woman's path to emotional growth.

Hmm, that basecamp food must have been worse than she imagined because he was already done by the time she was rolling little balls of dough. Hailey saved a small amount in the bowl.

"I have a weakness for raw cookie dough. Do you?" she asked.

He nodded and once again she was struck by how

handsome he was. He wore just a plain blue polo shirt matched with a pair of khaki shorts, but she enjoyed observing the strength of his bare arms. Tightly muscled, he didn't have the bulky shape of a body builder, just pure, broad-shouldered strength. It was intimidating.

And thrilling. She was sorely tempted to run her finger along the lines of muscles roping his arms. But those kinds of thoughts led women to playing hide and seek in the sheets.

Hailey pushed the bowl of dough between them, and they both reached inside at the same time, brushing hands. His fingers caught hers, stroked the back of her hand.

"Thank you, Hailey."

She glanced up, way up, and met his eyes. Steely and completely focused on her. The way he said her name, slowing it down in the middle with a hint of something Midwestern was sexy as hell. And then he smiled and she began to wonder if there was an expiration date on her Fate Delivery Card. Like could she kiss him again right now?

"How long have you been a Navy SEAL?" she asked, ready now to fill the air between them with rambling instead of heat.

"Six years," he told her, the smile fading from his lips. "Why'd you kiss me, Hailey?" he asked her quietly. If he hadn't tacked on her name at the end of his question, she could have responded in some glib, flippant way. But how he said her name drew her gaze to his.

"Because I wanted to." And it was true. From the second Nate emerged from the water she hadn't been able to take her eyes off him. His power, confidence and the non-aggrandizing way he took care of his buddy intrigued her.

Fiancé Failure Number Two would have been all about pointing to himself. "Hey, look what I just did. I saved that dude's life."

Yet Nate had calmly taken care of business and when it was over, he was ready to hit the water again.

His gaze settled on her mouth, and she could almost feel the heat of his lips. *Just lean toward him.* That's all she'd have to do, and those lips would be hers once more. No more remembering or imagining a second and a third kiss with him.

But she wouldn't. This was not the right time in her life to be canoodling with men who dropped out of helicopters for a living. When she did start dating, it would be with someone utterly stable. Like an accountant or insurance agent.

The timer dinged announcing that the cookies were ready. *Saved by the bell.* Oh, no, this time she saved herself. Hailey pushed off and away from the counter. Grabbing potholders, she swung open the oven door and pulled out the cookie sheet.

"Glass of milk?" she asked, as she slid the cookies over to the cooling rack.

"Is there any other way to eat cookies?"

With a laugh she opened the refrigerator door. "No, there's not." She poured the glasses of milk and served them two cookies each. As she'd done since she was a child, Hailey tore her cookie, loving the way the melted chocolate chip strung between the two halves.

Nate had already wolfed both his cookies down. "Would you like another?" she asked.

He raised an eyebrow. "What kind of question is that?"

So she served him two more cookies.

The mood had lightened between them.

"Why'd you kiss me? Tell me the real reason this time."

The man knew how to ruin a cookie moment. Suddenly she was back on that beach, feeling his lips take over the kiss she'd started.

"Have you ever heard of Fate Delivery Cards? No, I can see that you haven't. Actually, I have them right here." Hailey walked to the desk in the corner of the kitchen where she and her sister planned the meals for the week for The Sutherland. After grabbing the cards, she handed the packet to Nate.

"Don't wait on fate, jump start your life today." He read off the front of the package. "I always thought you made your own fate."

"Oh, me, too. I just went along with it because it was a party game." Said the woman with fifteen thousand self-help books. "But are you brave enough to take a card?"

"And your card said what? To kiss me?"

She nodded. "Kiss the first man I saw."

"Lucky me," he said, and her breath hitched at the sensual tone of his voice.

"Technically, the hurt guy was the first one I saw, but I didn't think it fair to kiss a defenseless man."

Something flared dark in Nate's eyes. "Feel free to kiss me whenever I'm defenseless."

She doubted this man ever was defenseless. Hailey crossed her arms over her chest, trying to block the attack his words had on her body. He was inviting her to kiss him again. What was that saying? That the best defense was a good offense? "Seems to me you're stalling. You backing down from drawing a card?"

"Oh, I never back down from anything." He made

his statement with straightforward matter-of-fact calmness. Hailey knew he wasn't trying to sound tough for her benefit.

Yeah, she'd bet money he didn't back down. The man jumped out of helicopters.

She pulled the cards from the deck and began to shuffle. Then she fanned the cards out in front of him. "Pick a card, any card," she said, mimicking a magician.

His callused hand rested on hers instead of the cards she offered.

"Go out on a date with me," he urged.

She wrinkled her nose. "I don't do relationships."

"Good. I don't do them either," he said, drawing a card from the ones she held.

Which begged the question…why not? Nate glanced down at the card and read. A smile tugged at the corner of his mouth.

"What does it say?" she asked, overwhelmed by curiosity.

He stood. "I'll bring the card with me when I pick you up Saturday morning."

A week away. Her heart pounded, and she realized she was enjoying the byplay between them. "I haven't said yes yet." She followed him out of the kitchen into the foyer. *No no no.* That *yet* just stole away how cool she wanted to play this.

Nate looked over his shoulder and shot her the sexiest look a man had ever given a woman. "Ten."

Hailey couldn't believe she was nodding. "Okay." Man, she'd really lost control of that one.

He bent and placed a quick kiss to her unsuspecting, but very appreciative lips. Before she could say anything, he closed the door behind him. Hailey leaned against the wall, hugging the cards to her chest. She knew she wore a goofy smile.

NATE WHISTLED AS HE readied his H-gear for the next day. When had he ever whistled? If anything, the Navy had taught him to be even more silent than was his natural affinity for it. And here he was, whistling all the same. And he knew the cause.

Hailey Sutherland.

The woman was even more beautiful this evening. With her hair in a messy knot on the top of her head as she'd easily made him cookies, he'd never seen a woman as sexy. He didn't know which he wanted more, the woman or the cookie. Actually, that wasn't true. The woman. However, the cookie was the prudent choice.

He hadn't any intention of asking her out tonight— he merely wanted an explanation about the kiss. Soon he'd be back up to a hundred percent and deployed, and like a lot of career SEALs, his line of work and women didn't always mesh.

But when she told him she didn't do relationships, it sounded a little too much like a challenge. Did he secretly want her to consider a relationship with him? Not that he wanted one.

Nate carefully inspected and attached his radio and medical kit to the standard issue H-harness. Tomorrow he'd demonstrate to the men how to get first, second and third line gear ready. They didn't know it yet, but then the trainees would be cut loose for some land nav exercises. He smiled in anticipation. The fun part.

He made quick work of his equipment. This was the easy part, and he'd been doing it so long he could do it without thinking. Unlike how he ended up with a date with the lady from the B&B. He'd had to put a lot of effort into that because Nate felt out of his element with Hailey, a situation he'd never found himself in before, and was irritated by it.

She wasn't like the women he usually spent his off-duty time with, women who knew what they were getting with the kind of man who liked playing sports, drinking a beer and keeping it casual.

Although the woman claimed she didn't do relationships, nothing about Hailey seemed casual. She glided around in a flowery dress with a ruffle at the bottom that drew his eyes to her great legs. She wore heels, and her toenails were painted a sexy bright pink.

This wouldn't be a bowling date. There wouldn't be an evening at the batting cages or catching the Chargers practice. With Hailey, he might have to wear a tie.

But then she may take it off. A more than fair tradeoff.

Why had he made their date so many days away? Since that afternoon on the beach he couldn't stop his thoughts straying to her sweet smile and concerned hazel eyes. If he'd made the date tomorrow he wouldn't have to think about how much he enjoyed talking to her as she bustled around in the kitchen. Or imagine what her lips would taste like if he were involved right from the beginning.

And he definitely wouldn't have to keep wondering about her reaction when she saw the suggestion on his Fate Delivery Card…and whether or not she'd deliver on it?

A SOFT RAP SOUNDED on her bedroom door, and Hailey scooted up against the pillows, tossing her book aside. "Come in," she called.

Rachel poked her head around the door. "Glad you weren't already sleeping."

Hailey shook her head. "I was just laying here."

With a smile, Rachel walked in and plopped herself on the pillows. Her sister had been plopping herself down on Hailey's bed since she could remember. Over the years and side by side, they'd played Barbies, talked about boys and made plans long into the night, or at least until their parents told them to knock it off.

She knew her sister was here for a play-by-play of her encounter with Nate.

"Did you leave any dough for me?" she asked.

Hailey laughed. They both had a weakness for the raw stuff. "In a leftover butter dish in the back of the fridge."

"Thanks. And don't think just because you left me some that I will be forgetting that you made the man cookies. Cookies. Bringing out the big guns right from the beginning? Didn't Mom caution about using her secret weapon too early?" she asked with a brow raised.

"Just to soften the blow for when I told him no about seeing him again."

"Ha. So when are you going out?" Rachel asked.

"Saturday. How did you know?"

"Nate looks like the kind of guy who gets what he wants, and big sis, that man wants you. Bad."

Every part of Hailey began to tingle. *This* was why she needed male isolation. Tingles equaled bad decisions. "You know, I've been thinking about that Navy SEAL."

Rachel's eyes grew wide. "Of course you have, I

knew it wasn't one-sided. That kitchen was about twenty degrees hotter after he left, and it didn't have anything to do with you baking cookies."

"Actually, I wasn't thinking of him *that* way," Hailey admonished. *Liar.* She wasn't thinking of him *that* way at *that* moment. "Do you remember how excited all those women got when the SEALs began climbing down that rope?"

"One practically knocked me over getting to the railing."

"Exactly. No one could take their eyes off them, and that was before the one got injured. I say, give the women what they want."

Rachel's head cocked to one side, the sure sign she was intrigued. "Tell me more."

"I'm thinking bistro stools and tables out on the terrace. We'd serve some of the finger food that The Sutherland used to serve at brunch."

"Maybe update it a bit, mojitos and champagne iced tea," Rachel suggested, clearly warming to the idea. Food was her specialty. "And then what, we just wait for the SEALs to show up?"

Sucking in her bottom lip, Hailey thought that could be too tricky, since she knew now from first-hand experience that SEALs could be a bit unpredictable, although she hadn't noticed they followed any set schedule. "We'll bill it as a party night. We'll play Texas Hold 'Em."

Rachel's expression turned questioning.

"Non-gambling poker, of course. Or that new game everyone likes, Bunco. The SEALs would be an added bonus."

"But we'd all know we were there for the SEALs,"

Rachel added, smiling. "I think this could actually work. We can offer a special reduced rate on the rooms during the weeknights since we're slower than on Fridays and Saturdays. We'd be out the expense of the terrace furniture, but eventually better off with the additional money coming in."

"SEAL night it is."

4

AIR WEEK FOR HIS TRAINEES was almost over. They'd begin land navigation next, Nate's specialty. Although with his bum leg, he'd need extra help to run the drills. He hated feeling like he couldn't take care of business.

Today they'd be practicing a Rubber Duck insertion. Men on The Teams performed this with ease, and so must these SEAL trainees.

Nate observed closely as his trainees pushed out their duck, or inflated rubber boat, now outfitted with large cargo parachutes. Then the trainees jumped from the plane quickly behind the duck. Soon parachutes filled the sky.

Now it was Nate's turn. As a SEAL, he felt most comfortable in the water, but there was something about free falling, before the jerk of the cord and the abrupt halt of descent, that was exhilarating. Like a fine whisky, or riding with the top down, even making love to a beautiful woman, the anticipation was every bit as good as the experience.

His thoughts conjured Hailey's lovely face. The parting of her lips after he'd kissed her. The joy of sinking his hands into her hair. Pulling her close without an audience.

Nate jumped.

The rubber ducks, or inflatable rafts, allowed them to cover more area and carry more gear than a fast line descent into the water, and already the trainees were taking care of business as they'd done over and over in the classroom.

In a flash, he was in the water, his body ready for the shock, although SEALs weren't strangers to being wet and cold. That was pretty much his status quo during BUD/S Hell Week. Even after obtaining his Trident, and becoming an official SEAL, he'd spent some quality time in the Alaskan glacier-fed waters of Chiniak Bay. The water here off the coast of California was about fifty-two degrees—what most SEALs called toasty warm.

"They're here, ladies!" was his welcome as he broke the surface of the water. Followed by…female catcalls?

Nate pivoted to face the beach and spotted about nine women waving and calling to him and his men. One carried a bullhorn. "Look at them getting into the boat," she said, and the others cheered.

He looked over, and sure enough, two SEAL trainees were hoisting themselves over the sides of the rubber boat with a minimum of effort.

Had these women been waiting for them? Nate couldn't believe it. One woman carried a sign that had what must be a phone number. All held martini glasses. Two more SEALs were approaching the boat to more cheers and catcalls.

"619-4—"

"Ensign." Nate's harsh tone cut the remaining phone number recitation. In irritation he turned toward the women. Didn't they understand these men were conducting training that might save their asses one day?

The ladies stood in the approximate area where he'd received the hottest, most surprising kiss of his life. That couldn't be an accident. He scanned the women mingling near the water, but did not see her. Where was Hailey? He'd recognize that body anywhere. He tamped down the inappropriate surge of disappointment.

Maybe she was working. His gaze switched to the large hotel, which stood several hundred yards behind the women.

And he spotted her. He sucked in a breath as his eyes alighted on her beautiful bare legs. He followed the smooth line of her thighs, interrupted by khaki colored shorts. Her midriff was also bare, and his fingers curved in the water in the same way as he ached to shape his hands around her waist. He suppressed a groan as his gaze traveled over her small, shapely breasts. Breasts he'd felt pressed against his chest and thought about as he lay in his bunk alone at night.

She lounged on one of the recliners, wearing large sunglasses and her beautiful light brown sandy-colored hair loose about her shoulders. Her lips arced in an inviting smile, and he almost returned one of his own. Then she lifted her drink glass in greeting and he knew. She was the person responsible for the shenanigans out there on the beach.

"Smile for the cameras, boys," one of the women called.

Out of the corner of his eye he spotted another one of his men wave.

"What the hell are you doing?" Nate demanded.

"Representing the U.S. Navy, sir."

Letting them off easy in the weight room had been a mistake. "Look," another one of his men said.

A woman lifted her top and flashed his men something they'd been missing for weeks due to training. Okay, he was pulling the plug on this. Order was disappearing. He'd planned for a slow drift through the water for the men to practice their patient silent approach. Now they'd be working on speed, and getting back to the base as quickly as possible.

Yeah, back at the base where he'd plan an attack of a different kind. He and Hailey had some business to discuss.

HAILEY WATCHED THE MEN in their boats until they were just tiny dots in the ocean. She needed someplace cool and she needed it now. Hailey felt hot and achy and restless. Her cheeks were flushed, and even where her clothes touched skin felt uncomfortable.

The commercial icemaker would do the trick. A few fell into her hand from the dispenser and she ran the cube along the back of her neck, then across her chest.

"Is it really that hot out there?" Rachel asked.

The ice dropped from her hand and fell to the floor. Hailey hadn't even realized her sister was in the kitchen. "I, uh, um…"

"Never mind. I know what that's all about. Well, you keep having your male-induced panic attack. Meanwhile, the women are calling for more mojitos," Rachel said, as she mixed limejuice and rum together in a pitcher.

"You saw that outside, right?"

"That display of capable male hotness?"

"Yes," she said, her breath came out in a rush. "They jumped out of a plane, Rachel! That's like the sexiest thing I've ever seen."

"Woo hoo, Hailey's living again. This calls for a drink," Rachel said as she poured herself a small glass of the mojito.

"What are you talking about?" Hailey asked, feeling defensive. This wasn't the first time her sister had implied she wasn't herself. Didn't her sister know that was exactly what she was trying to do? Remember who she was?

"You've been focused on nothing but getting The Sutherland back into shape and self-improvement for the last four months."

"Both of them need some work," Hailey responded drily.

"Maybe a little, but sis, you've taken it overboard. Completely distancing yourself from men, what's with that?"

This was unfair. "I'm resetting my inner attraction switch. It's outlined perfectly in *Stop Picking the Wrong Men*. That book really opened my eyes to my own destructive dating patterns. Cutting out men from my life has really worked out great. I can begin Step Two at the end of the month."

"I'm afraid to ask what that entails."

"It's dating myself. Relearning me. Who I am, what I want, what I'm attracted to."

"I think your body is telling you what you're attracted to."

"That's pure animal attraction," Hailey said with a brush of her hand. "I mean, what woman wouldn't be attracted to big broad shoulders and a tight hard body? Or that great smile of his? And Nate's gray eyes. When he looked at me all hot and..." Hailey sunk her head into her hands. "Ohmygod, you're right. I want him."

Rachel gave her a sympathetic squeeze to her shoulder. "It's not so bad. Listen, I'm going to give you the outline of my latest, Why Hailey Chooses Dumb Moves."

Hailey lifted her gaze. "I thought you told me it wasn't going to be so bad. You just called me dumb."

"I called your choices dumb. Let me keep going. You grew up watching mom and dad and their great relationship, and knew you wanted the same thing."

"How do you know so much about what I want?"

Her sister's expression turned ironic. "Because, honey, I have the same problem. It's just manifested itself in a different way. I became a waiter—waiting for Mr. Perfect, whereas you became a fixer. Take your first fiancé, the emo guy."

"Adam? He had such talent. What a painter, remember?"

"I remember you buying a lot of canvas and very expensive paints. He never seemed to have the money for the essentials of his trade, but he had a lot of dreams and not many plans."

"That was simply his artistic nature," she said, shrugging.

"So you planned it all, and worked so hard to make everything come out perfect, and hide all the problems so he wouldn't be so down all the time. So when that fizzled you went with the complete opposite. Mr. Efficient, businessman."

"Mason."

Rachel made a face. "I'd almost forgotten that controlling bastard's name. At least you had something in common with the last one—you both were in love with him."

Hailey rubbed the back of her neck, trying to prevent a knot wanting to form. "What's the point of bringing all this up? I'm trying to fix my life now."

"But honey, that's just it. The fixer in you is the problem. It's why you have a thousand self-help books upstairs in your room, but wind up at the same place every time."

"So how do I stop attempting to fix everything?"

Rachel flashed her a wry smile. "I know the problem, but I don't have the solution. That one you will have to figure out all on your own." Then after tossing in a few fresh mint leaves, Rachel slid the pitcher of mojitos across the granite countertop toward her sister. "But right now, Hailey, you can deliver more drinks. I think I hear the ladies out there getting restless since the SEALs are gone."

"This worked better than I thought it would, and we did this in under two days. Imagine what we could do with more than just phone calls and a few flyers."

"Amy really came through for us. We wouldn't have had nearly that kind of response if she hadn't gotten on the horn and invited her friends."

"Does she seem the same to you?" Rachel asked. "She seems more...subdued almost. I noticed it after the bridal party when we were loading her car with the gifts. I thought maybe she was tired, but today she seems even worse."

"Are those mojitos ready?" Amy asked as she pushed her way into the kitchen.

"Were your ears burning? We were just talking about you," Hailey said.

"Better be good things," Amy warned with a slight smile.

"You seem…not yourself," Rachel said.

"Don't worry. Rachel accuses everyone of that lately," Hailey teased as she picked up a dishtowel.

Amy shrugged. "No, everything's fine."

The two sisters looked at each other. Okay, maybe Rachel *was* onto something. Women excited about getting married didn't look mopey and tell everyone she was fine. Hailey should know, she had this engagement thing down pat. "You sure?" Hailey questioned.

Amy plastered a tight smile across her face. "Absolutely."

"We didn't mean to put you to work," Rachel said. "But as long as you are, how are we on the finger foods?" she asked.

"We're good," Amy said, laughing. "I'm heading out."

Once Amy had left the kitchen, Rachel blurted, "See what I'm talking about? Something seems off with her."

The doorbell rang. All this use, and still it sounded terrible. "I'll get it," her sister said, and headed toward the lobby.

Hailey put the dishtowel to use and began to wipe up the water some of the crushed ice had left behind. She'd always hated The Sutherland growing up, rejected the idea that she'd ever take her place behind the counter, making beds, preparing food and welcoming people. Okay, hate was a strong word. She just hadn't wanted this life, it hadn't seemed exciting to a fifteen-year-old wanting to travel the world and see everything.

But that fifteen-year-old hadn't yet had her heart broken. Three times. Hadn't realized the comfort of being surrounded by family, in a familiar place.

With a not so discreet clearing of her throat, Rachel announced her return. And there was a guest in tow.

Nate Peterson.

Unlike last time, the man didn't appear too happy about his visit to The Sutherland. However, his stern and tired expression only made him all the more appealing. She wanted to stroke the tension from him. Hailey's stomach did a little flutter. Now that she'd acknowledged how much she desired him, she didn't feel as bold as when they stood together on the beach. The idea of walking over to him and stealing a kiss filled her with shivers, not resolve.

"I guess I'll go check on the party, sounds like it's winding down," Rachel said as she exited.

Good Lord, there was the tunnel vision *Stop Picking the Wrong Men* warned about. Hailey hadn't even remembered her sister was in the room. Laughter drifted in from the other room.

"Actually, your guests are what I wanted to discuss with you," he said after dragging his gaze from her lips.

Yes. He felt it, too.

Except she had a suspicion this little discussion wasn't going to be pleasant.

Hailey had this handled. Would Nate like peanut butter cookies as much as chocolate chip? The man had definitely responded to the whole warm kitchen feeling of a few nights ago. Maybe she should work on writing a book on drawing a man's attention away from a problem. Why did women always find it so difficult dealing with men? Food and sex, sometimes they camouflaged most anything. Now, to find that peanut butter…

What was it her sister had said? That Hailey worked so hard to hide all the problems? That's certainly what she was doing now. She swallowed. Hailey could follow the same pattern she'd used with every other man in her life, or she could try something new.

She took a deep breath. Hailey met his gaze, instead of opening the cabinet for the peanut butter. She was done smoothing things over.

Nate leaned forward, balancing on the center island separating them. The sturdy muscles of his arms flexed as he moved, and once again she was taken in by his amazing physical side. Everything about him seemed to suggest leashed danger.

"So what happened on the beach this afternoon, that was a one-time occurrence, right?" he asked.

Hailey folded her arms across her chest. "Not so sure about that," she drawled, as if it was a standoff from the Old West.

He reached into his pocket and pulled out a neatly folded piece of paper. "You're done with these flyers, too." Nate spread out the flyer they'd quickly put together at the local copy shop announcing Spot A SEAL day at The Sutherland.

"We just made those yesterday. How did you find one so fast?"

"The U.S. Navy has excellent intel."

A little mojito would be great right about now. She sighed, blowing the wisp of her bangs. "Okay, how bad is this?"

"That depends," he said, his glance straying once more to her mouth.

"On what?"

Then that gray gaze of his slammed right into hers. "On how bad do you want it to be?"

5

NATE WOULD HAVE LAUGHED at Hailey's widened eyes if she didn't look so cute. Or so damn sexy. A slight flush began to spread down her neck and across her collarbone. The exact same path he'd take with his mouth. His tongue.

Hailey wanted him. She wanted him every bit as badly as he wanted her. His body tightened in response.

With a rueful shake of her head, Hailey reached for the handle of one of the cabinets. Cookies? His mouth began to water. Then a dozen possibilities filled his vision. Eating that cookie off Hailey's stomach was his favorite.

To his disappointment, she reached for a pitcher. "We need some more mojitos."

"I thought the party was winding down."

She sucked in the corner of her full bottom lip. Sexy as hell. "This one's for me," she told him.

He watched as she gathered fresh limes, sugar, rum and some sort of leafy thing that looked like raw spinach.

"I love the smell of fresh mint," she said.

That explained the green leafy thing.

She gently bent the leaf and held it to his nose. "Smell," she urged.

Nate reached for her wrist and drew her closer to

him. He breathed in the scent, never taking his eyes off her face. Hailey's skin was softer than anything he'd ever touched. Her breath hitched as he drew her closer still.

Hailey's other hand fluttered to his shoulder, her fingers curled into his shirt. He groaned and dropped her wrist and cupped her face. He didn't need to draw her lips to his. She met him, her lips easily willing against his.

The rush he felt when she traced his bottom lip with her tongue equaled that of fast lining out of a helicopter. He needed her. Now.

Hailey used the hand draped around his shoulder to push herself away. She turned her back to him, her chest raising and lowering as she drew in deep gulps of air. He thought he may have heard her mumble stop, "picking the wrong men," but his thinking must be muddled from that kiss she'd laid on him

She spun on her heel. "I'm so sorry."

"Wh-what?"

Hailey nervously wrung her hands. "I hope you don't think I kissed you just now to try to make you forget why you were here."

Kissing Hailey *was* why he was here.

She lowered her hands to her sides. "Nate, you look like the kind of man who appreciates a straight answer, so I'm going to give it to you. This was only our first beach party, and we brought in several hundred dollars. We recently rescued our family home from a management company determined to let it fail, and I busted my 401k on everything you see in the kitchen. You and the rest of the SEALs have already brought in money with a minimum of effort on our part and none on yours.

Each one of those women paid a cover charge. The next time there will be room bookings."

"Those men are in training." He gently traced her lower lip. "I'm sure I don't have to tell you how distracting a woman can be."

"How about if I put a stop to the signage and flashing?" she asked, and his stomach clenched at the hopeful tone in her voice.

This was why relationships were hard. Hailey needed the money, he knew it, and still he was going to ask her to stop. "Those aren't just games they're playing out there. They're learning how to protect themselves and to keep *you* safe."

"Maybe you could give me a schedule of your less dangerous exercises and we could work around that."

"They're all dangerous."

She slumped against the counter. "The money is just so good," she said, not even attempting to hide the disappointment in her voice.

He wanted to help. This woman had nearly made him senseless with a kiss grounded firmly in PG on the movie rating scale, tempted him with cookies, and now she triggered all kinds of protective urges. Looking into her hazel eyes, Nate admitted, "We can't make you stop, it's a free beach…"

She perked up immediately.

"*I'm* just asking you to do the right thing here."

Her shoulders slumped. He could fight his newfound desire to comfort or he could roll with it. Nate drew her forward, and Hailey didn't resist as she moved into his arms, warm and fitting perfectly against his side. Rolling with it…definitely the right way to go. "I know you will come up with something," he whispered against her hair. "Maybe we can think of something together on our date."

Hailey pulled away, and blinked up into his eyes. "Together? As in we come up with ideas…" Her voice trailed off.

Nate nodded. "Together."

Her jaw angled to the right. "You don't want me to fix this problem all on my own?"

"Why would I want you to do that?" As a SEAL Team, they repeatedly went over every detail of a dive together, ferreting out weaknesses, looking for ways to improve. It only made sense. What kind of man wouldn't do the same with a woman he wanted to help?

Her eyes softened, and Nate remembered his original intention in tugging Hailey close—to roll with it. He'd meant for the kiss to be gentle. Soothing. But as soon as his lips brushed hers, Hailey sunk her fingers into his hair and pressed herself against him. The tips of her breasts brushed his chest, and all he could think was heaven. And more.

The woman knew how to kiss. And that was his last thought before hunger for this sexy woman took over. Her hands moved up and down his back, and she hooked a leg over his thigh creating the perfect cradle for his growing erection. Hailey was a small woman, but her breasts filled his hands as if they were meant to be there. He groaned as he felt her nipples harden through the material of her bra and blouse.

She broke away from their kiss, and nibbled on his neck, then the lobe of his ear. Her soft sigh as his hand slipped under her shirt to stroke the bare skin of her stomach nearly did him in. Deployment and injury had kept him celibate long enough.

Then his knee gave out.

He groaned at the sharp pain attacking his joint.

Hailey's movements abruptly stopped. Her leg slid down to the floor. "That wasn't a good kind of groan, was it?" she asked, concern lacing his voice.

Nate squeezed his eyes tight, willing his thigh muscles to relax. But he wasn't in so much agony that he didn't miss her worried tone. The little massaging motions of her hands on his shoulders only confirmed her apprehension. Opening his eyes, he cupped her face and smiled. "Not a good kind of groan."

Now he could add one more label to the injury that took him off the Teams. Mood killer.

"What happened?" she asked.

He reached for her hand and she immediately twined her fingers through his. "It's not the most romantic of stories."

Hailey made a scoffing sound. "Don't worry, I'm not the romantic type."

"Not falling for it," he told her, making his way through the kitchen toward the door that led to the lobby, Hailey's soft hand still snug in his. "They may not want to admit it, but deep down, all women want romance."

"Believe me, that's so not true," she said, rolling her eyes.

"That sounds a lot like a challenge."

She held both hands up in surrender. "No, no challenge, it's a lost cause. I hate flowers, don't even think about stuffed animals, and never, *never* mix me a CD of cheesy love songs."

"I never think about stuffed animals."

"I just prefer deeds over gestures," she told him, and he got the feeling this woman had received plenty of talk but not a lot of substance.

They passed the stairs together. Did those stairs lead up to her bedroom? Hell, it was a B&B, the place was filled with beds. If he asked, would she take him upstairs?

Something hot burned between them, there was no denying it, but did he want to hound dog his way through life? He knew two minutes out the door, he'd regret not having her in his arms again. In ten minutes he'd want to kick his own ass. Being a SEAL had taught him patience; nearly getting killed had forced him to take life slower. Strange, he'd even missed the party tonight, and didn't care.

It wasn't so long ago that if a woman told him she didn't want a relationship he would have cheered. But with Hailey...she was the kind of woman to relish. To savor.

Nate forced his eyes off the tempting stairs and reached for the doorknob instead.

Hailey might not have realized it, but she revealed something to him tonight, something vulnerable. He sensed she wasn't the kind of woman who did that often. She'd already told him she didn't do relationships, now she was down on romance.

Nate wanted to change that.

"You didn't show me your card," she told him as he stepped into the cool night air.

"That's right," he replied, then quietly closed the door behind him.

AMY BRADFORD HAD A fire to start, and it was going to be a big one. Accidentally barging in on Hailey practically crawling on the SEAL in the kitchen had, well, sealed the deal so to speak.

She wanted *that*.

That passion, that hunger for another person so consuming neither even noticed that someone had walked in on you while in each other's arms.

Yearning for passion should probably not be on the wish list of a woman about to be married in a few days. She should already have the passion. Be looking forward to making that passion permanent.

Which was why she needed the fire. A fire so big the shuttle would be able to spot it from space. Hmm, maybe the backyard wasn't such a good idea. Neighbors tended to make phone calls. She quickly cleared the area around her sink, moving the dirty cups and spoons to a dishtowel. This cluttered area would just have to do, there was no time to get them clean and put away.

Her skirt swished around her knees as she opened and slammed drawers looking for a lighter or some forgotten book of matches. There were none. Desperate, she glanced down at the ruffle of her sundress. Okay, cool spring cotton with pastel flowers that she'd worn to the Spot the Seal party didn't seem appropriate for building an inferno.

Calm down.

She took a deep breath. Thought of the ocean. A bubble bath. Hot chocolate. *Control the panic. Make it subside.* Her heartbeat slowed, and now she could actually think.

Be smart about this.

Amy reached above her head and pulled down a glass to fill with tap water. After draining the contents, she placed it upside down on the dishtowel already filled with the dirty dishes from her sink. Her hand was shaking, but growing steadier. *Good.* Her cell phone rang, the special ringtone telling her it was Jake on the line.

A tiny prickle of the panic returned.

Jake Arkins, her fiancé, the love of her life, the man she had to avoid pronto. "Hello," she answered.

"Hey, I thought you were going to tell me what time to meet you back at our place," he said. His voice was a deep baritone that never failed to send shivers down her back. "Our place, that has a nice ring to it."

It did until that card. Now "our place" sounded a lot like "lack of privacy." "Mmmm," she managed as a response.

"How'd the party go?" he asked.

She nodded before she answered. "Good, good. We all had a good time," she said, her gaze examining each closed cabinet, as she tried to remember if a box of matches could be behind the door. Earlier this week, she'd sorted through every drawer and every cabinet combining her stuff with his. Now her mind was a blank.

"Thought maybe you could show off some of that naughty lingerie you got from the shower before dinner."

She'd need the fire extinguisher, too. She'd had the thing so long maybe it had expired. Did fire extinguishers go bad?

"Amy?" Jake asked, his voice uncertain.

Oh, hell, what had he asked? Dinner? "Yeah, I have it all in the crock-pot."

Jake chuckled. "Sounds sexy."

Under the kitchen sink. That's where they'd stashed

the extinguisher. She lowered to her knees and began to rustle through the cleaning supplies. Wait, a crockpot sounded sexy?

How could she forget? They'd made plans to hide out at their duplex and not worry about wedding details for the rest of the evening, and just be together.

Except she didn't have time for sexy right now. Although she yearned to have his strong arms around her. He always made her feel safe from the outside world.

Amy gave herself a quick mental shake. *Task at hand.* "Jake, I'm sorry I didn't call. With this party tonight and all the wedding details, I'm a little distracted."

"Ames, it's okay. You sound pretty stressed. I'm on my way home now, and we'll unplug the phones and I'll take your mind off of fittings and flowers and whatever else it is your grandma says a wedding must have."

The heat of his words and the promise in his voice made her heart pound again. For all the wrong reasons. "If I don't start cracking on these thank you notes, my grandmother will never forgive me. You know how she is about etiquette." And she had a fire to start, to put out and hide all the evidence.

"I love you," he said.

She closed her eyes, allowing herself to really feel the emotion. How had she been so lucky to find a man like Jake who loved her in return? Fate had really smiled—

Fate.

Her stomach clenched and all the warm feelings of just a moment ago vanished. "I love you, too," she said over the lump in her throat. Amy closed the phone and returned it to her purse. Something else was tucked there. The stupid Fate Delivery Card she'd been forced to take. The thing she'd been avoiding but had gotten her into this mess in the first place.

After the excitement of Hailey's kiss on the beach with the hot Navy SEAL everyone had forgotten that she'd drawn a card. It wasn't until she stopped off to get a soft drink at the drive thru that she'd found the Fate Delivery Card she'd stuffed in her purse.

With a smile, she remembered the hilarious things Tori and Hailey had to complete. What did fate have in store for her? In excited anticipation she'd turned the card over and read.

Amy wasn't smiling now. Her fingers crumpled the plastic coated card as she yanked the hated thing once more from her purse. She would read it again. Not that the last seven times she'd read it had changed the very clear message.

Set something you love free.

Its challenge was clear. Jake. Amy was supposed to set Jake free.

And that's why she was going to set that sucker on fire—pretending the card had never happened hadn't worked. She'd practically taken a second job at The Sutherland to avoid going home. Amy knew it seemed irrational, but it made some weird kind of sense that if she could just remove any trace that the card had ever existed, everything would go back to normal. No harm, no foul.

Except she couldn't find anything to use as a lighter. Jake was allergic to scented candles, there wasn't a fireplace in the new home and the stove was electric, not gas.

She was screwed.

Or maybe fate was telling her something. She slumped to the floor with her back against the stainless steel of the refrigerator door. She loved Jake, she really did…but something wasn't right. It had niggled her for weeks, months, and now, when she couldn't destroy the one thing that was trying to shed light on the problem she'd been hoping to ignore, Amy had to face it. All thanks to that stupid, stupid card. She buried her face in her hands for a moment, but no tears would come.

Only resolve.

Amy stood up, kicked off her pretty strappy sandals, and padded barefoot on the travertine flooring she and Jake had installed together not long ago. In the bedroom, one of her suitcases lay on its side. She'd only unpacked it two days ago. Quickly tossing it on the bed. She unzipped the top, and in a daze began to pack.

Where would she go? Her reasoning was too stupid to try and explain it to her grandparents. Besides, her grandma would be the last person to understand. Her old roommate already had someone moved into Amy's old bedroom.

But as she zipped her suitcase shut, she knew here was only one place to go.

"I CHECKED THE DOORS and set the alarm. The Sutherland is officially closed for the night," Hailey said, as she slumped next to Rachel on one of the rosewood couches in the lobby, newly reupholstered in a deep burgundy. The sisters had completed the work themselves, tackling one a week so the lobby wouldn't be bare for their guests. The sitting area could still use a bit of refreshing to its Victorian décor, but they could look at the condition of their childhood home with some pride.

"We keep having nights like tonight, we can buy

some new silk lampshades and fund the electrical wiring for that wall sconce idea you had." This area had originally been illuminated by candles along the perimeter, but when the house was wired for electricity, that charming Victorian detail had been lost. Faux electrical candle lights would do the trick.

But Hailey's stomach tensed at the mention of money. She hated the idea of disappointing her sister. Or Nate.

"Although we should probably hire someone to help with the serving," Rachel continued, "we won't be able to count on Amy, especially after she gets married."

Hailey nodded. "Yeah, I'm surprised she even showed up and stayed that long. Although I've never actually been a bride I've seen those to do lists in bridal magazines. It's brutal."

"Which is why I think something is going on with her and Jake." Her sister sat up, fully alert. "Speaking of relationships, what happened between you and the SEAL? I can't believe I forgot to ask."

"Right. I'm surprised you didn't pounce on me earlier."

"I'm going to blame it on the mojito." Rachel closed her eyes once more. "And don't think you're going to misdirect my attention so you don't have to answer the question. You can't fool me like you once did."

The good old days for sure. As the youngest, Rachel had always been so gullible and easy to manage.

"He came to talk to me about watching the SEALs."

Rachel's eyes snapped open a second time. "That's great. Maybe on your date you can fish around for when the SEALs will be training again. We could put actual times on our flyers."

"Actually, I wanted to talk to you about the party. He didn't like it."

Rachel's eyes narrowed. "Don't tell me. He convinced you to stop our SEAL watch party."

Hailey began to squirm. "I didn't exactly tell him we wouldn't do the parties again, but he did raise some good points."

"Which means we're not having the parties. I'd actually be impressed by his negotiation skills if I weren't irritated that we'll be out all that green. How'd he do it?"

"He appealed to my sense of duty, and how the women are distracting to the men while they were training."

"Sucker."

Probably. For the man. His argument and his grey eyes. Her lips still tingled. "Don't worry, I thought of another idea. Don't you have a friend who works at the San Diego Visitors' Bureau? Well, I'm going to need that number."

"This sound intriguing. I thi—" The rusty sound of the doorbell cut off Rachel's idea.

"We've got to get that fixed. Who'd be ringing now? All the guests are accounted for."

The bell sounded again.

"Whoever it is, they don't seem to be leaving. Better see who it is." Hailey quickly made her way to the large wooden front door that had welcomed hundreds of guests through the decades.

Hailey peered through the peephole. "It's Amy."

"Weird. Maybe she left something."

"We should probably just give you a key," Rachel said.

Their friend and happy bride appeared to be anything but. Her cheeks were blotchy, but a firmness lay across her chin.

"Oh, Amy, what happened?" Hailey asked.

"That stupid card of yours, *that's* what happened." Amy thrust the card at Hailey, then reached for a large suitcase which she rolled into the foyer.

"What are you doing?" Rachel asked.

Hailey was already turning over the card, a tight knot of dread growing in her chest. "Set something you love free," she read aloud. Damn, it was worse than she could have imagined.

Rachel gasped, then jumped up and curved her arm around Amy's shoulder. "Sweetie, it was just silly game. It didn't mean anything."

"I said that to myself the whole drive home. Then every day since. You want to know what happened today? Nothing. I tried to burn the stupid card but I couldn't find one thing to catch it on fire. I can't believe I let Jake talk me out of gas burners for the new range."

The two sisters looked at each other. Clearly they had a case of wedding jitters gone bad on their hands. It might not be in the job description of B&B owner, but surely friends could talk one overwrought bride into calming down. Rachel made a slight nod toward the kitchen.

"Follow me and we'll get you some warm tea and figure this out," Hailey said, as she touched Amy's elbow to direct her. A cup of chamomile tea had always been their mother's remedy, and Hailey fell back on it now. The soft warm brew soothed as well as encouraged talking.

Amy allowed herself to be led a few feet. "I don't even have a lighter in my car. Just an outlet to plug in electronics. Is that insane or what?"

Rachel opened the kitchen door. "Well, listen, if burning is the problem, don't worry about it. Plenty of matches in this place, and our range has eight burners. Each one of them gas."

Amy slumped into one of the chairs at the country style butcher-block table. "I appreciate it, but not being able to burn the card was just the tip-off. Maybe fate has been trying to clue me in all along. There's something fundamentally wrong in my relationship with Jake, and maybe taking seven days away from the wedding planning and the new place will be good for me."

Hailey had been down this road before. She'd aim for soothing tones. "Take it from a woman who has been engaged three times. Once you start thinking a break's a good idea, it soon becomes a reality. Jake probably doesn't even realize you're gone. You can head over there now."

Amy flashed her a tight smile, her face determined. "Oh, I'm not going. The card said set him free, and that's what I'm doing. I'm staying here."

Both sisters began talking at once.

"Oh, but—"

"We don't—"

"I'll pay you," Amy said.

Ahhh, those sweet, magic words.

"Welcome to The Sutherland," Rachel told her.

Hailey shot her sister a fierce look. "She's kidding. We don't want your money." The kettle began to whistle. "You drink your tea while I look at the register for an open room." She fled to the check-in area, and ran her finger down the computer screen. Having the party that afternoon, they'd skipped cleaning their newly-vacated rooms in order to take care of decorating the terrace and making sure it was in tiptop shape.

It had saved time, but now it severely limited which spaces were available. They had one room left. The bridal suite.

Hailey placed an "X" next to the room number and grabbed the key.

Fate did indeed have an ironic sense of humor.

6

NATE HAD NEVER BEEN a dinner and movie kind of guy, but he suspected that's the kind of date Hailey was used to. He avoided his natural inclination toward the water fun of San Diego. Although he would have loved to explore the tidepools at Point Loma or even surf, none of those seemed romantic. And that was his goal here today, lots and lots of romance.

He'd told Hailey to dress casually, and to wear good walking shoes. He could tell by the long pause on the phone she was surprised, but he didn't believe in retreat. He'd see these plans through, and once he'd had more of an opportunity to observe Hailey, he'd choose something better suited to her interests next time.

She opened the door for him quickly, not making him wait. He liked that. Dressed in jeans to her knees, white tennis shoes, casual pink polo shirt and her wavy hair in a high ponytail at the top of her head, Nate didn't regret the casual approach. Hailey looked sexy as hell, and when she flashed him a welcoming smile he couldn't help smiling back.

"I'm ready," she said. She held up a white sack with pink polka dots. "I even made some peanut butter cookies."

"You know how to keep a man coming around, don't you? But why don't you show me your place before we leave."

Her eyes widened in surprise. "You sure?"

"We're not on any kind of schedule."

"You weren't kidding when you said casual."

"My whole life is a schedule, so when I'm off it, I don't even want to see a clock."

"Duly noted." She reached around and closed the door behind him. The air current caught her perfume, sweet and flowery.

"Okay, well, you've been here, this is the foyer. Unlike many bed and breakfasts that have been converted, my family built this home specifically to be a guesthouse in 1889. We have photos of the opening in the Tea Room. It must have been something. Anyway, the income paid the bills and allowed generations of Sutherlands to avoid being nine-to-fivers."

"I can understand that sentiment," Nate told her. "I would suffocate in an office building. So you were born into the business."

Hailey made a scoffing sound. "Not that I wanted to be. In fact, that's how I got engaged the first time."

Nate almost tripped. The *first* time?

"Fiancé Failure Number One was a dreamer. Not so much of a planner. Or a money saver. Anyway, my grandmother firmly believed the first thing any guest should see when they stepped inside The Sutherland was beauty."

It was an extreme effort to keep his eyes off of Hailey as she spoke. Now *that* was beauty. She spoke of her home with such passion he wanted to see what she saw, so he tore his gaze away from her smiling face. Waves of yellow sunlight poured from the double transoms, warm and welcoming. Just like Hailey.

"But now you're back, and clearly happy to be here," he said.

"The Sutherland needed me, and it's funny, but I found I needed it, too. I feel connected to my past now. See the staircase?" she asked.

Nate nodded. True to his prediction, he'd wanted to kick himself for not following his first instinct and explore where that staircase led with the woman beside him.

"At seventeen, it was my job to polish that sucker. I hated it, but now, when I see it gleam, I think about how my mother would let us slide down it when our father wasn't around."

He laughed at the image of this utterly feminine woman sliding down the banister like a tomboy.

"As you can see, we began by concentrating on the kitchen, Tea Room and terrace. The lobby is where we want to concentrate next. There are a dozen little Victorian touches we want to add to this room, like brocade or maybe some porcelain."

Nate had endured near freezing night swims and bunked under the stars in the desert and woken up with a mouthful of sand, but until a few days ago, he might have preferred a tent on the beach if presented with the idea of sleeping in a Victorian B&B. And if Hailey invited him up to her room…he might just endure Hell Week again for that. Hell, he was already getting hard.

"What else?" he asked in an effort to distract his mind from his body. And hers.

"Wireless Internet. All over." Hailey waved her hands dramatically. "You don't want to know," she said.

But he wanted to know. Know about her job, those cards, what she liked…anything she wanted to tell him.

The service door from the Tea Room to the kitchen opened and Amy walked in, looking rumpled and a cell phone to her ear.

"Jake, I don't want to talk about it. No, this is the way it has to be. I'm sorry. Okay, I'm at The Sutherland."

With a sad expression, she closed her phone, disconnecting the call. She looked up, jolted. Her hand flew to her neck. "Oh, you scared me. I didn't realize you two were in here."

"How's everything with Jake?" Hailey asked.

Amy's eyes filled with unshed tears. "He's still caught up that it's the card thing. I'm just going to go up to my room."

"What was that all about?" Jake couldn't help but ask after she'd gone.

"Those dumb Fate Delivery Cards." Hailey gave a theatrical shudder.

"Those cards seem to have something to answer for," he told her.

"Tell me about it," she said, her tone rueful. "Okay, let me put on my professional voice. 'Our hallmarks here at The Sutherland are our friendly and personal service, desserts and easy access to the beach. Whether you're on a business trip, looking for a romantic escape or a fun weekend away, we'll have the mojitos waiting.' Or at least that's how we're hoping it will be. As you can see, it's a work in progress."

"I can see that," he said and she laughed. "Are you ready to go?"

"Sure, what do you have planned?" she asked.

"It's a surprise."

"I hate surprises," Hailey said as she wrinkled her nose, and he fought the urge to kiss the tip of it. Then to move down to her lips and keep kissing.

"That's what I was counting on."

"As long as you brought the card I'll endure the surprise. Just be prepared to pay up on that one."

HAILEY HADN'T EXACTLY TOLD Nate the truth. She actually liked surprises, but only if she were the one giving the surprise. Now she was eaten up with curiosity by two things—what his card had instructed and what were they doing. Nate escorted her to a car that could only be described as a hotrod. Black, sleek and with its top down. "Bought it when I first joined the Navy and had that first flush of cash. Thought it was cool and the chicks would dig it. Didn't realize it would mainly sit in storage because I was always overseas. I've toyed with the idea of having it sent to Missouri for my brother to use."

"How'd a boy from Missouri wind up in the Navy?"

"It's funny, but a good portion of our ranks come from the land-locked states. Probably because we yearn to see the ocean."

He helped her inside the car and she was engulfed by the plush gray leather. The color matched his eyes, but she doubted he'd appreciate her pointing that out. He may think the car kind of silly now, but it suited him. Streamlined and amazing to look at. The car smelled like him, too—ocean breezes with a hint of wood and sea salt. She took a deep breath, and dragged in the scent of him.

"How long are you home?" she asked, as he joined her inside the car.

"Not much longer, I hope. Right now I'm instructing Land Nav for SEAL SQT."

She tried not to appear clueless.

"It's the last training the men have before becoming a SEAL," he explained.

Apparently she hadn't done such a good job in not seeming clueless.

"After BUD/S." A slow grin spread across his face, and his eyes twinkled. "None of this is ringing a bell, is it? I thought you grew up in San Diego."

"Yes, but my mom didn't let me hang around sailors."

"Smart mom," he said, laughter in his voice.

Tell me about it. With his tight military-trained body, easy good looks and on the lookout for a fun time, he was like her kryptonite. "Sorry I'm so unfamiliar."

"Actually, I kind of like it."

After they fastened their seatbelts, Nate fired the powerful engine and they were off. He easily navigated away from Coronado toward old San Diego. She breathed deep as they crossed the Coronado Bridge linking the two areas. Soon she spotted the Victorian era buildings that could only be the historic Gaslamp Quarter. The city and its residents had done an amazing job restoring this area, and now it was a major attraction, from the Horton Grand Theater to antiques shops.

She turned toward him. "I've been wanting to visit Gaslamp since I came home, just never had the time."

"Thought seeing all this restoration would be inspiring."

"Me, too." And they shared one of those endless kinds of stares girls dreamed about as longing-for-a-boyfriend teenagers. The kind of gaze that never grew awkward, but instead only made them more aware of each other as a man and as a woman. And she was very much aware of him as a man. Her skin heated.

Nate had planned this just for her. He'd actually thought about it and attempted to come up with something for them to do that she would like.

She could be in some trouble with this one.

After Nate parked and put up the top, they strolled though Gaslamp. "I'll have to bring you back here at night. The Gaslamp Quarter sign is all lit up."

A warm tremble settled in her stomach hearing him suggest future times together.

More kryptonite.

They strolled through several unique stores of the Quarter and then Nate led her to an antique shop. She was intrigued by so many of the wares and displays that the only thing that had a hope of interrupting her was the growl of her stomach. Which it did. Loudly.

"One quick stop and then we can eat," he promised.

The crowds outside on the sidewalk were heavier now than when they first hit Gaslamp, and it seemed the most natural thing in the world for her to accept Nate's hand. The man was commanding in a crowd, people seemed to naturally get out of his way. The two of them walked together until they stood outside one of the oldest hotels of the area.

Irritation tensed her stomach, chasing away her earlier warmer feelings. Just what did he think was going to happen here? At a hotel? She followed him to the ornately carved front desk. The reception area was a classic example of Victorian-era American furnishings, with its dark woods and interiors. The Sutherland's front desk was not nearly as dramatic as the one here, but it was clear they were cousins. Although hers were the poorer relations.

"There should be a basket for Peterson."

That caught her attention. So he wasn't planning on checking in for a little first date horizontal time. That flash of irritation she'd felt, she now directed at herself. She shouldn't be so quick to judge on the basis of past bad boyfriends.

The woman behind the desk smiled and picked up the phone. "Let me just ring dining."

This was getting stranger. Nate reached for his wallet, and she discreetly walked away from the transaction. That move was squarely from her father's Rules of Dating 101. You never paid attention to how much or how little a man spent on a date. Instead she busied herself admiring the handpainted wallpaper with its stylized flowers and leaves the color of jasper—straight from the Victorian era. The fabric of the chairs in the lobby matched the wallpaper. What a good idea.

After a moment, a woman bustled up from the dining room carrying a large wicker hamper that looked a lot like a—

"Here's your picnic basket." She flashed a friendly smile toward Hailey. "Hope you enjoy your day."

"A picnic basket?" she asked as they were once more outside, her hand back in his.

"Unlike you, I'm not much of a cook."

He'd brought the romantic big gun, and Hailey realized she wasn't as immune as she'd suggested to Nate their last time together. Her heart, or stomach or something inside her seemed to soften. Hailey took a deep breath.

Then they were back in his car and this time they traveled up the San Diego freeway until she made out a familiar sign. "You're not taking me to Sea World?" she teased.

"I'm saving that for another day," he said with a wink. "We're going to Mission Bay Park."

The Mission Bay area had been a favorite of hers growing up. Acres and acres of nothing but green grass, palm trees and sandy beaches. The perfect place for a picnic. She had to reassess her beliefs about military men. Nate had whipped up something very romantic. For her. The predictable heartmelting reaction followed. This was even worse than softening. She really needed to avoid romance.

They took a winding path until they reached a shady spot. Nate spread out the traditional red and white-checkered cloth and they both sunk to the comfortable ground, softened by grass and blanket.

The basket contained delicious chicken salad, fresh fruit, croissants and wine, and since it was food she didn't have to prepare, cook or clean up afterward, Hailey was thrilled. "I have to hand it to you, Nate, this has been a really fun time."

"I'm glad. The hotel even tucked a kite inside the basket," he said.

Just to make sure every romantic date cliché had been covered. Unfortunately, it was working.

He stood, towering above her. Nate offered her his hand again, and although she'd held it before, she could dismiss that as an act of crowd protection. This time it would be more personal. Intimate. And why was she overanalyzing something like simply holding hands?

Nate had a man's hand. Big and callused and that easily engulfed hers. With little effort he tugged her to her feet. She grew increasingly aware of every inch of his body as he pulled her up. The wetsuit had only hinted at the strength of his legs, the utter flatness of his stomach and solidness of his chest. Without her heels, the top of her head was somewhere in the vicinity of his nose, and when she reached her full height she was staring at the jut of his chin. A chin with just a hint of a dimple.

It was one of the sexiest things she'd ever seen. She lifted her hand to trace it, then pulled away swiftly. Had she lost her mind? Hailey's eyes settled on the line of his mouth, his bottom lip surprisingly curved. Finally she met his gaze. And sucked in a breath.

He'd been waiting for her to meet his gaze. Where once she only saw the color of cool gray steel, his eyes had now darkened to a smoky slate. He wanted her. Hailey's heart began to pound. Her lips parted and she leaned into him. She wanted to kiss him so bad.

"This part of the park is perfect for kite flying. No power lines. No tall trees. You ready?"

She was ready for something, she just wasn't sure what.

That was a look of desire he flashed her, right? Hailey had chosen not to date for a while, but surely she wouldn't miss the mark that much? She'd certainly flashed him all the signs that she was ready for a little lip action.

"I can't remember the last time I flew a kite," she told him with a smile. Her voice tight.

He dropped her hands, then reached for the kite. It wasn't anything fancy—a few wooden poles, thin cotton material, but the tail…now that was cool. All the different, brightly colored fabrics tied to the string invited her enthusiasm.

"You want to toss up the kite or hold the string?" he asked.

"String."

He flashed her a boyish grin, handing her the string while holding the kite with excitement. Obviously she'd chosen correctly. "Okay, give it a little slack."

"Now what?" she asked when standing a few yards away.

"We wait for the wind."

A quick gust from off the ocean zoomed in, and Nate tossed the kite up. The air caught it at the right angle and the material poofed and lifted. She gave it more string, instinct or some muscle memory from childhood activated, and soon she had their yellow kite flying high in the air.

He returned to her side. His eyes were trained to the sky. "Pretty good teamwork," he said.

They stood together, side by side, watching as the kite went higher and higher. "Want to run with it?" she asked, feeling light and carefree and wanting the wind on her face and in her hair.

"Absolutely. We should lower it some. I'll help," he offered. Nate looped his arms over her shoulders and then his hands surrounded hers. Once again she was struck by just how big he was. How much larger he was than she. Like a mismatch. But with his tanned arms circling hers she had a great view of the hardened muscles of his biceps. Staring at the kite and running with it wasn't the same kind of temptation it was a moment ago. Now she battled leaning fully against him, closing her eyes and breathing him in.

"You know, I think there are easier ways to rein in the kite," she said over her shoulder.

He nodded. "Probably." But he didn't move.

She laughed and together they towed the kite lower until it bounced and waved only a few feet above their heads. Then he found her hand, and the two of them ran down the sandy beach, the water tickling their toes. They dodged children splashing in the foam and sea-shells and Hailey laughed, really laughed. Had she ever laughed this way with a man?

To her surprise the wind died, and their kite fell to the ground. "Oh, that's too bad," she said, her tone full of regret.

"Not really." And for her second surprise Nate brought her chin up and his lips came down on hers. Hailey didn't know how long they kissed under the sun with the waves lapping at her feet, but it was the most amazing kiss of her life. *This* was what it felt like to have Nate fully involved with a kiss from the beginning. That Fate Card sure knew how to deliver.

His lips moved along hers with a gentle confidence. She rose on her tiptoes and draped her arms around his shoulders. Nate's hands found her hips, and he nestled her closer into his body as his tongue found hers. He tasted like wine and a sunny day and she couldn't get enough of it.

The breeze picked up again, and she heard the kite kick and crash against the sand. Nate's hands slowly drifted up her waist and over her arms to cup her face. With a reluctance she wasn't quite ready to acknowledge, she allowed Nate to draw her away. He rested his forehead to hers and she felt him take a deep breath.

Hailey smiled, knowing the kiss had affected him as much as it had wrecked havoc with her.

"After BUD/S, I never thought I'd *want* to run on the beach again."

Warmth spread through her chest at his rueful words. She liked knowing she could change his mind.

"Of course then I'd just swam, jogged and then told to roll in the sand. I came out looking like a sugar cookie."

Now that held some strange appeal. Nate had conjured up in her mind two delicious images, cookies, and a wet, buff man in a swimsuit.

"You ready to finish off that wine?" he asked.

No, but it would have to do. She nodded, and after winding the remaining kite string up tight, they returned to the blanket.

They lay on the checkered material, facing one another. The breeze and warm sunny day lulled her, tempted her to lower her guard where Nate was concerned. Thoughts like, "what could it hurt to see him a few times?" and "he'll be gone soon, no harm, no foul, right?" kept popping into her head. And of course everything about him from his consideration to his tight butt lured her further into thinking about taking everything he offered and demanding more.

Soon the sex thoughts emerged. She'd had the emo artist guy, the business-suited manipulator and finally Mr. Hot who was as into himself as she was into him. But she'd never been intimate with the hard body, capable type. Broad shoulders, strong arms…she had more than one thing to be thankful to the U.S. military for. What would he be like in bed? Adjectives like maneuverable and robust popped into her head, and she fought a giggle.

Then words like powerful, strong and big pushed those other words aside. The man jumped out of planes, he dived under water with explosives strapped to his body with only his ability and equipment to trust. The man possessed that quiet intensity that both excited and unnerved her. What would it be like to have all that focused directly on her? As they made love? Hailey shivered. The idea was both delicious and intimidating. Actually, very intimidating.

"Grape?" he asked.

It was clear he planned to feed her. It was right up there on the romantic scale, and must have been his one-thousandth sexy move of the day. Why had she ever mentioned she didn't believe in romance? Hailey drained her wineglass. Now was the time to remind him of her no relationship stipulation because this felt very much like a relationship oriented moment. With a sigh she said, "I just want to make sure you know...I don't date."

He nodded, looking completely unconcerned.

"At all," she added for emphasis.

"I remember," he told her, his eyes growing curious. "How come?"

"I pick bad men."

His lips twisted, and he gave her a kind of lopsided grin. "It's a good thing you didn't pick me then. Your Fate Delivery Card did, remember?"

Exactly how much sexiness and allure was a woman supposed to take? Man, if ever the "life wasn't fair" assertion had come into play. This was it. When she didn't want a man, a funny hot one charged onto the scene. She had to put an end to this now, or she'd be back down that same road. She was supposed to be taking time off. Regrouping, and yes it was a cliché, but finding herself.

"Enough with the charm," she said with a good-natured, but very firm, grin.

"I balk at the word charm."

She knew his shmooze was all in an effort to prove her wrong. "Okay, attitude then. It's cute, but I've done the cute fiancé thing. In fact, I've had three."

"Three?" he asked, his voiced raised since the first time she'd met him.

Now he sounded a little concerned. He should be concerned. She'd tried to warn him.

"I thought I only had to contend with one former fiancé, but three?"

So, he'd put some thought into her brief mention of her former lover. It made her happy despite the fact that there would be no place for them to go with what they were doing.

"I'm taking time off from men."

"Strange, it seemed like I was getting a very different signal from you when you were in my arms, kissing me."

"I wasn't kissing you, you were kissing me."

"You were kissing my face off."

She propped her hands on her hips. "I was not. It was fun, I grant you that, but it was part of the mood—the kite, the beach, the running. It was the scenario, and I doubt the mood will strike again."

As soon as the words flew out of her mouth, she knew she'd said the wrong thing. Nate was the kind of guy who *enjoyed* a challenge. Hell, he probably lived for the adrenaline rush.

"Listen, if you want to try it again just to prove it didn't mean anything, you're welcome to." He flexed the muscles across his chest as if he was bracing himself.

She laughed, but quickly cleared her expression. "I think I've seen that ploy in a movie or something. Look, we're not going to act out any cutesy scene of you daring me to kiss you and if I don't respond then you'll go away."

"Kiss you again? I hadn't even thought of that."

"Liar. I'm just going to lay it all on the line here." Enough with the playful banter. It was time to get serious. "You are very good-looking, sexy even."

"Why am I not feeling flattered?"

Hailey smiled. "Ordinarily I'd be going for you in a snap, and therefore," Hailey held up her hands and said, "I'm not."

The humor faded from his eyes. "That makes zero sense."

"Believe me, you don't want to know how many mistakes I've made with men. Sure I could get involved with you, I mean, what girl wouldn't want to at least try to make something work with you? Normally, I'd be there in a shot and it would be great…for awhile. But then what would happen? My very prominent self-destructive DNA asserts itself."

Nate glanced around the park. Searching for an escape route perhaps? "Usually I follow one of two routes. Option one is me finding fault with every little thing you do. Men love a nagging woman, believe me."

"What if there's nothing to find fault with?"

Ah, more of that challenging spirit. She liked it.

"Well then, I go into my test mode. That's were I see how much of my nonsense you'd take. Either way, the sex gets really awkward, and eventually you'll have had enough. Then starts the dividing of our stuff, and…right now you should be thanking your lucky stars that I'm preemptively ending our relationship before it even starts."

"Huh, and here I was thinking maybe dinner. Did you say something about sex in all that?" he asked. He stroked down her forearm with the back of his hand. The warmth of his caress made her jolt.

Funny, sexy and charming…her doom. *Get away from him now.*

"Do I make you nervous, Hailey?" By the stunned expression on his face, he seemed surprised by his re-alization.

Yes. "No, uh, no. Of course not. Why do you ask?" She glanced downward, and began to play with the edge of the blanket.

His hands stilled hers, and she looked up. "You seem jumpy around me. Although you're awfully girly, you don't seem high-strung, so I'm guessing it's me," he said his tone light, but his expression serious.

And he got it in one. He made her nervous and jumpy and agitated in ways no man ever had. But she would not be intimidated by her primal reaction to the man. No, she'd give as good as she got. "Girly?" she questioned.

Hailey imagined some lean, athletic type woman who would look great with her hair in a ponytail, no make-up and jogging beside this very physical man. In school she'd always admired the girls on the soccer field running and laughing. Hailey didn't even have the coordination to do step aerobics.

"I take it you don't normally go for the girly types."

He shook his head, his smile turning rueful. "No one ever baked me cookies," he said, his voice low and raspy.

His tone told her he wanted to taste her cookies like he wanted to taste her.

"And those dresses you wear with the frilly little straps…"

Nate's voice trailed, and she imagined his lean fingers sliding those straps down her shoulders.

"Or worn an apron," he said, leaning closer. "I just want to reach for the strap and tug."

She swallowed, thinking of him taking off her apron…and more.

"And those ridiculous heels are sexy as hell," he whispered against her lips. Then his mouth settled on hers, warm and inviting and for way, way too short of a time.

After she caught her breath, she smiled up into his eyes. "I'm good with girly."

His eyes darkened, and his gaze made a pass to her lips, down to her breasts, then back up to meet her eyes. "I'm more than good with it."

7

SOMEHOW, SOMEWAY, Hailey found herself on the date that would never end. A date she didn't *want* to end. Nate seemed just as reluctant to leave because now he sat on the terrace of the Sutherland drinking a beer. She hadn't been able to convince him to sample the Mojito.

Alone with nothing but the breeze and the peaceful lap of the ocean, Hailey became utterly aware that she was alone in the dark with Nate. A man she couldn't wait to get her hands on. She'd never diss romance again because right now the butterflies were making an appearance in her stomach. Not even the moon was out to shed light between them, and her senses grew hyper-alert of every subtle shift of his body.

He stood, and Hailey sucked in a breath, instantly feeling foolish.

"Do I make you nervous, Hailey?" he asked, his voice like a caress to her already agitated senses.

"You…you asked me that once already."

"And then I got distracted, but I'm not distracted now. Now I'm focused on you."

That's what she was afraid of. To have all that single-minded SEAL determination and intensity focused squarely on her…heady.

With one quick, silent motion, he was beside her. His big body warm and oh, so tempting. "How'd you do that? I can't see a thing out here in the dark." Besides being night, the awning partially covering the terrace shrouded them in shadows.

"Most of my missions are after the sun sets. SEALs do their best work in the dark."

That's what she was afraid of.

He trailed a finger down her cheek, making her shiver. "So what's the problem?" he asked.

How like Nate to want to tackle a problem head on. Based on the several personality quizzes she'd taken over the years, she knew she preferred to be an avoider in bad situations.

Whoa, and there was another problem. She'd only known the man a few days, and already she was recognizing his personality traits. Hailey swallowed. She was on a mission to change, might as well take a cue from the man she found so intriguing. "You're a little…a little big."

Hailey could almost feel him smile. Yeah, yeah yeah, she knew where his thinking was headed because her mind had also gone *there,* too.

He gently cupped her face, kissed the tip of her nose. "I could never hurt you, Hailey."

She nodded. "I know."

"No, I mean, Hailey, I would never hurt you. Never *allow* anything to hurt you."

Her throat tightened. Nate's words were the sexiest, most amazing thing a man had ever said to her. And she knew, deep down, he meant it.

"I'll prove it," he offered.

He must have taken her silence for doubt. She

almost rushed to reassure him, but a very intriguing thought popped into her head. "How would you prove it, Nate?" she asked.

"You be in control. You tell me how to touch your body. Where to kiss. When to move."

Every nerve ending, every muscle, every sense she had popped into action. If she'd thought having all his intensity focused on her was heady, his offer now made her lightheaded. Her nipples tightened. Warmth pooled between her legs. "I just tell you what to do?"

"If anything you suggest shocks me, I'll let you know," he said, his voice teasing and yet filled with so much desire for her that Hailey's nerves began to subside.

What did she want him to do to her? For her? In the past, she'd concentrated on how to make the men in her life happy, but here was one wanting to see to her needs. "Kiss my face," she encouraged. "Gentle, but not on my lips."

Nate drew her head toward his mouth, and ran his lips lightly along the line of her jaw, kissed her chin, then the tip of her nose. Finally, he tenderly kissed her closed eyes. Heaven.

"Trace my lips with your tongue."

His strong arms circled her shoulders, bringing her nearer. Slowly, achingly slow, his tongue followed the line of her bottom lip, then the top. She wanted him to sink his tongue into her mouth, sensed he wanted to deepen the caress as well, but didn't. True to his word, he was waiting for the invitation.

"Kiss me," she urged. With a groan, his tongue slid past her lips and teeth to tangle with her tongue. How quickly she had become accustomed to his taste.

Her nipples tightened further. Her breasts ached for his touch.

"Caress my breasts."

Nate's hands flowed down her body until they rested at her hips. His fingers slipped under the material of her shirt, and she sucked in a breath at the exquisite feel of his warm fingers against the bare skin of her stomach. If this is what he could do with just a touch to her waist, imagine what the man could do when he had free rein of her body.

His hands slowly drifted up her sides, past her ribcage and finally cupped her breasts. "You fill my hands perfectly," he whispered against her lips.

Hailey had not always been a fan of her small breasts. Had even thought of augmenting them at one time, but right now she couldn't be happier with their size. "Take my bra off and really feel them," she said, surprised by the impatience she heard in her voice.

His fingers made a lazy trail to her back where he found the clasp. With a quick motion, he freed her breasts, cupping them once more.

"Does this seat lay back?" he asked.

"Yes."

Hailey felt cold as his hands left her body, but the idea of stretching out on the lounger with Nate beside her was just too appealing.

"Take my shirt off," she said. Nate's fingers tugged the material up and over her head, tossing it to the side.

Hailey slipped her bra off and reclined against the cushion.

"I wish I could see you," he said, his voice raw and filled with wanting.

"I thought you said SEALs worked best in the dark."

"After lots of practice. I'm going to need a lot of time with your body," he responded.

There were the shivers again. "Then have at it," she invited.

"No, you have to tell me what to do. Remember?"

If those weren't the sexiest words ever spoken by a man, she didn't know what would qualify. She swallowed, readying herself to tell this man in detail what she wanted him to do to her body.

"I want you to gently touch my breasts with the palms of your hands. Slowly. In circles."

The lounger dipped as he leaned toward her, and then she felt the heat of his hands, smoothing over her nipples.

"Lighter," she instructed, and sucked in a breath as the pressure of his stroking eased to just a hint of a touch.

"Mmm, I like that." And she wanted more. "Now I want you to lick my nipples then blow."

Nate followed her instructions as if he was born to do it; the sensations exquisite. "My nipples are so tight."

"I know, I want to suck them."

Moist heat flooded between her legs. "Well, you can't," she teased, feeling powerful and in control—exactly the way Nate wanted her to feel. "I want you to tease my nipples, gently with your teeth."

With a swirl of his tongue, he did just that. First one nipple, then the other. Her toes curled into the cushion, he was making her feel so good. Hailey felt the solid length of his erection against her thigh. Clearly, the man was big all over.

It took a moment for her to find her voice. "Now I want you to trace my entire body with your hands, making your circles smaller and smaller until you reach my…"

"Your what?" he asked against her ear. His warm breath tickled her neck and sent shivers through her body.

He was going to make her say it. "My clit."

"You have on too many clothes," he stated.

"Then take them off."

"As you command." She knew Nate was smiling in the dark because she was, too. His fingers found the waistband of her pants, and pulled them slowly down, down her legs.

Hailey sat up on her elbows. "But wait, you left my panties."

"Do you want me to take them off?" he asked, but his promising tone made her think she might want Nate to take her clothes off in stages.

She shook her head and lowered herself back against the soft cushion of the lounger. "No. Leave them."

Nate started with his circles, his hands not touching anyplace remotely sexual as he stroked her in a wide arc. Her heels dug deeper and deeper into the lounger as his circles tightened. He reached the top swell of her breasts, down her arms and across her thighs.

Now his hands were fully across her nipples making them tingle, then his brief touch moved lower to torment her thighs, getting closer and closer to the spot she knew he'd make her feel best.

Two more circles around her body and his hand settled between her legs. With a slow, tortuous glide his hand slid between her thighs to stop at the silk of her panties.

Frustration bubbled up inside her. "Take them off."

"How? With my hands or with my teeth?"

Her legs began to shake. "Teeth," she urged.

Hailey felt his lips at the place where skin met silk.

He gently kissed her hip, traced the edge of lace with his tongue, then he nipped at the material, drawing it into his mouth. She squeezed her eyes tight as the amazing sensations of those panties sliding down her body, dragged only by Nate's teeth.

He finally had her naked. His fingers started to slowly trace her again. This time he didn't stop anywhere. No, now his fingers slid up between her thighs. And up until his fingers tickled the curls. Then he stopped.

The waiting was agony. Why wasn't he doing anything? Then she realized he was waiting for her next instruction.

"Stroke me," she said, her voice strained.

And Nate slipped a finger inside her, and tenderly began to move. "Touch me more," she commanded, never feeling so raw. Nate slipped another finger inside and his thumb finally, *finally* touched her clit. A moan tore from her body and she began to writhe. Something was missing. She was astounded by her overwhelming desire to have him *fill* her. She'd never felt that way.

"Now, Nate. I need you now."

"I don't have a condom," he told her.

She almost groaned. "What? Why?" she asked.

"I was supposed to be romancing you tonight. If I'd brought a condom I'd be thinking about sex," he said with a laugh.

How like him to psych himself up that way.

"But don't worry, I can still take care of you," he promised, his voice sensual, his words sincere.

Hailey was wet now. Nate's lips touched hers at the

same time his thumb settled on her clit. His fingers began to slide in and out of her. She raised her hips toward his hand, not able to get enough of him.

"This is how I'll make love to you," he said against her mouth. "Gentle until you want it hard."

"I want it hard *now*." She was breathless. Sweat broke out along her forehead.

And Nate complied with her wish, his fingers all over, all in her until that sweet tension inside broke and she erupted. Her moan filled the air as she came.

After a few minutes, when her breathing returned to normal, Nate tenderly kissed her face. The tip of her nose. Her eyes. Just like her first instructions.

"Do I still make you nervous?" he asked.

Even more so. A man who could make her respond to him like she had with just one hand was a man to be concerned about.

But her worries about his bigness, about his overwhelming power had subsided. "Yes," she replied, nodding.

He sat up, flexing the muscles of his shoulder. The lounger was oversized, but it wasn't built for two, and with Nate's large frame, that had to have been a tight squeeze. "I better go," he said.

"Oh, but what about, uh, you." Nate had to be in a bad way.

He felt around at his feet until he found her clothes. "We'll take care of me next time."

Next time. His words made her skin tingle. Hailey couldn't wait until they took care of him.

He helped her with her clothes, and then walked her to the terrace door. The parking lot was as easily assessable from the terrace as it was the front door. "Nate, make sure you bring a condom."

A slow smile tugged at his lips. "I'll bring more than one. Now lock the door."

With a twist of her wrist, she made sure The Sutherland was secure for the night. Nate checked the lock from the outside then turned. She watched his retreating back until she couldn't see him anymore.

Hailey knew she wore a goofy grin, but she couldn't help it. The man made her feel amazing, but there was something else. That checking the door move made her heart skip a beat. What had her first instinct been about the man? That he was trouble?

Instincts usually seemed to be right.

"Oh, Hailey, there you are."

Hailey spun around to spot Amy at the entrance of the Tea Room and her hand went immediately to her hair. Did she look normal, or did she look like a woman who'd just—

"Do you have a few moments? I wanted to talk to you about Jake."

Whew, okay, maybe she didn't look too rumpled. Or sated. Hailey pulled out one of the Queen Anne chairs from the closest table and invited Amy to take a seat. "How are things with Jake?"

Amy's face crumpled, yet she managed to appear a bit defiant. "He's still pretty angry with me."

"Well, I can kind of see his point."

Amy gasped.

Okay, Hailey obviously needed a more tactful approach here. She schooled her features into what she hoped was an understanding expression, and faced her confused and upset guest and friend. "I mean, you won't even see him, Amy. That kind of sounds like you're following the instructions of the card rather than trying to discover the source of your problems together as a couple."

"I keep telling myself if it's meant to be then it's meant to be."

A trickle of unease slid down Hailey's back. What Amy had just said wasn't something she hadn't thought of herself half a dozen times, but now...now it seemed a little like leaving things in fate's hands. And she was pretty irritated with fate right now. First by delivering a man she couldn't stop thinking about, but knew she should stay away from, and now a friend turned guest whose life was in shambles because of what happened at The Sutherland. Not exactly a great restart for their B&B.

That reminded her. They were going to burn Amy's card and never had. Tonight would be a great time to do it. In fact, they could burn the whole deck right here at the—

"Do you ever have to fake it?" Amy asked.

Well, there'd certainly been no pretending with Nate. Hailey glanced toward the door, wanting to escape. Where was her sister when she needed her?

"Would you like me to brew some chamomile?"

Amy shook her head. "No, if I don't do this now, have a real conversation about sex, I might be miserable for the rest of my life." Amy grew flustered. "Jake's the only man I've been with, and I've never been particularly adventurous. Well, sometimes he would like me to be..."

Hailey reached for her hand and gave her a reassuring squeeze. Wow, what kind of freaky stuff was this man into to make Amy so upset? "It's okay, you can tell me anything. Go on."

"Sometimes he would like me to be on top," Amy said on a rush of exhaled breath.

Hailey turned skeptical. "Are you…kidding with me?"

"No, no. There's more. He once told me he'd like for me to initiate sex once in a while, can you believe it?"

Hailey chewed on her bottom lip.

"I know there are women, friends of ours who have no problem being so wild, but I've tried and I just can't do it."

Hailey let out a relieved sigh. "For a minute there, I was afraid you were going to tell me he was into something really weir—okay, I'm not doing such a good job here. Amy, it seems like you were born before the sexual revolution. What you've said doesn't even describe *my* mom. I know your grandparents raised you, but surely…"

"My grandmother told me sex—" Amy smiled, obviously proud she was able to say the word without stumbling "—was something you did to make your husband happy, and that was basically my entire education. When she had to buy me my first B, I thought I was going to die of embarrassment."

"Are you still calling it that?"

Amy nodded.

"I'm almost feeling sorry for Jake," muttered Hailey.

Amy looked hurt.

"I keep saying the wrong thing, don't I? I'm so sorry." Where was her sister?

Surprisingly, Amy chuckled. "Oh. My. God. What kind of grown woman can't say the word bra?"

The two of them laughed together, but Hailey quickly sobered. "Just so I'm clear, you've never had an orgasm?"

"I don't think so."

"Believe me, there's no 'think' about it if you've had one." Hailey's body warmed at the memory of the orgasm Nate had given her a little while ago. "I'll put that down as a no. You've never done anything other than the, uh, missionary position?"

Amy shook her head quickly, her cheeks glowing pink.

Hailey shook her head again. "I can't believe Jake even got you into the bedroom."

"To tell you the truth, I can't believe it either. I was liking it up to a point, all the kissing and the holding, but then I felt so dirty."

Hailey made a disgusted noise. "I can't believe you were ever taught to feel that way. Sex, making love, it's a wonderful thing. It can draw a couple together and be beautiful, or it can be playful and fun, and sometimes you could maybe make it dirty," Hailey said, and winked, "if you wanted to. But sex can also divide two people, and that sounds like what's going on between you and Jake."

"Like a wedge," Amy agreed.

"I'm guessing that you've never discussed this with your fiancé? Or anyone?"

"Oh, God no. I turn on the water faucet when I go to the bathroom, I certainly couldn't talk to him about *this*." She shook her head. "Even when I moved into the dorms at school, some of the girls made fun of me, so I kept my mouth shut."

Hailey sucked in her lip, feeling guilty all over again. "Have I apologized about laughing earlier?"

Flashing her an easy grin, Amy said, "Tori just thinks I'm shy. No one, but you, knows it all."

"I'm going to say it again. The person you need to be talking to is Jake."

"No I couldn't."

"You're going to have to do something. Believe me when I tell you this, Jake appears to be a hell of a guy, especially considering the water bill he must be facing. But sex is important in a relationship. You need to fix this now. Listen, I have an idea. I'm going to run up to my room and grab something for you. Be right back."

"Okay," Amy said, and Hailey bound from the room.

Hailey returned, holding a small red and yellow book. *Freeing Your Sexual Self.* Amy swallowed after reading the title.

Hailey gave Amy's shoulder a reassuring pat. "Don't let the title intimidate you. Also, maybe you're thinking about your Fate Delivery Card in the wrong way."

"How could I look at it any other way? Picking *that* card…it was just so strange. There's fate, and there's co-incidence and then there's plain cosmic weirdness. Surely there was a reason, two weeks before I'm supposed to get married, that I pull that card from the deck. Right? How many signs am I supposed to ignore?"

Hailey's head tilted. "Or those 'signs' just mani-fested in the form of silly little cards that mean nothing and you're in the middle of a sex wedge and some very understandable prewedding jitters and panicked."

Amy glanced down at the engagement ring twin-kling on her finger. "The card only made it clear to me that things have been off for a while."

Hailey held up her hands in surrender. "I've had

three failed engagements, maybe some of my bad luck is rubbing off on you."

Amy quickly looked up at her new friend. "Of course not, that's just silly."

"As silly as banking your future on some mass produced boxed card set? Anyway, this is what I meant about the card. Maybe you're not supposed to set him free as in letting him go. Maybe you're supposed to set something in your relationship free, as in exploring. Now, get to reading." Hailey stood. "I'll leave you to it."

8

"THOSE CHOCOLATE and strawberry waffles are to die for. The guests are asking for more," Hailey informed her sister, as she placed the serving tray on the tiled countertop. Nate liked good food. Would he feel like breakfast in bed?

"How's our latest guest doing?" Rachel asked. The line forming between her eyebrows told Hailey how worried her sister was.

"Relax, I set a few things in motion last night. I'm sure the self-help book I gave her really got her mind to thinking."

Rachel groaned. "Not another one." Her sister took a very deep breath. "It's okay. Not going to worry about it. What was it mom always said? Don't get involved with the lives of guests?"

"Amy is not a guest, she's Amy. And if that's a rule, we can add it to the long list of other ones I've broken. We stayed up pretty late last night talking."

"Get any closer to her real reason for being so upset?"

"Yes, and believe me, you don't want to hear it."

"Good, I don't. Did you see that? *That* is how you take sound advice."

Hailey laughed. She felt kind of sorry for Amy—not

having a sister to laugh with, talk about sex with, get advice from.

"By the way, how did everything go last night? I had the ice cream all ready," Rachel said.

Hailey heard the disappointment in her sister's voice and immediately felt guilty. Eating ice cream in the kitchen after a date had become a tradition when their mom was still alive. The three of them would joke, confide, eat and talk about their date until her dad would tease them that girl power hour was over.

"Rachel, I'm sorry. I guess I've been going on dates and dissecting them all on my own for so long, I completely forgot." Not that she hadn't already dissected every moment, every touch and every kiss she'd shared with Nate.

"Waffle batter is not as fun as hot fudge and sprinkles, but you're going to spill it all right now. Did you get lips?"

She shivered at the memory. "As in non-card-coerced-mouth-on-mouth action?"

"Stop stalling. I'm not afraid to splash you with melted butter."

"Okay, yes, I got lips." And so much more. "If I were the kind of girl that appreciated romance and romantic gestures, I'd say he scored himself a winner. A picnic on the beach." And she wanted even more than what she got although she knew she shouldn't. She was man transitioning here.

Rachel dropped the sponge in the murky water. "Wait, what? You did something outside? On purpose? And you liked it? With the bugs, and the probability of sweating and the potential to mess your hair?"

"I'm not that bad."

"Yeah, I'm actually giving you a little credit. Hailey, you're my sister and I love you, but you're the girliest girl I know. Pink is your favorite color and there hasn't been a pair of cute strappy sandals you could say no to. I didn't even know you owned a pair of tennis shoes until I saw you walk out of here in them with Nate."

"I'd just bought them," Hailey confessed. Then busied her hands arranging the glasses on the top rack of the commercial dishwasher.

Rachel shook her head. "Wow, I get more and more impressed by this SEAL the more I hear about him. He got you into something totally ungirly."

He could probably get her out of something just as easily.

"So, when are you going out again?"

Hailey stopped loading the dishwasher. "He didn't exactly ask me for another date." He'd just referred to *next time*.

The teasing smile faded from her sister's face. "Hmm, that's odd. He seemed pretty into you."

"I told him I didn't do relationships." She almost wished she'd kept her mouth closed.

Her sister clucked her tongue. "I knew you wouldn't take my advice. Feel free to ignore the little sister. He didn't seem the type to be discouraged that easily."

No, Nate was clearly one of those over-achiever types. And where were all these conflicted feelings coming from? She didn't want to date right now. Did she? She'd had to remind herself of that several times last night when he reached for her hand as they strolled on the sidewalk. She clearly recapped her resolution as they raced down the beach with the kite. Okay, she forgot during the kissing part, but that was a minor slip off course. She was back, repeating the no-dating mantra, when they were lying on the blanket together, enjoying the wine.

But then all hell broke loose out there on the terrace.

"You're smiling," Rachel said.

"What?" she asked. Playing it dumb was the best course of action here.

"You don't look like he took your words at face value. Like maybe something a little more than lips happened last night."

"I don't know what you're talking about," she insisted as she closed the door to the dishwasher. A little too forcefully.

"Listen, if you can't be honest with yourself, at least be honest with me. You like him."

Hailey pressed the button to get the machine started, then propped her hip against the counter. "Now is not the best time for me to be seeing him. To be seeing anyone."

"So why did you agree?"

Because when he was sitting here in this kitchen it seemed like a really good idea. Nate was funny, and charming and so, *so* hot.

"You're going to hate it when I tell you. He took a Fate Delivery Card, and…" Hailey's words trailed away on a gasp. "All the time he never told me what it said on his card," Hailey blurted, feeling really naive.

That kiss he'd given her had really messed with her priorities.

"Maybe that was his plan," Rachel said.

And it was a pretty good one. Her curiosity ramped even higher now, and it wasn't only about the card.

She was intrigued about the man, his motives and how he'd make love.

"Well, anyway. Enough about Nate. I have some good news, too. My friend at the Tourism Bureau came through. We have at least twelve guests for coffee and cake. Operation Spot a SEAL two point oh is on."

TONIGHT'S TRAINING EXERCISES would take them late until the evening. They'd fast rope from the helo at sunset, swim for two hours, then ascend to the helicopter in the dark. SEALs conducted the majority of their operations at night to avoid detection. These men would not only have to get used to the dark, but qualify to where they operated in the shadows just as easily as in the daylight. For Nate it was his everyday job, but the training had to reflect the realities of life as a SEAL. The new moon would give them no help.

No one spoke, each man concentrating on the job. They were getting closer to completing SQT, closer to earning their Trident, which finally made them a SEAL. Still, even at this level, some would fall short.

In a few minutes, The Sutherland would come into view. Nate couldn't imagine the B&B without thinking of the action that took place outside between him and Hailey. Damn, that woman was hot. He could still hear those quick breaths she took. Or that sexy slow moan she made as she turned to fire in his arms. Adrenaline rushed through him, searing his focus. He was always like this before a jump, but this time he was more tense because he wanted to see if Hailey had kept her word about no more women on the shoreline.

Truthfully, he expected his men to operate as trained

regardless if a hundred flashing women waited for them at the beach. Good experience for his men to work through the distraction. His hand fisted around his harness. Except that it would mean something—something *to him,* if the ladies weren't there all scantily clad and cheering. Hailey would have placed his request above her own financial gain. Long before she'd told him, it was obvious that she needed the money and he knew what it would cost her not to have the extra cash from those women.

He held his breath and glanced down at the beach, but the helo was still too far away for him to get a clear picture. Nate noticed some of the men were also straining to see if their cheerleaders were on the beach. Didn't matter. The rush provided by the thought of those women might give the men an edge.

He shifted in his seat, his gaze never settling for very long. What waited or didn't wait on the beach would answer a lot of questions. Like whether he should go with his gut, instead of his head, and pursue Hailey.

The military life suited him. He liked the discipline, the clear-cut lines. None of that was Hailey. Yet she was the sexiest, most mix-signaled woman he'd ever met. She'd tell him she didn't date, then plant the hottest kiss with that same mouth. He'd left Hailey at her door, but he craved her sweet-smelling softness the rest of the night.

Next time he wouldn't be forgetting the condoms.

The pilot signaled their approach, and he readied his gear. In orderly fashion each man quietly plunged into the ocean. Cold and bracing. As soon as Nate resurfaced, the distorted sound of some kind of patriotic music blasting from a cheap set of stereo speakers hit his ears. He ground his teeth. The men, searching for the source of the sound, rotated in the water.

But he knew the source. The Sutherland.

People lined the shore once more, but he had to hand it to Hailey, she'd kept her word, but still got her way. Instead of rowdy single women, couples waved to them. The crowd held signs, but they didn't encourage phone calls. No, these signs read "We're proud of our son!" and "Keep up the good work!"

"I think that's my mom," one of the men said, clearly horrified.

For a woman who'd stated she didn't want him in her life, Hailey knew how to make certain he did just that. He found himself smiling in anticipation. Then he quickly propelled forward…should get that two-mile swim started as soon as possible. He had a long night ahead of him.

"WELL, OUR GUESTS HAD their SEALs for the night," announced Rachel as the men swam out of sight. "This went even better than when we had the ladies only. All but two of the parents booked a room. We're almost at capacity."

Hailey nodded, unable to shake her feeling of apprehension as she cleared the tables of napkins and glasses.

Amy pointed to an empty bottle. "Except some of the dads are wanting something other than mojitoes. We'll definitely need more scotch." She then yawned and stretched out on one of the loungers. "All this time on my feet. The B&B business is hard work."

"Tell me about it," Hailey said.

"What's wrong, Hailey?" Rachel asked. "You don't seem excited. We had a great night."

Hailey swiped a tabletop with a cloth. Technically, she'd kept to her agreement with Nate. No distracting women.

"Hailey?"

She shrugged. "I don't know. Inviting the parents seemed like a good idea at the time. A nice alternative to that all-female meat market feel from the other day, but now…"

Rachel gave her sister's hand a squeeze. "Now is the balance sheet. Give that a quick scan, and you won't have any doubts."

And yet, somehow she felt as if she was letting Nate down.

The doorbell rang. "All that use, and the thing still sounds terrible," Hailey grumbled.

"Another couple of SEAL Watch Parties, and we'll be able to afford a whole new announcement system, never mind a new doorbell. You see who it is, I'll take all these glasses to the kitchen."

As Hailey happily avoided kitchen duty as much as possible, she gladly took that deal. Tossing the cloth over her shoulder, she headed for the lobby. With a tug, she swung the wide oak door open wide and was surprised to see a tall, blond man at the threshold. His expression was a combination of worry and anger.

"May I help you?" Hailey asked.

"I'm here for my fiancée. Amy?" he answered.

This must be Jake.

AMY WAS DRAINING THE last of her drink and enjoying the soft cushion of the lounge chair on the terrace. She could stay like this forever. The light gentle breeze, the lull of the ocean as it lapped at the sand all helped to ease her stress. The tension that had been building in her shoulders in the form of tight knots for weeks released more every day. Today was even better. Alone she could enjoy the warm San Diego weather without having to worry about fittings or wedding plans, Jake or diets. Or orgasms.

As long as she didn't let her thoughts drift to the complete mess she'd made of her life, she was totally fine.

"Amy!"

She sprung upright, the muscles lining her back already returning to knots. Her eyes went wide, hoping the sound she'd heard was a trick of too much mojito.

Not a trick. Her stomach pitched and she scrambled to her feet. She was not ready to deal with this. Not yet. She knew Jake was mad, but she'd never wanted to hurt him, would do anything to make him feel better, make up for deserting him like this…but in a few days. Not now. She wasn't ready.

He burst through the door leading from the Tea Room to the terrace. Hailey mouthed, "I'm sorry," and Amy gave her friend a quick nod of understanding. *This* was not her fault.

"Jake," she said, her voice almost breathless. Amy hadn't expected to feel the tightening of her chest when she saw him. She'd practically fallen in love with him the day he'd walked in late to their freshman English class at San Diego State. Now his eyes were filled with pain. Pain she'd caused.

He looked her square in the eye. Dauntless conviction rested in those green depths. "We need to talk."

Amy nodded, knowing there had to be some kind of confrontation. "Let's go to the beach."

Together they took the tiled steps from the terrace to the sand below. Together, but very much apart.

As poor college students, walking the beach had been the only thing they could afford. Since it was free. Along this very shore, they'd talked and dreamed and planned their life together. Tears pricked the back of her eyes.

"When was the last time we were here?" she asked.

Jake shrugged. "I don't know. Feels like a long time ago." He sounded frustrated and a little sad.

"To me, too." They continued to walk in silence, both staring straight ahead. "We shouldn't go too far. There's not much sun left."

He stopped walking and faced her. "Are you ever going to tell me why you left me?"

The hurt in his voice made it hard for her to breathe. The selfishness of what she'd done had fully hit her.

"I had no hint, no clue that anything was wrong," he began. "You never said a word. I think you owe it to me to say something now."

She struggled to find the right words. To make them match her thoughts. "Things haven't felt right in the last few months."

She heard him swallow, watched his Adam's apple move up and down.

"Since we became engaged?" he asked.

"Before that. I was hoping getting married would help that."

Jake made a strangled sound in his throat. "I can't believe this. How could marriage help relationship problems?" he asked, waving a hand in the air.

"You don't understand," she said, looking away, focusing on where the sun met the water's edge in the horizon. As a kid she'd listen to see if she could hear it sizzle.

"I'm trying to understand," he said, drawing her close. "Make me understand."

It felt so good to lay her head on his chest. To feel his arms around her body. *Freeing Your Sexual Self.* The title of the book popped into her mind. Could she be the kind of woman who did the things the book suggested? Amy shivered and felt goose bumps along her arms and the back of her neck.

Jake rested his hands on her shoulder and pushed her away slightly to peer into her eyes. "Are you okay?"

She nodded, not able to find her voice. The warmth from her face spread throughout her body, as the idea of his body moving within her grew more carnal. Her mouth dried. She needed a drink. Maybe she needed him.

His eyes seemed to scan her face, search her eyes. She must have failed at whatever it was he sought because his hands fell to his sides. "Maybe we should head back," he told her, already turning.

Alarm raced through her. That was it? He was ready to let this conversation go so quickly? She was losing him, and suddenly she knew losing Jake was the last thing she wanted. Something strong and urgent forced her to try again. To make him understand. To make herself understand why she did such a crazy thing as leave the one she loved. "All the bridal magazines advise you should never lose the man you're marrying because the wedding has overtaken everything else, but I felt like I'd lost you long before you put that ring on my finger." *The first night he'd taken her to bed.*

"I think I know what you mean."

Her feet wouldn't take another step. "You do?"

"Until you said it just now, I hadn't realized it, but in some ways I think we've just been going through the motions. The steps of life, you know? You graduate from college. You get a job. Then you get an apartment. Finally you get married."

Her stomach began to clench. Jake's words made her feel more like a convenience. Like he didn't really love her. The blow felt almost physical. She hated that damn card right now. "Maybe drawing that fate wasn't such a bad thing after all," she mumbled, feeling bitter.

"Maybe not," he agreed. "It seems as if I've been ignoring things too long."

So what did she do now? Hand the ring over? It felt so final, and suddenly she knew she didn't want final. She didn't want Jake to be feeling the same feelings she'd been having about him.

Back at The Sutherland, Hailey was clearing tables in the Tea Room. She couldn't take her ring off in front of Hailey. It might embarrass him. It would certainly embarrass her.

But Jake surprised her by walking directly to Hailey. "I'd like to book a room," he told her.

Hailey propped her hand on her hip, her flustered gaze zig-zagged between Amy and Jake. "Oh, well, uh…"

"Jake, what are you doing?" Amy asked, shocked. Weren't they breaking up?

He turned to her, a sexy gleam in his beautiful green eyes. A look she'd hadn't spotted in at least six months. "You're setting me free, well, I'm not setting you free." His hands cupped her face. "I love you."

Amy blinked. A rush of emotion made her eyes prickle with unshed tears.

"Put me in the room next to Amy's."

Next to? Her heart beat kicked up a notch.

9

HAILEY SHOULD HAVE BEEN PREPARED. She acknowledged it, yet she was still surprised to open the door and see a not too pleased Nate standing there. Wearing black shorts and a grey polo shirt that matched his eyes, she stopped herself just in time from sucking in a breath at how gorgeous he was.

If fate hadn't already proved what a jerk she could be, dropping into Hailey's lap the perfect specimen of man concluded the matter. He was smart, he knew what was important in life, and could she please stop and admire his body again? Surely he wouldn't mind. Those firm biceps, broad shoulders and trim hips were too cruel.

And she hadn't even gotten to the part where he made her body burn with a mere touch.

"Hailey" was all he said, his voice all business.

She sighed. "Yeah, I know."

Surprise flickered in his eyes as if he'd expected her to play coy or argue. "Noticed that your guys swam through it all. Well done," she told him.

"It was better than just the women, but—"

"Yeah, I know," she said again. She slumped against the doorframe. "We could really, really use the money."

The harsh lines of his face relaxed, and he took the

two steps to stand in front of her. Tower over her, in fact. She looked up, directly into his eyes. He had that straight-from-the-shower appeal to him. Freshly shaven and squeaky clean. There was something very tempting about a squeaky clean man, something inside her wanted to make this man very, *very* dirty.

He reached up and cupped her cheek, his thumb lightly rubbing her chin.

"Would you stop, though, if I asked you to?"

When had she ever thought gray eyes cold? This man's stare burned.

"Yes," she said. And she wouldn't examine why. Wouldn't try to figure out why she was willing to throw away a bundle of cash simply because this man asked her to.

Wait, she knew why. Because she was stupid with men.

And completely dumb about this one.

His gray eyes darkened with pleasure at her answer and something else. Nate leaned forward and he gently kissed the tip of her nose. "Thank you."

Her breath hitched.

He kissed both her closed eyes. "Thank you."

Her stomach hollowed and her heartbeat shifted into high gear.

Then she felt the warmth of his lips on hers. He didn't deepen the kiss, simply moved his mouth against hers. Hailey couldn't breathe, couldn't think. She'd never had a kiss seem so innocent yet affect her so intensely as this soft caress.

"Thank you," he whispered against her lips, then moved away.

She wanted to give him some flip response. Or a

fully confident, "You're welcome." But something about that kiss changed whatever it was building between them. Made it more personal than two people hooking up for mutual pleasure. It scared her a little. She wanted more.

"Maybe I can help. If it's SEALs bringing in the guests, I could ask a few off-duty buddies to stop by."

Her eyes flew open, the dejection of a moment ago evaporating. "Really? Nate, that's perfect. We could have like a speed dating tea thing right in the Tea Room. The women would love it. We could charge a fortune."

His expression grew a little panicky.

"Not what you had in mind?" she asked, not able to hide her excitement.

"They may never speak to me again."

She put a hand on her hip. "Let me make the picture a little clearer. This room will be filled with a lot of SEAL-loving women. Beforehand, I'll feed the men all they can eat of my mom's famous pot roast. It's delicious."

"You make pot roast?" he asked, and she heard the hunger in his voice.

"With new potatoes and lots and lots of corn bread."

"Done."

"Wow, I can't believe how easy that was."

"Yeah, I can't believe I just offered," he said as he made his way toward the front door.

She laughed at his chagrinned expression. This, the fun byplay between them was way more comfortable for her than the charged sexual energy of before.

"By the way, don't think I forgot that you didn't show me your Fate Delivery Card."

He smiled. "All part of the plan."

Of course it was.

"I'll show my card the next time we go out."

Despite the fact that her pulse skipped at the promise in his voice, Hailey felt the need to make it clear once more about her dating status. Regardless of how great his kissing was. Hell, maybe she was reminding herself. "Nate, you know I don't do relationships."

"I remember you *said* you don't do relationships."

"Well, I want you to take my word at face value."

He nodded, but his determined expression told her he didn't believe her. Or that he planned to change her mind.

"Son," someone called from across the lobby.

Nate's face drained of color. There was a man crossing the lobby toward them. Tall, with a full head of dark blond hair, killer smile and grey eyes.

Eyes exactly like Nate's.

"This is your dad?" she managed to choke out.

"That would imply some kind of parental responsibility," Nate said drily. He stiffened as his father stopped to stand right beside him. All military formality. "Sir."

Nate's dad raised his glass, the scotch sloshing within. "You don't have a hug for your dear old pa?"

Nate stuck out his hand. "Good to see you, Jim."

Hailey watched the interaction between the two men who looked so much alike. Nate called his father by his given name, and for the first time didn't seem completely comfortable with a situation. How unlike the warm and caring byplay she'd always shared with her own parents.

"Started calling me Jim when he hit fourteen. Couldn't have a kid crashing my style," Jim told her with a wink. The man oozed the kind of charm that said he'd been fawned over by women since an early age. Getting older hadn't changed his expectations. "Good show out there in the water, son. These ladies sure know how to throw a great party," he said, with a leering wink directed at Hailey.

"Don't," Nate growled.

Jim gave her a quick once over, his gaze staying overly long on her chest. "Got good taste. Just like your old man."

Nate's intake of breath was like a snarl. "You here for the day, sir?" His words were phrased like a question, but sounded more like an order.

Jim raised his hands in surrender. "I won't crash your PI, kid."

"PI?" she asked.

"Stands for public image. Jim's taken to talking in text."

"Hey, Bailey here has a sister. Maybe we could double date."

Hailey's lips twisted into a smile. What do you know? Her big, bad Navy SEAL needed a little saving. "Sorry, I think my sister will be too busy." *Forever.* "Besides," she said as she tucked her arm around Nate's waist, "I like to keep this bad boy all to myself."

Jim raised his glass to his son.

MAYBE YOU'RE NOT SUPPOSED to set him free as in letting him go. Maybe you're supposed to set something in your relationship free, as in exploring.

Could Hailey be right? Had Amy been looking at the card's message all wrong?

Amy decided that yes, she was. She was going up

those stairs. She was going to knock on her fiancé's door and she was going to have her first orgasm.

Um…tomorrow.

No, she really wasn't avoiding the issue…she was setting the stage. Chapter four in Hailey's book had some great suggestions and she'd need a few props to put her plan into action.

The next day, Amy finally worked up the courage to walk inside The Toy Box. She'd been visualizing Jake's body all day long, and was ready for the next chapter. *Undress for His Pleasure—And Yours.*

And that's why she was here now. Earlier on her lunch break, she'd purchased a baby blue, frilly and very very expensive nightie.

But that didn't really seem to fit into the theme of the book. Ducking her head, she returned and scurried to a rack of women's lingerie, each sexier than the last. French Maid, sweet coed, even a referee. But then she spotted a leopard print teddy complete with a thong and naughty cutouts.

Amy could only imagine the shocked look on Jake's face when she revealed herself to him wearing that. She fingered the soft fabric, wanting to prance around his hotel room for his eyes only.

Thinking about the possibility of experiencing her first orgasm Amy threw in a pair of matching leopard print gloves. *I can't believe I'm doing this.* Now to check out.

"We're having a sale on lubes and vibrators," the girl at the register said casually.

Her eyes widened. Amy cleared her throat. "I'm good in that area."

The saleslady took the outfit off the hanger. "I love this set. Have you thought about shoes?"

Amy nearly panicked. She'd taken a major step just walking into this store, but she was definitely ready to get out of here. She shook her head.

"We have a nice selection. I'll show you." With an easy smile, she led Amy to a mirrored area lined with boots and shoes of every color, style and height.

"I think these would go great with the print you chose. They're a six-inch platform, so if you're not used to walking around in heels, we can look at something else."

Platform shoes were the exact opposite of anything she'd ever worn before. Now was the time to go with different.

"I have these in black, silver and gold. Don't let the vamp strap or ankle cuffs throw you, there's a zipper on the back that allows for easy access."

Amy was sure some of what that lady had said would have made sense to someone. When she heard "zipper," the only words out of her mouth were, "If you have them in a seven and a half, I'll take them in black."

The woman smiled. "I'll meet you at the counter."

Now she pulled into the parking area of The Sutherland. She stopped her car right beside Jake's, her heartbeat picking up the pace. She scrambled out of the car, and quickly carried both of the lingerie sets up to her room without being stopped in the foyer, in the stairwell or on the landing that led to her bedroom.

Once inside, Amy arranged each outfit on the top of her bed, which was stupid, because she knew the leopard print was the only choice. And she had to put it on as soon as possible or she'd lose her nerve. She'd tackle her own sexuality. She shimmied out of her work clothes and after a quick shower she slid those thong panties up her thighs.

Okay, not the most comfortable article of clothing she'd ever worn, but what had she expected?

Hopefully, she wouldn't be wearing them long.

A slow smile crossed her face. The gloves were next followed by the teddy. The shoes were even less comfortable than the thong, but a change came over her after zipping them up and standing. Her pulse hammered as she crossed to the mirror. Uncomfortable, but the results...

Not only did they make her legs looks damn good, but they were kind of empowering. For the first time ever, she felt sexy. And that was a very good feeling.

She fluffed up her hair, then donned her navy terry-cloth robe. Jake hated the thing, but maybe after tonight he'd gain a new appreciation for it. She lightly knocked on Jake's door, and heard some fumbling around in his room. She smiled.

"Who is it?" he grumbled.

"Amy. Were you asleep?" she asked, trying to keep it light between them. So unlike how their last conversation had gone.

He opened the door a crack, and she watched as he ran his fingers through his rumpled blond hair and down his whiskered face. He looked her up and down.

"Are you okay?" he asked.

She nodded, her heart skipping at the concern in his voice. Even after everything she'd done to embarrass him, he still had her well-being in his thoughts. "I just wanted to talk," she told him, but then opened her robe slightly.

"Amy?" he said.

She pushed the door open, stepped inside, then shut the door firmly behind her. Jake had only occupied the room for a short time, but already it held his scent. She hadn't realized how much she craved breathing him in.

Now she was ready for action. Chapter Seven was all about the strip tease, and she was prepared to try it.

Jake opened his mouth at the same time she let of her robe fall to her feet.

"Wra...wow." His gaze now traveled up and down her body like he couldn't get enough.

A flicker of something she could only describe as feminine power strengthened her resolve. She couldn't stop the smile from curving her lips. Amy liked this feeling.

Jake's hands reached for her, grazed her hips, but she pushed at his shoulders. "Not yet," and she lightly shoved him away.

With a long, lingering glance at her barely covered breasts he walked backwards until his legs hit the high Victorian bed.

She stepped out of the pile of terrycloth pooled at her feet and moved toward him, stopping just out of his reach.

"Amy, before we get any further into this, I think we should discuss—"

"You can't just...run with it? Enjoy it? I plan to strip for you. After that, I'm going to take off all your clothes."

He swallowed.

"Then I'm going to..." *Say it.* "Ride you like a..." *Say it.* "Ride you like a cowgirl."

"Okay." Jake scrambled onto the bed.

She raised a brow? "Who told you to get up on the

bed? If I'm going to strip, don't you think you should be in a chair? You'd like a lap dance, wouldn't you, Jake?"

A lap dance might sound pretty tame to the girls from her wedding shower, but to her it was one of the dirtiest things she could do, and she planned to enjoy the hell out of it.

She sauntered over to the desk, and drew the chair out to the middle of the room. Jake's hands brushed hers. "Here, let me help you with that."

"That's the last time you get to touch me until I say." Earlier, she'd gone on the Internet to find out how to give a lap dance, and that was one of the first principles. "House rules. No touching the dancer."

Amy placed both her hands on his shoulders and thrust downward. Jake settled into the chair, his legs spread. He wore an expression that was a combination of incredulousness and thinking he was one lucky guy.

She planned to *make* him one lucky guy. Loved that he thought himself that way because of her.

"Hands behind your back," she whispered, the scent of the exotic and spicy perfume he'd given to her for her birthday wafted between them.

Jake immediately complied.

She'd downloaded a few sexy songs onto her iphone, which she'd left in the pocket of her robe. Not a smooth move, but maybe she could make this work. She pranced around Jake, drawing her fingers along his arm, across his neck and to the other arm. "Be right back," she said and licked behind his ear.

She quickly grabbed her phone, and soon, sound filled the little room. The mood still wasn't completely right. She *needed* him to see her, but not in full light.

Amy snapped on the bedside lamp and flipped the bright overhead light off. Now this warm soft radiance set the perfect tone.

Dancing had never come naturally to her, although in this instance she was more than determined. She approached Jake with a look in her eyes that she hoped would say, "I plan to give you a good time." Between the V of his legs, she simply moved her hips side to side, and he moaned deep from his chest. As each moment passed, she felt less awkward, more empowered. Amy slinked closer. So near she felt the heat from his thighs.

She began to bend her knees, getting lower and lower. Evidently, this move made a man think of a blowjob. She couldn't imagine Jake ever thinking that since she'd never given him one, but she certainly spotted his reaction. He bulged beneath the zipper of his khakis.

Raising herself, Amy turned and did the same sinking motion with her back to him, only bending over. He groaned at the sight of her thong.

"You are so sexy," he said, his voice rough.

She smiled, for the first time believing that he found her sexy.

Straightening, she backed up. The next suggestion was to caress her own body. *Think of it as slathering on lotion.*

Amy bent forward, giving him a full view of her cleavage. When she reached her ankles, she made lazy circles and strokes up her calves. She brushed her thighs with her fingertips and—

"I want to be doing that so bad."

She glanced up. Oh, hey, this touching herself thing *did* work. Their eyes made contact and what she saw burning in his green depths sent another flood of warmth between her legs. She straightened, taking the opportunity to thrust her breasts at him. Her fingers trailed up her stomach, to touch her skin where the cutouts were, around her breasts, then down her arms. First to remove one leopard print glove then the next. Both landed in his lap.

The next move was to actually do the "lap" part of the lap dance. With slinky moves, she sauntered once more between his legs. She turned and rubbed her backside against his lap. The force of his erection floored her. She'd never felt him so hard. And it was all for her. *Because* of her. She settled against him, giving him more of her weight with a moan-inducing grind.

"Do you like this?" she asked.

"Yes." His reply was a long drawl, like it was difficult for him to get the word out.

"I have more." Her fingers reached for the straps of her teddy, sliding them over her shoulders and down her arms.

Out of the corner of her eye, she spotted his hands move. "No touching," she warned.

Amy lifted off him and backed a few feet away. With the straps no longer a barrier, she peeled the teddy over her breasts and down to her waist. She found Jake's eyes had narrowed to slits.

"Look at me," she said, loving how her nipples hardened as his gaze touched her skin. Amy caressed her breasts then, cupped them and molded them the way Jake did in the dark under the sheet.

It felt good, but it would feel better with his hands on her breasts. Amy approached him once more. She teased his lips with her nipples, but when he opened his mouth, she backed away. "Not yet."

She shimmied the teddy down her legs, standing

before him in only her thong and shoes. "I could make this a full body dance if you were on the bed."

Jake needed no second urging as he leapt out of his chair and was flat on the mattress in seconds. There was that curl of feminine power again that she'd been missing. With a slow gait, she walked to the side of the bed and pushed the thong down her legs. Amy would leave the shoes. Doing Jake with her shoes on sounded just like the kind of naughty thing she'd love to try. So did referring to making love as "doing it."

But what sounded even more wicked was to leave all of Jake's clothes on, just exposing the one part of him she really needed. She lowered her body to his, slowly sliding upwards until she cradled his hardness between her legs. His eyes closed and lines formed across his forehead.

She found the sensitive place above his collarbone and kissed. Then she shifted to the buttons of his shirt. Alternating between a kiss and a lick, she had that whole shirt unbuttoned and his body for her pleasure in no time. Amy gave a quick swipe of her tongue under his bellybutton.

"Keep going," he urged. "This is really getting interesting."

As adventurous as she was prepared to be, Amy was not quite there yet. So she smiled and shook her head.

Jake propped on his elbows to tug the shirt off.

"No," she told him. "Leave it."

Her hands fumbled for just a moment with his belt buckle, but then she had it loose around his waist and his zipper down. Only the black cotton of his boxer briefs separated her hands from his cock. Her hands were impatient as she tugged the material down and she reached inside. He fit perfectly in her hand.

"Pants staying on, too?" he asked.

With a nod, she straddled him. Despite being lovers, there were a lot of things she'd never done. Never initiating sex was one of them. She felt a little awkward, but soon she was teasing herself with the tip of him.

"You're so wet," he said. "I've never felt you so wet."

She squeezed her eyes tight in anticipation.

"I want to taste you," he whispered. The sexy, carnal words nearly did her in right there. They'd never done oral play. The one time Jake had brought it up, she'd been so horrified he'd spent their next date apologizing.

Now she wanted him to taste her, ached for him to. And more, she wanted to feel the hard length of him against her lips. In her mouth.

But the oral stuff would have to wait for another night because the sensation of caressing herself with his penis was exquisite. She positioned him in place and slowly sunk down on him.

When he was fully inside her, he groaned. "You feel so good."

Those were the exact words she wanted to hear. She squeezed her eyes tight again, but this time she was trying to stop a tear from sliding down her cheek. Amy needed to know that she made him feel good. That he wasn't turned off by her sexual needs. The book had said a caring and tender lover would want to hear her desires, and it was right. Jake seemed more sexually excited and charged than she'd ever seen him before.

His hands fisted at his sides, and she felt the struggle within him to let her keep the lead. Amy began to move. The angle, her control of the angle was all new to her, and it felt amazing. She forgot all about books, and mortification and thoughts and just felt. Enjoyed the sweet friction of his body sinking into hers. A tension coiled inside and soon her motions grew erratic. She was so close, so close to something, but she needed a little help.

"Jake. You can touch me now. I *need* it."

With a powerful burst of released his energy, Jake gripped her hips and began to pump inside her. Amy felt him grow even harder. With a gasp, her inner muscles began to clench and she ground against him harder still.

"Now, now now," she urged. "Deeper."

She wanted more. Needed more. And Jake delivered.

Amy couldn't stop the cry that came from some primal part of her body as wave after wave of pure ecstasy hit her.

The sound of their labored breathing filled the room. Amy felt sweaty and relieved and very, very dirty.

"Wow, I've never heard you come so hard," Jake said, his voice sent a trill of sensation down her neck.

Yeah, there was a reason for that. She kissed his cheek. And even though this night was all about talking, some words were better off not spoken.

10

"DID YOU SEE THE LOOKS those two were flashing each other this morning?" Hailey asked as she brought the last of the breakfast dishes in from the Tea Room, where they'd served Amy and Jake this morning.

"It looked to me like she couldn't figure out whether to pounce on him or run away as fast as she could," Rachel replied, putting away cups and saucers.

"She apparently opted for the running away because Jake is out there all by himself."

Rachel gave a quick peek out the door. Jake sat alone in the Tea Room, pushing aside the made-to-order omelet Hailey had worked so hard to create.

"Now *that* is just ridiculous," she said to Rachel. "I mean, I know he's a little confused about life right now, but to waste the delicate fluffiness of the egg like that... It was the kind of omelet mom would have made, and he's ruining it."

Rachel shrugged and took a step back. "Don't look at me, I never turn down food."

Hailey reached behind her to untie the apron strings. "I'm going to talk to him."

"Hailey, maybe that's not such a good idea. It's just an egg."

Hailey almost laughed out loud. "Silly. I'm not going in there to confront him about his omelet. We're going to discover why he's wasting food like that, and work toward a solution together."

Rachel's eyes widened.

Flashing her sister a wink, she looped her apron on the hook by the door. "I'm messing with you."

"Still maybe we should maintain a policy of staying out of our guests' lives."

"It wasn't exactly on purpose, it just sort of happened. Besides, I think I did a pretty good job with Amy. At least there's a little more going on now than just those two arguing. Looks like he's trying to hide a hickey."

Rachel gasped, then she squinted, trying to catch a better glimpse of Jake's neck.

Hailey picked up the coffee pot off the warmer. "Here's what I was thinking we could do for tonight. We'll set up a nice little romantic dinner in the Tea Room…then the champagne and the Fate Delivery Cards will do the rest. Or better yet, we can set the meal up in the Bridal Suite. Cuts out all the work of walking up the stairs to get to the bed."

Rachel shook her head. "Oh, no. I'm not letting those cards anywhere near guests of The Sutherland from now on."

"Don't worry. I'm taking out any of the potentially dangerous cards before I let them loose on that couple."

Rachel gasped. "But that's cheating. I'm not sure we should be messing around with fate like that."

Hailey shrugged. "Maybe fate wants me to 'fix' the cards. Maybe fate put the idea in my head in the first place."

Rachel sighed heavily. "I hate it when you're like this."

Hailey gave her sister a little salute with the coffee pot then headed in Jake's direction.

"Refresher?" she asked.

Jake glanced up, startled. "No, I'm good," he told her.

"The eggs not to your liking?"

The man had the character to look a little guilty. That should prove that Amy had herself a good man. A man who knew good food, and felt remorse when he didn't appreciate the hard work that went into preparing the meal, demonstrated true integrity. He cleared his throat. "No, I—"

"Hey, it's okay. You're having a rough time with it. It's perfectly reasonable you're not hungry." *Sort of.*

He dropped his napkin to the table. "I don't understand how something that could be going so great could fall to shi—er, crap so quickly."

Excellent. Her opening. "What's Amy saying?"

"Other than the first night, she hasn't said much." A touch of red tinted his cheeks, and Hailey could guess that the book she'd given Amy had inspired her to take action that didn't involve a lot of talking. That hickey simply confirmed it. "And I can't get her to open up to me. Really talk."

As the woman who knew exactly what Amy's problems were, Hailey realized she must proceed carefully. She wanted to point Jake in the right direction, but not reveal all of her guest's confidences.

"Amy told me she was raised by her grandparents," she said, aiming for the right conversational tone. "Sometimes I thank my lucky stars I was never born in that generation. We have a lot to be thankful to the women who stood up and paved the way. Our lives have so many more options. And freedoms. Come to think of it, men have benefited in a lot of ways, too. Remember those old black-and-white shows where the couple slept side by side in twin beds? Some of our old records indicated The Sutherland had a few rooms with that set-up."

Jake didn't appear to be particularly uncomfortable with the conversation, the sexual repression problem was clearly Amy's. However, the cluelessness trouble rested squarely on Jake's shoulders. Hailey should probably press further.

"I actually had this one friend who thought her boyfriend would be put off if she showed him her sexual side. They eventually broke up."

Too heavy-handed? Maybe, although something seemed to be spinning inside his head because suddenly Jake started eating. A good sign.

"How could she think that?" he asked after nearly draining his coffee cup.

"You'd be surprised what some women are told about sex and their bodies. That double standard is still alive and well. In fact, I have the perfect book upstairs in my room. You might find it very interesting. Be right back."

Owning Your Bed, Owning Your Orgasm was written by a woman for women, but even the chapter headings should give Jake the right hint. All her life Amy had been given mixed messages about her sexuality and how her worth as a woman was tied into that. Hailey had a feeling Jake was exactly the guy for Amy to work out all her frustrations and confusion with. And on.

Nate looked like a man who could handle something like that. Come to think of it, she had a lot of frustrations...

Focus on Amy and Jake.

Five minutes later, Hailey was charging down the stairs, book in hand when the guest doorbell rang. It had been three days since Hailey had seen or talked to Nate. The fact that she'd noted that it had been three days was a bad sign. Even the Navy hadn't seen fit to grant her a training exercise in the ocean outside The Sutherland, despite the fact that she'd strained her eyes trying to catch a glimpse of a swimmer or a helicopter.

Turned out it was Nate at the door looking tall, and gorgeous and someone she couldn't wait to get her hands on. Her breath caught. He was early.

Definitely her kryptonite.

"Nice book by the way," he said, as he strode through the foyer.

Her gaze slipped to the title in her hand. Perfect. "It's not for me."

"Hey, anytime you want to own your orgasm, I'm your man."

She laughed. "I'll keep that in mind. Is something wrong?" she said. Their SEAL speed-dating night wasn't for several more hours.

"I came to help."

And he ladled on a whole new layer of kryptonite. She would be ignoring that little skip to her heartbeat that thought gave her.

Hours later, the Tea Room was buzzing and Hailey had to marvel at Nate. He'd delivered—boy how he'd delivered. A buffet of men, some dark and handsome, some fair and striking, they all shared that powerfully built swagger of a man who knew how to take care of himself. The women would be thrilled. And better yet—word would get out.

Now those men were polishing off the last of the pot roast and by the compliments she'd received, her mom's recipe still delivered.

Amy, Tori and a few of the other wedding shower guests had come through as well. Over twenty women waited in the lobby. A lobby that would soon have a new sound system thanks to these ladies' money. She could almost jump, Hailey was so excited.

Rachel cleared the dishes in the Tea Room while Hailey stood at the kitchen counter putting the finishing touches on the mojitos they were to serve when she felt, *felt* Nate's presence.

This was super bad.

"Thought I'd stick around for crowd control."

Her lips twisted into a grin as she turned to face him. "Those big, tough Navy SEALs afraid of a few women?"

Nate shuddered. "Terrified."

She laughed out loud. Nate probably wasn't afraid of very much, if anything. Their eyes met and she felt her heart softening. Her resolve to keep things light and uncomplicated dimmed. She swallowed past the tightness in her throat. "Thanks, Nate. I can't tell you how much this means to me. You've gone to a lot of trouble, I can't imagine it was that much of a fair trade."

"I'm getting another date out of this, too." Then the smile faded from his face, and he reached for her hand, his thumb lightly stroking her skin. "I would have done it even without the trade, Hailey. All you had to do was ask."

Then Hailey Sutherland did the craziest thing she'd done in a long while. Overwhelmed by the moment, his gray eyes, and by his words, Hailey reached up and planted her mouth on his.

Nate didn't meet her lips with any sort of surprise or hesitation. His kiss devoured her. And made her stronger, all at the same time. His hands wrapped around her hips and he dragged her close. If he'd hoisted her up on the counter, drew her panties aside and plunged inside, she would have wrapped her legs around his waist. And wouldn't have let him go until he'd given her the pleasure his every look, every word, every kiss had promised her since they'd met.

The buzz coming from the Tea Room broke through her concentration. The click clack of heels and the excited laughter of women poured in from the lobby. With an effort, Hailey pulled away. The sound of their labored breathing filled the large kitchen.

A light sheen of sweat broke out on his forehead, and her stomach tightened, thrilled that her kiss affected this big strong man as much as it had changed the way she planned to deal with Nate. The last time they were together, she'd told him to bring the condoms. Had he? The idea shot a tiny thrill to her heart.

"We'll finish this later," he assured her.

And that's what she was afraid of.

AMY NOTICED SHE HADN'T had a moment to think all evening. The Tea Room was filled with men and women. The numbers were off with more gals than guys, but the time system Hailey had implemented gave each woman a few minutes alone with every SEAL to see if a connection could be made.

As she walked around the room refreshing mojitos,

Amy couldn't help thinking of the connection she'd forged with Jake. The red number circled on her calendar signaling their wedding date loomed still. Well, hadn't they worked out their problems? Sure they hadn't yet had their long overdue conversation, but things were back on track between them, right?

Jake circled the perimeter of the room, picking up empty glasses and scooting in chairs. She loved him so much, she ached with it. When he'd raggedly told her he wanted to taste her, she hadn't been ready.

Tonight she was.

And she was going to taste him. As if he felt her staring at him he glanced up, blinked at the hotness of her look. She gave him a wink. Tonight she would rock his world.

THE NIGHT HAD BEEN an unqualified success. Hailey was relaxing on the terrace, the cool night breeze chasing away the heat from her skin. With Jake, Amy and Nate chipping in, there wasn't even a lot of clean up. What was left could wait until the morning.

Nate dropped onto the chaise lounge beside her. He spread out his long legs, and crossed his arms underneath his head. She expected him to say something, but he didn't. Instead, he joined the silence, staring up at the stars. It was the easiest, most relaxed time she'd ever spent with a man.

And it scared her to death. More than the kiss.

She squeezed her eyes tight and sucked in a breath. After releasing it slowly she rolled over on the lounger to face him. He turned his head, and she was struck by the almost overwhelming urge to touch him. To run her fingers along the line of his nose, the angle of his jaw and the curve of his eyebrow. Hailey wanted to explore his mouth and…

"Thanks for your help tonight, Nate. I really—"

He reached for her hand, stopping her words. Obviously he was as uncomfortable with thank yous as she was. Another thing they had in common—

She wasn't going there.

"What's your weekend look like?" he asked. "I'm ready to call in our date."

Her stomach turned all fluttery at his question. "Amy and Jake should both be gone by Friday, so will a number of the other guests, so it looks like a weekend of painting and trim work for me."

"Any way I could talk you out of that?"

"In a second." The words rushed from her before Hailey realized what she was revealing.

"I'd like to take you up to Anzo-Borrego. Spend the night out there and really see the stars."

"Like camping?"

"And hiking," he added with a nod. "But don't worry, we'll spend the night in Vallecito at one of their tent sites."

This sounded horrific, but then he'd just arranged for a dozen of his buddies to hang out at The Sutherland, and he cleaned up afterwards. "Have I ever given any indication that I'm the kind of girl who likes to rough it?" Because she wanted to identify whatever it was she was doing and put an end to it immediately.

Even in the dark, she could see him eyeing the ruffled, pastel sundress, her painted toenails and dainty shoes. A smile spread across his handsome face and he leaned back against his chair. "No, in fact, I would put you firmly in the girly column." But there wasn't a drop of disappointment in her.

That was a relief. Hailey sighed.

"I'd just like to see you dirty."

With the carnal way he said it, she immediately craved exactly that.

"You can choose the next date," he offered.

"Just so you understand that date will feature a mani, pedi party," she said, her voice a grumble.

Another smooth move by Mr. Peterson. Now he had her agreeing to two dates. Two points for him.

"I'd love to have your feet in my hands," he said in a low, rumbly voice that made her shiver.

"I'm taking a point away from you since you know what a pedicure is," she told him, not being a very good sport.

"What?"

Hailey sat up. "Nate, why are you doing this? Wanting to go out with me? I've told you I'm not at a place where I can do relationships."

The man looked completely unconcerned. In fact, he closed his eyes and took a deep breath. "I'm thinking I can change your mind."

Now if that weren't the sexiest, most irritating thing a man had said to her, she didn't know what it would be. Although whatever Nate did next would probably tie.

"What if I never change my mind?"

The chair squeaked as Nate sat up and dropped his feet to the terrace floor. He stood, reaching for her hands, and helped her stand. The small space between the two chairs didn't leave much room, and the solidness of his chest gently grazed her nipples, making them taut.

He cupped her face and gave her a quick, over-before-she-had-a-chance-to-respond kiss on her lips. But it still tingled. And it still made her warm all over. "Hailey, hopefully I won't be here in San Diego long."

Her stomach clenched. As a result of how much she'd miss him? "Where would you go?"

"Back with my platoon. Overseas. But while I'm here, I want to spend my time with you. You're funny and beautiful and I know we'll be so good together. I can still hear your moans in my head. I want to get you alone, away from here and really be together."

She knew sex between them would be amazing, which was why she'd been avoiding it. Because she'd just want more, more of *him,* and then where would she be? "Maybe we should avoid sex," she hedged.

He dropped his hands and winked. "Then bring your cookies. I liked the peanut butter best."

Sex with her or cookies…and he thought that an even exchange? Her cookies were great, sure, but somehow she felt this was a little insulting. Hailey opened her mouth, but Nate was drawing out a familiar black and red card from his back pocket.

His Fate Delivery Card.

"We talked about showing you this on our next date, but if you want to see it now, here it is. No date attached." Their fingertips brushed as her passed the card to her. "I'm accepting my fate," he said, his warm breath teasing her hair. "You call me if you want to do this." He kissed her temple, then walked down to the beach.

After straightening their chairs, Hailey headed to the Tea Room. *She,* however, needed light to read his card.

She shut and locked the door behind her, then leaned against the wall for extra support. With jittery fingers, she turned the card over. A smile crossed her face as she read *Don't take no for an answer.*

_11_

AMY LEFT HER DOOR SLIGHTLY AJAR. She'd draped one of the leopard-print gloves over the doorknob to invite Jake into her bed.

The significance of the glove and leaving her door open for him wasn't lost. By inviting him inside her domain, she felt exposed and vulnerable. He'd have all her secrets because tonight she also planned to talk. And more…

By now, she knew just about everything a woman could know about a man. Her man. All except one. How he tasted. After tonight that wouldn't be the case. Once again she acknowledged her plans for tonight weren't such a big deal between lovers, but to her, it was the final reveal.

A knock sounded at her door, and Amy turned, seeing Jake. Her heart contracted. She loved him so much, and she was lucky to have such a guy.

Wait, not lucky, smart. What had the book said? Choice? She was smart to choose such a man to lose her heart to.

Her skin grew achy for his touch. She was anxious to move onto this next step, but still some small part of her wanted to hide something of herself from his eyes. Then he smiled, and every worry, every fear disappeared.

With a purposeful stride, she walked across the room and shut the door firmly behind him. "Remember that first night when I came to your room and you said you wanted to taste me?"

Jake only nodded.

"I want you to. And I want to taste you, too."

She heard him release his breath on a slow exhale. Amy loved it when he made that sound. It meant that she'd surprised him. And turned him on.

"Not freaked out yet?" she asked.

"Never," he told her, his voice rueful.

Amy began to slowly unbutton his shirt, revealing the soft curling hair of his chest, and the flatness of his stomach. He allowed her full rein over his body, and she touched and tasted every part of him.

When her hands found his belt buckle, they began to shake. But she rallied her courage and took control of the metal and leather. Once loose, she shoved his pants down to the floor, followed by his boxer briefs.

The length of him sprang up, and with one promising glance at him, Amy sank to her knees. He was groaning before she had him fully in her mouth. His hands tangled in her hair as she ran her tongue along his shaft and around the head, teasing him. His knees began to shake as she drew him completely into her mouth, and out again. The movement mimicked his when he was in her body.

"Am—" He swallowed. "Amy, how far are you planning to take this?" he asked, his voice sounding raw.

"All the way," she said against his cock.

His hands touched her shoulders. "It's going to kill me to have you stop, but my legs can't take it." He tugged her upward. "To bed."

"Don't think you can handle me?" she asked. Amy had never teased him about sex, and she liked the cha-grinned expression that passed across his face.

"Not after three hours on my feet serving restless women drinks and fending off advances. You sure made me work hard to get you into bed."

"But worth it now?"

"Hell, yes." Then Jake apparently found a little extra strength because he swept her into his arms and carried her to the bed. "What was this about me tasting you?"

"Later," she assured him.

"I'll never forget the night your roommate was away and I stayed the night. You told me you didn't do oral. After that, it's all I've been thinking about. Like the for-bidden fruit I can't get my mind off of. Let me." His hands trailed up her thighs under her skirt until they reached her panties. "Easy access. You have to wear dresses from now on."

Jake threw up her skirt, then lowered himself between her legs. She wanted to cover her face, to pull him back up, but she didn't. She also wanted to be a woman who could enjoy everything with this man she loved. Amy felt his teeth on the satiny fabric at her hip. He tugged the material down first on one side, then the other. With her panties gone, Jake lifted her legs and tucked them over his shoulders.

His head lowered, and he kissed her gently, drawing her inside his mouth. It was unlike anything she'd ever felt before. Warm and wet and tender. He made a long swipe with his tongue then encircled her, her...clit. "Jake," she whispered, not sure what she wanted to say or ask.

Then he began the tasting part, teasing every part of

her with his tongue. She locked her legs, keeping him in place, and lifting her hips toward him. Her orgasm wasn't a slow buildup like it had been since the first. This climax came out of nowhere, surprising her and making her gasp and call his name. She quaked and trembled and when he sucked her clit once more she came again.

Finally, it was over. She'd never felt so sexually drained. Every muscle lay lax.

"Jake, if you give me a moment, I'll return—"

"If I don't have you right now…"

Amy's eyes flew open. She was going to give him the same kind of pleasure he'd given her, but where she was relaxed, his muscles were visibly strained. She widened her legs and Jake settled himself between them again. "I love you," he said as he entered her.

The rest of the evening they made love, and right before dawn, Amy shared everything about growing up and her fears that he wouldn't want her anymore after the newness of the intimacies they'd shared had worn off.

With a heavy sigh, he folded her into his arms. "Amy, you have to promise me that if we ever have a daughter, you won't let her anywhere near your family. I can't believe how warped you are about sex. Uh, sorry."

She gave him a hug. "No, it's okay."

Pinning her beneath him, Jake's gaze caught hers. "It just kills me that you were taught to be ashamed of your inherent desires. Hell, I *want* you to enjoy sex with me. Demand it anytime. I'm yours for the asking. The taking. Am I making myself clear?"

Amy began to giggle. "Very," she said, feeling

sexual, sensual and very loved. He held her in his arms until her wake-up call from the front desk.

"Let's go home."

Home with Jake. The thought genuinely excited her.

Amy snuggled into the embrace. "Let's go home," she said.

HAILEY FINGERED THE CARD Nate had given her last night. He'd paperclipped his phone number to the back. She lifted up the scrap of paper and read his fate once more.

Don't take no for an answer.

Nate's card wasn't a fate, it was his way of life. A description of his personality. The man didn't need extra help from fate.

Except he would accept a no from her if she chose to give him one. His number. All she had to do was dial the digits and tell him yes. Camping. She sighed. Could he have chosen anything she would have hated more?

No, probably not.

"How long are you going to twiddle that card in your hand?" Rachel asked, carrying a basket of The Sutherland napkins fresh from the dryer.

Hailey wanted to bury her face in the clean fresh scent and forget about making tough decisions. Instead, she dropped the card, washed her hands, and reached for the napkins. Her sister needed help folding.

"If I call him, it changes everything."

"Of course it does," Rachel said, giving her a strange look for stating the obvious.

"I don't want a relationship with him."

"Liar. You may not have observed the looks you toss that man's way, but I have. You can't get enough of him.

Personally, I'd like you to get on with it, so I can stop watching you mope. I don't remember you ever being this moody."

"I'm tired of you giving me such a hard time. I'm in a transitional phase of my life right now."

"No, you're in a won't-make-a-decision-in-life phase because you're afraid of getting hurt. What happened to the girl who left San Diego? She was charged up, ready to hit life with both feet running."

"She came back to San Diego with a broken heart times three."

"Yeah, well, I'm officially putting an end to the moping. A lot of people get their heart broken. A lot of people make mistakes. You're not the only one. I think Nate is a great guy, and you're not exactly making it easy on him. Look at what he's put up with, and yet he's willing to have more."

"I obviously didn't tell you he wants to take me camping this weekend."

Rachel laughed. Hard. "Man, the mental image I have of you is cracking me up. You'll be out there with the bugs, and the dirt and with your antibacterial wipes."

"That proves right there that he doesn't know the first thing about me. How could he expect me to do something like hike? Are there bears in Vallecito Park?"

"No, there's desert," Rachel told her, shaking her head. "Hmm, I actually think this camping thing is kind of sweet."

"You are out of your mind."

"No, listen to me for a minute. He planned your first date all about you. Show that he could fit into your interests. Now he's trying to share what he likes with you, to show you what he's about. Nate must really be into you."

That filled her with excitement and dread. "It's times like these I really miss Mom. I could sure use her advice now."

"I guess we'll have to rely on each other," Rachel said. "And Hailey, I don't need a self-help book to see you're pushing Nate away because he's a man you could really fall in love with."

Her throat tightened and her eyes filled with tears. "I'm not sure I could handle having my heart broken again." Especially since he would be leaving soon.

"Then just make it fun. You said he wants to redeploy. A man like that doesn't necessarily want a relationship either. When you're with him, I see glimpses of my old spunky sister."

Hailey kind of missed her old self, too. Missed the person who left The Sutherland with dreams and hopes and a lot of excitement. Maybe she had been wallowing for too long. "You don't have a sleeping bag or a backpack, do you?"

"Ha, now that's funny. But I'll start a load of sheets in the washer, then we can shop online."

Nothing like shopping to lighten the mood. Or the anticipation of spending time with a sexy man. Hailey dialed.

Nate picked up on the second ring.

"You do realize there's like a million cool things to do in San Diego," she told him.

"Good thing Vallecito is not in San Diego then," he said, and she heard the laughter in his voice, laced with maybe a hint of surprise at her phone call. Pleasant surprise.

"I'm just saying there are other things we could be

doing than camping and hiking." Normally she'd never complain about a date, but she knew Nate was getting a kick from her teasing.

"You're right," he countered. "We'll be geocaching as well."

"Sounds great." Geocaching?

HER NEWLY PURCHASED BACKPACK and sleeping bag waited by the front door. She'd packed plenty of wipes, hand sanitizer and bottled water. Nate told her not to worry about meals, which only made her even more concerned. The man didn't have a good working knowledge around a kitchen and who knew what he thought cooking at a campfire should entail.

She met Rachel at the front door, who'd left early to buy a combo bottle of bug repellant and sun screen. She opened the lid and took a whiff. "I know why bugs stay away. This stuff smells awful. Thinking it might repel Nate, as well."

"Well, then tuck it into your backpack. Bugs might not even be an issue in Vallecito."

The doorbell rang and Rachel gave Hailey a hug. "Here, I'll be mom. Have a good time and be sure to drink plenty of water."

Hailey laughed, nervous and excited, but happy to be looking forward to something.

"Now I'll be me. I slipped in a few packets of condoms, so really have a good time." Then her sister scrambled up the stairs.

Wiping her hands on her new khaki shorts, Hailey reached for the doorknob. If she'd been nervous about the clothes she'd chosen, Nate's very appreciative looks at her bare legs and rugged pink T-shirt chased those concerns away. He looked incredible. The outdoors, and the anticipation of being manly under the sun brought out the sexiness in him.

Hailey expected the hiking boots, and his tan camo shorts, but was surprised to see the pink ballcap in his hands. "This will protect you from the sun," he told her, and placed it on her head.

"Did you buy this specifically for me?"

"Well, I didn't have it hanging around."

She was touched by his gift. Once again she was struck by his effort to take the time and pick out something that she needed, but that she'd also like. His hands rested at her shoulders and she leaned forward. That was all the encouragement the man needed. His lips found hers in a firm heart-stopping kiss. Suddenly, the idea of camping didn't sound too bad.

"This your gear?" he asked, and she loved hearing the anticipation in his voice. "Nice backpack."

"When I spotted the little pink skull and crossbones, I knew this beauty had to be mine."

"Let's go." He easily hoisted her stuff over his shoulder, draping his free arm around her.

They made it to their destination in just under two hours, the terrain becoming dryer and the desert taking over the landscape. As they drove, he asked her about her plans for The Sutherland, and he shared some of his funnier stories about becoming a SEAL and spending most of his time cold, wet and without a lot of sleep.

"So this is going to be a breeze for you?"

"Beats running with a telephone poll."

Nate didn't talk much about his time overseas, but

she heard the pride in his voice when he talked about his fellow SEALs.

"So you never told me why you're teaching," she asked, sipping from one of the bottles of water Nate had packed in an ice chest.

"I was hit by explosives."

"Good Lord, what?" He'd said it so casually, like the way other people mentioned they'd had their bangs trimmed, it caught her completely off guard.

"In the leg."

Hailey had given his muscular legs quite an inspection, and she'd never noticed a scar, although come to think of it, she had spotted him rub his thigh on a few occasions.

"It's higher up," he said quietly, as if he'd read her mind. "In the water I can push through any pain, but I'm point man in my Team, and they can't have someone do land nav when they can't hike."

"But you're okay now?"

"I'm better. My muscles are responding to the physical therapy, but this weekend is going to be my first test."

Hailey wanted to wrap her arms around him, but she sensed the last thing he'd want was to draw anymore attention to himself like this. "So tell me what we're going to search for?"

He raised an eyebrow. "Found out what geocaching is?"

"I looked it up on the Internet."

"But it's not what we're going to search, it's what we're going to find."

Now she was intrigued. "Don't take no for an answer, huh?"

"Got you in that seat beside me, didn't it."

She hid a smile, liking that he didn't want to hear a *no* where she was concerned.

He angled his head toward the dashboard. "There's a printout of what we're looking for in the glove box."

"Are these the coordinates for the GPS?"

He nodded, turning off the main highway. They passed fewer cars now, and the desert seemed never-ending. To the west lay the San Diego mountains, and that was about all she could supply in terms of geography.

"Do you use a lot of GPS when you're deployed?"

"We can, but it's not always something you can count on. Give me a compass and a map and I can get you anywhere."

They entered the campground, and after being assigned a tent site, Nate parked his car near a fire ring. "Like a five-star hotel," he teased.

Desolate was the best word she had to describe it. Sand and brush and more sand and brush.

"You ready to go?" he asked.

"What about the tent?"

"It's a pop up, so we'll have that up in only minutes. I'm anxious to get out there with you and test my leg." He held out a hand, and Hailey eagerly took it. He might just make a camper out of her after all.

Then some kind of flying bug rammed itself against her cheek. Hailey squealed, jumping and trying to get away from the insect. Scratch that whole camper idea.

Nate struck a pose like Superman. "I'll save you from the bug." Then he nibbled where the bug had touched her skin, making her want to shriek for a whole

new reason. Nervousness set something off inside her.
When they returned, what would he do? Draw her to
him? And how would she respond?

Not take no for an answer?

12

AN HOUR AND A HALF later, Hailey was sweaty and no longer squealed when a bug buzzed by. About ten minutes into their hike, Nate put away the GPS and they just enjoyed the scenery together. Although she sensed he ached to challenge himself, he'd taken her on a number of the easier trails. The paths were clearly marked with signs describing the different kinds of cacti and desert wildflowers.

Nate brought her to a tiny oasis and showed her the archeological digs. "This area is filled with fossils."

No longer did she see the bleakness of the sand, but a vibrant desert of amazing vistas filled with hawks flying overhead and even a roadrunner or two. They'd trekked to the top, the view inspiring. Looking down, not seeing another soul, Hailey could image they were the only people on the planet.

"This is one of the few places left in America where you can just pitch a tent in the park."

"Have you ever watched any of those Bizarrely Enough TV programs where they show the petrified remains of missing people? I'm pretty sure pitching a tent below is how it all started."

She'd meant it to be funny. Being hot and sticky, she

needed a little comic relief. But Nate didn't laugh, instead he gently gripped her chin, drawing her toward him. A line formed between Nate's eyebrows, and his gaze grew intense. "I'd never let anything happen to you, Hailey. Never put you in a situation where you could be hurt."

The quiet sincerity, the utter conviction touched some, up-to-this-point shriveled, part of her heart.

And she knew.

Knew Nate would never let anything bad happen to her. It was a strange understanding for her. He was so different from the men in her past. And it was so unexpected to have stumbled upon someone like him.

That's when she decided Nathaniel Peterson was getting lucky that night. Well, as lucky as a man making love in a tent could get.

Hell, he was probably into that.

His thumb caressed her chin, and she leaned into his light caress. She met his gaze, and she nodded. "I know." A brief, sexy smile lifted his lips and she knew he was about to plant one of those amazing kisses on her.

Then she felt the prickling sensation of little tiny legs on her arm. A sensation she'd felt about a million times since leaving Nate's car. The moment lost, Hailey flicked a bug off her arm. She was long past shrieking when one touched her. "I read somewhere that the average person swallows eight spiders in their lifetime. I suspect all those people were campers, and they just skewed the results."

"Beetles kind of taste like apples."

"A. I don't even want to know how you now this. And B. I'm going to pretend that you're joking."

A deep rumble sounded in Nate's chest. He tugged

her closer and looked down into her eyes. She just wanted to keep melting into the steel depths of his. She'd hike, geocache, even sleep in a tent with this guy.

"Don't tell my sister, but I never thought I would enjoy this so much," she admitted, delighting in their water break.

"Your secret is safe with me," he promised, wiping a smudge of dirt from her face.

"Thanks for bringing me, Nate. It's been fun."

"Day's not done yet. We have an appointment at Nineteen hundred."

"What did you just say?"

"Nineteen hundred, er, seven o'clock. Military time. Hard habit to break. It's just adding or subtracting twelve."

"If math is a requirement for dating you, I see why you're single."

He snuck a quick kiss. "Duly noted. No math required. You ready?" he asked.

"Where are we going?"

"We're near Agua Caliente. The state park has two naturally-fed hot springs, like pools. I've been told they're very therapeutic."

"I didn't bring a bathing suit," she said, feeling a rush of disappointment.

"Not a problem."

What did he mean not a problem? Was he suggesting that they go buck naked? Skinny dipping with Nate? Despite the heat, she felt herself grow warmer. "I remembered what a girly girl you are and scheduled a couple's massage in town."

"I fell for that one, didn't I? All right nav man, if there's a day spa somewhere, I expect you to lead me to it."

It took another twenty minutes to hike back to where they'd parked. The air conditioning of Nate's car was heavenly against her hot, dusty skin. Drowsy from the sun, she must have dozed off because the next thing she knew Nate was at her door, gently shaking her awake.

He helped her out of the car, and never let go of her hand as they entered the day spa. The woman behind the desk must see quite a lot of hikers in from the park because she didn't blink at their windblown and dusty appearance. "I booked a couple's massage for Peterson."

The woman scanned her appointment book, then flashed them a smile. "Right this way. There's a sauna shower in the room along with towels and robes."

"Sauna shower?" Nate whispered to her as they walked down the hall.

"How come you didn't know what we were getting?"

"I just asked for the works."

She looped her arm through his. "Now it's my turn to give you an education. Nate, you are going to be a changed man after this. You can have your choice of dry or wet heat. Since the desert was so dry, I'm going wet heat all the way. Over your head will be a rainfall shower, but the best part are the jets that line the wall."

They found their room, the low lights and soft music already relaxing. He popped his head in the stall. "That doesn't look big enough for the two of us."

"This is supposed to be relaxing, not pornographic," she told him playfully. Although a shot of heat pooled between her legs at the idea of showering with this man. Sudsing him all up, then washing it all away.

"How's your leg?" she asked.

He rubbed at his thigh, a move she'd seen him do

often now that she knew what to look for. "Holding its own," he replied, and from the pleased voice, she knew he wasn't just acting tough for her sake.

That might mean he'd be leaving San Diego soon. Hailey hated the pang that thought gave her. She would just have to enjoy him while she could. She busied herself finding a robe and towel and hanging them on the wooden pegs beside the shower. "Okay, first things first. Are you a talker or a shut up and feeler during a massage?"

"I don't know, I've never had one."

"You've never had a massage?"

"No."

"Nate, you have missed out on so much of the truly great things in life."

He squeezed her hand. "Then it's a good thing I hooked up with you."

"For sure. Since you've never done this before, you go first," she said, turning her back to him. "Time to strip."

She heard the sound of his clothes rustling, sliding down his skin and hitting the floor. Hailey held her breath. Knowing that she planned to have sex with him tonight made him undressing now feel all the more intimate. The door opened and closed and she relaxed for a second knowing he couldn't see her reaction to him being naked and so very close.

But him beneath the water raised a lot of questions. Did he shave in the shower or at the sink? Was he a soap or shower gel guy?

Definitely soap. Gel didn't seem manly enough.

Wash his hair first or last? Soon, she planned to discover all that for herself.

After a few moments, the water stopped and she

heard Nate rustle with the towel. Her imagination went into overdrive as she thought about that towel moving across his skin. The way she planned to tonight.

She gave him triple enough time to get dry and in his robe before turning around.

Damn, she should have peeked. Nate hadn't even bothered to get in the robe, simply draping the towel around his hips. If life were fair, that towel would drop. He was something to stare at all right. Little droplets of water held on for dear life onto his chest. She didn't blame them, she'd want to stay perched there forever, too.

On second thought, a few of those droplets began to roll down his chest, over his ribcage and over the flatness of his stomach, roped with muscle. Happy water droplets. Wow, she'd definitely had way too much sun.

"Have I thanked the Navy lately?"

His laugh was deep and sexy and sent shivers all up and down her back.

"You can thank *me* later."

Trying to distract herself from his magnificent physique and how he made her feel, she asked, "How was the shower?"

He raised a brow. "Would have been better with you in there with me. Not as warm as a shower I would have at home, but very refreshing."

"Your turn to turn around."

His gaze rested on her breasts. "Do I have to?"

No. "Yes," she said firmly to him and for herself. A couple's massage was supposed to be a promise of what was to come…not a full blown party in the shower.

"It's a shame," he said, but turned around anyway.

Hailey was out of those clothes and under the water

so fast she didn't have time to change her mind. The water raining over her was just as heavenly as she remembered. Maybe they should install these in a few suites of The Sutherland? She opened the bottle of shower gel, inhaling the floral freshness. The scent was like aromatherapy in a coin-sized dollop, and she felt instantly invigorated. She could have stayed under that water forever, but she had a massage waiting for her.

And a man.

After patting the water off her body, she knotted the towel around her head and reached for the robe.

Nate looked decidedly disappointed by the full coverage of the white terrycloth. Her fingers itched to reach for the ties and slowly pull the material free to expose herself to him. Or better yet…Nate would reach for those ties.

"Now what?" he asked.

"We hop up onto the tables and wait for our masseuses."

He instantly frowned. "You know, when I booked a couple's massage, I thought we'd be doing it to each other."

"Ha, you did not."

"Too bad I returned my Fate Delivery Card."

If the man wanted her hands on his body, he didn't have too long to wait. Their masseuses walked in and Hailey realized Nate was a shut up and feeler. Good to know. He'd closed his eyes, giving her the chance to really look at him. He hadn't shaved in the shower, a light stubble crossed his cheeks and over the cleft of his chin. Hailey didn't mind, she liked the feel of manly skin against hers.

His masseuse began to work and knead on the thickness of his shoulders, and Hailey almost told her to stop. *She* wanted her hands there. To trail along his shoulder blades to smooth the aches away.

She'd never noted how sensual a man's back could be. Just like the rest of Nate, he was lean and lined. The urge to follow the drop of his spine to the small of his back with her tongue had her turning away. She wanted him too much.

But out of the corner of her eye, she saw his hand reach out for hers. She gripped his fingers, and he gave her a tight squeeze. She'd slept with a few men in her day, but none of her experiences ever felt as intimate as holding Nate's hand, knowing they'd soon be touching every part of one another.

After an early dinner in town, Nate drove them to the campsite. As promised, he had the tent up in a matter of minutes. Right now, that two-person red and black canvas looked as inviting as a feather mattress. All that buildup, all this time…she was ready.

He unzipped the front of the tent and she crawled inside. Actually, it wasn't too bad, with plenty of room to stretch out and maneuver. The meshy material of the tent allowed for a breeze, and she began to unroll her sleeping bag.

"Still the girly girl," he said, laughing.

"What gave it away?"

"The fancy deluxe sleeping bag."

"Not something they issue in the Navy? Too bad because when I ordered it online it very specifically mentioned the horizontal quilting made it extra comfy. Way comfier than the bedroll you have."

"That pad won't let a single rock or stick poke me in the night, so we'll see who's more comfortable. Of course, feel free to crawl on over. I'll make room."

She bet he would. "Never thought you'd be with a girly girl, did you?" she teased.

The humor left his eyes. "Actually, no."

Her back straightened.

"Now I can't imagine it any other way."

His words were like a pierce to her heart. Here she was trying to keep things light before he left, but his words, the way he touched her, made her wish for something more than just a fling.

He rubbed his hand through his hair. Looking for the right thing to say? He seemed to think she needed to be romanced. "I want you."

It was the right thing to say. His simple words punched through any remaining doubts.

"I want you, too."

"Then you get me."

With a light groan he finally, *finally,* lowered his head, and her body decided not to take no for an answer. She met his mouth as hungrily as his lips found hers. Everything, from the moment those women prodded her to kiss him on the beach, their picnic, to the massage seemed to be leading to this point.

Ordinarily she liked a man to undress her slowly, but Hailey didn't want to wait another second to get him naked. To be naked with him. Their lips moved in a frenzy. She opened her mouth, and his tongue thrust inside. On her knees, she pulled at the yellow cami she'd changed into at the day spa, their kiss only interrupted when she tugged it over her head.

His hands were everywhere on her body, stroking her back, her bare legs, her arms. "You're so soft," he told her as his fingers trailed down her spine.

Now she wanted that shirt off his back, those shorts off his body and whatever lay beneath. Hailey lost most of her finesse as she yanked at his clothing. At last she could touch and taste him until she got her fill. She loved the sound he made as she ran her tongue down his collarbone, and lower, to suck his nipple into her mouth.

With her cami off, Nate cupped her breasts, teased her nipples with his fingertips. They tightened, and a wave of utter desire slammed straight to her core.

"Pants off," she said, sounding hoarse and very, very aroused.

"Whose?" he asked. "Yours or mine?"

"Both."

His fingers moved to the zipper of her shorts, sliding it downward until the material gaped open. She expected him to slide her clothes down her legs, but instead, he slipped a hand underneath the lace of her panties.

Her breath hitched when he lightly grazed her clit. Then his finger sunk between her legs.

"You're so wet," he said against her temple. "You turn me on so bad."

Good. She wanted to be bad with him. Hailey wanted to feel him, to know what she did to his body. After tugging at the button and the zipper, she pushed his shorts down his thighs.

Nate sucked in a breath, and that wince told her it wasn't from desire.

She glanced up, feeling panicky. "Did I hurt you? That's where you were shot, isn't it?"

He looked embarrassed. "I'm fine, I'm just not used to someone touching me there."

"Sort of like bracing yourself?"

He nodded.

"Then brace yourself." With a push at his shoulders, Nate fell against the downy comfort of her sleeping bag. She tugged his shorts all the way off, then found the scar on his leg. The skin was red, and slightly puckered and she understood why the muscles of his leg tightened on him.

She knew he wouldn't want her to acknowledge his injury, or offer to kiss it and make it all better. Nate was the kind of man who'd want her to accept it and move on. And right now she wanted to move on to his underwear. The black cotton was her only barrier to getting him completely naked.

Hailey could do something sexy, like tug it down with her teeth, but she was just in too much of a hurry. She'd never had a man undressed as quickly as she had Nate. Now he lay totally revealed to her, and she drank him in. She swallowed. Had she thanked the Navy yet? Nate didn't have those big bulky muscles of a bodybuilder; instead he was fit and trim, and very powerful. He'd said he'd never let anything hurt her, and she believed him.

He also wasn't very passive, not content to allow her to gaze at his magnificent body. "Come here," he said and tugged her down until she lay across his chest. In one quick move he had her rolled over onto her back, his mouth at her breasts.

"I can't tell you how many times I've wanted you like this. Those strappy dresses you wear make me want to slide that strip of material down, and do this." He circled her nipple with his tongue, and she felt another flood of warmth between her legs.

"What else?" she asked. Hailey desperately wanted to hear all the ways she made him hot, so she could do them again and again.

"Those flirty little skirts, I can't tell you how many times I wanted to slide my hands up your legs." Nate did exactly that until he reached the soft lace of her panties. His fingers hooked around the material and slowly removed it. "Sometimes this was all I could think of."

"What's the best way to make love in a tent?" she asked.

"I don't know. Let's find out."

"I have condoms in my backpack," she told him, and crawled on all fours to reach it.

Nate groaned behind her. "You are so damn beautiful."

She'd forgotten men typically liked this view.

Seconds after she had the packet in her hand, Nate pulled her backward, her back to his chest, his hands on her breasts. He nuzzled her neck, his tongue making her crazy. She wiggled against him, feeling his hard cock press against her bottom.

"How do you want me?" she asked.

"Every way," he told her, as he took the condom wrapper from her fingers. She turned and watched as he slid the latex in place, then crooked his finger.

With a smile she straddled him, his mouth at her breasts. Gently, she lowered herself, loving how he stretched and filled her. He grabbed her ass, and drew her closer. When he was fully inside her, she wrapped her arms and legs around him.

"Kiss me," he said, and she met his lips forcefully.

The connection she felt to him during the massage couldn't compare. Never had she been this close, this intimate, emotionally, with a man.

At Nate's first push of his hips she moaned, harshly drawing his tongue into her mouth. She ground herself against him, careful to keep her weight off his injured thigh. He lay back, and now she had better leverage, and she planned to make full use of it.

Hailey sank up and down his shaft, and he groaned. "This is better than I'd ever imagined."

She loved that he'd imagined what she'd thought about so often.

"One more," he said and rolled her to her back.

She looped her feet together behind his back and jerked him to her. His thrusts were powerful and fierce, and Hailey couldn't get enough. "Harder," she urged. Nate gave her exactly what she asked for.

Her every nerve ending felt on fire. The force of him against her finally drove her over the edge. She used her legs, her arms to urge him on. "Nate," she cried out as she reached her peak.

He grew rock hard inside her, his every muscle tightening and clenching. He groaned out her name as he came. Hailey smiled at the sound. She could listen to that all day.

Nate collapsed to his side, tucking her against his chest.

"I changed my mind. This beats your cookies hands down."

13

WHY WAS IT ALWAYS easier to tell a man secrets in the middle of the night? It probably had something to do with resting her head in the crook of his shoulder after making love. The reassuring lull of his heartbeat. The quiet moments of sharing as she ran her finger along his skin all enveloped her in one big tempting urge.

"You know that phase where you think members of the opposite sex are gross?" she asked.

He dropped a kiss on her nose. "Yeah, in fourth grade I thought girls were yucky." He even added a faux shudder.

She gave his arm a playful push. "Well, I never went through that stage. I always liked boys." She'd had at least six self-help books tell her she'd missed out on some elusive yet important socializing factor that helped women know the good men from the bad.

She leaned on her arm, loving the way the light from the lantern played on his face, deepened the cleft in his chin. "That's why you're dangerous."

His lips turned up at the corners. "I'm irresistible, am I?"

Pretty much, yes. Instead of telling him that, she shoved at his shoulder. "Be serious. You can't charm your way around being harmful to women."

"I hate the word charm," Nate said, his smile waning.

She took a deep breath, was ready to admit why she needed to keep him at a distance. She remembered his dad. The tension between them. His dad was full of charm; now she understood why Nate hated the word applied to him. "You know how I said I didn't do relationships?"

"How could I have forgotten? You reminded me of it every time you kissed me."

"*I* kissed *you?*" she asked, incredulous.

"All the time." Then he leaned forward. "But I didn't mind," he whispered in her ear.

Somehow his playful attitude made this late-night confession easier. "I like you. A lot. I want to spend time with you, get to know you better. And then I'll really be in trouble."

He twined his fingers through hers. "You're saying it like that's a bad thing."

Hailey nodded. "It is. You see, I follow a very predictable pattern. I'll take your interests for mine, come to depend on you, and then where will I be when you leave?"

"Where am I going?" he asked, placing a kiss on her cheek.

"You told me yourself you couldn't wait to rejoin your team…wherever."

"That doesn't mean—"

"Don't say it." Whatever pacifying thing that was about to come out of his mouth she didn't want to hear it. It would make leaving him all the more difficult.

His expression grew concerned. "Why is it so hard for you to believe that I'll stick around?"

Reaching around him she snagged her T-shirt, and slipped it over her head. There should be a warning about sharing secrets in the night; all the sloshy romantic feelings would be lost. "Because first, you're a man, and second, take a good look at yourself, Nate. Look at your job, you're itching to go overseas now. You're practically *designed* not to stick around."

"The job moves around a lot, yeah, but that doesn't mean I don't want to come back to you. A guy would be an idiot to *want* to leave you behind."

Her throat tightened, and Hailey closed her eyes. It would be so easy to believe. So easy to allow herself to get sucked in by his gray eyes, easy manner and gentle words. His *charm.* But she wouldn't. Because Hailey couldn't trust her feelings. Her feelings had gotten her into a lot of trouble in the past. Even now they were telling her that a long-distance relationship would work. Go ahead and let yourself move beyond just a fling.

This was the lesson she was supposed to have learned. Feelings messed up her life.

Usually, in a situation like this, with Nate half naked and making her beautiful promises, she'd be lobbing herself into his arms and telling him that she loved him. And maybe a Fate Delivery Card had delivered him into her arms, but it still didn't change the fact that her instincts were off where men were concerned.

So she wouldn't be falling in love, but she would be falling in fling. Friends with benefits. Platonic sex.

Nate was an unselfish lover who made her feel incredibly good in and out of bed. So, yeah, she'd enjoy him while he was around, be sad when he left, but his life wouldn't become hers.

Hailey cupped Nate's face. "Make love to me, now."

STRIKING THE TENT Sunday morning and clearing camp wasn't as easy as setting it up.

"It never is," Nate drawled, pouring the last of the water on the fire. This morning he'd made them something called scramblesmash, which was basically eggs, cheese, peppers and onions all cooked over an open fire. And it was delicious.

They had an easy drive into the city, and Nate helped carry her backpack and sleeping bag into The Sutherland. And here was where the awkwardness started. Usually, she'd invite her man inside, offer to share her bed for the evening…but that was relationship territory, and as he liked to tease her, she'd told him she didn't do relationships plenty of times.

Nor was she going to hint around to find out when she'd see him again. From now on when she wanted to go out with him, she'd call. Not wait around for him to dial.

The lobby couldn't have looked any less welcoming, so she turned to her SEAL instead. "I had a great time, Nate."

A slow, sexy smile found his lips, and she couldn't help responding to it.

"Me, too," he told her. Then his smile wavered. He scrubbed his hand down his face. "We'll be out doing drills for the next three days, so I won't be in touch."

"I understand." See? It was already working out great. Already the intense intimacy they shared this weekend was cooling. Him going away fit perfectly into her comfort zone.

Brave words. Stick with them.

"I'll call you when I get back."

He might…he might not. It was all good. *She wasn't even a proficient liar.* But she had to do something to distance herself. Fling not feelings.

With a lingering glance at her lips, Nate then turned and walked out. Her breath released in a large exhale. The clamoring footsteps down the stairwell let her know Rachel had been waiting to pounce.

"So, how was it?" she asked before even taking the last step.

"It was good."

Rachel crossed her arms against her chest. "Good?" she asked, with a lift of her eyebrow.

Hailey felt the heat of a flush on her cheeks.

"That's what I thought," Rachel said after spotting Hailey's obvious reaction. "Just tell me one thing, am I going to have to buy a new box of condoms?"

With a laugh Hailey nodded, and Rachel gave her a high five. "Amy called after you left. She'd like us to host the wedding as well as the reception afterwards. I couldn't turn them down."

It probably would come to no surprise that a woman who'd been engaged three times loved weddings. Truthfully, she didn't really need a lot of convincing. The prep work might keep her mind from straying to Nate. "We've never hosted anything that big."

"We have to start sometime. I've already made a to-do list. Why don't you look it over while I call Amy back. She has to get the information to the printers for the invitations."

Yes, invitations were important. She'd recycled over four hundred of them. Luckily she'd ended it with Fiancé Failure Number Three before placing her order.

Hailey quickly scanned the list, noting a lot of carpentry. Not her strong point. Her thoughts drifted to Nate. Was he good with a hammer?

No. Not going there. That was relationship thinking, and she wasn't having it.

NATE WAS BACK AT BASE at 0500. He smiled, remembering Hailey's remark about him still being single and attributing it to the way he told time. Thoughts of his single status never popped into his head. He'd dated women, but they'd never lasted through a deployment. The idea of a woman waiting for him back home sounded like a burden. What did he have to offer, but a string of lonely nights? Nate was born to be a SEAL, and his career came first.

Only now he wondered if he had room to add one more thing.

The dull ache in his thigh taunted him. What was after his time with the Teams? Still, he had years to go before his body couldn't meet the physical demands, and he gave up his place to younger men, but that time would come eventually. Would he start looking for someone to share his life then? It sounded ridiculous. He guaranteed that no one like Hailey, who baked him cookies and looked at him as if she couldn't wait to rip his shirt off, would be hanging around that long.

"Nate."

He turned from where he was preparing his gear to see Riley, charging toward him. "Just wanted to give you a heads-up, a couple of the guys who couldn't make that dating thing at The Sutherland are looking for you. They want to know when the next one is."

And here he'd thought he'd pulled every favor with

his buddies to get them there. Apparently they wanted more. He couldn't wait to tell Hailey and watch her eyes light up. Those three days loomed large now.

"I'll pass along the word," he said.

"I've got a date tonight, and another tomorrow."

"Doesn't sound like it's the same girl."

Riley shook his head. "When you're in demand, you gotta give the women what they want."

"Sounds like dangerous living."

"Good thing I'm a SEAL."

Nate laughed as Riley walked away. Funny, there was a time when he felt much the same way as Riley. He kept things light with women, always after a good time.

Hailey was a good time, but she was so much more. She made him laugh, she made him hot and she made him think. And it didn't scare the hell out of him that he wanted to discover how much more she was to him.

OF COURSE, TELLING HER thoughts to stay away from Nate was a lot easier in theory than it was in practice. Hailey swiped her lemon oil filled cloth across the wainscoting of lobby walls. "I think the ceiling color looks awful. Maybe we should repaint."

Rachel heaved a dramatic sigh. "I'll be glad when Nate gets back. Maybe you won't be so gripey."

"I'm not gripey," she snapped at her sister.

"Okay, you just keep believing that. Remember when I said I hated seeing you all mopey? I'm taking it back. I'd way rather deal with mopegirl than Ms. Nothingisright."

Hailey stopped wiping the wall. So far her fling idea

wasn't working out so well. She couldn't stop thinking of Nate, and that made her mad. Really angry. With herself, at Nate—both of them.

She turned and faced her sister. "Isn't there some saying that as soon as you decide love sucks, it comes to bite you in the ass?"

Rachel was clearly trying to hide a smile. That made Hailey even more irritated. "I don't know if that's the exact wording…"

"Well, it should be." She'd been resisting the idea of Nate for so long, she'd almost missed out on how good it felt to fall in love with someone.

"I'm glad you're finally admitting it. That whole fling thing sounded pretty desperate."

"But I don't want this. I don't want to care about him, and focus on him all the time. I'm finally getting things back to normal in my life."

"I hate to break it to you, but they weren't that normal."

"How about more normal for me?" Hailey slumped on the stairs. "I should never have taken that card."

"Really?" Rachel asked. "I know you're feeling rough, but would you rather have never met Nate at all?"

Her mind flashed to him pulling that injured man onto the beach, racing down the beach with a kite blowing in the breeze behind them, teasing her about revealing his card, laying across from her at the day spa, making love to her in the tent. "No."

"I'm glad you said that because I think that's Nate coming up the walk right now."

"Now?" Hailey surged to her feet. She looked terrible. Her hair was wrapped in a lavender bandana and she was covered in cleaning products. They'd left the doors and windows open for some air circulation so all she had to do was face the doorway and watch him walk through.

Had it only been three days? It felt much, much longer, and her heart beat faster at the sight of him. Nate appeared exhausted. Lines fanned from his eyes, and his shoulders drooped. As an instructor he did almost everything his men did, and whatever it was they'd done had nothing to do with sleeping for the last three days.

Her irritation and frustration with falling in love with this man faded when she saw him smile and a fire behind the steel eyes of his.

"I'll just, uhm, be in the kitchen," Rachel said, leaving them alone.

How could a man look so good? She had no idea. She allowed herself to drink him in with her eyes. Hailey didn't want to seem too anxious, but she raced across the room, ladylike, of course, but she wanted him. Right now.

"You seem tired," she said, stroking his pale cheek.

"And when you look at me like you're doing right now, all I want to do is find the nearest bed as fast as I can and stay there." He hauled her up his body, smelling of soap and the outdoors.

"What do you know, we just happen to have quite a few beds upstairs."

"Show me the way."

After seventy-two long hours she was hungry for him. She didn't want a slow, explorative experience. She wanted him with the desperation of a woman who'd just realized she loved the man she was with and their time together surely would be short. Their clothes were off the moment her bedroom door closed behind them. She tugged his head down to her breasts, arching toward him.

His mouth circled her breasts, finding her nipple and sucking. She ran her tongue over his ear and down the side of his neck. With a groan he hoisted her against the wall, his cock between her legs.

"I want this to be good, but I'm so hot for you, Hailey," he said roughly, his lips at her collarbone.

And that's how she wanted it. Against the wall and fierce. She wrapped her legs around his waist, feeling his erection already probing her.

He groaned. "You're killing me, Hailey. I've got to get a condom."

She released him. "Just come back. Quick."

Nate flashed her a sexy look that told her all she needed to know. He dug around in his wallet, making impatient sounds and she smiled. Then he was back, raising her to his waist, and she locked her feet behind him. With one stroke he was in her, and her moan matched his.

"Open your eyes," he insisted.

Her lids drifted open, and her gaze collided into the warmth of his. He pulled away and thrust again, his eyes never breaking contact with her. "You feel so good," she told him. "You make me feel so good."

Her words must have triggered something deep inside him because his shoulders tensed. "I can't hold out any longer."

"Then go."

Afterward, they lay on the bed, Nate drawing lazy

circles on her arm and staring at her wall. "What would you say that color is?" he asked.

"When I picked the sample out at the store, they told me it was called blush."

With her head on his chest, she felt and heard him laugh. "I knew it had to be something like that. Can I ask you another question? What's with all the horse stuff?"

Hailey rolled over and smiled. "You remember our talks about me being a girly girl?"

"I see the evidence all around me." There were a lot of things here leftover from her childhood.

"Well, one of the side effects is a love of all things equine. I have half a dozen notebooks filled with nothing but drawings I made of horses."

"Just horses?"

She shrugged. "Some were ponies."

He chuckled softly, hugging her closer.

"Okay, now I get to ask you a question."

"Shoot," he said, looping his arms behind his head.

"I'm trying to figure out what's wrong with you. I mean what is your issue?"

"My issue?" he asked, his brows drawing together in confusion.

She began twisting the fitted sheet with her fingers. "Yeah, what is it that you want from me? What makes you want to be with me? My first fiancé wanted me because—"

His hands stilled hers. "I don't want to discuss who you were with before me. They let you go, so believe me they were all idiots."

Hailey battled a smile. Everything inside her screamed now was not the time for honesty. No time was good, in fact, but she had to run with this. "I worry about who I choose. The engagement thing, it's there. It will always be there."

"How about, those guys just weren't right for you. I am." Nate peered into her eyes, his gaze a steely gray. "I want to be with you because I like you."

"Why are you still single?"

"I hadn't met you yet."

The perfect answer.

AFTER A LONG POWER NAP, Nate followed Hailey downstairs, and for the price of spaghetti and meatballs and oatmeal cookies, The Sutherland had neatly clean baseboards. Nate turned out to be handy with a hammer, and fixed a few that were loose.

That evening, she mixed him a mojito and they lazed together out on the terrace.

"This is one of the worst things you've ever served me," he told her after a single sip.

She raised a brow. "One of?"

He raised his hands in surrender. "Okay, okay. The only bad thing."

"That's better. Would you like a beer?"

Nate shook his head. "No, I have to drive back to my apartment."

Hailey stared out into the surf, knowing she was about to make that next big step. "You could always stay here for the night."

He cut her a sideways glance. "I have to get up pretty early in the morning," he warned.

She nodded, still not taking her eyes from the beach. "Doable," she told him.

Nate surged to his feet, drawing her up with him. "In that case, forget the beer, let's go to bed."

The next two weeks followed a very similar pattern. On his days off, Nate was at The Sutherland helping them with all the little things that needed to be done before the wedding. Amy and Jake joined them. For meals, they sampled Rachel's creations. Her sister had a lot of plans for a new menu, most of them fantastic. For the first time in a long time, she felt hopeful about the future.

On those evenings when Nate didn't have to get up so early the next morning, he stayed over. Sometimes he made tender love to her. Other times it was as fast and wild as that first time in her bedroom. After the initial night when her invite had come out of the blue, Nate had always brought his beat-up old Duffel bag.

When she opened the door to him, her eyes always strayed to his hand to see if he clutched it. She'd grown to love seeing that Duffel bag because she knew her night would be filled with the pleasure only he could give her.

That was why she was so surprised to see what he'd left on her dresser. Panic burned in her chest. "Rachel," she called. "Come quick."

"What? What?" Rachel asked, rushing into the room. "At some point you're going to have to learn how to take care of the spider yourself."

"No, look!"

"What?"

Impatiently, she pointed to her dresser. "Don't you see it? It's his comb. He left it here."

Rachel propped her hand on her hip. "What's the big deal? You're having sex with him, right? That *is* Nate Peterson I see leaving sometimes in the morning?"

"Well, yeah, but that's in a platonic, uh, way…"

Rachel began to laugh. "Did you almost tell me you're having platonic sex? I mean, that sounded like what you were about to say, but even you can't be *that* delusional."

Hailey flopped onto the bed clutching his comb to her chest. "Oh, Rachel, I'm in trouble here. Everything I'm feeling I don't trust. I have to end this right now."

14

NATE FINALLY HAD THE ORDERS he'd been waiting for. In less than a month he'd be back in the Teams, this time out in the Indian Ocean. Strange, Nate always knew where he belonged, how he fit in this world, but with Hailey in his life things had changed. She'd changed him.

"I heard the good news," Riley said. "Got my orders, too. I'll be sad to kiss all the ladies goodbye, but it's where I belong."

"I know what you mean," Nate replied.

"Doesn't sound like it. All those free meals at The Sutherland softening you up?"

Nate shut his locker with enough force to be considered a slam. "No."

Riley held up his hands, backing off.

"Sorry," Nate mumbled. He was acting like a jerk.

"No problem. I've seen this before. Have you dirt dived her yet?"

Nate didn't bother pretending he didn't understand Riley's meaning. Twelve men saw her kiss him on the beach, so word got around when he spent less time in the weight room. No, he hadn't dirt dived her. SEALs planned, tested and retested every action, every drill, so that it would become second nature. With Hailey, he hadn't planned his next step. He couldn't even anticipate her reaction to his wanting more. It was a stretch to bring his Duffle bag that first time. Nate shook his head.

"Figure something out without making the ladies mad, would you? I don't want to miss out on pork chop night." Riley's laughter echoed down the hallway.

He was kind of partial to Hailey's pork chops, too. He was partial about everything where that woman was concerned. He'd learned to tread carefully when it came to the relationship they *weren't* having, but his orders created a sure problem.

He loved her. It wasn't something that he'd planned, but he liked it. Now he wanted things differently in his life, things that included her. And today was the time to act.

HAILEY WAS STAPLING THE last bit of fabric to one of the high-back chairs she'd pulled out of storage. As furniture goes, it was sound, just needed to be reupholstered. She'd saved their budget a cool two-thousand bucks with that afternoon's work. She dusted off her knees at the sound of the doorbell. The staple gun slipped from her fingers because she knew Nate would be on the other side of that door.

And he wouldn't like to hear what she had to tell him. She ignored how good he looked as she opened the door. Instead, she pulled the comb from her back pocket, and slapped it in his hand.

"You found it," he said, following her into the foyer. He tossed the black plastic in the general direction of where he'd already dropped his Duffle bag.

She closed her eyes and felt her chest tighten. That bag almost did her in. Knowing she could spend one last night in his arms loomed so tempting. But it wasn't fair to him or to her. Hailey opened her eyes, and faced him with resolve. "You can't leave your stuff here, Nate. It's not like that…it's not like that between us."

Nate squared his jaw, obviously full of resolve himself.

Don't take no for an answer. Fate had given him the wrong card.

"How is it between us, Hailey?" he asked.

His voice sounded odd. Cold. She also noted a hint of a challenge. "We're just friends," she said with a shrug.

"Friends who make love?"

She shook her head. "Friends who have sex."

He scrubbed a hand down his face. "That's crap, and you know it."

Now she was mad. "I told you right from the beginning that I didn't do—"

"Do relationships," he finished for her. "Yeah, I know. You've told me a million times."

"You obviously weren't paying attention."

"How could I over all the mixed signals you've been sending my way." Nate stormed toward her, dragged her tight against his body. "You make love to me like a woman who can't get enough." She felt his every straining muscle. His erection almost made her cave. "Tell me you don't want me, Hailey."

She met his eyes, saw the raw intensity, the raw emotion he felt for her in those depths.

"I love you, Hailey. That's all you need to know. I love you."

Her eyes filled with tears, and she turned her head

away. "I don't want you to love me." It made it harder
to say since she knew she loved him, too.

He released her carefully. "If it's any consolation, I
don't want to love you, either."

She gasped, swiping at her cheek.

"Actually, it's not true. I'm glad I love you, Hailey,
even though you don't make sense a lot of the time."

Something that sounded similar to a sputter came out
of her mouth.

"But I'll tell you what does make a lot of sense. You
and me. At first I thought I wanted what you wanted. A
quick, fun fling. Someone to spend my time with between
deployments like every other woman I've had in my life.
But that all changed because I fell in love with you."

"How do you know you actually love me? That it's
not the heat of the moment?" Three other men had told
her they loved her, too. But none of them had…not
really. She couldn't bear it if Nate did the same. He was
too special. She loved him too much.

"Because I've never been in love before."

"Never?" she asked, shocked.

He shrugged as if it was no big deal. "I was never
looking for it. You saw my dad. The kind of man he is.
I didn't want to be like him."

"All guys want to be like him. A different woman
every night," she challenged.

"Maybe hearing my mom cry so much made me not
want to be like all the *guys*."

And here he was stuck with her. With her past relationships, she was more like his dad. Fate had its irony
too, that was for sure.

He cupped her face. "I wasn't looking for love, but you

made me realize how lonely my life has become. I know it's probably not the life you imagined, Hailey, but we have something special, so I'm asking you to wait for me."

"Wait for you? What do you mean?"

"I got my orders. I'm shipping out."

"When?" she asked, her throat feeling raw.

"End of the month."

Hailey tugged away from his grasp and wrapped her arms around her waist. "I'm happy for you."

"You're not going to wait for me, are you?" he asked slowly, like he needed to hear her say the words.

Hailey shook her head.

"Why? I know you have feelings for me, Hailey."

"You're right." She couldn't lie to him to make this easier on herself. She owed him more than that. "I do have feelings for you."

"Then what's the problem?"

"I don't trust those feelings. After my last breakup I left my job and my home in Dallas, but it was more like running away. I can't risk my heart again."

He gently wiped a tear away from her cheek. "I told you I'd never let anything hurt you."

Hailey gripped his hand, needing his warmth even though she was being selfish. "You wouldn't mean to. I'm sure right now your intentions are all good. But so were theirs, and look where it got me."

"So that's it? You're giving up?" he asked, his hand falling from her face.

"I think this is just the way it has to be."

He looked like a man who wanted to argue with her. To try to convince her everything would work out. As a SEAL he was used to making things work his way.

Nate drew her chin up toward him and kissed her. His warm lips soft against hers. It was a goodbye kiss.

She watched as he turned away from her, reached for his Duffle bag and walked out of her life. Hailey almost called him back. Almost ran toward the door so she could block his exit. Instead, she stood planted to the hardwood floor of the foyer, praying she hadn't made a mistake.

TWO HOURS LATER, Hailey joined Rachel in the kitchen where her sister was shelling peas for their dinner. "Where's Nate?" she asked. "I thought he'd be joining us. I bought chocolate chips so you could make him more cookies."

"He got his orders. He's leaving." Hailey felt dead inside.

Rachel's face was a picture of sisterly outrage. "So that's it? He's done with you? That jerk."

Hailey swallowed over the lump in her throat. "No, he, uh, he asked me to wait for him."

"Well, that's just great. You're supposed to wait on him and he gives you nothing?"

"He told me he loved me. I think he would have asked me to marry him if I'd given him the chance." How she'd wanted to give him that chance.

Rachel huffed so hard her bangs blew. "Big sis, you're making it really hard to be on your side here. So what did you do?"

"I told him it was over."

Rachel tossed the remaining peas in the strainer. "I knew this was going to happen. Have you ever thought that maybe one day you're going to push the wrong someone away, and they might stay pushed?"

Fighting tears, Hailey busied herself wiping the kitchen counter where water had splashed. "Easier for them not to break my heart that way."

"Not that you're interested in my opinion, but I think this is bad. Nate is different from all those other guys you dated."

"How so?" she asked, trying not to sound defensive.

"First off, he doesn't want anything from you other than to be with you. To share his life with him."

Hailey sighed heavily. "What's the point of bringing this up?"

"Because besides being total losers, not one of your other guys ever made you truly happy. Nate did. He wanted to. *That's* what makes him different."

THE NEXT WEEKS PASSED in a blur of wedding preparations. Amy's complete happiness only highlighted how miserable Hailey had become. At some point she realized she hoped Nate would ignore what she'd told him and contact her anyway. But he wasn't like that. He respected her wishes. Ugh.

Stop thinking about him.

"Hey, I hope it's not awkward for you, but Jake invited Nate to the wedding. They became friends when Jake and I were working here," Amy said.

Hailey gave her a blasé shrug. "No, it's fine."

But it wasn't fine. She couldn't walk along the beach without seeing Nate pull a man there to safety.

She couldn't eat in her kitchen without thinking how easy it was to get him to see things her way, after she placed a plate of cookies in front of him. Even the lobby and foyer had his touches, from opening the front door and seeing his smiling face, to the baseboards he'd helped repair.

And her bedroom? There the memories were the worst.

The idea of sleeping in one of the guest bedrooms popped into her mind, but could she ever forget what it was like to snuggle next to Nate, no matter which bed she was in. Besides, with their increased bookings, they didn't have a lot of rooms to spare.

Three failed engagements, yet none of them ever devastated her the way asking Nate to leave her life had.

She was in love with him.

Hailey breathed in the feeling, loving that she could finally admit it to herself. Wanted to shout it to her sister. Whisper it in his ear.

Only she'd hurt him pretty badly. It didn't take a lot of experience with men to know that when one of them told you he loved you, and you told him to go away, it would be tough to win him back.

Shoving off her bed, Hailey marched down the stairs and into the kitchen. There on the desk lay the box of Fate Delivery Cards she'd vowed to burn at least a dozen times, but never had. With trembling fingers she drew every card until she found the one she really wanted. His card.

Don't take no for an answer.

THE MORNING OF THE WEDDING was a typical San Diego beauty. The Sutherland was a bustle of activity the way Hailey remembered it growing up. The florists arrived on time with gorgeous centerpieces for every table. The Tea Room had never looked better. Bows and greenery wound around the railing on the trellis and the rented chairs fit perfectly on the terrace. An arch of flowers marked where the bride and groom would share their vows and candles perched nearby. It was simply stunning. Rachel draped her arm over Hailey's shoulder. "Mom would be proud."

Hailey nodded. "I think she would be, too."

"Don't worry about Nate. In fact, I think you should look at this as closure. One more time to see him, and then it's over. You'll never have to lay eyes on him again," Rachel said. After stating her opinion that she was a fool to push Nate away, her sister had stood by her faithfully the way she always had.

Hailey gave her sister a reassuring smile, but knew she couldn't fully agree. This time when she saw him, she'd be at a disadvantage. Nate had something she wanted, him, and she doubted he'd still be too interested in her after everything she'd said. The doorbell rang.

"Our first guests!" her sister excitedly announced.

Hailey, however, was filled with trepidation.

The guests seemed to arrive in clumps, and after escorting them through the lobby and to the Tea Room and terrace, Jake's groomsmen took over with the seating. And Nate came alone. She'd seen the man in a wetsuit, T-shirt and shorts, and naked, but he was *amazing* in a suit. What was it about a tie that made her want to pluck at the knot and tug that thing loose?

He greeted her sister with a kiss to the cheek, but seemed reluctant to face her.

Remember the card. Remember the card.

Finally, he turned toward her and Hailey met his

gaze. She heard his sharp intake of breath and felt a tiny spark of hope. His gaze ran up and down her body. He wanted her, and she went weak inside. *Yes*. Maybe, just maybe she could pull it off.

"Hailey," he said, his tone impersonal.

"Nate."

Rachel had offered to escort him to the Tea Room, but Hailey knew she wanted him to herself. "Follow me," she told him.

He matched her steps through the lobby, both of them silent.

"How have you been?" she asked, knowing he probably wouldn't initiate any conversation.

"Fine."

"I'm glad."

"You?" he asked.

"Fine." *Lie.*

"I'm glad." Ugh, this conversation was horrible. And painful. She didn't have much time before she had to turn him over to someone else. Hailey cleared her throat. "I hope you don't mind, but would you stand in the back with me? I, uh...need help with something."

Okay, as excuses went, it could be plausible, and very doable as it was so off the cuff. Nate nodded, and she flashed him a quick smile before she had to return to the front door. The final guests filed in and Hailey and her sister headed for the Tea Room.

"Nate looked pretty good, don't you think?" Rachel asked.

"You don't have to keep rubbing it in. I made a big mistake."

"Huge," Rachel told her, nodding in agreement.

"I'm going to fix it right now."

"How?"

"Like I do everything. Make it up as I go along. Wish me luck."

"I'll do more than that," Rachel said, and gave her a hug.

Hailey just hoped she'd be getting a congratulatory hug after the wedding, and not one out of consolation because Nate had turned her down flat.

Nate was waiting against the wall like she knew he would be. He'd always be there for her. She knew that now. Rachel was right. The difference between him and all those other men was that she could depend on him, lean on him. And he wanted her for who she was.

He didn't glance her way, as she took her place beside him. Hailey understood. She'd hurt him. She caught a whiff of his cologne—rugged and masculine and all him. She ached to have his arms around her. To breathe in his scent. To breathe in Nate. The piano music began and the guests stood. Hailey was a huge crier for anything even resembling a wedding, but she stood beside Nate dry-eyed.

Amy looked beautiful dressed in an ivory gown and on her grandfather's arm. Though neither the flowers in her hair, nor the dress or the veil made her truly beautiful. It was her smile. Her smile, knowing she was walking toward the man she loved, and would spend the rest of her life with. Hailey ached to have that, too. To have Nate look at her with the same kind of palpable love Jake's gaze held for Amy.

The music ended, and the guests found their seats.

Her heart began to pound. This was it. If she didn't make her move, didn't give him at least some indication of how she felt, she'd lose him forever.

Don't take no for an answer.

"Dearly beloved…"

Hailey slipped her hand in his.

At her side, Nate jerked in surprise.

He glanced her way. This was the moment she'd been waiting for.

"I love you," she mouthed.

She saw his shoulders visibly relax, a slow smile cross his face. He squeezed her hand. It was all she needed. All that trepidation and angst and worry, man he was easy. A lightness filled her heart.

They returned their attention to the bride and groom, who were now sharing their vows.

Then her tears came. So many times Hailey had wished she'd never met one of those prior duds, but then she would have missed this moment, this feeling with Nate. She could appreciate him the way he deserved to be appreciated.

Amy and Jake kissed and the happy couple walked back down the aisle together. The guests followed them into the Tea Room where the reception would be held. Hailey stayed where she was, never letting go of Nate's hand.

"Do you need to help serve?" he asked.

Hailey shook her head. "We hired extra stuff for that." It was a last minute Rachel idea. Hailey wondered if her sister had guessed she'd changed her mind, knowing that if things worked out with Nate, she'd be too excited over her man to work in the kitchen. And that if things didn't work out, the last thing Hailey would want to do is serve wedding cake.

The bridal party and their families returned to the terrace so the photographer could take pictures.

"Come on," Nate said, and led her down the stairs. At the sand, she kicked off her sandals, and walked beside him. He led her almost to the exact location where they'd first met—where she'd first surprised him with a kiss.

"Tell me," he urged.

"I love you," she said, her smile as wide as it could possibly be. "I love you so much, Nate, and I'm sorry if I hurt you. I was scared."

He brought her into his arms, drawing her to his chest. She heard the solid thump of his heart. "I love you, too." And with those words he placed a kiss on the top of her head.

She squeezed her eyes tight. "I wasn't sure that you would ever say those words to me again, but I grabbed a little insurance just in case."

He looked down into her eyes. Warmth and love turning the gray almost to blue. "What kind of insurance?"

She pulled the familiar red and black card out of the pocket of her skirt. "Your Fate Delivery Card."

"Don't take no for an answer. I should have held on to that, and saved myself a lot of agony."

"But this way I came to you, and you'll never have to doubt me."

"I never doubted you ever," he said against her lips. Then his mouth took over. He ran his tongue along her lips until he sensually slipped it into her mouth.

"I take it this means you're engaged to my sister?" Rachel hollered from the terrace.

Hailey and Nate quit kissing and began laughing.

"So Hailey, will you marry me?"

"Doable," she told him.

* * * * *

Celebrate 60 years of pure reading pleasure
with Harlequin®!
Just in time for the holidays,
Silhouette Special Edition® is proud to present
New York Times *bestselling author*
Kathleen Eagle's
ONE COWBOY, ONE CHRISTMAS

Rodeo rider Zach Beaudry was a travelin' man—
until he broke down in middle-of-nowhere South
Dakota during a deep freeze. That's when an
angel came to his rescue....

South Dakota, big time. He'd have given his right an

to be climbing into a hotel hot tub instead of a brutal

"Don't die on me. Come on, Zel. You know how much I love you, girl. You're all I've got. Don't do this to me here. Not *now*."

But Zelda had quit on him, and Zach Beaudry had no one to blame but himself. He'd taken his sweet time hitting the road, and then miscalculated a shortcut. For all he knew he was a hundred miles from gas. But even if they were sitting next to a pump, the ten dollars he had in his pocket wouldn't get him out of South Dakota, which was not where he wanted to be right now. Not even his beloved pickup truck, Zelda, could get him much of anywhere on fumes. He was sitting out in the cold in the middle of nowhere. And getting colder.

He shifted the pickup into Neutral and pulled hard on the steering wheel, using the downhill slope to get her off the blacktop and into the roadside grass, where she shuddered to a standstill. He stroked the padded dash. "You'll be safe here."

But Zach would not. It was getting dark, and it was already too damn cold for his cowboy ass. Zach's battered body was a barometer, and he was feeling South Dakota, big time. He'd have given his right arm to be climbing into a hotel hot tub instead of a brutal blast of north wind. The right was his free arm anyway. Damn thing had lost altitude, touched some part of the bull and caused him a scoreless ride last time out.

It wasn't scoring him a ride this night, either. A carload of teenagers whizzed by, topping off the insult by laying on the horn as they passed him. It was at least twenty minutes before another vehicle came along. He stepped out and waved both arms this time, damn near getting himself killed. Whatever happened to *do unto others?* In places like this, decent people didn't leave each other stranded in the cold.

His face was feeling stiff, and he figured he'd better start walking before his toes went numb. He struck out for a distant yard light, the only sign of human habitation in sight. He couldn't tell how distant, but he knew he'd be hurting by the time he got there, and he was counting on some kindly old man to be answering the door. No shame among the lame.

It wasn't like Zach was fresh off the operating table—it had been a few months since his last round of repairs—but he hadn't given himself enough time. He'd lopped a couple of weeks off the near end of the doc's estimated recovery time, rigged up a brace, done some heavy-duty taping and climbed onto another bull. Hung in there for five seconds—four seconds past feeling the pop in his hip and three seconds short of the buzzer.

He could still feel the pain shooting down his leg with every step. Only this time he had to pick the damn thing up, swing it forward and drop it down again on his own.

Pride be damned, he just hoped *somebody* would be

answering the door at the end of the road. The light in the front window was a good sign.

The four steps to the covered porch might as well have been four hundred, and he was looking to climb them with a lead weight chained to his left leg. His eyes were just as screwed up as his hip. Big black spots danced around with tiny red flashers, and he couldn't tell what was real and what wasn't. He stumbled over some shrubbery, steadied himself on the porch railing and peered between vertical slats.

There in the front window stood a spruce tree with a silver star affixed to the top. Zach was pretty sure the red sparks were all in his head, but the white lights twinkling by the hundreds throughout the huge tree, those were real. He wasn't too sure about the woman hanging the shiny balls. Most of her hair was caught up on her head and fastened in a curly clump, but the light captured by the escaped bits crowned her with a golden halo. Her face was a soft shadow, her body a willowy silhouette beneath a long white gown. If this was where the mind ran off to when cold started shutting down the rest of the body, then Zach's final worldly thought was, *This ain't such a bad way to go.*

If she would just turn to the window, he could die looking into the eyes of a Christmas angel.

* * * * *

*Could this woman from Zach's past
get the lonesome cowboy to come in
from the cold...for good?*
Look for
ONE COWBOY, ONE CHRISTMAS
by Kathleen Eagle
Available December 2009
from Silhouette Special Edition®

Silhouette Desire

FROM *NEW YORK TIMES*
BESTSELLING AUTHOR

DIANA PALMER

THE MAVERICK

A BRAND-NEW
LONG, TALL
TEXAN STORY

SD76982

REQUEST YOUR FREE BOOKS!

2 FREE NOVELS PLUS 2 FREE GIFTS!

HARLEQUIN®

Blaze™

Red-hot reads!

HARLEQUIN *Blaze*

COMING NEXT MONTH
Available November 24, 2009

#507 BETTER NAUGHTY THAN NICE Vicki Lewis Thompson,
Jill Shalvis, Rhonda Nelson
A Blazing Holiday Collection
Bad boy Damon Claus is determined to mess things up for his jolly big brother,
Santa. Who'd ever guess that sibling rivalry would result in mistletoe madness
for three unsuspecting couples! And Damon didn't even have to spike the
eggnog....

#508 STARSTRUCK Julie Kenner
For Alyssa Chambers, having the perfect Christmas means snaring the
perfect man. And she has him all picked out. Too bad it's her best friend,
Christopher Hyde, who has her seeing stars.

#509 TEXAS BLAZE Debbi Rawlins
The Wrong Bed
Hot and heavy. That's how Kate Manning and Mitch Colter have always been for
each other. But it's not till Kate makes the right move—though technically in the
wrong bed—that things start heating up for good!

#510 SANTA, BABY Lisa Renee Jones
Dressed to Thrill, Bk. 4
As a blonde bombshell, Caron Avery thinks she's got enough attitude to bring a
man to his knees. But when she seduces hot playboy Baxter Remington, will she
be the one begging for more?

#511 CHRISTMAS MALE Cara Summers
Uniformly Hot!
All policewoman Fiona Gallagher wants for Christmas is a little excitement. But
once she finds herself working on a case with sexy captain D. C. Campbell,
she's suddenly aching for a different kind of thrill....

#512 TWELVE NIGHTS Hope Tarr
Blaze Historicals
Lady Alys is desperately in love with Scottish bad boy Callum Fraser. And
keeping him out of her bed until the wedding is nearly killing her. So what's
stopping them from indulging? Uhh...Elys's deceased first husband, a man very
much alive.

www.eHarlequin.com

When they reached the front door Elle turned to him. "I'm not expecting this to take too long. You'll be okay here with Bonnie?" she asked.

Anders nodded. "We'll be fine. Just be safe."

She smiled at him. "Always."

She started to walk out the door, but he stopped her by grabbing her by the arm. She turned around to face him and he leaned in and captured her startled lips with his.

He hadn't expected it; he certainly hadn't planned it. But once his mouth took hers, he remembered just how much he'd wanted to kiss her and how often in the past two days he'd fantasized about it.

His fantasies had been woefully inadequate. The real thing was so much better. Her lips were soft and warm and welcoming. It shot instant desire through his entire body. He could kiss Elle Gage forever.

* * *

The Coltons of Red Ridge:
A killer's on the loose and love is on the line

* * *

If you're on Twitter, tell us what you think of Harlequin Romantic Suspense! #harlequinromsuspense

Dear Reader,

A sexy, macho cowboy and a tiny baby always tugs at my heartstrings. There's something about a strong man made vulnerable by the innocence of a child that I find incredibly attractive.

When Anders Colton finds a baby on his doorstep, the mystery of the identity of the infant brings rookie police officer Elle Gage into his life. Elle is a strong woman who only wants to focus on proving herself as a cop. Neither of these two are looking for romance.

I loved writing this book with these characters. I found it exciting to write not only the scenes that showed them growing closer to each other but also the scenes of danger closing in on them.

I hope you enjoy reading this book as much as I enjoyed writing it!

Happy reading,

Carla Cassidy

THE COLTON
COWBOY

Carla Cassidy

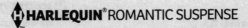

HARLEQUIN® ROMANTIC SUSPENSE

Special thanks and acknowledgment are given to Carla Cassidy for her contribution to The Coltons of Red Ridge miniseries.

ISBN-13: 978-1-335-45642-7

The Colton Cowboy

Recycling programs for this product may not exist in your area.

Copyright © 2018 by Harlequin Books S.A.

Printed in U.S.A.

www.Harlequin.com

Carla Cassidy is an award-winning, *New York Times* bestselling author who has written more than 120 novels for Harlequin. In 1995, she won Best Silhouette Romance from *RT Book Reviews* for *Anything for Danny*. In 1998, she won a Career Achievement Award for Best Innovative Series from *RT Book Reviews*. Carla believes the only thing better than curling up with a good book to read is sitting down at the computer with a good story to write.

Books by Carla Cassidy

Harlequin Romantic Suspense

The Coltons of Red Ridge

The Colton Cowboy

Cowboys of Holiday Ranch

A Real Cowboy
Cowboy of Interest
Cowboy Under Fire
Cowboy at Arms
Operation Cowboy Daddy
Killer Cowboy
Sheltered by the Cowboy
Guardian Cowboy

The Coltons of Shadow Creek

Colton's Secret Son

The Coltons of Texas

Colton Cowboy Hideout

The Coltons of Oklahoma

The Colton Bodyguard

Men of Wolf Creek

Cold Case, Hot Accomplice
Lethal Lawman
Lone Wolf Standing

Visit the Author Profile page at
Harlequin.com for more titles.

This book is dedicated to all the editors who
showed a special kind of patience with me!

Chapter 1

Anders Colton jerked awake, his heart racing and every muscle in his body tensed with fight-or-flight adrenaline. From the nearby open window a cool night breeze drifted in, and crickets and other insects clicked and whirred with their usual night songs. They were familiar sounds and wouldn't have awakened him. So what had?

He remained perfectly still, and then he heard it…a faint shuffle of feet against wood. In one quick movement he slid out of bed and grabbed the nearby rifle that rested against the bedroom wall. He stalked out of his bedroom clad only in a pair of navy boxers.

Tonight he was going to catch the culprit who had been stealing from him for the past couple of weeks. He'd dubbed the person the "Needy Thief" because of the strange things that had come up missing.

Last night it had been fruit from the bowl on the kitchen counter and a jar of peanut butter and a loaf of bread from the pantry. A week before that it was a mattress from the bunk barn and an old baby cradle from the barn.

Anders didn't mind the loss of the food, and he'd already replaced the mattress, but one of his grandmother's quilts had also been taken and he definitely wanted that back. His heart now beat with the sweet anticipation of finally catching the culprit.

Was the person a runaway in trouble? A criminal hiding out on the property? Was it possible it was his cousin Demi, who had been on the run from the law and had a newborn baby?

Tonight he hoped to nab the thief red-handed and find out exactly who he or she was and what in the hell was going on.

The kitchen was in complete darkness except for the shaft of moonlight that danced in through the window above the sink. It was just enough illumination to see that nobody was there.

The cabin was fairly small and it took him only seconds to check in the guest bedroom and bath and realize the thief wasn't anywhere inside. Then he heard it...retreating footsteps outside. The porch!

He threw open the front door, expecting to see a person running away. Instead he nearly stumbled over a pale yellow tote bag and the stolen wicker baby cradle. He stared at the cradle in stunned surprise. Had the thief suffered a twinge of guilt and returned it? A faint noise sounded, and he leaned over the basket and then straightened up with a new shock. Nestled in a pink blanket was a sleeping baby. What the hell?

The moonlight overhead was bright. He gazed around the area and then looked a quarter of a mile in the distance toward the main house where his parents and his kid sister, Valeria, lived. He could barely see the huge place through a thick stand of trees. There didn't appear to be any lights shining from the mansion and there was nobody lurking around his cabin. It was just him and a baby.

Why on earth would anyone leave a baby with him? He picked up the tote bag and the cradle and carried them into the living room. He placed the cradle on his sofa and then turned on the lamp on the end table.

A tuft of strawberry blonde hair topped rosy, chubby cheeks. The baby was very small and he would guess she wasn't more than a couple weeks old. He couldn't tell the baby's eye color because she was sound asleep. Then he noticed a note pinned to the pink blanket. He carefully plucked it off and opened it.

She's a Colton.

His heart stutter-stepped. If she was a Colton, then who did she belong to? Was it possible she was his? He sank down on the sofa next to the sleeping baby.

Yes, he supposed it was possible she was his child. There had been a few women in his recent past, but nothing deep or meaningful. He didn't do deep and meaningful since he'd been betrayed two years ago. What he had now were occasional hookups. Had one of those hookups created this baby?

He stared at her little rosebud lips and tiny features and then looked away. He couldn't do this again. He couldn't get emotionally involved with a baby. The last one he'd loved so desperately had been cruelly snatched away from him and his heart had never quite healed.

Still, if she really was a Colton, he also wasn't overly eager to hand her over to social services until he knew who she was. So, what should he do with her? Should he call somebody now? In the middle of the night? Where would she be placed if he did call social services? He didn't even know if there were any foster parents in town.

Somebody had left her here with him for a reason. But he was torn. He didn't really know anything about taking care of a baby and she'd be better off with somebody who had more experience than he did.

He opened the tote bag to find formula, bottles, diapers, toys, clothing and several other items. There was everything he needed to take care of her. He could smell the sweetness of her, that baby-powder-fresh scent that was so achingly familiar.

Who would have left her here and why? Was it possible the Needy Thief was her mother? Now the theft of the food items and the cradle and quilt all made sense. But why hadn't the mother just come to him and asked for his help? Damn, he wished he would have caught whomever it had been.

Why leave the baby here? He was a bachelor, a workaholic who spent hours out working on the ranch and chose to live in a small cabin rather than in the family mansion. He'd made the old foreman's cabin his home. He'd made the decision first of all because he was the ranch foreman, and secondly because his parents drove him crazy.

Of all the places and with all the people in the

entire town of Red Ridge, South Dakota, the baby could have been left with, why him?

He found it hard to believe that it had anything to do with somebody who worked for him. All his ranch hands lived in the bunk barn in small apartments. He supplied the men who lived there not only everything they needed but also some extras to keep them happy. Besides, the note said she was a Colton.

He needed to call the Red Ridge Police Department and get somebody out here. He didn't know why the baby had been left on his doorstep, but she couldn't stay indefinitely and in any case he needed to make some kind of a report.

Was it possible her mother would return later tonight? Maybe sometime tomorrow? He couldn't take the chance of waiting around for her to come back to retrieve the baby. Eventually the baby would wake up and need something and he wouldn't know what to do.

He made the call and when he finished, the baby opened her slate blue eyes and gazed at him. Her rosebud lips curled upward and she released a soft coo. He closed his eyes and steeled his heart. No matter how cute she was, he absolutely refused to care about her.

Rookie K9 Officer Elle Gage hunkered down behind the back of a pickup truck in the warehouse parking lot. Next to her was her partner, her bull-dog named Merlin, who was trained in protection.

Merlin had entered her life eight months before, after going through an intense ten weeks of training at the Red Ridge K9 Training Center. He was not only her partner, but also her best friend and companion. As far as she was concerned he was the best dog in the whole entire world.

The pavement smelled of grease and oil baked under the June sun that day. Her heart beat quickly in anticipation and her blood sizzled through her veins as she stared at the warehouse in the distance.

Tonight she was hoping to finally prove herself, not only to her chief, but also to her brother and fellow officer, Carson. She also wanted to prove herself to her brother Lucas, who was a bounty hunter.

In her mind she always thought of her brothers as South Dakota's Most Overly Protective Brothers. She was more than ready for them to trust that she could take care of herself and stop watching over her so carefully.

She stared at the warehouse that belonged to the Larson twins, suspected mobsters who were involved in everything from money laundering to drugs and gunrunning. This was where the smooth, handsome

men held their meetings and it was suspected that tonight the place was packed with illegal guns and drugs.

The parking lot was filled with vehicles belong-
ing to the twins' known associates. She'd love to be
part of the team who took them down, although she
hated the fact that whenever she was assigned to any
job, her brother Carson made sure he was assigned
to the same job. She was twenty-six years old. Jeez,
couldn't a girl get a break?

She wanted to be the one to cuff one of the twins,
not just because they were a menace to society, but
because they stole a prized German shepherd named
Nico from the RRK9 Training Center and got away
with it, and they were also suspected of having one
of their thugs steal a puppy from the center. Evan
and Noel had clearly had an immoral veterinarian
remove Nico's microchip and replace it with one declaring them the dog's owner. Nico had been a day
or two from being paired with a K9 handler; that's
how highly trained he was. Now he was in the wrong
hands. And the puppy had cost the center a small
fortune. Elle knew the Larson twins were slimeball
criminals, but stealing a dog? For that crime alone,
the two should be jailed for the rest of their lives.

Crouching, she moved a couple of steps closer,
still hugging the body of the pickup that was her

cover. All she was waiting for was the official word to go in.

Tonight she would prove to everyone that she was a good cop and could hold her own under any circumstances. Tonight she would prove to her brother that she didn't need them babysitting her anymore.

Her cell phone vibrated in her pocket. She pulled it out, unsurprised to see her brother Carson's number. She punched the button to answer, but before she could say anything, Merlin released a deep, loud grunt, his trained alert for danger.

Elle whirled around in time to see a big man barreling down on her. She dropped her phone and raised her hands in a defensive posture, her heart nearly beating out of her chest.

He was about to make full-body contact with her. She had no time to think but could only react. She quickly sidestepped and when he brushed by her body, she used her elbow to chop him on the back. Obviously surprised by her quick action, he went down hard on his hands and knees.

She gave him no time to recover. She kicked his midsection as hard as she could once, twice, and a third time. He groaned and attempted to regain his footing, but before he could get to his feet, she had drawn her gun.

"Raise up slowly and turn around," she commanded. "Ignore my instructions and I'll shoot you," she warned. He turned and she quickly snapped cuffs on his wrists. It was only then that she leaned over, breathing hard, but not as hard as her prisoner who, even though he was winded, managed to gasp out some ugly language directed at her.

"Shut up," she said as she picked up her phone from the pavement. "All I have to do is say one word and my partner here will tear out your throat."

He'd obviously thought she'd be an easy takedown because she was a woman. The joke was on him for underestimating her skill and clear focus. She'd had the same training as the men and she was as good as any one of them…including her brother.

Footsteps slapped pavement, coming toward her. She held her gun tight, unsure if it was more danger approaching. She relaxed as she saw her brother and his partner running toward her.

"Elle, are you okay?" Carson asked, his eyes blazing with concern. He stopped abruptly at the sight of her prisoner.

"Elle, why didn't you yell for help? I was on the phone with you," he said angrily. "All you had to do was say that you were in trouble."

"Cool your jets, Carson. I didn't need any help

from you. He attacked me and I handled the situation." A sense of pride swept through her as she watched his panic turn to grudging respect.

"Good job," he replied. "I heard the commotion on the phone and knew you were in trouble."

"Like I said, I handled it. This is one bad guy—a thug associate of the Larson twins—who will be off the streets for a while," she replied. At that moment her phone vibrated again. Carson took control of the prisoner while she answered her phone.

It was Chief Finn Colton. "I want you to get over to the foreman's cabin on the Double C Ranch. A baby has been abandoned there with Anders Colton. Your brother can handle the surveillance without you."

An abandoned baby. It was a nonthreatening job and if she didn't know better she'd swear that her brother had talked to the chief and told him to pull her off this more dangerous case.

She hated to leave the surveillance at the warehouse. She really wanted to catch one of the Larson twins red-handed and put at least one—if not both—away.

At least her sense of pride stayed with her as she and Merlin got into her car and headed for the Double C Ranch. She'd taken care of the thug all by herself, with-

out the help of one of her Overly Protective Brothers.
She hadn't even had to set Merlin into motion.

She wasn't particularly happy to be going to inter-
act with any Colton other than the police chief and
her fellow officers. The feud between the Coltons
and the Gages was legendary. It began a century
ago when the Gage family lost a good plot of land to
the Coltons in a poker game. There had been cheating accusations, and the bad blood between the two
families remained today.

Most recently she had a wealth of rage directed
toward one particular Colton...Demetria "Demi"
Colton, the woman she believed had murdered her
brother, Bo.

On the night before his wedding he'd been found
shot through the heart and with a black cummerbund
stuffed in his mouth. It was supposed to be a bachelor
party at the Pour House, a dive bar in a sketchy area
of Red Ridge, but there had been no party, only the
murder of her brother.

Bo. Bo. His name blew through her on a wind of
pain and terrible regret. The last time she'd seen him
they'd had a terrible fight...and then he was dead.
How she wished she could take back some of the
things she'd said to him. How she wished he were

still alive instead of the first victim of someone the police and press were now calling the Groom Killer.

She cast all of these things out of her mind as she pulled into the entrance of the Double C Ranch. She drove slowly past the huge mansion where Judson and Joanelle lived. The lights in the house were all dark, so apparently Anders hadn't disturbed anyone there.

Anders Colton. The only thing she really knew about him was that he was a wealthy cowboy and definitely a piece of eye candy. He was a tall, muscular man with dark hair and bright blue eyes.

Elle was immune to all men right now. At twenty-six years old, her entire focus was on her work and the need to prove herself to everyone in her family and on the police force.

In any case Anders Colton would be the last man she'd have any interest in. First of all, he was a Colton and that was enough to make her keep her distance. But, secondly and more important, it was possible he was aiding and abetting his cousin Demi, who was still on the run from authorities. Had Demi killed Bo? Was she the Groom Killer? Evidence said she was. Witnesses said so, too. And the fact that she'd fled town before she could be arrested and had been on the run ever since made a lot of people, her own relatives on the force included, think she was guilty. But the FBI had caught sightings of her far from Red Ridge on the night of subsequent murders with the same MO. Some said Demi had been framed. Others said she was smart and setting it all up herself.

All Elle wanted was for the murders to stop. And justice for her brother.

Although she didn't know specifically where the foreman's cabin was on the property, she followed the dirt road that took her past a huge barn and a wooded area.

Then she spied the cozy cabin with the porch light on. Seated on the porch was Anders Colton, rocking the baby in his arms. He didn't move as she parked her car and then got out with Merlin at her heels.

As she got closer, her heart flipped just a bit at the sight of a hot, handsome cowboy holding a bundle of pink. It didn't help that he was clad in a pair of worn jeans and a blue shirt that was unbuttoned, putting on display his firmly muscled chest.

"Looks like you've got yourself a baby," she said in greeting.

He smiled. "Looks like you've got yourself an ugly, fat baby of your own." He looked pointedly at Merlin.

Oh no, he didn't, she thought with irritation. "My

baby can protect me from getting killed. What can yours do?" she asked coolly.

"Touché," he replied, and stood. His arms still rocked the baby with a gentle motion. "I'm not quite sure what to do with her. She's awakened twice and started to cry, but if I rock her she goes back to sleep. Come on inside."

She followed him into a homey living room with a beautiful natural stone fireplace and casual brown leather furniture. He placed the baby into a wicker cradle. He straightened and then motioned for her to have a seat in a recliner. "Even though my sister and your brother are together and I've seen you around, we haven't ever officially introduced ourselves. I'm Anders Colton."

She sat on the edge of the chair and tried to avoid looking at his broad chest. "I'm Officer Elle Gage and this is my partner, Merlin. Now, tell me about what's going on."

She listened as he told her about the thefts that had been occurring and then stepping outside to find the baby on his porch. While he spoke he buttoned up the blue shirt that mirrored the beautiful blue of his eyes. *Thank goodness*, she thought. She didn't need to be distracted by the sight of his bare chest.

"These thefts…were they break-ins? Do you

know how the person is getting inside the cabin?" she asked.

"I never lock my doors. I'm pretty far off the beaten path and I've never had a reason to lock up," he replied.

"Even after the first theft you didn't start locking your doors?" she asked in surprise.

He shook his head. "It was obvious the thief wasn't after anything valuable. I figured if somebody was stealing food then they must need it. He or she only came in at night so I intentionally left the doors unlocked hoping I'd catch them. I just want to know who it is and if they're in some kind of trouble."

"And you have no idea who left the baby here?"

"Not a clue, but she had a note pinned to the blanket." He pulled a small piece of paper out of his pocket and then walked over and handed it to her.

She's a Colton.

Elle's heart nearly stopped as her brain worked overtime. Demi Colton had been pregnant when she'd gone on the run to avoid being charged in Bo's murder.

Was it possible? She stared at the sleeping baby. Suddenly the baby's eyes opened and she began to fuss. Elle jumped to her feet and picked her up.

She held the baby close to her heart and breathed

in the sweet baby scent. If this little girl was a Colton, then it was possible she was Bo's baby. Bo and Demi had been engaged to be married for a week, and then he had dumped her for Hayley Patton, a K9 trainer.

Bo's baby. For a moment she believed she felt his spirit swirling in the room, surrounding her with warmth and love. She stared down at the baby who couldn't be older than a couple of weeks. A part of Bo...a gift from heaven. She looked up at Anders, wondering if he'd put it all together in his head.

"She may be a Colton but that means she's also probably a Gage," she said. "And if I find out that you're helping Demi stay hidden on this property, I promise I'll have you arrested so fast your head will spin."

Chapter 2

Anders didn't know whether to be amused or irritated. Elle Gage was definitely a hot number in the neatly pressed uniform that hugged curves that were all in the right places.

Her honey-colored blond hair was caught in a low ponytail that shone with a richness in the artificial light. But her pretty brown eyes stared at him with more than a hint of distrust and dislike.

Still, her pronouncement about the baby possibly being a Gage had surprised him. He hadn't considered that the baby might be Demi's and that Bo was the father. But it was definitely a possibility.

He was so damned tired of people thinking he was hiding out Demi here, although he did believe in his cousin's innocence. "I don't know anything about Demi being here on the property. All I know is that I had a thief and now I have a baby."

"But if this is Demi's baby, then Demi has to be on the property someplace," Elle replied. She studied him as if he were an insect under a microscope. If she was looking for signs of deception from him she wouldn't find any. He hadn't seen Demi anywhere around his ranch.

"It's possible she was on the property about an hour ago, but who knows where she might be now," he finally conceded.

"I know she was in touch with her brother, Brayden, declaring her innocence. She texted him on a burner phone that the baby was fine and that she's working to find the real killer. If she's so innocent, then why is she on the run? Why do so many clues point to her?"

She placed the baby back in the cradle and then faced Anders once again. "Demi isn't exactly a shrinking violet. She's a bounty hunter and is known to have one heck of a temper. She thought Bo was going to be with her, but then he dropped her to marry Hayley."

Anders considered what he'd heard and read about

the murder. There was no way his cousin was capable of such violence against another human being. "Despite some of the evidence to the contrary, I still believe she's innocent, but I'll leave the investigation to the authorities," he replied.

"Right now this authority is going to take her partner and do a sweep of the area. We'll be back when we're finished." She headed for the door with the sturdy brown-and-white bulldog at her heels.

Anders released a deep sigh as they went out the front door. Was it really possible the baby was Demi's?

The answer was easy. Absolutely it was possible. Everyone knew that Demi was pregnant—and very likely with Bo Gage's baby—when she went on the run six months ago, and the timing was right for her baby to have been born within the last couple of weeks. And even though Anders and Demi had never been close, she definitely would have trusted him to take care of the infant. Demi *had* been close with Anders's sister Serena, and though Serena had sworn multiple times she hadn't heard from Demi, who knew if she had or not? Serena was romantically involved with Detective Carson Gage, so it wasn't as though Demi could ask Serena to hide her or for help with the baby. But if Anders's name had come up in their conversations, Serena would have told Demi that if she needed someone to count on, Anders was the guy.

Unfortunately Elle was right about clues pointing to his cousin's culpability in Bo's murder.

The rumor mill was rife with stories that Demi had snapped in a fit of rage over being dumped by Bo. Anders didn't listen to gossip, but he'd heard that Bo had written Demi's name in his own blood at the crime scene. He shivered at the thought. Plus, a gold heart necklace with Demi's engraved initials had been found near the crime scene and a witness had put her there, as well. When a warrant had been issued for her arrest, she'd run.

It was much easier to be on the run from the law without a newborn baby in tow. A surge of unexpected protectiveness welled up inside him as he looked at her. She was so tiny, so achingly vulnerable.

And it was also a possibility that the baby could be his. He'd always tried to make sure he had protected sex; however, he also had occasionally trusted when a woman told him she was on the pill and didn't want him to wear a condom.

He would make a good target for a woman to trick. Although his uncle Fenwick Colton and his branch of the family were filthy rich, Anders's father had done all right, too, and Anders certainly didn't have to worry about money.

Yes, he'd make a good target for an unscrupulous woman to intentionally get pregnant in anticipation of some sort of a big payoff. He looked back at the baby.

He had to figure out something to call her besides "the baby." Even though he intended to give her a name and despite the protectiveness that had welled up inside him, he refused to be drawn into caring or loving the baby in any way.

For just a moment his thoughts threw him back to a place when he'd been so happy. It had been a time when he had loved with all his heart, when baby giggles had been the sweetest sound he'd ever heard.

Damn, he couldn't even think about that time without grief pooling inside him.

He sank down on the sofa, his thoughts turning to Elle Gage. He'd occasionally seen her around town but had never really noticed how attractive she was.

It had been acutely obvious that she didn't particularly like him and she definitely didn't trust him. Of course, he was a Colton and she was a Gage. Forbidden fruit, so to speak. Not that he was interested in a romantic relationship with anyone at the moment. He'd loved once and had been devastated. He certainly wasn't eager to go there again. He had a ranch to run and plenty of work to keep him occupied.

A little cry alerted him that the baby was awake

once again. He froze and waited to see if she would go back to sleep, but her cries got louder.

He picked her up in his arms and began to rock her, hoping that the motion would calm her down as it had before. It didn't. Her little face screwed up and grew more and more red as her wails filled the cabin.

He could handle a bucking bronco or an enraged bull, but the crying baby in his arms scared him half to death. Why was she crying so hard? What was wrong with her?

The door opened and Elle and her dog came back in. "I can't make her stop crying," he said with an edge of panic. "I've tried rocking her, but that isn't doing the trick."

"Has she been fed? Have you checked to see if she needs a diaper change?" Elle walked over to the sofa and opened the tote bag. She pulled out a diaper, a bottle and a can of powdered formula.

"Give her to me. I'll change her diaper while you make her a bottle." She took the wailing baby from him and handed him the formula and the bottle.

"But I don't know how to do this," he protested.

"Read the side of the can. It isn't rocket science." She turned around and placed the baby on the sofa. "And make sure you warm it."

He hurried into the kitchen where he managed to make a bottle and warm it in the microwave. He carried it back into the living room where she was seated on the sofa and rocking the still-sobbing baby.

He handed Elle the bottle and noticed the exotic, floral scent of her, a scent he found wildly attractive. The baby latched onto the bottle's nipple and drank greedily.

"Poor little thing must have been starving," she murmured.

An edge of guilt filled him. He should have thought about the baby being hungry. "I'm assuming you and your faithful companion didn't find anyone outside," he said.

He moved to stand in the doorway between the kitchen and the living room. It was easier to concentrate if he was far enough away from her that he couldn't smell her evocative fragrance.

"No, but we both know somebody was here to leave the baby."

"You know, it is possible she could be mine."

Elle's dark eyes studied him solemnly. "If that's the case then you should know who her mother is."

"Actually, it could be any one of several women."

The look she gave him made him believe he should feel some sort of shame. He was thirty-three years old and he'd be damned if he'd let some hot canine cop make him feel guilty about his past relationships or any future ones he might enjoy.

"But she could also still be Demi and Bo's baby," she replied.

"We have to stop calling her 'she.' She needs a name, at least for tonight, because I intend to keep her here through the night," he said.

She pulled a cloth diaper out of the bag and threw it over her shoulder and then raised the baby up and began to pat her back. She looked like a natural. Merlin sat at her feet like a sentry guarding both her and the baby.

"I'll stay here for tonight to help."

A rush of relief washed over him. "Thanks, I really appreciate it."

"I'm not doing it for you," she replied. "I'm doing it for the baby and because she might be a Gage." The baby gurgled and once again she gave her the bottle.

All of her features softened as she gazed down at the baby. He'd always thought Elle was pretty, but she looked utterly gorgeous with all her features relaxed and a soft smile playing on her lips.

"Bonnie," she said suddenly. She looked up at him. "Let's call her Bonnie."

"Sounds good to me," he replied. "Does that name mean anything special to you?"

"No, it just sprang into my head when I was gazing into her beautiful blue eyes."

He didn't care what they called her. He was just

grateful Elle was staying through the night to help him with the newly named Bonnie.

"I need to call the chief and let him know we're keeping her here for the night but we'll bring her into RRPD in the morning so we can decide what the next move will be where she's concerned."

The baby had fallen asleep once again, and Elle returned her to the cradle and then pulled out her cell phone and made the call to Finn. He agreed with the plan.

"It's late," Anders said when she finished with the phone call. "I'll show you to the guest room."

"Before you do that I'm going to take one final walk around outside with Merlin." She stood and Merlin did the same, his gaze focused on Elle in what appeared to be utter devotion. "We'll be right back."

When she walked out of the door it was as if she stole some of the energy from the cabin. A weariness fell heavily on his shoulders. It had been a wild and crazy night. Thank goodness the small spare bedroom was clean and ready for a guest.

She was only gone a couple of minutes and then returned with a duffel bag in hand. "I always keep a change of clothes and some toiletries in my car. Now you can show us to the guest room." She walked over and picked up the wicker cradle. "I'll keep her with me for the night. She'll want to be fed again before morning."

"I really appreciate your help," he replied. "I don't know much about babies."

"That's fairly obvious," she replied drily.

He didn't respond, but instead led her into the room that held a double bed with another of his grandmother's quilts covering it. There was also an easy chair in one corner and a dresser.

She carried the baby to the chair and set the cradle down. "She should be okay to sleep right here for the night." She tucked the blanket around Bonnie and then straightened. "Before I go to sleep, I'd like to get another bottle ready."

"I can take care of that," he replied. He didn't intend to just dump the baby in Elle's lap and not do what he could to help her. He couldn't forget that this was his problem and not hers.

He took the near-empty baby bottle from her and then went into the kitchen. He ran hot water in the plastic bottle to make sure it was all cleaned out and then measured out what was needed to refill it again. Once he was finished he placed it in the refrigerator and then went back to the guest room.

She had unpacked the tote bag and all the items were laid out on the bed. "Whoever packed this pretty much thought of everything," she said. "As you can see, there are five sets of onesies and several little knit hats. There's an extra bottle, another can of formula, diapers and toys that she won't be old enough to play with for another month or two."

She gazed at Anders, that straightforward, sober look he found more than a little bit sexy. "Whoever left her here obviously loves her. That means she must have thought you'd take good care of the baby and keep her safe."

"I will...with your help."

"I couldn't help but notice the quilt on the bed. It's beautiful."

He smiled. "One of my grandmother's. I had another one, but the thief managed to pluck it right off the bed in here and get away." His smile faded. "Uh...do you have anyone you need to call, maybe a significant other or somebody like that?"

"No, nobody. Merlin is the only significant other I have in my life," she replied.

His gaze swept down to the bulldog sitting on the floor. "Does your dog require anything special for the night?"

"Merlin. His name is Merlin and no, he doesn't need anything special. I keep dog food in my car so I'll be able to feed him in the morning."

"I didn't know bulldogs made good police dogs." He stared at the thick-bodied brown-and-white dog whose tongue was hanging out. Thank God the floor was wooden, he thought as he spied a string of drool slowly making its way down the side of the dog's mouth.

"Bulldogs make great protection dogs. They're a lot more agile than they look. Merlin can jump almost six feet in the air. This breed bonds to people and I know he would give his life for me, although I hope that never has to happen." Her affection for the dog was evident in her voice.

"Uh...does he sleep in the bed with you?" He winced at the idea of all that dog slobber on his grandmother's quilt.

"Absolutely not," she replied. "I'm the leader of Merlin's pack. I'm the master and he knows it. I sleep in the bed and he sleeps on the floor."

A small smile curved the corners of her mouth and shot a wild unexpected heat through him. "I can tell by the look on your face that you're relieved my fifty-pound drooling dog partner won't be sleeping in your bed."

"Guilty as charged," he replied. What he'd really love to see was a real, full-out smile from her.

At that moment the baby began to fuss again. "She might have a little more gas." She picked Bonnie up once again. "She didn't really give me a good burp after drinking the bottle." She began to pat Bonnie's back once again. Merlin let out a low, long grunt, as if he were the one being burped.

Elle's eyes widened and she thrust the baby toward him. "Here…take her," she exclaimed. At the same time he heard a noise coming from the living room. He whirled around and ran out of the bedroom.

Across the living room a tall, slightly burly man in a ski mask stood several feet inside the front door. He appeared to be looking around the room.

Adrenaline shot through Anders. "Hey!" he yelled. "What in the hell are you doing in here? What do you want?"

All he could think about was Elle and the baby in the next room. The last thing he would allow was any harm to come to them.

For a long moment the two men faced each other. Anders tried to discern facial features under the mask, but all he could see were glittering dark eyes.

He rushed forward, ready to take the creep down, but he turned and ran for the front door, which was standing open.

Anders ran out the door after him, cursing as he tripped over the side of the recliner. When he finally made it outside to the porch, the man had disappeared into the night. What in the hell was that all about? He stared out into the darkness, fighting against a cold chill. Who was the man and what did he want?

* * *

Elle stood in the bedroom doorway and waited for Anders to return. She was positively livid. Her entire body trembled with her anger. Anders Colton was just like all the other men in her life. Leave the little lady holding the baby while the big, strong man took care of any impending danger.

"A baby on the doorstep and a masked man in the living room, could this night get any more strange?" he said as he came back into the house.

"What in the hell do you think you were doing?" she asked.

"What are you talking about?"

"Have you forgotten that I'm the cop here? That I'm the one with the training and a gun? You should have taken the baby from me when I told you to and let me handle the situation out here."

"I acted on instinct, and as a man my instinct was to protect you and the baby. So shoot me," he replied with a touch of humor.

"Don't tempt me," she retorted. She drew in several deep breaths and then continued, "Contrary to the beliefs of my Overly Protective Brothers and every other man in my life, I can take care of myself and others. I'm a cop, not a piece of fluff. Now, tell me what just what happened."

"There was a man in a ski mask in the living

room. When he saw me he turned and ran out the door. I couldn't get to him in time. By the time I reached the porch, I didn't even know which direction he'd run." He sat down on the sofa.

She walked across the room to the front door. "Come on, Merlin," she said, and then walked outside. The night was dark, with clouds chasing each other across the moon. She knew it was a futile search; the man was probably long gone by now.

Still, she and Merlin walked around the wooded area. There were a lot of places someone could hide, but he couldn't hide from Merlin's nose. When Merlin didn't alert, she headed back into the house. At least her burst of aggravation with Anders was over.

When she went back inside he was still seated on the sofa. She sank down in the chair facing him and released a sigh of frustration. "Whoever it was, he's gone now. Did you lock the door after I came in the last time?"

He shook his head. "It was unlocked. The man just walked in."

"So do you have any idea who he was or what he was doing here?"

He shook his head. "Not a clue."

"Do you think he was looking for the baby?" She couldn't help but think it was odd that on the same night the baby had been left, a masked man had broken in.

"I don't know what he was doing here or what he might be looking for," he replied, the line of frustration across his forehead doing nothing to detract from his handsomeness.

"Is it possible this guy is the needy thief you told me about earlier?"

"I don't think so." His frown line deepened. "This guy didn't look like he'd be interested in stealing a quilt and a cradle, and his mask definitely didn't make him appear like somebody in need."

"I'll tell you one thing, I was ready for bed fifteen minutes ago, but now I'm not a bit tired." The appearance of the intruder had shot her full of adrenaline and given her a second wind.

"How about I make a small pot of coffee?" he suggested. "I'm definitely not ready to call it a night, either."

"Coffee sounds great." Maybe over coffee she could figure out what was going on here because there was definitely something going on. "I'm going to bring Bonnie into the living room so we can hear her if she cries." She also wanted the baby in her eyesight.

She left the room to get the baby and once the sleeping Bonnie was in her cradle on the sofa she returned to the kitchen. What was a masked man doing inside Anders's cabin? What did he want? And it was definitely strange that he had broken in on the same night that a baby had been left on the doorstep. Did the baby have something to do with him?

If he was the baby's father, then why wear a mask and break in? Why not just knock on the door and introduce himself? Maybe the father was a bad guy who didn't have custody of the baby. But then where was the mother? Or maybe the mother was trouble and the father just wanted his baby back. These were the thoughts that shot through her head as she sat at the kitchen table and waited for the coffee to brew.

And then there were the totally inappropriate thoughts that had intruded among the more important ones. Did Anders always smell so good? Like sunshine and wind and a faint woodsy cologne?

His broad chest made her wonder what it might feel like to be held tightly against it…against him. And that sexy smile of his…he was just so hot.

Jeez, what was wrong with her in entertaining any of those kinds of thoughts? She wasn't even sure she liked him and she definitely hadn't appreciated his taking over the situation when *she* was the cop. She wasn't into macho men who felt they had to protect the little lady of the house.

"Cream or sugar?" he asked.

"No thanks, black is fine," she replied.

She was grateful when he placed a red mug of coffee before her and then sat at the table across from her with his own mug. At least when he was seated she couldn't see the entire length of his sexy physique.

"So, tell me about these Overly Protective Brothers of yours," he said.

She wrapped her fingers around the warm mug. "No matter what job I'm assigned to Carson is always there shadowing me. I think he's told the chief that he wants to be on the same assignments as me and that makes me crazy. Then there is Lucas. Neither one of them trusts me to be capable to do my job or live my life and I keep telling them to back off."

"I think I heard Demi once say that Lucas was her number one competition in the bounty-hunting business," he said.

"He often told me the same thing about her. I just wish he would stop trying to talk me out of being a cop."

"I understand them wanting to keep you safe. I feel the same way about my kid sister," he replied.

"Valeria is a real sweetheart."

He nodded and a smile curved his lips. "We haven't been close in the past, but I'm working hard to build a close relationship with her now."

"How come you live out here instead of in the big house with the rest of your family?" she asked curiously.

"My parents wanted me to live in one of the wings there, but I prefer to be out here. To be honest, my parents make me more than a little crazy."

"How?"

He took a drink of the coffee and then leaned back in the chair. "I know my parents love me, but my mother has always been kind of cold and my father definitely tries to be overbearing. Growing up it always felt like they were more interested in what people thought about them and how many tacky objects they could buy for the house than parenting." He grimaced. "I shouldn't have said all that."

"I'm not a gossiper, Anders," she said in an effort to let him know his words were safe with her.

"So, tell me more about your family."

Since he had shared so much about his, she decided to open up a little about how she felt. "With two older brothers and three younger siblings, I always felt like I wasn't seen or heard much. I guess you could say I suffered from typical middle child syndrome. There were a lot more boisterous voices than mine in the family." She looked down into her coffee, thinking about the one family member's voice she would never, ever hear again.

"I'm so sorry for your loss," Anders said softly.

She looked up at him sharply. "What are you, some kind of a mind reader?"

"No, no mind reader, you just looked incredibly sad and I took a guess that you were thinking about Bo."

"I was." She took a sip of her coffee and drew in a deep, painful breath. "The night before his murder we had a terrible fight." Emotion pressed tight against her chest, but she swallowed hard in an effort to maintain control. The last thing she wanted was to break down and appear weak, especially in front of Anders Colton.

"We fought and then he was dead and there was no way for me to tell him I was sorry or take back the words I said to him that night."

"What did you fight about?"

"It was stupid really. We got into an argument about ethics. I told him that there were times I thought he was ethically challenged, and he told me I was an uptight, boring straight arrow. That really made me mad. I got heated and he got heated and it got ugly. Of course I didn't know that would be the last time I'd talk to him and I hate that I never got a chance to tell him I was sorry."

"I'm sure he knew how much you loved him," Anders said softly.

She nodded, suddenly exhausted. It had to be after

two and the night had been filled with action, but it was the emotional drain of thinking about her brother that had her finally ready for bed.

"I think I'm going to call it a night," she said. She drank the last of her coffee from her mug and then stood.

"I'm with you," he replied, and also got up from the table. He took the mug from her and set them in the kitchen sink, and then they both walked back into the living room where Bonnie was still sleeping soundly.

"Thanks for the coffee," she said.

"No problem."

"Don't be surprised if I'm up again with the baby. I don't want you to hear me and think I'm another intruder," she said as she picked up the cradle.

"Got it. The bathroom is in the hallway. Feel free to use towels or whatever you need from the linen closet." He walked with her to the bedroom door and gestured to the bathroom across the hallway.

"Thank you," she replied.

He held her gaze for a long moment and her breath hitched in her chest. There was something soft, something sensual in his gaze. Lordy, but the man was a handsome devil. "Elle, I'm so glad you're here."

"Me, too," she replied. She broke the gaze by looking down at Bonnie. "I would definitely hate to leave this precious girl with a man who didn't even know to feed her when she cried. Good night, Anders."

"Good night, Elle."

She closed the bedroom door and then placed the cradle on the chair and stared down at the sleeping Bonnie. Right now she was a total mystery. Was she Anders's baby or was she Bo's? She desperately wanted her to be Bo's.

She didn't have the answer as to who the baby belonged to, but the appearance of the masked man in the cabin definitely made her wonder if little Bonnie might be in some kind of danger.

If she had to she would stay here with Anders for however long it took to make sure the baby remained safe. And she told herself her commitment to stay here had nothing to do with Anders's impossibly blue eyes or his sexy smile.

Chapter 3

Anders took the fried bacon out of the skillet and placed it strip by strip on a plate covered with a paper towel. He knew Elle was up because he'd heard the shower in the bathroom running a few minutes ago.

Elle Gage. He'd thought about her way too much the night before. Sleep had been elusive and she'd filled his thoughts in decidedly inappropriate ways. He'd wondered what she'd look like with her hair loose instead of tied in the ponytail. And just how sexy would she look *out* of that uniform?

She intrigued him with her serious brown eyes that had softened so beautifully when she'd gazed at

Bonnie and spoken of her brother, Bo. Anders had spent far too long before going to sleep wondering what it would be like to see that soft gaze directed at him.

Then he'd remained awake and wondered when, since he'd met Officer Elle Gage, had he lost his mind? It had been a very long time since a woman had made him curious about her, but he was definitely curious about Elle.

Then he'd thought of the baby, wondering why she had been left with him and if she was his. Or was she Demi's? There had been so many rumors about Demi's whereabouts, he didn't know what to think.

When Elle walked into the kitchen a few minutes later clad in her uniform and with the cradle in tow, it was like déjà vu from two years ago when Rosalie had appeared on his doorstep with a dark-haired, blue-eyed baby she'd told him was his. The only difference was the bulldog who walked close at Elle's feet and the fact that they had no idea who baby Bonnie's parents were.

At that time he'd not only opened his home to Rosalie and little Brooke, but he'd also opened his heart. He wasn't about to make that same mistake again with Elle and Bonnie.

"Good morning," he said.

"It's always a good morning when you wake up to the smell of bacon," she replied.

"I hope you're a breakfast eater." He pointed to the coffee machine. "Help yourself to the coffee."

"Thanks, and yes, I'm a breakfast eater as long as somebody else is cooking it," she replied. She placed the cradle in one of the chairs at the table and then scooted it in so it was secure. "Bonnie had her breakfast about an hour ago at five thirty, and right now I'm going to take Merlin out and grab his dog food and bowl."

"How do you like your eggs?" he asked.

"Any way you want to cook them is fine with me. I'll be right back." She disappeared from the room and a moment later he heard the front door open.

Despite the smell of bacon and toast, he thought he caught a whiff of her fresh perfume. He hadn't had a woman in the cabin since Rosalie. He'd forgotten how nice it was to smell a feminine fragrance, to have somebody here to share morning coffee and pleasant talk.

The baby made a noise and he turned from the stove and walked over to make sure she was okay. Her blue eyes gazed at him and she released a soft coo as her little arms waved in the air. And then she smiled at him.

It shot an arrow of warmth straight through to his

heart. Did she know he was the man who had rocked her in his arms last night when she'd fussed? No, he told himself. He backed away from the table and returned to his breakfast work.

No, there was no way in hell he was going to allow her any access to his heart. Bonnie could look all cute in her little pink outfit and she could coo and smile all she wanted. He was not going to fall in love with her in any way until he found out for sure that she was really his. He was not going to get his heart ripped out again.

He was grateful when Elle returned. She carried a big dog bowl full of food and set it just inside the back door. As Merlin began his meal, Anders cracked four eggs into a bowl, added a little milk and shredded cheese, and then transferred the mixture to the awaiting skillet.

"It's a beautiful morning," Elle said as she poured herself a cup of coffee.

"Normally I would have left here an hour or so ago. I'd be on horseback and out on the ranch checking in on my men," he replied.

"It's much nicer for you to be here fixing me breakfast," she said as she sat down at the table.

"I'll make breakfast, but I definitely will demand you pay me back and cook dinner tonight." He then shook his head. "That was silly for me to say. There's no reason for me to think that you'll still be here at dinnertime."

"We'll see what Finn has to say when we take Bonnie into the police station this morning."

He took up the eggs, divided them on two plates, added bacon and toast, and then carried the dishes to the table. "Hmm, looks good," she said. "Oh look, Bonnie found her thumb."

Sure enough, the little girl's thumb was in her mouth and she looked delightfully happy. "Should we stop her from doing that?" he asked worriedly. Didn't that cause buck teeth?

"No, although we might want to buy her a pacifier."

"How do you know so much about babies?" he asked. And how could her hair look so pretty in the sunshine, so soft and touchable despite the severe style of the low ponytail at the nape of her neck?

"When I was a senior in high school one of my close friends got pregnant. Her parents encouraged her to have an abortion, but she decided to have the baby. When the baby was born I spent a lot of afternoons and weekends with them helping her out."

"What about the father?" he asked.

"Just another deadbeat dad," she said in disgust. "He swore he loved her and then dropped her like a hot potato when she told him she was pregnant."

"Was her family supportive?" he asked.

"Financially, yes. They didn't kick her out of the house or anything like that, but they weren't real emotionally supportive. The good news is last I heard she'd married a great guy and was finally living happily-ever-after."

"That's nice," he replied.

"Anyway, I learned all kinds of things about babies when I was there with her, although she had a boy, not a girl."

As they ate breakfast the conversation was light and easy. They didn't talk about whether little Bonnie was a Colton or a Gage. They didn't speak about the intruder from the night before; instead, they spoke about the weather.

She loved the spring and he liked the fall. They both liked winter if it involved a fire in a fireplace, cozy blankets and plenty of hot cocoa.

He told her a little about his normal day on the ranch and by that time the meal was over. They worked side by side to clean up the kitchen and then it was time for them to take the baby in to the Red River Police Department.

Immediately the first problem they encountered was they had no car seat for Bonnie. "There's the discount store just before we get to the police station. If you'll stop there I'll run in and get a car seat,"

Elle said. "In the meantime you'll just have to drive very carefully."

"I always drive carefully," he replied. "In all my years of driving I've never had a single traffic ticket."

"Then you're either a good, law-abiding man behind the wheel or we just haven't caught you yet," she replied with a small grin.

Her humor surprised him. His initial assessment of her had been that she was a bit uptight and way too serious. But the impish grin proved him wrong.

Thirty minutes later Bonnie was secured in a new infant car seat and sleeping peacefully next to Merlin, who was probably slobbering up his back seat. Elle had also picked up a pacifier in the store and had tucked it into the tote bag for whenever Bonnie might need it.

The Red Ridge Police Department was a large one-story brick building. Anders had never been arrested nor had any run-ins with the law, although he'd been inside the building a couple of times in the past to bail out some of his men. The charges were usually the same—drunk and disorderly—and their pay was docked until they'd paid Anders back.

Of course he knew he'd been under a lot more police scrutiny in the past six months since Demi had disappeared. And now with the baby showing up, he'd probably be under even more. He didn't care. He had nothing to hide. He had no idea where his cousin might be.

He parked in the lot and then went to the back seat and got Bonnie out. She rode on his arm in the carrier that pulled out of the car seat. Elle fell into step with him, carrying the tote bag and with Merlin by her side.

"Babies require a lot of equipment," he said.

She released a small burst of musical laughter. "Trust me, this is just the beginning. There are bassinets and bouncy chairs and toys to aid in their development. Then a crib and another car seat and more clothes, diapers and toys."

"Whoa," he said with a laugh of his own. "Let's take this one step at a time."

They walked into the building where a receptionist sat behind the front desk. "Hey, Lorelei. How's it going?" Elle greeted her.

The pretty brunette with chin-length hair and silver-framed glasses smiled at Elle. "It's going. They're all waiting for you."

He followed Elle down a hallway and into a large room, suddenly worried that little Bonnie's fate just might be out of his hands. And then worried why that bothered him.

* * *

The names of the victims of the Groom Killer were written on a large whiteboard in the front of the room. The first name was Bo Gage and Elle's heart ached as she saw his name up there. Unfortunately, his name wasn't the only one.

Michael Haydon, Joey McBurn, Jack Parkowski and Zane Godfried were all men who had been killed the night before their weddings by a gunshot wound to the heart. Cummerbunds had been shoved in their mouths, identifying them as victims of the serial killer now known as the Groom Killer.

As a result, the town of Red Ridge had become anti-wedding. Engaged couples didn't go out in public, and Elle believed some of the public breakups between couples were staged and fake to hopefully make the man in the relationship less of a target.

Businesses relating to weddings were also taking a big hit. Nobody was rushing out to buy wedding dresses or ordering wedding cakes. Printers weren't printing wedding invitations and the popular venues for a marriage ceremony remained empty. June was the month of brides, but there were no brides in the town of Red Ridge right now.

Finn Colton stood at the head of the room. Dark-haired and with piercing dark eyes, Elle knew him to be smart and serious and focused on his job.

Besides Finn there were six other officers in the room, including Elle's brother Carson. Elle and Anders greeted everyone and then sat in the folding chairs lined up in front of the whiteboard. Merlin sank down at Elle's feet.

"Give me a report, Elle," Finn said.

She filled him in on everything that had occurred the night before and when she was finished, Finn frowned. "So, do you think the intruder was looking for the baby?"

"I have no idea what he was looking for," Anders replied.

"And we don't know who the baby belongs to," Finn said.

"Demi," Carson said. "She's got to be Demi's baby. From all we know, the timing is right. That means she was on your property last night." His voice held more than a little suspicion.

"I've told you all before, I am not hiding her out anywhere on my ranch," Anders said firmly. "I'm not helping her in any way stay hidden from the authorities. I have no idea if the baby is hers. I haven't seen or talked to her since she took off, despite what some of you think. It's also possible the baby could be mine."

"Then what you need to do when you leave here

is go to the lab where we can conduct a DNA test. I want to know if that baby is Demi's," Finn replied.

Of course a DNA test between Anders and Bonnie wouldn't answer if the baby belonged to Demi, but if Anders was ruled out as the father, then the odds were good Bonnie belonged to the runaway bounty hunter who'd needed to leave her infant somewhere safe.

"In the meantime, we need to figure out what to do with the baby," Finn continued.

"I'd like to take her back home with me," Anders said. "She was left on my porch with a note saying she is a Colton. She was left with me for a reason and until I know that reason, I'd like her to stay."

"It's also possible if she belongs to Demi, then Demi might return for her. I'd like to stay on this, Chief. If I stay at Anders's place, it's possible I can make an arrest and bring her in," Elle said.

"I could definitely use Elle's help," Anders added.

"I don't think that's a good idea," Carson protested. "Elle is still a rookie. Surely we have an officer with more experience who could stay at Anders's."

"I'm definitely up for this job," Elle said with a heated glare at her brother. This Overly Protective Brother stuff was definitely getting on her last nerve. "Didn't I prove to you last night that I can take care of myself during the stakeout when that thug came out of nowhere at the Larsons' warehouse?"

"Speaking of last night, we got nada," Finn said in obvious frustration. "When the team finally went in, they found no drugs and no guns. There was absolutely nothing illegal in the building."

Elle shared Finn's frustration. The Larson twins were definitely slick. "Then where are they keeping their stash?"

"Wouldn't we all like to know that," one of the other officers grumbled.

"Back to the Groom Killer case," Finn continued. "We are still investigating Hayley Patton's admirers. As you all know Noel Larson has come up with an alibi for all of the murders so far. We need to look hard at those alibis."

"He knows a lot of thugs. Isn't it possible he hired somebody to commit the murders in some twisted obsession because he wasn't going to be the groom?" Elle asked.

Hayley Patton was the woman Bo had dumped Demi for. The day after his murder was supposed to be his wedding to Hayley. She was a pretty blonde who worked as a trainer at the RRK9 Training Center. Elle liked her okay, but hadn't really gotten close to her.

"That's what we need to find out," Finn said.

"I'm still trying to find out who is sending Hayley flowers every week since Bo's death," Carson said. "It doesn't help that the florist was murdered and his record books are missing."

"I think the creep is feeling the heat of us getting closer to identifying him," Officer Brayden Colton said.

"I wish we were close enough to make an arrest today," Carson replied.

"Let's get to your assignments for the day," Finn said briskly. "Okay, Elle…you stay out at Anders's place…at least for the next couple of days. I'm sure that you and Merlin can protect the baby since we don't know for sure what's going on or what the masked intruder wanted. You update me daily or as needed, and Anders, don't forget to stop by the lab for the DNA testing," Finn said.

They left the room as Finn continued to hand out the daily assignments to the other officers. It didn't take long in the lab for swabs to be taken from Anders and Bonnie, and then they were back in his car and headed to the cabin.

"Are you okay?" she asked him.

"Why wouldn't I be okay?"

"It's not every day you get swabbed for a paternity test." She was curious how he'd felt, what had been going on in his mind when he'd gotten tested. He'd definitely appeared tense in the lab.

"First time for me," he replied.

"Have you thought about what you want the outcome to be?"

"No, and I don't intend to think about it. I'm not into speculation. I'll see how I feel when we get the results."

"So, I guess this means I'm on dinner duty," Elle said, and looked at Anders once again.

He flashed her a quick smile. "And don't think I'm going to let you off the hook."

Why did his smile make her heart do a little happy dance in her chest? He wasn't the first handsome man to smile at her. So why did his smiles somehow feel different to her?

"You might be sorry. Cooking is definitely not in my repertoire of things I do well," she replied.

"We'll figure it out," he replied. "How long do you think it will take to get back the DNA results?" he then asked.

"If we're lucky then maybe within a couple of days, but I'm sure the lab is really backlogged with all the evidence from the groom killings, so who knows."

"The sooner the better," he replied. "Do you ever think about marriage?"

She looked at him, surprised by the question that seemed to come out of nowhere. "Not really. I mean,

I'd like to be married at some point in my future, but right now I'm totally focused on my career. What about you?"

"I entertained the idea for about a minute and then decided I'm definitely a confirmed bachelor. Maybe that will change if I find out Bonnie is mine, but right now marriage definitely isn't on my mind. What were you talking about when you told your brother that last night you proved you could take care of yourself?"

She blinked at the abrupt change of topic. She explained to him about the warehouse stakeout and the takedown of the man who had been about to attack her. "I handled the situation without anyone else's help. I might just be a rookie, but I'm good at what I do," she said with a little more confidence than she felt.

"I have no doubt of that," he replied.

"I'll need to leave for a little while this afternoon so I can go by my apartment and grab some additional clothes."

"Why don't I swing by there now so you don't have to go back out?"

"Okay," she said, unsure how she felt about Anders seeing her personal space. She gave him the address to her apartment and within minutes they were there. He carried the baby and Merlin followed behind as they climbed the steps to her second-floor apartment.

The door opened into a fairly large living area with an island separating the living space from the kitchen. Her furniture was simple, a black sofa with bright yellow and turquoise accent pillows. A large wooden rocking chair sat in one corner of the room. Her flat-screen television was small and in a large bookcase that also displayed a few other items, including lots of books, both fiction—mystery and crime drama—and nonfiction police procedurals.

"I'll just be a few minutes," she said as she left the living room to go into her bedroom.

"Take your time," he replied.

She grabbed a duffel bag from her closet and opened it on her bed. She then returned to the closet and began to grab T-shirts and jeans along with several more clean and neatly pressed uniforms. She added underwear and two nighties. She wasn't a girlie girl, but she did love sleeping in silk nighties that made her feel wonderfully feminine.

She grabbed some toiletries from the bathroom and then zipped up the suitcase and carried it back into the living room. Anders sat in the rocking chair with Bonnie in his arms. "She's starting to fuss a little bit," he said as he stood.

"She's probably getting hungry again." Elle set her suitcase down and then dug into the tote bag to find the pacifier she'd bought. Once she found it, she quickly took it out of the packaging and then took it to the kitchen sink and ran it under hot water. Bonnie's fussing turned into full-fledged wails.

"She definitely has a good pair of lungs on her," Anders said.

"Let's see how this works." Elle placed the pacifier in Bonnie's mouth. She immediately latched onto it and sucked happily.

"That's a magic cure," he said in obvious pleased surprise.

"It's a cure that will only last so long. We should get going back to the cabin. I'm sure she probably needs a diaper change, too."

"Here, you carry her and I'll get your duffel bag," he offered. As she took the baby from him, his inviting scent filled her head.

It continued to be with her in the car as they traveled on to his cabin. "I hope I didn't overstep by suggesting I continue to stay with you and the baby," she said when they turned into the Double C Ranch entrance.

"Not at all," he replied. "I'm grateful to have you with me, not just to help with the baby but also to help me figure out what that man last night wanted."

"You know if I see Demi, I do intend to take her down." She looked at his profile as she spoke.

"I know." He released an audible sigh. "To be honest, I almost wish she was behind bars. At least I'd know she was safe there. I worry about her being out on the run and trying to prove her innocence. What happens if she does manage to find the murderer?"

"Demi's tough and she's obviously smart and lucky. She's managed to evade arrest for the last six months," Elle said.

"Yeah, but sooner or later her luck is going to run out." Anders pulled up in front of the cabin. They had just gotten out of the car when Merlin alerted and stared at the cabin.

"Stay here," she commanded. She pulled her gun, grateful that he'd grabbed the baby and she hadn't yet gotten her duffel bag.

She approached the cabin cautiously, her heart leaping into her throat as she saw that the front door was ajar. In a defensive crouch with her gun leading the way, she swept into the living room.

Chaos greeted her. Sofa cushions were on the floor; the contents of Anders's desk were dumped out. It was obvious a search had gone on, but was the intruder still in the house?

She checked her bedroom first. Merlin was on point next to her, his quickened breathing letting her know he was alert and looking for trouble.

Her bedroom was trashed as well, but there was nobody in there. The bathroom took no more than a glance to clear and then she headed for Anders's bedroom.

Her heart beat frantically and even though Merlin gave no alert, she didn't know if somebody was in there or not. His door was closed and as she curled her hand around the doorknob. her heartbeat accelerated even more.

She twisted the doorknob and mentally counted to three and then exploded inside the room. Her breath whooshed out of her in relief as she saw there was nobody there.

But somebody had definitely been there. She had no idea what Anders's room had looked like before it had been tossed, but now the king-size mattress had been displaced and all his dresser and end table drawers had been dumped on the floor. Clothes had been pulled out of the closet in what she was fairly certain had been a search. But a search for what?

Was this the work of the man who had come in last night? Whoever had been here hadn't been looking for Bonnie. He wouldn't have found her in a desk drawer or a closet. So what had he been looking for? And was it possible Anders wasn't telling her something?

She holstered her gun and headed back outside where Anders remained standing next to the car with the baby. "Prepare yourself," she warned him. "The whole place has been ransacked."

He frowned and she followed him back inside. He paused on the threshold and looked at the shambles. He shook his head and walked on through. He came to a halt at his bedroom door. He turned back to look at Elle. "What in the hell is going on here?" he asked, his eyes narrowed with anger and his jaw tightened.

At that moment Bonnie spit out her pacifier and wailed as if she wanted an answer, too.

Chapter 4

Elle immediately took Merlin for a walk around the property while Anders fixed a bottle and then sat on the sofa to feed Bonnie. As he gazed around his living room he was positively shell-shocked, and he hadn't even begun to process the mess in his bedroom.

There was no question somebody had been looking for something, but what? Initially he'd believed the intruder last night might have been looking for the baby, but this obviously had nothing to do with Bonnie.

So what did somebody think he had? What were

they searching for with such an intensity? Hell, he was just a ranch foreman. What on earth was this about?

He glanced over to his desk where his expensive computer and printer still remained, letting him know this break-in wasn't a robbery but something else altogether.

Remembering how Elle had burped Bonnie earlier when she'd fed her, he pulled the bottle from Bonnie's mouth and raised her up to his shoulder.

He'd only patted her three times when she not only burped but also spewed a milky mess on the shoulder of his shirt. Great, he had baby puke on his shirt, dog drool all over the place and an intruder who had turned his house upside down searching for who knew what.

He gave Bonnie the bottle once again and at that moment Elle and Merlin walked in. "Nobody," she said in disgust. "Whoever was in here is long gone from the immediate property now. I called the chief and he's assigned me to follow through on this."

She picked up the chair cushion and placed it back in the chair. She started to sit but instead straightened back up. "Are you aware..." She brushed at the right shoulder of her blouse.

"Am I aware that I have baby puke all over my shoulder? Yes, I'm quite aware of that," he said more sharply than he intended. He drew in a deep breath.

"Sorry, I didn't mean to snap at you. Needless to say I'm a bit upset about the condition of my cabin right now."

She disappeared into the kitchen and returned a moment later with a handful of paper towels. She leaned over him and wiped at his shirt. "It's not baby puke, it's baby spit-up," she said, her voice a caressing warm breath on the side of his neck.

"In my world if it goes down and comes back up again, it's puke."

She smiled and he noticed not only the pretty gold flecks in her eyes, but also her beautifully long lashes. "In the baby world it's spit-up and now it's all cleaned up." She straightened and looked around. "And hopefully if we work together we can get everything back where it belongs by bedtime."

"Your job isn't to clean up this mess," he said. "I've already got you taking care of a baby, and that's not your job, either."

"What I should be doing is seeing if I can pull any fingerprints from this mess," she said as she looked around the room.

"Do you really think a guy bold enough to do something like this in broad daylight didn't think to wear gloves?" Bonnie had fallen asleep and he set the bottle on the end table and then stood to place her in the cradle.

"You're right," Elle replied. "There's no way this guy didn't wear gloves. By the way, he came in through the back door, which he jimmied. The door still locks, but it's pretty flimsy now. He must have gone out of the front door."

"I've got another lock around here someplace. I'll replace it this afternoon. Security has never been a big deal around here…until now."

"He had to have been watching the cabin. He spent quite some time in here so he must have come in shortly after we left to go to the police station," she said with a frown.

"I think we can safely say now that he isn't after the baby," he replied.

"And we can also safely say that this wasn't a robbery attempt," she said, echoing what he'd thought about earlier. "You have a lot of pricy computer equipment sitting on your desk and it's all still there. But as we get everything straightened up you need to tell me if you find something at all missing. Why don't you start in your bedroom and I'll clean up mine and then we'll work together on the living room and kitchen. Bonnie should be fine right here."

"Sounds like a plan," he replied.

"Merlin…stay," she said to the dog, who promptly sat at the foot of the sofa where Bonnie slept. *"Beschermen,"* she said.

Anders looked at her curiously. "What language is that?"

"Dutch. Most of his commands are in Dutch. I just told him to protect the baby."

"Why are his commands in Dutch?" he asked curiously.

"The obvious reason is because we don't want other people being able to direct the dogs to do anything. But the original reason for the use of Dutch language is because many police dogs are imported from Holland. Merlin wasn't and his commands like sit and stay are in English…" She trailed off. "Sorry, we don't need to talk about dogs right now. We need to get to work."

A few moments later Anders stood in the doorway of his bedroom, his knees almost weakening as he stared at the mess. Who had done this…and why?

First the intruder last night and now this shambles. He couldn't for the life of him figure out what was going on. Right now it didn't matter. All that mattered was righting the chaos that had been left behind.

It took him a little over two hours to put the room back the way it had been. As he worked he kept an eye out for anything that might have been missing. When he finally finished up he was pretty sure that nothing had been stolen from the bedroom.

He kept an envelope of cash in his dresser and it was still there, tossed to the floor with his socks and boxers. A nice gold watch was also still there. So it was obvious the break-in hadn't been about money or items that would be easy to pawn or sell.

He walked into the kitchen to find Elle putting plates back into the cabinet. She offered him a tired smile. "At least whoever it was didn't break all the dishes."

"Thank God for small favors. Did you get your room back to order?" He felt guilty that he hadn't helped her. After all, it was his cabin, not hers.

"It's all back to normal. What about yours?"

"The same," he replied. "So far I haven't found anything that's missing. In fact, I had cash and several pieces of nice jewelry that are still there. I did find the new doorknob to replace the one in the back door."

"That's good," she replied. "I hope it's a stronger model than the last one."

"It will do for now."

For a few minutes they worked in silence. As he replaced the doorknob she continued to work putting away dishes that had been pulled out of the cabinets. There was no question that whoever had been in Anders's home appeared to have looked for something in every nook and cranny.

"I'll let you off the hook for dinner tonight," he finally said. He closed the door and locked it and then turned to look at her.

"So you're going to cook?" she asked.

"I was thinking this is a good night for nobody to cook except maybe Chef Chang, if you like Chinese food."

"I love it," she replied. "I've never had a bad dish from Chang's restaurant. Are you going to have it delivered?"

He laughed. "No, there aren't many places who will deliver to me all the way out here in the middle of nowhere. I'll drive in and get a carryout order."

"The sooner, the better, as far as I'm concerned."

"Do you and Bonnie want to take the ride with me?"

"No, we'll stay here," she replied.

"Will you be okay here alone?" he asked worriedly. She shot him a look reminiscent of the one she'd given her brother earlier in the day. He winced. "That was a dumb question, wasn't it?"

"Definitely dumb," she agreed. "I'll take an order of sweet-and-sour chicken. While you go get the food, I'll keep working at the cleanup. Maybe by the time you get back I'll have found your living room floor beneath all the papers and things from your desk, and then you can check to see if anything is missing."

"My gut instinct is this guy won't be back again tonight," he said. "What do you think?"

"I would have thought my patrol car parked out front this morning would have kept any bad guys away, but that didn't stop this creep, so what I think is that we have to stay on our toes. We don't know if or when he might return." Her brown eyes held his in a sober gaze. "And you swear you have no idea what that man might be looking for?"

"What exactly are you asking me? Do you think I'm involved in doing something criminal?" Her question touched a sore spot from long ago, when a Colton had spent time in prison after being framed by a Gage. That Colton, Shane, was now together with Elle's sister, Danica.

"I swear I have no idea what's going on here." It hurt his feelings just a little bit that she had any doubt, but he supposed if their roles were reversed he'd have some doubts, too. "Elle, I swear on everything I hold dear that I have no idea what's going on."

"It was a simple question, Anders. You have to remember I don't really know you, but I trust your word." She gave him a reassuring smile. "Now, go get dinner. We'll be just fine here."

He hated to leave her, but they hadn't eaten lunch and it was already close to five o'clock. She had to be as hungry as he was, and he was starving. Besides, he had to remind himself that she wasn't a piece of pretty fluff, she was a police officer with a gun.

Minutes later he was in his car and headed back to Red River. As he drove a million thoughts flew through his head. Who had broken into his home and what in the hell had they been looking for? More important, had they found what they wanted? Or would they come back?

The thought of Elle and Bonnie somehow being at risk tensed all the muscles in his stomach. Oh, he knew Elle was a trained officer of the law, but that didn't mean something bad couldn't happen to her.

Once again he reminded himself that she could take care of herself and she could always depend on Merlin. After all, the dog was trained to protect her.

He turned down Rattlesnake Avenue. He passed Bea's Bridal, a couple of ritzy restaurants and several popular boutiques and then arrived at Chang's Chinese, a relatively new eating place in town.

Already he was eager to get back to the cabin. He hurried inside the popular restaurant, placed his order to go and then sat on a bench in the entrance to wait.

His thoughts instantly went back to the DNA test.

If Bonnie was his, then who was her mother? He'd dated Vanessa Richardson around the right time, but he'd heard she had gotten married and moved someplace back east.

To be honest, he couldn't remember all the women he'd been dating at the time. Not that there had been so many, but because he'd had no reason to remember who he'd been with before now.

If the baby was really his, then why hadn't the mother simply knocked on the door and told him she was in some kind of trouble or needed help?

He considered himself to be a good guy. He would have done whatever was necessary to help her out. But the mother hadn't been on the front porch. Only the baby had been there.

It was much easier to contemplate these thoughts than try to figure out who had broken in and why.

Thankfully by that time his order was ready and he got back into his car with the scent of the Chinese food wafting in the air and making his stomach rumble with hunger pangs.

There was something else he was hungry for. More than once during the day he'd found himself wondering what Elle's lips might taste like. He wanted to touch the silkiness of her hair and kiss her until her eyes darkened with passion. He wanted her in his bed with her exotic scent filling his senses.

These were totally inappropriate thoughts, but they had floated around in his head nevertheless for most of the day. He had to remind himself that she wasn't in his cabin because she had some sort of a romantic interest in him.

She was there solely to do her job. He didn't know what was going on. He had no idea how much danger they might be in. He just hoped that in trying to prove herself to her brothers and other officers, she didn't manage to get herself killed.

Elle sank down in the living room chair with a framed picture in her hand. The picture hadn't been on display before the break-in and had been mixed in with the items that had been pulled out of Anders's desk drawers.

It was of him and a beautiful dark-haired woman Elle didn't recognize. He was holding what appeared to be a two- or three-month-old baby in his arms. They all were smiling, even the baby girl, who sported a bright pink ribbon in her dark hair.

Who were this woman and the baby? It was obvious they were, or had been, important in Anders's life. If the baby was his, then where was she now? Where was the woman?

Was she responsible for Anders's confirmed bachelorhood? Had she broken his heart? Why did Elle care if Anders's heart had been broken in the past? It was really none of her business.

She placed the photo on the bottom of a stack of

paperwork she'd picked up off the floor and then once again sat in the chair. She reached down and petted Merlin.

"I know it isn't part of my job, but I wish I knew him better," she said to her canine partner. All she should want to know from Anders was if he was somehow helping Demi stay hidden from the authorities or not and what was going on out here.

But the picture had stirred a new curiosity. She was stunned to realize that as a woman, she was curious about Anders the man.

At least it was easier to think about this than dwell on the conversation she'd had with Finn since they'd been home, which she'd found depressing.

Merlin alerted and she got out of her chair. A few seconds later Anders walked through the front door. "Wow, you've been busy while I was gone," he said as he looked around the living room.

"I just made the piles on top of your desk instead of having them all over the floor," she replied. "Hmm, that smells delicious."

"Let's go eat." He carried the food into the kitchen and she carried Bonnie. Since the break-in she didn't want the little girl out of her sight.

They grabbed plates and silverware and then filled their plates out of the cartons of food. For a few minutes they ate in silence. She felt his gaze on her and looked up. "What?" she asked.

"You've seemed a little subdued throughout the afternoon," he replied.

"I have? I guess I've just been busy working the cleanup," she replied. She stabbed a piece of the chicken with her fork and released a deep sigh. "And to be honest, the chief kind of depressed me when I called him earlier about the break-in."

"Depressed you how? What did he say?"

The heat of embarrassment and a touch of humiliation warmed her cheeks. "He basically said since I was a rookie I could handle things here because everyone else was busy doing the important work of finding the Groom Killer and getting the goods on the Larson twins. He didn't use those exact words…" Of course the implication was she wasn't good enough to be working on something big.

"This *is* an important case," Anders protested. "Maybe not on the same level as the other two, but we don't know what's going on here. Somebody broke into my house and I don't know if the person will be back or not. I have no idea if the person is dangerous, and in the midst of all of this is a baby who suddenly appeared on my doorstep."

He reached across the table and covered her hand

with his. "I can't think of another officer of the law I'd rather have here with me and Bonnie right now."

She flushed with unexpected pleasure. She wasn't sure if it was because his hand was big and strong and wonderfully warm over hers or if it was his words of confidence in her that pleased her.

He pulled his hand back from hers. "Now, tell me about Merlin."

"Are you really interested or are you just passing time?" she asked. He'd scarcely looked at the dog since they'd arrived. At the mention of his name Merlin left his food bowl and came to sit at her feet.

"A little of both," he admitted.

"Okay then, you asked for it. I have always loved dogs and from the time I was young I always wanted to be a K9 officer. I was lucky that the training center is right here in Red Ridge."

She intended to keep the conversation short, but she wanted Anders to understand how great police dogs were in general. She told him about the Greeks, Persians, Babylonians and Assyrians being the first cultures to use dogs for policing.

She also explained to him how a K9 dog's sense of smell was at least 10,000 times more acute than humans, that they could search an area four times faster and with more accuracy than human beings, and that dogs identified objects first by scent, then by voice and then by silhouette.

"Oh my goodness," she finally said. "I've been going on and on. I'm so sorry."

"Don't apologize for showing your passion about the subject," he replied with a smile. "No offense, but I haven't seen Merlin do anything yet."

"He's alerted several times since I've been here."

One of Anders's eyebrows shot up. "He has? How?"

"He gives a long, deep grunt," she replied. "He did that this morning when we got back to the cabin and the intruder had been inside."

"I remember now," he replied. His eyes lit with humor. "To be honest, I just thought he had gas."

Elle laughed. "Oh, trust me, you'll know when Merlin has gas."

The conversation through the rest of the meal was light and pleasant. "Why don't you get comfortable and relax and I'll clean up here," he said when they were finished eating.

"I need to take Merlin outside and then I'd definitely love to take a quick shower." She was still clad in the uniform she'd put on first thing in the morning and she was more than ready to put on something a little more comfortable for the rest of the evening.

"Take as much time as you need." He nodded toward Bonnie, who was still sound asleep. "I've got this covered."

"Then I'll see you in a few minutes." She and Merlin went out the back door.

As Merlin did his business, she looked around the area. The cabin was located in a beautiful wooded setting. Unfortunately the trees would make it easy for somebody to hide. Beyond the trees she knew there would be miles and miles of pastureland.

The Double C Ranch was one of the most prosperous around, and she knew that spoke highly of Anders's skill as the foreman. She needed to let him know that there was no reason he couldn't go about his business as usual while she was here.

There was absolutely no reason for him to hang around the cabin when he had a business to run.

Once Merlin was finished, they went back inside and she headed to the bathroom for a shower. As the hot water pummeled her, she tried to keep her mind focused on the break-in, but it kept taking her into dangerous territory.

She'd liked the feel of his hand around hers and she enjoyed the way his eyes crinkled slightly at the corners when he smiled. His laughter was deep and melodious and she was surprised to realize she liked Anders Colton...she liked him a lot.

She could like him, but that was as far as it would

go. She couldn't help the way her heart lifted and how her breath caught just a bit in the back of her throat at the sight of him. Okay, the guy was definitely hot. Any woman would have that same kind of reaction to him.

But she wasn't just any woman. She was an officer of the law and a Gage. She wasn't about to get sidetracked in her goals by a sexy Colton.

She dressed in a pair of gray sweatpants and a pink-and-gray T-shirt. She left her hair loose and it fell in soft waves to her shoulders. She always wore it pulled back when she was working, and even though she was working every minute that she was here, she liked to keep it loose in the evenings. Otherwise, if she kept it pulled into the tight ponytail for too long she wound up with a headache.

When she came back into the living room Anders was seated at his desk and sorting through all the papers, and Bonnie was in her cradle on the sofa, still sleeping.

"You look nice," he said. His gaze felt far too warm as it lingered on her.

"Thanks." There went her heart again, doing a little dance in her chest. Why did this man have such a crazy effect on her? She sank down next to Bonnie. "You know, Anders, I realize this ranch doesn't run itself, so I was thinking tomorrow you should get back to business as usual."

He frowned. "But what about you and the baby?"

"What about us? We'll be fine here."

"But what if this creep comes back?"

"Merlin will alert me if anyone comes close to the cabin and I'll be ready for him. I'd love for him to come back here so I can get him into custody and find out exactly what's going on," she said. "And get that worried look off your face."

He laughed. "I can't help it. It's a natural instinct for me to want to protect you and Bonnie."

"Well, put your alpha away. I don't need your protection…and speaking of Bonnie…" Bonnie was awake and blinking her pretty blue eyes as her fists waved in the air. "Do you have a small blanket I could place on the floor? Bonnie could use some tummy time. She's been in that cradle far too long."

"I'm sure I have something." He got up from the desk and disappeared into his bedroom. Meanwhile, Elle got Bonnie out of the cradle and set to changing her diaper. When she was finished she picked her up and nuzzled her sweet little cheek.

Poor little thing, Elle thought. Everything had been so crazy over the past twenty-four hours that she'd forgotten that what Bonnie needed more than anything was cuddling and love.

There had obviously been little bonding time between mother and baby, so it was vital she and Anders give Bonnie as much stroking and holding and rocking as possible. A baby who didn't get that might grow up with attachment disorder, a condition that would make relationships difficult for her throughout her life.

"Here we go," Anders said as he returned to the living room carrying a small brown-and-gold quilt. He spread it out on the floor.

"That's darling," Elle said as she gazed at the blanket. It was a patchwork quilt and in each square was a cowboy with a big hat riding a horse.

"My grandmother made it for me when I was born," he replied, a touch of wistfulness in his voice.

"You and your grandmother were close?"

He nodded. "I was her firstborn grandson and she spoiled me rotten."

She frowned. "But what about Finn? He's older than you, isn't he?"

"Finn and I are actually half brothers. He belongs to my dad and his first wife. When she passed away, Dad met my mom, and she had me and my two sisters."

Elle gestured to the quilt. "Are you sure you want to use it?"

He smiled. "My grandmother made me several quilts and each time she gifted me with one she told me the same thing. She said she didn't want them wrapped up in plastic and stuffed in a closet. She didn't want them saved for a special occasion. She wanted me to use and enjoy them."

"Your grandmother sounds like a wonderful woman."

"She was. She died seven years ago. She used to tell me that when she was gone her sons would fight over her money and her daughters-in-law would fight over her china, but nobody could take away the quilts she'd made with love for me."

"That's really nice," she replied. "All right then." She knelt down and placed Bonnie in the center of the quilt on her tummy. "Just ignore us," she said to Anders, who had returned to his seat at the desk.

Elle then stretched out on her stomach at Bonnie's head while Merlin took a position right next to Bonnie. "Hey, sweet baby girl," she said softly. "I'll bet your mother misses you desperately. I wish we knew why you were here and not with her."

She continued to softly talk and occasionally reached out to stroke first one tiny arm and then the other. She watched as Bonnie struggled to raise her head to find the voice speaking to her.

"Is that good for her?" Anders asked.

"It's very good for her. See how she's working her neck muscles to try to raise her head and look at me? This is an exercise that makes her stronger."

To Elle's shock, Anders got up from the desk and then stretched out on the floor next to her. Instantly, every one of her muscles tensed. His body heat warmed her and the scent of his cologne made her half-dizzy.

"I'm constantly amazed by your knowledge of babies," he said. "I'm surprised you don't already have a baby of your own."

She laughed and fought the impulse to jump up and get some distance from him. He was far too close to her. "It isn't time yet for married life and babies," she replied. "I want to establish myself in my job before I fall in love and have a baby." She turned her head to look at him. "What about you? Why aren't you married with a couple of babies of your own? I know you said you were a confirmed bachelor, but why?"

"As far as I'm concerned love is just a way to manipulate other people's emotions. I don't believe in the fairy tale of love and that's why I'll never marry." He abruptly pulled himself up off the floor. "And I certainly don't intend to love that baby, either."

He returned to his work at the desk and she continued to play with Bonnie. Was his seeming bitterness toward the idea of love rooted in whatever had happened between him and the woman and baby in the picture? What could have gone wrong between them? They looked so happy in the picture. It didn't matter to her if he loved Bonnie or not, although she suspected if he found out she was his he'd embrace her with all of his love. Still, it certainly didn't matter to her that he didn't believe in love.

Elle had been in love once. Two years ago she'd been mad about another rancher. The handsome Frank Benson had swept her off her feet and after six months of dating she was certain he was going to ask her to marry him.

And she had desperately wanted to marry him. She wanted to have his babies and have her career. They'd even talked about how that might work out.

She remembered the night he'd sat her on his sofa and had taken her hands in his. Her heart had beaten with the quickened rhythm of excitement and she was certain she saw her future in the depths of his green eyes.

Then he told her that while he'd been dating Elle he'd also been seeing somebody else and he was in love with the other woman. He'd told her that the other woman was exciting and intriguing and everything Elle wasn't. She had been utterly blindsided and it had taken her months to get over him.

Love wasn't on her radar at all. After Frank she had made the decision that she would devote herself solely to her work. Work wouldn't betray her. Frank might have found her inadequate, but she was going to give her all to the job and nobody would find her wanting in that capacity.

She was here in the cabin to do a job, and once the job was over she'd probably never see Anders again except for in passing. Nope, it certainly didn't matter that he didn't believe in love, because the last thing she was going to do was fall in love with him.

Chapter 5

Anders mounted his horse and headed out to the pastures. The morning sun was warm on his shoulders and he was glad to be away from the cabin if only for a couple of hours.

He wasn't accustomed to the pleasant scents of floral perfume and fresh baby powder and at the moment he felt as if he were drowning in it.

In particular it was Elle's slightly exotic scent that half distracted him, that tormented him more than just a little bit. Would he find the source of it at the base of her throat? Between her well-shaped breasts?

When he'd stretched out beside her on the floor

the night before what he'd really wanted to do was reach out and pull her into his arms. He'd wanted to taste her lips and stroke his hands down the length of her very shapely body.

Last night when he'd finally fallen asleep, his dreams had been of her. They had been hot and erotic and it had taken a very long, cold morning shower to finally get them fully out of his head.

He urged his horse to run a little faster, as if he could outrun his growing lust for Elle. It hadn't helped that he'd awakened in the middle of the night and had started into the kitchen for a drink of water.

He'd been about to walk into the moonlit room when he spied Elle fixing a bottle. He'd backed up and gone back to his room, but not before her vision was emblazoned in his brain.

She'd been clad in a short nightie that had showcased her long, shapely legs and hinted at a curvaceous derriere. If he would have guessed what kind of nightclothes she wore, the sexy silk would have been his last guess. Before last night he would have guessed that she wore a pair of pajamas or a cotton nightshirt to bed.

Oh yes, he was developing a real good case of lust for the rookie cop who was his temporary houseguest. He felt as if his stomach muscles had been tensed since the first full smile he'd received from her.

He consciously shoved thoughts of her and Bonnie out of his mind and instead focused on his surroundings. Everything was a beautiful spring green and pride filled him as he saw the healthy cattle herd milling in the distance. The air was fresh and clean and he drew in several long, deep breaths.

He'd worked on this place since he was ten years old, shadowing first his grandfather and then his father and learning everything he could about ranching. He'd never wanted to do anything else. He'd never wanted to be anyplace else. This land was his heart and soul and he couldn't imagine ever leaving it.

He headed toward the big house, deciding he should probably tell his family about what was going on at the cabin. Heaven help him if they only got some silly gossip off the street. It was early enough that his father would probably be the only one up, but that was fine with Anders.

Anders loved his mother, but had never really felt close to her. She was beautiful and she'd been a young mother who had employed a series of nannies to raise him.

Joanelle Colton was also more than a bit of a snob who spent far too much of her time worried about other people's opinion of her and her family. If she knew Elle Gage was staying at his cabin, she'd have a fit worrying about gossip.

He rode around to the back door of the mansion and dismounted there, where there was a hitching post. If his father was up and around he would be in the breakfast nook having coffee and reading the morning paper.

Anders tied up his horse and then went to the window and indeed, his father was at the table. He saw Anders through the glass and gestured him to the back door.

"Good morning, Mr. Colton," Angie, one of the kitchen maids, greeted him as he came inside.

"Morning, Angie. It sure smells good in here," he replied as he swept his hat from his head.

Her dark eyes twinkled merrily. "I just pulled a tray of cinnamon rolls out of the oven."

"Ah, Angie, you know how partial I am to your cinnamon rolls," Anders replied with a grin.

"Go sit and I'll bring you one with a cup of coffee," she replied.

"Sounds good." He walked into the breakfast nook.

"Son! Sit down. Angie, bring my boy some coffee," Anders's father bellowed out as though he hadn't heard a word the woman had just said.

"Coming now," Angie replied. Before Anders had even sat down she was at the table with huge cinnamon rolls for them both and a cup of coffee for Anders.

Judson Colton was a tall, strapping man who could be a bit overbearing. Anders had gotten his father's blue eyes, but where Anders's hair was dark, his father's was blond...and receding, much to his chagrin.

"I've been waiting for you to come up and tell me what's been going on at your place. Valeria told me she saw a cop car parked out front for most of the day yesterday. Thank God Valeria didn't mention it to your mom. So, what's going on?"

"The patrol car is still parked there," Anders replied. He told his father about everything that had happened since the baby had been left on his doorstep. "Officer Gage has been assigned to the job and is staying with me."

"Carson?" Judson asked.

"No, Elle," Anders replied.

"Hmm, I've seen her around town. She's a damned attractive young woman." He narrowed his eyes. "Just remember son, she's a Gage. It's bad enough your sister Serena is involved with a Gage and won't listen to reason. We don't need you falling for one, too."

"She's there to do her job, Dad. And I definitely appreciate her helping me out with the baby."

"Is the baby yours?"

"I don't know. It's either mine or Demi's."

"Got careless, did you?"

"Maybe once or twice," Anders admitted. "We did a paternity test down at the police station so we should know if she's mine in the next couple of days or so."

For the next few minutes the two talked about ranch business. Although Judson had pretty much turned over the running of the ranch to Anders, he still liked updates often.

Then the conversation turned to the Groom Killings and Demi. "I don't know what to think about that girl. She was always a bit wild, but it's hard for me to believe she's a coldhearted killer," Judson said. "Rusty certainly wasn't a great father. You can't blame the kids for that. Hell, all four of them were raised by different mothers."

Anders knew his parents were embarrassed by his uncle Rusty, who owned the Pour House bar. The place was a dive on the wrong side of town and Anders couldn't ever remember seeing his uncle without a beer in his hand. Rusty had been married and divorced from four different women and at least for now didn't seem to want to add a fifth wife to the mix.

"Your mother will have a fit if she finds out Elle Gage is staying at the cabin with you. She was so upset when Serena got engaged to Carson Gage. Now with your younger sister deciding she's madly in love with Vincent Gage, your mother is about to lose it. You know Coltons and Gages were never supposed to mix. She thinks the family is going to hell in a handbasket."

The last thing Anders wanted to do was spend any more time engaged in a conversation about how upset his mother was by current events. In any case by that time Anders had finished the cinnamon roll and coffee and was ready to get back to work. He once again assured his father that Elle was merely at his cabin to do her job.

"Thanks for the coffee," he said. He grabbed his hat from the empty chair next to him and got up from the chair.

"You'll keep me posted about what's going on?" It was posed as a question, but Anders knew it was a command.

"Of course," he replied.

Minutes later he was back on his horse and headed out to the pastures. Once again he breathed in the clean, fresh air, relaxing with each deep breath he took.

The relaxation only lasted a few minutes as he saw in the distance a few of his men working on a portion of downed fence. He urged his horse faster and then pulled up and dismounted as he reached them.

"Hey, boss." Sam Tennison, one of the ranch hands, greeted him.

"What happened here?" Anders eyed the length of downed white fencing.

"Don't know. It was down when we made first rounds this morning," Sam replied.

"Did we lose any cattle?" Anders asked.

"We don't think so," Mike Burwell, another of the men, replied. "A couple of us rode out to look but we didn't see any."

"It looks to me like it was pulled down on purpose," Sam said in obvious disgust. He cocked his hat back on his head. "I'm thinking maybe it was Seth Richardson. I've seen him lurking around the past couple of days."

"Yeah, I saw him at the Pour House the other night and he's still ticked off about getting fired," Mike added. "It wouldn't take many drinks for him to try to get a little revenge with some of the other lowlifes that hang out in the bar."

Seth Richardson. Anders wanted to kick himself in the head. Why hadn't he thought of the man before now? Damn, he needed to tell Elle about Seth.

"Don't worry, we should have all this back up in the next couple of hours," Sam said.

"I'm not worried, I know how you guys work. If you need any extra supplies just let me know," Anders replied. He remounted, suddenly eager to get back to the cabin to talk to Elle about Seth.

Thankfully he had good men working for him. They were all well-versed in what it took to keep the place running smoothly and most of them were self-starters who didn't need anyone standing over them and cracking a whip.

Sure, he'd had to bail a couple of them out of jail over the years, but he always gave them a second chance. There hadn't been too many men he'd had to fire and even though he'd given Seth more than enough opportunity to clean up his act, ultimately the man had let him down and Anders had had to fire him.

He headed toward the stables, vaguely surprised at his eagerness not only to share the new information with Elle, but also just to see her again.

He didn't like the feeling. He definitely didn't want the feeling. He'd felt that same way about Rosalie and Brooke, and he never wanted to give a woman and a child that kind of power over him again.

He arrived at the stable and unsaddled. He then stalled his horse and got into his car to drive back to the cabin.

When he reached it, he got out of the car and went to the front door. He was pleased to find it locked. He'd told her before he'd left that morning to make sure and keep the doors locked, which had earned him another dirty look.

She opened the door before he could even pull his keys out of his jeans pocket. She had her gun in her hand.

"Let me guess, Merlin let you know I was here," he said as he walked in. Merlin stood at her side and Anders could swear the dog was smiling at him.

"What are you doing back here so early? I didn't expect to see you here again until about dinnertime."

"I thought of something I should have thought about before," he said.

"What's that?" She placed her gun on the coffee table and then sank down on the sofa next to Bonnie, who was sleeping. Elle wore that serious expression that made him want to do or say something to make her smile.

He fought the impulse and sank down on the recliner. "Last week I had to fire a man named Seth Richardson and he didn't take it very well."

She leaned forward, as if he were the most fascinating man in the entire world. Unfortunately he knew she was interested only in the information he had for her.

"What do you mean, he didn't take it very well? What did he do?"

"He threw around a lot of stupid threats."

Her brown eyes narrowed slightly. "What kind of stupid threats?"

Anders shrugged. "He couldn't wait to meet me in a dark alley and show me who was really boss. He was also going to destroy my good name around town and ruin the ranch's business. Keep in mind the man was drunk as a skunk at the time."

"Is that why you fired him?"

Anders nodded. "I'd warned him half a dozen times that if he didn't clean up the drinking then I was going to have to let him go. Needless to say he didn't clean up and so I fired him. I think it's possible he pulled down some fencing in the pasture sometime last night. My men found it down this morning and it appeared to have been deliberately pulled down."

"So you think he might have been the same person who broke in here yesterday? Maybe it wasn't a search at all but instead a trashing of the place in some childish attempt at revenge?" she asked.

He frowned thoughtfully. "I don't know. I just thought you should know about him."

Elle leaned back again into the sofa, a dainty frown appearing across her forehead. "So then do you think he was the masked intruder who came into the house after the baby was left here?"

He thought about the masked man he'd seen in his living room. "No, I don't think that was Seth. That man was physically bigger than Seth."

"But it's possible this Seth might have broken in here and tossed things around," she replied. "Where does he live?"

Anders shrugged. "I don't know. Up until a week ago he lived here in the bunk barn. He did tell me to send his last check to the Pour House and he'd pick it up there."

"Are you going to be here for a while?" she asked.

"Yeah, why?"

"I need to go change my clothes. Can you keep an eye on Bonnie? She's been fed and her diaper was just changed so she should be good for a couple of hours."

"Sure," he replied. He didn't know why she thought she needed to change clothes. She wore a pair of jeans that hugged her long legs and a navy T-shirt that clung to her full breasts. She looked more than fine to him.

The minute she left the room, Bonnie awakened. She stretched her little arms out and released a soft coo that reminded him of a dove's call.

Her sweet coo turned into a little bit of fussing. He looked toward Elle's closed bedroom door, wondering how long she would be. He mentally shook his head. He couldn't depend on Elle every time Bonnie fussed.

When the fussing turned to actual crying, Anders got up and picked the baby up from the cradle.

He returned to his chair with her cradled in his

arms. She was so tiny she fit perfectly in the crook of his elbow. Instantly she stopped crying and instead she looked at him steadily.

She held his gaze and in the depths of her eyes he saw such pure innocence and a trust that humbled him.

And then she smiled at him.

He found himself smiling back. "Hey, little Bonnie," he said softly. She waved her arms and cooed as if happy just to hear his voice. He had no idea if she was his or not, but at the moment it didn't matter.

"Are you trying to talk to me?" He smiled again as a bit of baby babble left her lips. "You're a pretty little girl and you're going to have a wonderful life filled with lots of love," he said softly.

"She seems very happy in your arms."

He looked up to see Elle standing in her bedroom doorway. She was clad in her neatly pressed uniform. Her beautiful hair was pulled back in the low ponytail at the nape of her neck and she wore a somber expression.

He frowned at her. "Why the official look?"

"I'm going to do some official business," she replied. She walked over to the coffee table, picked up her gun and then put it into her holster.

"What kind of official business?" He frowned at her, not happy with this turn of events.

"I need to check out Seth Richardson and see if he has an alibi for yesterday when we had the break-in here."

"Do you really think that's necessary?"

She looked at him with a touch of surprise. "Of course. It's not only necessary, it's my job. We need to know if Seth was the one who broke in here for some sort of revenge. If he was, then one mystery is solved, but if he didn't do it then we know it was an actual search of the place."

He stood with Bonnie in his arms. "How are you going to find Seth?" He walked over to the cradle and put Bonnie there. "He could be anywhere."

"If he told you to send his final check to the Pour House, then I'm going to have a talk with Rusty. He'll probably know where Seth is staying."

He walked with Merlin and her to the front door and tried to quash his worry. She would hate knowing he was worried about her. She'd remind him that she was a trained officer of the law and this was what she did.

When they reached the front door she turned to him. "I'm not expecting this to take too long. You'll be okay here with Bonnie?" she asked.

He nodded. "We'll be fine. Just be safe."

She smiled at him. "Always."

She started to walk out the door, but he stopped

her by grabbing her by the arm. She turned around to face him and he leaned in and captured her startled lips with his.

He hadn't expected it; he certainly hadn't planned it. But once his mouth took hers, he remembered just how much he'd wanted to kiss her and how often in the past two days he'd fantasized about it.

His fantasies had been woefully inadequate. The real thing was so much better. Her lips were soft and warm and welcoming. It shot an instant desire through his entire body. He could kiss Elle Gage forever.

But the kiss lasted only a couple of moments and then she stepped back from him.

"I'll see you later," she said, her eyes dark and mysterious pools. She turned on her heel and headed for her patrol car. Merlin padded along beside her.

He watched them get into the car and he continued to watch until her car drove away. It was only then he closed and locked the door and sank down on the sofa next to Bonnie.

He probably shouldn't have kissed her, because now all he could think about was hoping he'd get an opportunity to kiss her again.

That kiss. That damned kiss burned her lips as she headed into town. He shouldn't have done it, and worse than that, she shouldn't have allowed it.

But his mouth had been so hot, so demanding and hungry against hers. It had momentarily taken her breath away and made it impossible for her to think.

She'd wanted to fall into him and feel his strong arms wrap around her. She'd wanted him to carry her into his bedroom and make passionate love to her.

The moment she'd wanted him to deepen the kiss was the same moment her good senses had slammed back into her and she'd backed away from him.

The kiss didn't change anything between them. It couldn't. She just had to forget it ever happened. Besides, she had business to attend to. She needed to make a call to Finn and let him know what she was doing.

She made the call. "Hey Chief, just wanted to check in with you," she said when Finn answered.

She explained to him about the disgruntled, fired ranch hand and that she was on her way to the Pour House to see if she could find him.

"You know to watch your back in that area of town," Finn said.

"I know. I just want to know if this guy spent his morning yesterday trashing Anders's cabin or if we're dealing with something else altogether," she replied.

"Make sure you keep me in the loop," Finn said.

"Will do, Chief."

The call ended and still Anders's kiss played in her head. Why had he kissed her? What had caused his moment of temporary insanity, for that was surely what it had been?

They'd both made it clear to each other that they weren't looking for any kind of a relationship. He was a Colton and she was a Gage, further complicating things. And she still didn't know if she could fully trust him when it came to Demi, although she realized she desperately wanted to trust him.

It didn't take her long to arrive on the seedier side of town with its abandoned storefronts and tattoo shops and liquor stores. She pulled into the rear parking lot of the Pour House but remained in the car.

Bo. His name instantly leaped into her brain. It was here, in the back of this parking lot, that he'd been found, half on the asphalt and half on the grass. He'd come here to celebrate his bachelor party and instead been brutally murdered.

Her grief was still so tangled up with her wild sense of guilt. If she could just go back in time and instead of fighting with Bo, she would have hugged him. She would have told him how much she loved him.

It was an important lesson to remember. You never knew how much time you had with your loved ones, so it was vital to tell them how much they meant to you each time you left them. But it was too late for her and Bo.

She shoved aside her grief and got out of her car. It was noon so she knew the bar would be open although surely not too busy at this time of the day. All of her senses went on full alert.

This was an area where police weren't particularly wanted and she scanned every inch of her surroundings as she walked around to the front of the building. Merlin walked beside her, constantly working to keep her safe.

The bar's front door was open and all the neon beer signs were lit up and flashing. She stepped inside with Merlin at her heels.

"Officer Gage." Rusty greeted her by raising his mug of beer. He sat at the bar alone, his unruly reddish-brown hair gleaming in the artificial lights overhead. "To what do I owe a visit from one of Red Ridge's finest?"

There was only one other man in the establishment. He sat alone at a table and hadn't even bothered looking up when she'd entered. He didn't appear to be any kind of threat.

"I was wondering if you could help me out," she said, keeping her tone light and pleasant.

She'd try a little honey first to see if that would get her the answers she needed. If that didn't work, she'd come on a little harder.

"Help you out how?" Rusty asked.

"I'm looking for Seth Richardson. Can you tell me where he might be staying?"

"He's staying at the motel, but if you wait ten or fifteen minutes he should be here." Rusty paused to take a drink of his beer and then continued, "For the last few days Seth has been doing some handyman work for me around here."

"Was he here yesterday?" she asked.

Rusty nodded. "He was. I had him paint the ladies' room. It definitely needed it and ladies are way pickier about those kinds of things than men are. Got it painted a nice light blue for the women."

"What time did he get here yesterday morning?"

Rusty frowned. "It was about nine thirty or so in the morning. Why? What's he done now? He's already lost his job at the Double C Ranch."

Before Elle could reply the door opened and a short, stocky, dark-haired man walked in.

"Ah, there he is now, the man of the hour," Rusty said. "Seth, Officer Gage here has been asking about you."

Seth narrowed his dark eyes. "What's the problem?"

Rusty stood and got a second beer. "Here, sit," he said to Seth.

Seth approached the bar and slid onto a stool, his gaze never leaving Elle. "I ain't done nothing. Why are you asking about me?" Rusty set a beer in front of Seth.

"We had some issues out at the Double C Ranch yesterday and your name came up," Elle said.

"What kind of issues?" Seth's tension was evident in his tensed broad shoulders and in the white-fingered grip on his beer mug.

"The foreman's cabin was trashed yesterday morning."

Seth's eyes widened in what appeared to be genuine shock. "I had nothing to do with something like that. I was here yesterday. Go ahead, ask Rusty. I painted for him all morning."

He wasn't their guy. She'd known it before Seth had even walked into the bar. Rusty had no reason to alibi the man and they certainly hadn't had an opportunity to talk about an alibi before she walked in. Nobody had known she'd show up here today.

"What about last night?" Elle asked, remembering what Anders had told her that had brought the man to his mind in the first place.

"What about last night?" He averted his gaze from hers and instead looked down in his beer mug.

"There was some downed fencing on the property. You wouldn't know anything about that, would you?"

"Jeez, Seth, did you do something stupid last night?" Rusty asked the man.

Seth took a long drink of his beer. "I don't know anything about it," he said, but there was definitely a lack of conviction in his voice.

Elle figured it was probable that he was responsible for the fencing, but he hadn't broken into the cabin. She stepped closer to him, close enough that she could smell his sour body odor and see the pores and broken vessels across his broad nose.

"Let me give you a little bit of advice, Seth," she said. "Stay away from the Double C Ranch. You have no business anywhere near the place. You're on my radar now. If anything goes wrong there, you'll be the first person I come looking for. You got it?"

"Yeah, I got it," he replied.

Answers gotten and message delivered, Elle nodded to Rusty and then turned and headed for the door with Merlin by her side. She stepped out into the sunshine and practically ran into her brother.

"Carson, what are you doing here?" she asked in surprise.

"The chief mentioned that you were here and I was in the area and thought you might need a little backup," Carson said.

She stared at him for a long moment, irritation quickly taking hold of her. "You have to stop." She grabbed her brother's arm and pulled him farther away from the bar's door. "Carson, this Overly Protective Brother stuff has gotten way out of hand."

"I was just checking in on a fellow officer," he protested.

"That's a lie and you know it," she replied heatedly. "It's bad enough that I'm assigned to a babysitting job instead of working on the Groom Killer case. I can't have you constantly shadowing me and you've been doing it since the day I was sworn in, and you're getting worse instead of better about it."

He looked off into the distance for a long moment and then looked back at her. "I don't want anything to happen to you, Elle," he said. "We've already lost Bo." For a moment his eyes were dark and haunted.

Carson had been the first one to stumble on Bo's body minutes after he'd been murdered and Elle could only imagine how absolutely horrifying that had been for him.

She reached out and took his hand in hers. "Yes,

we lost Bo. But Carson, I knew the risks when I became a cop. Just like you, this is what I want to do and it's important to me that you believe in me and just let me do my job."

"I do believe in you," he replied.

"But every time you shadow me, each time you show up to 'help' me with my job, you undermine my confidence in myself. And you know that a cop with no confidence isn't a good cop." She squeezed his hand and then released it.

"Let me grow up, Carson, and let me be a good cop."

He gave her a nod. "Did you get what you needed here?"

"Yes and no." As they walked back to their patrol cars she told him about Seth Richardson and why she'd come here to check him out. "I am pretty sure he isn't the person who broke into Anders's cabin, which leaves us still with a mystery," she said.

"Keep your eyes open and watch your back," he replied.

"Don't worry, I've got this," she said.

Minutes later she was back in her car and headed home. No, not home, she corrected herself…rather back to Anders's cabin. Once again her thoughts filled with Anders. Not only had he stunned her with his kiss, but before that he'd surprised her with Bonnie.

He'd been so clear that he had no intention of loving the baby, but his actions spoke louder than his words. When she'd come out of the bedroom and seen him holding Bonnie and talking to her, she'd heard the love and affection in his voice. She had seen it shining from his eyes as he gazed at the baby girl.

He had vowed so adamantly that he wasn't going to love the baby and yet there he was, with a warm smile on his face and wrapped around little Bonnie's pinkie.

It had been an unexpected turn-on...the big sexy cowboy sweet-talking a tiny baby girl. Add in that very hot kiss Elle had received from him and she was feeling more than a little vulnerable.

She had to stay focused on her job and right now her head was also filled with a lot of questions. She firmly believed Seth and some of his drunken friends might have pulled down the fencing in the middle of the night.

She also believed Seth was not the man who had broken into the cabin. She was positive that had been a search and not a trashing by a disgruntled former employee.

So who had broken into Anders's cabin? And what had they been looking for? More importantly...was the person dangerous and would he be back?

Chapter 6

Two days had passed since Elle returned from the Pour House. Nobody had come forward to claim the baby and they still had no idea who the intruder had been or what he'd wanted.

Just because nothing had happened in the past forty-eight hours didn't mean they had let their guard down. Anders was just spending a couple of hours each morning away from the cabin and the rest of the time he was inside with Elle and Bonnie.

He didn't feel right leaving Elle alone to take care of Bonnie. She wasn't here to be a full-time babysitter and he didn't expect her to be, especially if little Bonnie turned out to be his.

The one thing that hadn't happened in the last two days was any mention of the kiss they had shared. It was almost as if it hadn't happened. But it had, and he'd thought about it far too often.

She was now stretched out on the floor in the living room having tummy time with Bonnie and he was in the kitchen cooking their evening meal.

Last night he'd fried up burgers for dinner. Tonight he was making chicken and rice. In the past two days they'd fallen into a comfortable routine.

He made breakfast for them each morning and then went out to ride the range and take care of chores. When he returned about noon she had lunch ready. He'd eat and then remain in the cabin. He'd pulled out an old chess game, delighted to learn that she knew how to play, and they had passed the afternoons in hot challenges. Then in the evenings, he cooked while she played with Bonnie.

It all felt so effortless and it almost scared him just how comfortable they had become together. It felt like playing house, only at night they went to separate rooms.

Her laughter now drifted into the kitchen, tightening his stomach muscles with its pretty melody.

He'd love it if for just one night they wound up together in his bed.

He opened the oven door to check on the chicken; the heat wafting out had nothing on the heat of his thoughts. Why was she under his skin so much? What was it about her that had him so off-balance?

Another half an hour or so and the chicken would be ready and then they could eat. After dinner they'd sit in the living room and talk until bedtime. So far he'd enjoyed their evening talks. He felt as if he was getting to know her better and better.

Even though he was in the kitchen, he heard Merlin's alert. Instantly every muscle in his body tensed and he ran into the living room to hear a knock on the door.

Elle was already at the door, her gun in hand. She looked at Anders and then opened the door. Anders relaxed as he saw his sister Serena, holding her nine-month-old baby, Lora, in her arms. His little niece had Serena's dark hair and eyes, although at the moment her eyes were closed as she slept.

"Whoa, this is some kind of welcoming committee," she said.

Elle lowered her gun and instead offered a smile. "Sorry about that, but we're a little bit on edge." She waited for Serena to come inside and then Elle closed and locked the door behind her.

"What are you doing here?" Anders asked as he gestured her to the chair. "You usually don't drop in this time of the day."

"Carson is still at work, so I thought it was about time I had a look at the mystery baby," she replied.

"We've named her Bonnie for the time being," Elle said. She set her gun down and then leaned over and picked up Bonnie in her arms and stepped closer to Serena.

Serena gazed at Bonnie and then looked at him and shook her head. "I know everyone is wondering if she's Demi and Bo's baby, but she doesn't look much like either of them. Of course I guess the strawberry-blond hair and blue eyes might change over time."

"Have a seat, Serena," Anders urged his sister. "Surely you can stay and visit for a few minutes."

"Just a couple of minutes and then I need to go." She sank down in the chair and smiled at Elle, who had placed Bonnie back in her cradle. "I'll bet Anders is glad to have you here."

"You've got that right," he replied. "I don't know how I'd handle all the baby stuff without her."

"I wasn't really thinking about that," Serena replied. "I was talking about the fact that she's a police officer and is here to watch your back. Father told me about the break-ins that have happened here."

"There is that, too," Anders agreed. He looked at

Elle, who had a warmth in her eyes and a smile curving her lips. He wondered if it was because Serena had seen her as a cop first and a baby helper second.

"And you don't have any idea what's going on?" Serena asked him.

"I don't have a clue," he replied.

"Have you heard if there's anything new in the Groom Killer case?" Elle asked. "I'm kind of out of the loop right now."

Serena shook her head. "Unfortunately, the answer is no. They're still trying to find out who keeps sending Hayley Patton flowers each week and they're still on the lookout for Demi. You know there are a lot of people who think she's someplace on this property, especially since the baby was left here." She shook her head again.

Anders remembered how Elle's brother, Detective Carson Gage, had been sure Serena was hiding Demi months ago, when Demi first fled town. They had become close, but as she'd said before, there was no way Demi could have risked leaving the baby with his sister, now that Serena was seriously involved with a cop.

"If she's on this property I haven't seen any sign of her and I wouldn't have a clue where, exactly, she could be," he replied.

"That goes double for me," Serena said. "I do hope Demi's okay out there on her own."

For the next few minutes they talked about town gossip and then Serena stood. "I need to head home. Elle, please take good care of my brother."

"Always," she replied.

He walked his sister to the door and dropped a soft kiss on little Lora's forehead. "Take good care of my niece," he said.

Serena's brown eyes twinkled. "You know we will," she replied. Then with goodbyes said, she left.

It was over dinner that Elle asked about baby Lora. "Is the father not in the picture at all? Carson has never told me and I haven't felt comfortable enough to ask."

"No, he isn't. My sister had an uncharacteristic one-night stand with a man she met at a horse auction. She didn't know his last name or really anything about him. The next morning when she woke up he was long gone, along with her cash and credit cards. He managed to rack up thousands of dollars of debt before she even knew he was gone."

"Oh my gosh, that really stinks," Elle said.

"It does. Anyway, fast-forward a couple of months and she realized she was pregnant. Despite my parents' having a fit about the whole thing, Serena chose to have the baby."

"She's obviously one strong lady. I'm so glad she and Carson found each other. She's good for him and he absolutely adores her and the baby."

"And as you know, she's more than a little crazy over him." He took a bite of the tender chicken.

"This is really good," she said.

"Thanks, it's got a little white wine in it."

"Do you cook like this a lot?"

"Yeah, actually I do," he replied. "I like to eat more than just the typical bachelor food of pizza and anything cooked in the microwave. I started experimenting with cooking when I moved out here by myself and discovered I really enjoy it."

"That makes one of us," she said with a laugh.

"I know you haven't fought me over dinner duty. Do you really not like to cook?" He loved the sound of her rich, musical laughter.

"It's something I've never had an interest in doing. Maybe it's because it's just me. It's always been easy to pick up fast food on the way home from work. I much prefer cleaning up the dishes after a good meal that somebody else has cooked than actually cooking one," she replied.

He grinned at her. "Then we make a good pair."

She held his gaze for a long moment and then looked back down at her plate. "For now," she replied.

For now? What did she mean by that? Did she

expect them not to be a good pair as time went on? Or was she referring to the fact that she was only here temporarily?

She looked so pretty with her hair loose and clad in a coral-colored T-shirt that complemented her honey-blond hair and beautiful brown eyes.

"What are your feelings about one-night stands?" Oh God, had that question really just left his lips? What was he thinking? He couldn't believe he'd just asked that.

Her gaze shot back to him in obvious surprise and her cheeks were dusted with a pretty pink hue. "I really haven't thought about it much." She carefully set down the fork that had been poised between her plate and her mouth.

"I've never had one, but I guess I wouldn't be completely against it as long as both people were on the same page," she said.

"And what page is that?" he asked. His breath was trapped in his chest and a wild anticipation gripped him as he waited for her response.

"I guess I'd want the understanding that it wouldn't mean anything, to be clear." She looked down at her plate again. "It would just be an expression of a physical attraction and nothing more than that."

Lordy, he could so be on that same page if it meant a night in bed with her. Did she find him physically attractive? Did she share even a modicum of the desire for him that he felt for her? He was sure that a single one-night stand with her would effectively get her out of his system.

Thankfully he didn't blurt out those questions. But he was aware that he'd made her uncomfortable and so he turned the conversation to a topic he knew she loved…Merlin.

Her eyes lit up as she told him how the breed was very sociable and loved people and especially children. She told him that Merlin loved to fetch a red ball she carried with her. And that there were times that, despite his large size, he acted like a lap dog.

When they were finished eating she cleaned up the kitchen while he rocked Bonnie and talked to her. The little girl seemed to change just a little bit each day. She was awake more and appeared more alert to her surroundings than she'd been only a few days ago.

As he heard Elle in the kitchen, he wondered if this would be what it was like if they were married and had a baby. He immediately mentally berated himself for the direction of his thoughts.

What was he thinking? Elle had made it clear she wasn't interested in any romantic relationship and he certainly wasn't ready to trust another woman in his life. He definitely wasn't looking for marriage.

So why did it feel so right to have her here? Why did he look forward to waking up in the morning and knowing her face would be the first one he'd see? Why did he spend his time out in the pasture wishing he was back in the cabin with her and Bonnie?

He needed to stop these crazy thoughts. More than anything he definitely needed to stop wanting Elle. He just had to figure out how to do it.

"I don't think I'll be in this afternoon for lunch," Anders said the next morning as they finished up breakfast.

"Okay." She looked at him with a bit of surprise. He'd been in a strange mood over the meal, unusually quiet and distant. "Problems on the ranch?" she asked as she walked with Bonnie in her arms to the back door.

"Something like that," he replied. He leaned over and gave Bonnie a kiss on the forehead and then straightened and grabbed his hat from the hook on the wall. "I'll be home in time to cook for dinner." He didn't wait for a response but rather turned on his boot heel and headed outside.

If she didn't know better she'd swear he was mad at her, but for the life of her she couldn't figure out why. She hadn't said or done anything out of line.

Not that she cared if he was mad at her. In fact, it

would probably make things a little easier on her if he showed a bit of a hateful bad side.

As things were he was way too attractive to her. He was so much more than a sexy piece of eye candy. He was also intelligent and funny. He had a softness inside him that he tried to hide, but it came out in his tenderness with Bonnie. And it was that particular characteristic of his that shot such warmth straight through her heart.

Things had definitely gotten a bit too cozy between them over the past couple of days. She felt a breathless anticipation around him and she wasn't sure what exactly she was anticipating.

She shoved thoughts of Anders out of her mind and instead focused on Bonnie, who was awake and waiting for a bottle. Once Elle had it ready she sank down on the sofa to feed her.

"This wasn't what I thought police work was going to involve," she said to Merlin, who was always a rapt audience for her. "I don't know how much longer I'll be assigned here. Finn can't keep me here strictly as a babysitter and if the danger is over, then there's really no reason for me to stay on."

She looked down at Bonnie and any desire she had to be anywhere else melted away. If this baby belonged to Bo and Demi, then she wondered what Bonnie's future held.

Bo was dead and Demi was on the run. If Demi was caught, she'd be arrested on any number of charges, leaving the baby to be raised by whom?

When she was finished eating, Bonnie fell asleep and Elle placed her back into the cradle. Elle sat on the floor and gestured for Merlin. He came into her arms and tried to sit on her lap, making her laugh.

"You're my big baby boy, aren't you?" She ran her hands over the soft fur of his back, scratching him the way he liked. With Bonnie in the house, she'd neglected giving Merlin the attention she knew he loved.

He raised his big head and closed his eyes as she continued to scratch his back, then he flopped over to bare his belly for more scratching.

This dog was who she could depend on, who would never let her down or tell her she wasn't good enough. He offered her unconditional love every single day. Merlin would protect her with his life and love her until one of them died.

It was a beautiful morning and she decided to take Merlin out for a game of fetch. She went into the bedroom and put her holster on. She then grabbed the little yellow knit hat for Bonnie. Then with her gun at her side she carried Bonnie outside.

She went first to her car trunk where she grabbed the red ball. Merlin spied it and began to dance with excitement around her feet.

He chased her back to the porch where she set Bonnie's cradle down. The morning air was a bit cool, but Bonnie was warmly nestled in her pink blanket with the hat covering her head and ears.

Besides, with the sun rising higher in the beautiful blue sky it wouldn't take long for the temperature to warm up. "Merlin." He sat at her feet and stared at the ball in her hand. "Fetch," she said and then threw the ball.

He took off like a rocket, running as fast as his short legs could carry him. He grabbed the ball and then brought it back to her and set it at her feet. Even though he was having some playtime, Elle knew that if anyone came near he would still alert and would choose her safety over his ball.

As she continued to play fetch with him, she couldn't help but admire the beautiful setting and the peace and quiet. She would love living in a place like this with the beauty of nature surrounding her. Not that she wanted to live here, she told herself, just a place like here.

She couldn't count the number of times her neighbors at her apartment building woke her with loud music or raised voices. Or somebody set off a car alarm in the parking lot.

She and Merlin played fetch for about a half an hour. Finally she called a halt to the fun. The three of them returned to the house, where she pulled the hat off the still-sleeping baby and took off her holster.

It was just after ten when Merlin alerted. Elle grabbed her gun from the coffee table, her heartbeat accelerating.

A knock fell on the door. She opened it quickly, her gun level in front of her.

"Oh…my," the young woman on the porch exclaimed.

Elle smiled at Valeria, Anders's younger sister, and the woman her brother Vincent had been dating and vowed to marry. "Sorry," Elle said, and lowered her gun.

"I guess Anders isn't here?"

"No, he's out doing his cowboy work. Why don't you come on in?"

"I just thought I'd come by and…" Her gaze fell on the sleeping Bonnie on the sofa. "Oh, she's so beautiful." She walked closer to the baby.

"She's also a really good baby," Elle said. "She only cries if she's hungry or needs a diaper change. We've been calling her Bonnie while she's been here."

"I heard that it's possible she might be Demi's baby," Valeria said.

"And Bo's," Elle replied.

"Of course," Valeria said quickly.

"Please…sit." Elle gestured to the recliner and she sat on the sofa next to Bonnie.

"I also heard there was some trouble out here. Do you think my brother is in any danger?" Valeria's dark eyes filled with concern.

Elle hesitated for a moment. "I don't know, but I don't think so. We aren't really sure what's going on, but that's why I'm here."

"And I'm so glad you're here for him," Valeria replied. "Anders and I have gotten so much closer over the last couple of months and I would hate to see anything bad happen to him."

"I promise I'm going to make sure he's safe," Elle assured her, and then hoped it was a promise she could keep.

"Is your dog friendly?"

"Ridiculously friendly," Elle replied. "Merlin, go make friends."

Merlin approached Valeria with his back end wagging to and fro with happiness. Valeria held her hand out to let him sniff it, then she stroked down his back. "He's beautiful. What's his superpower?"

"Protection. So you see, I'm not the only one protecting Anders from harm. Merlin is on the job as well."

"That's good to know." She straightened in the chair and Merlin padded back to Elle. Valeria's gaze returned to Bonnie and then slid to Elle. "If she's Bo and Demi's child, then Vincent and I would love to raise her."

"You two are just barely out of high school," Elle said.

"That doesn't matter. You know we're mature for our ages and we are going to be married soon. I already spoke to Vincent and he agrees that Bonnie would be a wonderful addition to our family. Then she'd be raised by a Colton and a Gage."

"Valeria, I don't really have any say in where Bonnie is going to end up. And remember, it's still possible the baby might be your brother's."

"If that's the case, then she's one lucky baby," Valeria replied. "I know Anders, and when he loves, he loves hard."

Those words played in Elle's head, but she quickly shoved them away as the conversation continued.

The two chatted for the next twenty minutes or so. Bonnie awoke and Elle let Valeria give her a bottle. "She really is so sweet," Valeria said when Bonnie had finished the last drop and had been burped. "I meant what I said about Vincent and me raising her."

"I know you meant it. We'll just have to see how things turn out. Anders took a paternity test and we should have the results any time now."

Valeria stood with obvious reluctance. "I'd love

to stay here all day with her, but I need to get going. I'm headed into town to run some errands."

Elle walked with her to the door and the two women hugged. "Anders will be sorry he missed you," Elle said.

"Tell him I'll see him soon."

"And tell my baby brother I said hello," Elle added.

Valeria's face lit with love at the mention of Vincent. "I will," she replied.

Minutes later Elle was once again alone in the cabin and thinking about the conversation she'd just had. Vincent and Valeria might be madly in love, but Elle didn't believe they were anywhere near ready to take in and care for a baby.

They were only nineteen years old. Not only did Elle believe her brother was too young to become a husband, but she definitely believed he wasn't ready to become an instant father to an infant.

There was no question the two were crazy in love with each other, but Elle hoped they didn't plan a wedding until the Groom Killer was caught. The last thing she wanted to do was lose another brother to the murderer.

I know Anders, and when he loves, he loves hard.

Valeria's words echoed inside Elle's head. Somehow she believed that about him. She wondered if he'd loved hard the woman and the child in the picture she'd found.

She thought the answer was yes. That woman had hurt him badly and now he had one-night stands that assured his heart wouldn't ever get involved again. It all made sense.

She remembered the shocking question he'd asked her about one-night stands. Why did he want to know what her opinion was of them?

Did he want to have a one-night stand with her? Her heart stuttered at the thought. Just his kiss had rocked her world; what would it be like to actually make love with him?

She jumped up off the sofa, refusing to entertain such ridiculous thoughts any further. She'd barely made it into the kitchen when Merlin gave his low grunt alert again. She grabbed her gun and opened the door to see her sister, Danica, standing on the porch.

Before Danica could reply, Merlin jumped at her, as if aiming for her arms. Danica laughed and fell to her knees to love on the dog.

Danica had been Merlin's trainer at the Red Ridge K9 Training Center. Her red-blond hair gleamed in the morning sunshine and her green eyes sparkled as she looked up at Elle.

"Hi, sis," she said, still remaining on her knees.

"Hi, yourself," Elle replied. "Are you going to get up and come inside like a normal person?"

Danica laughed again and rose to her feet. "Actually, I'm not going to come in. I was on my way to work and just decided to stop by to see how this guy is getting along." She scratched Merlin behind one ear.

"He's doing great, as you can see," Elle replied.

"This is the first time he's staying with you someplace other than your apartment. Any signs of trauma?"

"None at all. He's an amazing dog."

"How are you holding up? I've heard about the trouble out here."

"I'm doing fine. What about you?"

"Staying busy. I'm working with a new dog out at the training center."

"What kind?" Elle asked curiously.

"Another bulldog." She pulled her phone out of her pocket and checked the time. "And I really need to get going so I'm not late to work."

The two sisters hugged and then Danica left.

For the rest of the afternoon Elle kept herself busy. It had been nice to see both Valeria and Danica, even if just briefly.

It was just after four when Merlin alerted and she heard the back door in the kitchen open and close.

She stepped into the kitchen in time to see Anders hang his black cowboy hat on a hook by the door.

He turned and for just a moment his features registered an open pleasure at the sight of her, but then all expression of any emotion left his face.

"How was your day?" she asked. She walked over to the counter where a flick of a button set the coffee to brew. She knew he liked a cup of coffee about this time in the afternoons.

"It was fine. What about yours?" he asked.

"Fairly quiet except both Valeria and Danica stopped by for brief visits."

He walked over to the sink and began to wash his hands. "I'm sorry I missed them. Anything new with Valeria?"

"Not really, but she told me she and Vincent would step in to raise Bonnie." Elle sat at the table.

"That's the most ridiculous thing I've heard today," he replied. He grabbed the hand towel and dried off. "They're just a couple of kids."

"I know that and you know that, but I'm not sure how you get through to a pair of starry-eyed, madly-in-love teenagers."

"I've been trying to talk some sense into Valeria for months." He walked to the cabinet and pulled out two coffee mugs. "I don't have anything against

Vincent, but those two shouldn't be planning a wedding right now."

"Nobody in this entire town should be planning a wedding right now," Elle said. "Until we catch the Groom Killer all weddings in this town should be illegal."

He poured the coffee and then brought the mugs to the table. She murmured a thanks, still trying to get a read on his mood.

"Any new news on the case?" he asked.

"Not that I've heard."

There was a tension in the air between them and it emanated from him. His shoulders were bunched and a knot pulsed in his strong jawline.

"Has something happened on the ranch?" she asked.

"No, why?"

"You appeared a bit distracted this morning and you look a little tense now," she replied.

He rolled his magnificent shoulders and drew in a deep breath. "I've just been working through a few things in my head."

"Have I done something to upset you?" she asked.

"No, it has nothing to do with you." His gaze didn't quite meet hers. "Don't worry about it."

But it was difficult not to worry about it as the evening unfolded. They warmed up leftovers from the night before and ate in relative silence.

If she were a really good cop she'd be able to figure out what was bothering him, she thought as she cleared the dishes after dinner.

Whatever it was, it didn't seem to affect the way he interacted with Bonnie. His deep voice now drifted into the kitchen, not quite loud enough that she could hear the actual words he was saying. However, the tone was light and at one point his deep laughter rang out.

He sat in the recliner with Bonnie in his arms. He looked up as Elle entered the room and laughter still lit his eyes. "She just blew a big spit bubble and then smiled," he said.

"Oh, I hate it that I missed her first spit bubble," Elle replied with a laugh. She sank down on the sofa and sobered. "I really hate it that no matter how this turns out I'm going to miss a lot of firsts with her. She's definitely wormed her way into my heart."

"If she's mine, her home will be here and I'll fight for the right to raise her here with me," he replied with a touch of determination.

"If she's yours then I have to confess I'm surprised her mother hasn't shown up yet," Elle replied.

He frowned. "That makes two of us. I can't imagine why any woman I've seen in the past would just leave her baby on the porch. If she was in trouble,

I'd help her. I've been expecting somebody to call about Bonnie or return for her each day."

She wanted to ask him about the photo she'd seen, about the beautiful dark-haired woman and the cute baby. But it was really none of her business. She reminded herself she didn't have the right to ask him those kinds of personal questions.

"At least she's sleeping a little bit longer through the nights," she finally said, aware that the tension was back in the room.

It remained, making conversation slightly awkward throughout the rest of the night. She was almost grateful when she gave Bonnie her final bottle of the evening and then tucked her into the cradle for bedtime.

She was about to pick up the cradle and carry it into her bedroom when Anders stopped her. "I'll get that," he said, and hurried to the sofa.

But instead of picking up the cradle he turned back to face her. "Do you really want to know what's been bothering me?" he asked. His eyes glowed bright as he held her gaze.

"Of course," she replied.

He stepped closer to her, so close he invaded her personal space, so close his body heat warmed her. "You," he said, his voice deeper than usual. "You've been bothering me with your sexy smell and wonderful smiles. I'm losing sleep thinking about you and when I dream, I dream about having you in my bed and making love to you."

Her mouth had gone dry and an inside tremor took possession of her body at his words. "So, wha-what are we going to do about it?" she finally managed to say.

"Let's start with this." He pulled her into his arms, intimately tight against his body, and then his mouth crashed down on hers.

Chapter 7

What are your feelings about one-night stands?

Anders's question played through her head at the same time his lips on hers electrified her.

In the back of her mind she knew she should stop things right now, before they got out of control. But it was so difficult to hang on to that thought with his mouth plying hers with such heat, with his wonderfully muscled body so close against her.

As his tongue sought entry, she opened her mouth to allow him to deepen the kiss. She'd told him she thought a one-night stand would be okay as long as both people were on the same page.

Why stop this feeling? This intense desire she had to be with him? She was pretty certain they were both on the exact same page. Neither of them was looking for a relationship. Still, there was no question that there was a crazy physical attraction going on between them.

As his hands caressed up and down her back, she gave herself permission to stop thinking and just be in the moment, and in the moment she desperately wanted Anders.

She fell into a sensual haze as the kiss continued. Everything else faded away and there was just Anders, driving her crazy with his mouth, with his touch.

His lips slid from hers and trekked down her jaw and to her neck. He nuzzled just behind her ear, and her knees threatened to weaken with the sweet sensations that swept through her.

He finally released her and took a step backward. He then held out his hand to her, his eyes blazing with his desire.

She could stop this right now. If she didn't take his hand, then it would all be over right here and right now with nothing else happening between them. That would the best thing...the smart thing to do.

She leaned over and looked at the still-sleeping Bonnie and then she reached out and placed her hand in his. For the first time in her life she didn't want to do the smart thing. She desperately wanted Anders.

He led her into his bedroom and kissed her once again as they stood at the foot of his bed. The man definitely knew how to kiss. His lips demanded a response from her and she couldn't deny him. Their tongues swirled together in a dance of hot desire.

His hands caressed down her back and he gently grabbed her buttocks and pulled her more intimately against him. He was aroused and the fact that she could get that kind of response from him heightened her pleasure. When he released her again she was half-breathless.

"I want you so much, Elle," he said. "It's all I've been able to think about since the night you came here."

His naked hunger for her stirred her like nothing else ever had in her life. On unsteady legs she walked to the head of the bed, where she set her gun on the nightstand. She then pulled her T-shirt over her head not only to let him know, but to confirm to herself that she was ready to make love with him, that this was really going to happen.

He immediately pulled his T-shirt off, exposing his magnificently muscled and bronzed chest. And then they were on the bed, kissing with an intensity that spun her senses.

His hands went around her back, where he unfastened her bra. It fell away from her and then his mouth left hers and instead he licked one of her erect nipples.

She gripped his shoulders as he continued to love first one nipple and then the other. The sensations shot a flame straight through the center of her, leaving her gasping with pleasure.

But the pleasure didn't stop there. He pulled her sweatpants off and then took off his jeans, leaving her in a pair of silk panties and him in a pair of black boxers.

The faint light drifting in from the living room seemed to love each muscle and every angle on his body. He was truly a beautiful man.

When he pulled her back into his arms, she savored the skin-on-skin contact. His was so warm and smelled of his woodsy cologne. As they kissed once again their legs tangled together, hers sleek and slender and his long and strong.

He rolled her over on her back and as his hand caressed down her belly she tensed. His fingers slowly slid across the silk of her panties. Instantly the cool of the silk warmed with his intimate touch.

"You are so beautiful, Elle," he whispered into her ear.

She was about to reply, but then his fingers found the very center of her and she moaned. Oh yes, she wanted him there. She suddenly needed the kind of release she believed only he could give to her.

She arched her hips and he whisked away her panties. And when he touched her again it took only seconds before the waves of pleasure washed over her, leaving her gasping and half crying with her climax.

He rolled away from her and reached into the top drawer of the nightstand. When he turned back to her he was fully erect and wearing a condom.

Despite the thin latex covering, she stroked him, loving his sharp intake of breath at her touch. He gasped with obvious pleasure as she continued to caress him.

She kissed his neck and then down his taut stomach, loving the taste of him.

"Elle." Her name fell from his lips on a half-strangled groan.

She looked up at him. All his features were taut and his eyes glowed like a wild animal in the dark.

He shoved her hand away from him and instead moved between her thighs. He hovered there for a long moment, his gaze locked with hers.

Her entire body quivered with anticipation as he slowly eased into her. She closed her eyes, filled with him in every way. His scent invaded her head, and the sound of him whispering her name over and over again was like sweet music.

He moved his hips against hers, slowly at first and then faster and more frantic. She dug her fingers into his shoulders as the pleasure became so intense she could scarcely catch her breath.

Then the waves of a second climax crashed through her and at the same time he stiffened against her and moaned deep in his throat.

They remained locked together for several long moments. She could feel his heartbeat against hers, racing and then slowing to a more normal rhythm.

He finally rolled off her and to his back. When his breathing had evened out, he propped himself up on his elbow facing her.

He stroked a strand of her hair away from her face and then took her lips in a gentle, tender kiss that moved her far more than what they'd just experienced together.

When the kiss ended she sat up and reached down for her T-shirt on the floor. Now that it was over the need to escape him was strong.

"Don't go," he protested softly as she pulled the T-shirt over her head. "Elle, stay here with me. Sleep with me."

"No, I need to take Bonnie and go back to my room," she replied without looking at him. She was afraid that if she saw a soft appeal on his face she might relent and stay. She moved her feet to the floor and grabbed her sweatpants.

"Bonnie can sleep in here with us." He sat up and reached over to the bedside lamp. He turned it on, creating a small, intimate glow in the room.

"But I can't." She pulled her sweatpants on and stood. "I'll just see you in the morning." She picked up the rest of her clothing and her gun.

Oh, she wanted to stay. She desperately wanted to snuggle down in his sheets and cuddle against him as they fell asleep. She would love waking up in his arms in the morning. She would love to stay with him and that frightened her, and that's why she wouldn't...that's why she couldn't.

Merlin lay on the threshold of the room. It was as if he was keeping one eye on her and his other eye on the baby in the living room.

He got up as she approached and together they padded into the living room, where she picked up the cradle and then went into her bedroom.

She kept her mind blissfully blank as she took a quick shower. She needed to wash off the pleasant smell of him and the memory of his touch.

It was only when she was in bed that she allowed herself to think about the lovemaking they'd just shared. It had been more than wonderful and so intense that he'd taken her breath away over and over again.

But she couldn't let it mean anything. It was a one-night stand and nothing more. And she seriously doubted that it meant anything to him. He was accustomed to this kind of thing. He was used to making love with a woman and then walking away from her without any emotional ties.

Had he found her wanting? A bit boring like Frank Benson had apparently found her? This thought sent a wave of depression over her. Why could she never be enough?

Tomorrow she'd contact Finn and see how much longer she would be on this duty. Things had been quiet and there was no guarantee any real danger was imminent. She couldn't stay here forever playing house with Anders and Bonnie.

She was surprised that this thought sent another wave of depression through her. She moved to the edge of the bed and dangled her arm over the side. Her hand was met with Merlin's warm fur and he snorted his pleasure as she worked her fingers across his back.

At least she was always enough for Merlin. He loved her unconditionally, and right now in her life that was all she needed or wanted.

She must have fallen asleep, for she awakened to

Merlin's alert. She was instantly filled with adrenaline as she grabbed her gun and jumped out of bed.

Merlin led the way out of her doorway and into the darkened living room. He sat at the front door and alerted once again. Somebody was outside. It was the middle of the night. There was no reason for anyone to be lurking outside in the darkness of the night.

She gripped her gun firmly in her hand as her heart beat a wild rhythm of uncertainty. With the other hand she unlocked the door and then gripped the doorknob.

Drawing a deep breath, she flung open the door, thankful that her eyes were already adjusted to the darkness. She quickly scanned the area and tensed as she spied a figure standing beneath a nearby tree.

"Who's there?" she called out.

The figure remained nearly hidden in the dark shadows.

"This is Officer Gage of the Red Ridge K9 unit. Step forward and identify yourself." She waited a minute but the figure still didn't move. "You'd better step forward and identify yourself right now or I'll set my dog on you."

Merlin was next to her, his sturdy body poised for action. "What's going on?" Anders voice spoke softly from just behind her.

"I'm giving you to the count of three," she yelled

out, ignoring Anders's question. It was the question of a man roused from sleep and the answer was self-evident.

"One…" she said.

"No, don't. I don't want your dog to come after me," the man said. He took a step forward but was still shrouded in darkness too great for a visual iden-tification. His words were followed by an incoherent noise that sounded like crying.

What in the heck, she thought. The noise got louder as he took another couple of steps forward.

"Seth Richardson, is that you?" she asked. What on earth was the man doing out here in the middle of the night?

"Don't let your dog bite me. I just wanted to talk to Anders," he said. His voice was slurred and it was obvious he was drunk and blubbering. "I want my job back. I need to get my job back, Anders. Please," the man cried. Elle lowered her gun with a sigh of disgust.

"Go home, Seth," Anders called out. "It's the mid-dle of the night and you're drunk."

"I had a few drinks, I won't lie. I…I needed some liquid courage to come out here and beg you for my job." The words were half-garbled and said between deep, wrenching sobs. "Please man, I'm begging you. I need my job back."

"Go home, Seth," Anders repeated with a firm tone. "You don't belong on this property anymore."

"What about my job?" Seth asked, and then blubbered some more.

The sigh Anders released warmed Elle's back. "Okay, meet me at the barn tomorrow about ten and we'll talk. Come sober or there will be no discussion."

"Thank you, man," Seth replied. "Thank you so much. I'll be there. I swear I'll be there."

"Don't thank me yet," Anders warned. "Now get out of here. You've disturbed our sleep."

"I'm sorry," he replied. "I'll leave you be and talk to you tomorrow."

Elle remained on the front porch until Seth disappeared from sight. It was only when she sensed Merlin relaxing that she did the same.

"Nothing like being disturbed in the middle of the night by a man who is drunk as a skunk," Anders said as she closed and locked the front door.

"What time is it?" she asked.

"Just after two."

"Bonnie should be waking up any time for a bottle. I think I'll go ahead and get one ready for her."

Anders followed her into the kitchen and sat down at the table. She felt his steady gaze on her as she fixed the bottle. "You knew he was out there because Merlin alerted?" he asked.

She nodded and put the bottle in the microwave to warm it.

"Good boy, Merlin," he said. Merlin walked over to him and eyed him expectantly. Anders laughed and scratched the dog first behind one ear and then behind the other.

This middle-of-the-night scene was far too intimate, far too familiar for her. Him in his boxers and petting her dog while she was in her nightie and making a baby bottle, the whole thing made her want to run and hide.

Because she liked it. She liked it way too much. It was a glimpse into a fantasy that until now she hadn't realized she'd entertained. It was definitely a fantasy that had no basis in reality.

She grabbed the bottle from the microwave. "Come on, Merlin. The excitement is over for the night." She looked at Anders. "And I'll just say good night once again."

She didn't wait for a reply as she quickly exited. Her timing was perfect, for at that moment Bonnie began to cry.

Anders sat in his office in the barn waiting for Seth to arrive, but his head was filled with thoughts of Elle. She was like no other woman he'd ever known before.

She hadn't wanted to cuddle after making love and that morning she hadn't said anything about what they shared the night before.

Most of the women he'd been with in the past had clung to him both after sex and again the next morning. They'd wanted him to tell them how awesome he thought they were, how great the sex had been between them.

Elle had wanted none of that and it confused him. She had been an amazing partner and her silence about the whole thing made him wonder if she hadn't found him so amazing.

During breakfast she'd acted like nothing had changed between them. It was as if she'd already forgotten about their lovemaking.

But things had changed. He now knew where to touch her to make her moan with pleasure. He now knew that nuzzling her just behind her ear drove her half-crazy. Yes, no matter how much she wanted to pretend nothing was different between them, she was wrong.

What surprised him more than anything was the tenderness he felt toward her, a strange tenderness that had no place in a one-night stand and had lingered through a quiet and slightly uncomfortable breakfast.

What was happening to him? He'd thought that

all he'd felt for Elle was a good dose of lust and once he had her, it would be over. But it wasn't over. He still wanted her.

He, the confirmed bachelor who always had his relationships his way, was suddenly off-balance because of a woman who delighted him, enchanted him and intrigued him more than any woman ever had.

What was even worse was that he didn't just want her again in bed. He wanted her all day long, in and out of the sheets. She had not only gotten into his bed…she was slowly worming her way into the very center of his heart. And somehow he had to stop it.

He closed his eyes for a moment and thought about how she'd looked the night before standing on the front porch clad only in a midnight-blue silky nightgown and holding a gun. She'd looked so sexy and strong and he found it ridiculously charming that the sober-eyed police officer slept in silk. He opened his eyes with a sigh.

Any further thoughts he might have entertained were interrupted by Seth appearing in his office doorway. The man held his battered cowboy hat in his hands and looked down at the floor in what appeared to be genuine contrition.

"Seth, come in and take a seat." Anders gestured him to the folding chair in front of his desk.

"First off, I gotta say that I'm sorry about all the

bother last night," Seth said, still not meeting Anders's gaze. "I should have never shown up at your place in the middle of the night. I know you've given me a lot of chances and I've screwed up each time, but I'm begging you to please give me one more chance."

He finally looked up and in his eyes was a quiet desperation. When Seth was sober he was one of the best workers Anders had. Unfortunately, he wasn't sober as often as he was drunk.

"I've been working here for a long time. I don't want to work at another place," he said. "I liked working for you. You're a fair boss."

"You have a problem, Seth, and I can't have somebody working for me who is drinking on the job. That not only makes you a danger to yourself, but also a danger to all my other men."

"I know, but I swear I'm going to get help. When I woke up this morning the first thing I did was call Lester Banks. You know he runs those meetings in the basement of the Baptist church. I'm going to start attending them and he's agreed to sponsor me."

Anders reared back in his chair and studied Seth. He'd always believed in giving people a do-over, but Seth had had more than his share already. But the difference this time was the man had actually reached out for help on his own.

"You're a good, hard worker when you're sober and present," Anders said.

"Then give me another chance, boss. I swear I won't mess up again." Once again the desperation was in Seth's eyes.

"And you're really going to go to the meetings and clean yourself up? It can't just be about the job. You've really got to want it, Seth."

"I do want it. To tell you the truth I'm tired of drinking. I'm sick and tired of waking up with little or no memory of what happened the night before. I'm sick and tired of being sick and tired all the time. I'm fifty-two years old and I have nothing to show for my time on earth except a bunch of empty beer bottles."

There was a real passion behind his words. "I got stupid drunk last night and that's the truth," he continued, "but losing my job here was rock bottom for me. I want to get sober once and for all."

"I believe you can do it, Seth." Anders released a deep sigh. "Okay, I'll give you one more chance. You can move back into your room in the bunk barn, but if I catch you drinking on the job or if one of the men tells me you are, then you're out of here for good."

Seth jumped out of his chair as if eager to leave before Anders could change his mind. "I can't thank you enough," he said.

"You don't have to thank me. Just get sober."

Minutes later Anders remained at his desk, thinking about the decision he'd just made. He truly hoped Seth would succeed, that he'd fight whatever inner demons he might possess. But Anders couldn't do it for him. Seth had to believe in himself and recognize that he deserved better in his life.

His thoughts once again filled with Elle. She couldn't stay at his place forever. Nothing had happened for almost a week and he was sure Finn could better use her on the Groom Killer case instead of basically babysitting for him.

Of course he supposed it was possible Finn wanted to keep her at the cabin on the off chance that Demi would show up. If the baby was hers, then it was reasonable that she might return for the little girl.

He had no idea who had broken into his cabin and searched it. He also had no idea what they'd wanted and if they'd gotten what they'd been looking for. But everything had been quiet since the break-in and there was really no reason to believe the person would be back or that he or Bonnie might be in any danger.

When Elle left he wasn't sure what would happen with Bonnie. Anders couldn't run a ranch and take care of her at the same time. But with the possibility of her being his, he wasn't just going to hand her over to social services. He'd hire a nanny or do whatever necessary to keep her with him.

When Elle left…the words thundered in his brain. He was surprised to realize just how much he'd hate to see her go. She'd brightened the cabin with her smiles. Hell, she brightened him with her smiles.

She not only was beautiful, but she challenged him with her intelligence. She and Bonnie smoothed out the rough edges inside him and brought laughter to his lips. Hell, he even liked Elle's dog.

Happy. He was also surprised to realize he was happy with them in his space. He hadn't thought about happiness in a long time, not since Rosalie and Brooke had ripped his heart out. This all felt like history was repeating itself.

He got up from his desk. He refused to allow that to happen. He refused to put his heart on a platter for another woman to slice into pieces.

What he needed right now was to climb on the back of his horse and take a long ride. He wanted the wind to blow out any longing he had for the woman and any affection he had for the baby; they were really nothing more than temporary houseguests.

He rode for almost two hours, stopping occasionally to talk to his men when he came upon them. The downed fencing was once again up and in place and the herd of cattle all looked healthy.

He then returned to his barn office once again where he sat at the desk and did the payroll and ordered supplies. It was after three when he finally headed back to the cabin.

Before he even opened the back door he heard Elle's laughter. It instantly warmed his heart.

"What's going on in here?" he asked as he stepped inside. Bonnie was in her cradle in the middle of the table. Elle looked at him with her laughter still warming her beautiful brown eyes.

"Watch…" she said. She leaned over the table so she had Bonnie's full attention. "Hi, Bonnie baby," she said in a slightly higher-pitched voice. "Hi, sweet baby."

Bonnie's lips curled up into a smile and she waved her arms up and down as if in great excitement. Elle paused and Bonnie's smile faded.

"Hi, Bonnie," Elle said again in the same slightly exaggerated voice. And once again Bonnie grinned and her arms pumped. Anders found himself smiling.

"Let me try," he said. As Elle stepped back from the table Bonnie's smile once again disappeared. Anders leaned over and made eye contact with the little girl.

"Hi, Bonnie," he said. No smile curved her rosebud lips. Instead she continued to eye him soberly, a tiny frown in the center of her forehead. "Hi, baby girl." Still no smile.

"You're doing man talk," Elle said. "You have to do baby talk."

"Baby talk?"

"Act excited and raise the tone of your voice," Elle instructed.

"Hi, Bonnie," he tried again, doing what Elle had said. "I feel totally silly talking to you this way." Bonnie smiled and waved her arms and he and Elle laughed together in delight.

He looked at Elle and white-hot desire shot through his heart, through his very soul. It wasn't just the desire to kiss her or make love to her again. It was far more complicated than that and it was at that moment he knew that despite his wish to hang on to his heart, it was already too late. He was in love with Officer Elle Gage.

Chapter 8

Thunder rolled and rain pelted the windows. Elle studied the chessboard in concentration. It had been raining all day, keeping Anders inside. After breakfast he'd pulled out the chessboard and at the moment they were in a hot competition. He'd won the first game and she'd won the second. This was the playoff to determine the house chess champion.

"Who taught you how to play?" he asked her.

"Bo taught me some and then in high school I joined the chess club," she replied.

"I'll bet you were cute in high school," he said. "I

can just see you strutting the halls with your backpack in a short skirt and your chess club sweater."

She gave him a baleful look. "I didn't have a chess club sweater and stop trying to distract me. It's not going to work. I intend to beat your butt."

He laughed and then leaned back in his chair. "Do you intend to make your next move anytime soon?"

"Great moves take time," she replied. The truth of the matter was even if he didn't talk to her she found him ridiculously distracting.

His scent wafted in the air and she wasn't oblivious to the way his gaze lingered on her a little too long. Thunder once again boomed overhead and she finally made her move.

"Ha, not such a great move," he said as his bishop took her queen.

"A truly great move," she replied. She moved her castle. "I believe that's checkmate."

He stared at the board in obvious astonishment. "Well, I'll be damned," he exclaimed.

"I believe that makes me the chess champion of the cabin," she said. "And I also believe that puts you on diaper duty for the rest of the day." She leaned back in her chair and grinned at him.

He chuckled once again and stood. "But you're still on lunch duty and I'm starving."

She got up from the table and began to pull cold

cuts out of the refrigerator while he put the chess-board and pieces away.

Minutes later they sat at the table with ham-and-cheese sandwiches and chips. "If it stops raining later this afternoon, what do you think about the three of us going into town for dinner?" he asked.

The idea of getting dressed up and going out for a nice meal was appealing. Too appealing. It would feel like a date. It would feel like a family having a night out. And she wasn't dating Anders, nor was she part of his family. She was here working on a case.

"I really don't think that's a good idea," she replied. "I don't want to leave the cabin. We don't know if whoever was in here before might not come back."

He looked disappointed. "I guess you're right. I just thought it would be nice to get out of these four walls for a little while. Oh well, I'll just have to make a really special dinner here tonight."

"Anything is fine for dinner," she replied. "You don't have to go to any trouble on my account." She looked out the window and sighed. "I really hate rainy days."

"Why?"

"I just do." She wasn't about to confess to him that it had been raining on the day Frank had told her he didn't love her. She remembered running out of his

Dear Reader,

IT'S A FACT: if you answer 4 quick questions, we'll send you 4 FREE REWARDS!

I'm not kidding you. As a leading publisher of women's fiction, we value your opinions... and your time. That's why we are prepared to **reward** you handsomely for completing our mini-survey. In fact, we have 4 Free Rewards for you, including 2 free books and 2 free gifts.

As you may have guessed, that's why our mini-survey is called **"4 for 4".** Answer 4 questions and get 4 Free Rewards. It's that simple!

Thank you for participating in our survey,

Pam Powers

To get your 4 FREE REWARDS:
Complete the survey below and return the insert today to receive 2 FREE BOOKS and 2 FREE GIFTS guaranteed!

"4 for 4" MINI-SURVEY

1 Is reading one of your favorite hobbies?
☐ YES   ☐ NO

2 Do you prefer to read instead of watch TV?
☐ YES   ☐ NO

3 Do you read newspapers and magazines?
☐ YES   ☐ NO

4 Do you enjoy trying new book series with FREE BOOKS?
☐ YES   ☐ NO

YES! I have completed the above Mini-Survey. Please send me my 4 FREE REWARDS (worth over $20 retail). I understand that I am under no obligation to buy anything, as explained on the back of this card.

240/340 HDL GMYJ

FIRST NAME

LAST NAME

ADDRESS

APT.#

CITY

STATE/PROV.

ZIP/POSTAL CODE

READER SERVICE—Here's how it works:

▲ If offer card is missing write to: Reader Service, P.O. Box 1341, Buffalo, NY 14240-8531 or visit www.ReaderService.com ▲

BUSINESS REPLY MAIL

FIRST-CLASS MAIL   PERMIT NO. 717   BUFFALO, NY

POSTAGE WILL BE PAID BY ADDRESSEE

READER SERVICE
PO BOX 1341
BUFFALO NY 14240-8571

NO POSTAGE
NECESSARY
IF MAILED
IN THE
UNITED STATES

house, so broken, and it was as if the skies wept with her. Since then rain always reminded her of sadness.

"The rain is a good thing when you're working on a ranch. It makes everything grow and get green. It's life. We could always go out dancing in the rain," he said with a twinkle in his eyes.

She laughed. "No way, not with all that lightning out there. It isn't safe for man or beast."

"Do you play poker?" he asked.

"I know the game." She got up from the table to carry her empty dish to the sink. "Why?"

"I thought maybe we could play some cards to pass a rainy afternoon."

"Ha, you're just looking for something you can beat me at," she teased.

Merlin jumped to his feet and alerted. Elle grabbed her gun off the counter and turned toward the back door where a man in a rain slicker and a cowboy hat pulled low on his forehead stood just outside.

"I got it," Anders said. He opened the door and motioned the man inside. "Sam, what's going on?"

"That big old tree in the east pasture got hit by lightning. We lost about ten head of cattle to the strike. The rain has let up so the tree is going to continue to burn and the lightning strikes are still pretty intense. We thought you'd want us to move the cattle into the north pasture where there are fewer trees."

"Go ahead and get started and I'll be out there to help as soon as possible." Anders closed the door and headed for the coat closet, where he pulled out a long rain slicker and put it on.

"I hate the idea of you being out in this," Elle said as he strode back to the door and pulled his hat from the hook. She looked at him worriedly.

"This is what I do, Elle." He shoved his hat low on his brow and then he was gone.

The thunder continued to shake the cabin and the lightning slashed the darkened skies. At one particularly loud boom Bonnie awakened, crying.

Elle quickly picked her up in her arms and murmured soothing words. For the next hour Elle was on pins and needles as she drifted from window to window, hoping to see Anders's return.

She hated to think of him on horseback, a target for an errant lightning strike. *This is what I do, Elle.* His words played and replayed in her mind.

A rancher's life wasn't all riding the range under sunny skies. He had to face all of nature's elements and unpredictable animals, and a ton of other difficult situations. But he loved what he did. Just as she loved what she did, a job that could be dangerous at times.

She sat down with Bonnie in her arms and Merlin at her feet and turned on the television to catch a weather update. Thankfully there was no tornado warning splashed across the screen. She then put Bonnie on the blanket in the middle of the living room floor.

She didn't relax until Anders walked back in the house two hours later. The brunt of the storm had moved away, leaving behind a gentle rain that was forecast to fall for another hour or so.

His features were drawn and he looked completely exhausted. She helped him off with his rain slicker and then ordered him to the bathroom for a hot shower.

Minutes later he walked back into the kitchen, smelling like minty soap and with his hair still damp. "Did you get the cattle all moved?" she asked.

"We did, and the men are taking care of the dead." He released a weary sigh.

"Go sit in your recliner and I'll bring you a cup of coffee," she said. "And I've got dinner duty tonight."

He cast her a weary smile. "Should I be afraid?"

"Maybe a little. Now go and relax," she replied. As he left for the living room she hurried to the refrigerator to see what kind of meat he'd pulled out of the freezer that morning for dinner. Chicken breasts. Surely she could handle that.

She moved over to make the coffee and when it was finished she poured him a cup and then carried it into the living room. She took two steps into the room and then stopped, her heart expanding in her chest.

Anders was reared back in the recliner and sound asleep. Bonnie slept on his chest, her little body rising and falling with each breath he took. She wished she had her cell phone in hand so that she could take a picture of them, but she knew no simple phone photo could capture the utter beauty of man and child.

She silently backed out of the room. She sat at the kitchen table and drank the coffee she'd poured for him. She couldn't get the vision out of her head.

If Bonnie was his, then Elle had no concerns about the kind of parent Anders would be. Bonnie would never have a minute of feeling unloved.

Would some woman he'd had a relationship with in the past suddenly show up on the doorstep? Would she thank him for watching Bonnie for a few days and then take the baby and leave?

She had a feeling Anders had no idea how all in he was in loving Bonnie, and she feared his heartbreak if she was taken away from him.

* * *

Anders didn't know how long he slept, but he awakened to the scent of chicken in the air and Bonnie beginning to fuss in his lap.

He righted his position in the chair and as her fussing got louder Elle appeared with a bottle in hand. "Oh, I was hoping to get her before she woke you."

"It's fine. How long have I been asleep?"

"About an hour." She sat on the sofa and fed Bonnie the bottle.

"Is that dinner I smell?"

"It is," she said with a proud look on her face. "It's a spicy chicken breast with spicy rice on the side."

"Hmm, sounds good. Is there anything I need to do to help?"

"No, I've got this." She gazed at him with her sober expression. "Sorry about your cows."

"Yeah, me, too. But it is what it is. We always lose some cattle. Coyotes or wolves get them or they get sick. It's part of ranch life."

"I was thinking the other day that someday I wouldn't mind living in a place like this. It's so nice and peaceful and no matter where you look that landscape is beautiful."

"That's why I wanted to live out here instead of a wing at the house. I'm a simple man and I live a fairly simple life here."

"Don't you ever get lonely?" she asked.

He thought about the question before answering. It was impossible to think of loneliness when Elle and Bonnie filled the cabin with such life. "I guess there were times I'd get a little lonely, but all I have to do is drive up the way and visit with my parents or Valeria." He eyed her curiously. "What about you? Do you ever get lonely?"

She took the bottle from Bonnie's mouth and lifted her up to her shoulder. "Maybe occasionally." She gave the bottle back to Bonnie. "But that doesn't mean I want somebody in my life right now. With the Groom Killer still out there somewhere and the Larson twins running their illegal rackets, all I'm focused on is working."

He wasn't sure why, but her words depressed him just a little bit. "How long until dinner?" he asked.

"Probably another twenty minutes or so."

"I'm going to do a little work until then." He moved out of the recliner and into the chair at his desk. The dreariness of the rain had cast the cabin in an unusual darkness for this time of the year. He turned on his desk lamp and punched on his computer.

He needed to make notes about the storm and the loss of the cattle, but it was hard to concentrate with Elle sweet-talking Bonnie and with Elle's evocative scent eddying in the air.

He was almost grateful when she took Bonnie and went back into the kitchen. Fifteen minutes later she appeared in the doorway. "Dinner is ready," she announced.

"Good, I'm starving." He got up from the desk and entered the kitchen where the table was set. A red chicken breast sat on his plate, along with red rice and corn.

He sat and she did as well. "It looks...interesting," he said.

"I just hope it tastes okay." She didn't pick up her fork to begin eating but rather watched him intently.

He cut into the chicken breast, pleased that it appeared to be cooked perfectly, although it looked like she had gone overboard with the paprika.

He took a bite and instantly his mouth filled with the fires of hell. Cayenne pepper...not paprika. He chewed despite the fact that his eyes threatened to water and his throat was tightening with the need to cough. As he swallowed he reached for his water glass and chased the bite with a large swig.

"How is it?" she asked. She held his gaze steadily.

"It's definitely spicy."

She frowned and cut herself a bite. She popped it into her mouth. Her eyes widened and her cheeks reddened. She reached for her water glass. "Holy hell," she exclaimed after she'd taken a drink. "I didn't know that pepper would be hot."

"It's not that bad," he protested.

"It's awful," she said miserably. "I just wanted to make the chicken tasty, but it's not edible." Her eyes grew glassy and she jumped up out of the chair and carried her plate to the counter. She stood for a moment with her back to him.

"Elle," he said softly. "It's just dinner."

She turned around and marched over to him and grabbed his plate. "You can't eat this." She carried it to the sink and once again remained standing with her back to him.

He got up from his chair and walked over to her. "Elle, it's not a big deal. Don't be upset."

She turned around slowly and her eyes held the sheen of unshed tears. "I hate cooking."

He laughed and pulled her into his arms. "I don't care if you ever cook again."

"But what are you going to eat for dinner?" she asked, and to his dismay quickly stepped back from his embrace.

"I've got a frozen pizza in the freezer that will be ready in about twenty minutes. I don't want you to fret about this. If you'll smile for me I'll give you an A for effort."

The corner of her lips moved upward.

"You can do better than that," he teased. "Come on, give me one of those Elle smiles that light up a whole room."

"You're silly," she said.

"I'll show you silly." He reached out and grabbed her by the arm. "I'm going to tickle you until you're silly." He tickled her ribs and was delighted when she squealed with laughter.

She ran into the living room to escape him, but he chased after her. He grabbed her and wrestled her to the ground where he sat on top of her and continued to tickle her.

"Stop," she protested breathlessly. "Please…you have to stop."

She looked so beautiful with her cheeks pink and her eyes sparkling with laughter. He so wanted to kiss her. He stared down at her and her smile slid away. "Anders, go put the pizza in the oven," she said.

Reluctantly he got off her and helped her up from the floor. "At least I now know one of your weaknesses," he said. "You are wonderfully ticklish."

"And if you tell another soul, I'll have to shoot you," she replied with humor still lighting her eyes. "Now, you put the pizza in and I'll clean up the chicken mess."

A half an hour later they sat at the table sharing the pizza and talking about inconsequential things.

He discovered her favorite color was purple and she hated horror movies. She loved cold pizza in the morning and going barefoot.

He felt as if he could have a hundred…a thousand more dinners with her and not know everything there was to know about Elle Gage.

After dinner they turned on a movie and she entertained Bonnie while he played a game of tug-of-war with Merlin and a length of rope with a small ball on either end.

Before he knew it the day was over and it was time to go to bed. For the first time in a very long time he was reluctant to end the day.

Despite the lightning strike, the dead cattle and the red chicken, it had been a good day. Every day with Elle and Bonnie in the cabin was a good day.

And sooner or later it was all going to come to an end.

Chapter 9

The next evening Elle and Anders sat at the table eating the meat loaf, mashed potatoes and corn he'd prepared while catching up on each other's days. He'd worked later today than usual and had immediately gotten busy cooking so they'd scarcely had time to talk before now.

"Seth has gotten through the last two days working hard without a hint of alcohol," he said.

"He should be so grateful to you. It was darned good of you to give him another chance," she said. It had oddly touched her heart when he'd come home after the morning meeting with Seth and told her he'd rehired the man.

"I just hope he can toe the line and build something healthy and good in his life," Anders replied.

"That would be nice. On another note, I got some news about Demi today," she replied, and pushed her now-empty plate aside. "When I called this morning to check in with Finn he told me Demi had texted her brother Brayden from a burner phone."

Anders looked at her with interest. "I hope she said she left her baby with me."

"Unfortunately, no. She didn't mention the baby at all. She told Brayden to get Lucas off her back. I guess Lucas is trying to track her, and if anyone can, it's her biggest local rival in the bounty hunter business. She again said that she was innocent and getting closer to unmasking the real killer."

"Well, that worries me," Anders replied. "I hate to think of her being anywhere close to such a vicious killer."

"If she thinks her text is going to get Lucas off her back, then she doesn't know my brother very well," she said ruefully. "That will only light a new fire in Lucas to find her and bring her in."

"What a mess. It feels like this killer is keeping the whole town hostage." He got up and carried their plates to the sink.

"We'll get the killer. It's just a matter of time before it happens," she said with confidence.

"Hopefully it's before any more men are murdered." He returned to the table.

"It would have been nice if Demi had mentioned the baby—given an idea whether or not Bonnie is hers. I did ask Carson to ask Brayden to text her back and ask for a photo of her baby. If she has one and texts it to us, then we can see if it's Bonnie or not."

"I have to confess, I've gotten a little attached to her," he admitted.

"I know." Elle smiled at him.

He looked at her in surprise. "How do you know?"

"I see the way you look at her and the way you talk to her. I know you told me that you didn't intend to care about her. Does that have something to do with another woman and baby?" She held her breath, knowing she was pushing into personal territory, but too curious not to ask.

"What are you talking about?" He asked the question slowly…cautiously.

"When I was picking up the living room floor the night of the break-in, I saw a photograph of you and a woman and a baby."

"Oh, that." His eyes appeared to darken and he leaned back in his chair.

"You don't have to talk about it if you don't want to," she said quickly.

"No, it's fine. It was a long time ago." He stood abruptly. "Let's go sit in the living room where we'll be more comfortable."

She followed him into the room where instead of sinking down in the recliner, he sat on the sofa next to Bonnie. She sat in the recliner, wondering what can of worms her question might have opened.

"The woman in the photo is a woman I dated for a while. Her name is Rosalie. We dated for about six months and then she broke it off." Once again he didn't make eye contact with Elle, but rather looked down at Bonnie.

"Were you in love with her?" Elle asked softly.

He cocked his head and stared just over her shoulder as if in deep thought. "I think maybe I could have been in love with her if there had been more time, although she could be impulsive and insanely jealous. She also liked to play mind games, and when it comes to relationships, I'm not a game player. We were working on things, but then she broke it off. In any case, one night a little over a year later she showed up on my doorstep with a baby she told me was mine."

He released a sigh. "She told me she wanted to try to make it work between us for the baby's sake.

So she moved in. And that's when I really fell in love." He finally looked at Elle once again. "Not with Rosalie, but with Brooke, the baby."

He shook his head and his lips curved up in a smile. "Brooke was a couple months old and not only entertaining, but also a little charmer." His smile faded. "I never knew I could love that way...so incredibly deeply."

"What happened?" He looked so vulnerable at the moment. Oh God, had they been killed in a car accident? Had some tragedy happened that had taken them away from him? Her heart ached with the pain that glimmered in the very depths of his eyes.

"They'd been here about three weeks when Rosalie confessed to me that she wasn't here to try to make things work between us. She'd just needed a place to stay because she and her boyfriend had had a big fight and she wanted some time away from him. And that's when she also told me she'd lied about Brooke, that she wasn't mine. The boyfriend was Brooke's father. She walked out that day two years ago and I haven't seen or heard from her since."

"Oh Anders, what a horrible, wicked thing for her to do. I'm so sorry." She wanted to run to him, to hold him and somehow take away his pain. Her heart broke for him and what he'd been through.

He shrugged. "It's over and done, but going

through something like that changes who you are at your very core." He gazed down at Bonnie. "It's why I can't give this little one my heart. If she isn't mine she's just going to be snatched away from me like Brooke."

There was a very real possibility that Bonnie wasn't his, that she did belong to Demi and Bo. There was also a wild, crazy possibility that she didn't belong to Anders or Demi, but then who else's would she be? She was so torn. On the one hand she hoped Bonnie was Anders's daughter, but on the other hand she wanted the baby to be Bo's, a part of him that would continue after his death.

"So you will never love anyone again? Is that really the answer?" she finally asked him.

He looked back at her. "I don't know what the answer is. All I really know is that I never want to hurt like that again." He cleared his throat. "So now you know the skeleton in my closet. Do you have any in yours?"

She was about to tell him no, but he'd shared a piece of his painful past with her; wasn't it only fair that she open up to him?

"My skeleton is a lot more common than yours," she began. She tried to ignore the tight press of emotions that suddenly filled her chest. It was grief, combined with an anger she'd never allowed herself to feel before.

"I was dating a man named Frank. We dated for about seven months or so and I thought everything was going wonderfully well." She cast her gaze to the wall just over Anders's head as memories cascaded through her mind.

She'd been so happy, so sure of Frank's love for her. She'd given everything she had to the relationship and his betrayal had changed her forever. She'd never be that young, naive woman again.

"And things weren't going wonderfully well?"

Anders's deep voice jerked her out of her memories and into the present.

"He sat me down one night and I was certain he was about to propose to me." The emotion once again filled her chest. "I was ready to be his wife and to have his children. But instead of a proposal, he told me he'd been cheating on me the whole time with another woman and he was in love with her."

She stared at Anders for a long moment and then to her horror she burst into tears.

"Hey, hey," Anders said. He jumped up off the sofa and walked over to her. He took her hand and pulled her off the chair and into his arms.

She was mortified that she was crying in front of Anders...that she was showing any kind of a weakness in front of a Colton. But she was unable to control the deep sobs that choked out of her.

"It's all right," he said as his hands caressed up and down her back. "Let it all out."

She buried her face in the front of his shirt and wept the tears she hadn't released at the time her heartache had happened.

The funny thing was she wasn't crying over the loss of Frank. Rather she cried over the loss of herself. Somehow she had allowed him to steal away all of her self-confidence. He'd taken pieces of her that she could never get back...her innocence and her belief in herself.

"I'm so sorry," she gasped as the tears began to abate. She tried to step back from him, but he held her tight.

"Don't apologize," he said. He kissed her tenderly on the cheek. "He obviously hurt you badly."

The tears finally stopped but she remained in his arms. His heart beat strong and steady against hers, calming her after the unexpected storm of emotions that had gripped her. All that was left inside her was embarrassment and humiliation.

"Are you still in love with him?" His soft question jerked her back from him and she couldn't help a bubble of laughter that escaped her lips.

"Goodness, no," she replied. "I stopped loving

that jerk the night I discovered he was nothing but a two-timing cheat who played with my emotions."

"Then why all the tears?" he asked curiously.

She hesitated a moment, wondering if she could make him understand. "I was crying because it reminded me that I'm never enough. I wasn't enough to get attention from my parents when I was younger, and I wasn't enough for Frank. I'm not enough for my brothers to trust that I can do my job competently. Let me tell you, all of this definitely chips away at a girl's self-confidence."

Tears began falling once again and she angrily swiped at them, but apparently she wasn't finished with them yet as they chased faster and faster down her cheeks.

Once again Anders pulled her back into his arms. "I don't know why I can't stop crying," she said into his chest. "I feel like such a fool. I don't ever cry."

"It's all right. Just let it all out." Once again his hands caressed her back in slow, soothing strokes. "I just want to let you know that you're more than enough for Bonnie and you're more than enough for me."

His words did nothing to help. Bonnie was just a baby and anyone with a bottle and clean diapers would be enough for her. And in the case of Anders, she was just a woman helping care take for Bonnie.

It was easy to be enough if you were only a one-night stand.

Slowly the tears dried up and she became aware of the clean scent of his T-shirt, the smell of fabric softener combined with a hint of his cologne.

His strokes up and down her back became more languid and instead of comforting her, they stoked a flame deep inside her. She finally looked up at him and he captured her lips with his.

The kiss was soft and tender, but tasted of his hungry desire. It moved her in a way that was frightening, but that wasn't enough for her to stop it.

As the tip of his tongue sought entry, she opened her mouth to him and the kiss deepened. His hands moved beneath her T-shirt, warming her back each place he touched.

His lips left hers to trail a blaze down her neck. *Don't be a fool*, a little voice whispered inside her brain where there was still a modicum of rational thought left. *Don't go there again.* She pushed against him, grateful that he immediately dropped his arms from around her.

"Elle, I want you again." His deep voice washed over her and increased the fire that wanted to be set free inside her.

"We can't, Anders." It would be so easy to go into

his bedroom and let passion sweep away all remnants of her temporary breakdown.

"Why not?" His dark eyes held his hunger for her.

"Because it isn't right. I'm here in an official capacity and we shouldn't go there again. We shouldn't have gone there to begin with. It wasn't the right thing to do." She was babbling and she knew it, but she couldn't stop herself. "It will only complicate things between us. Besides, you're a Colton and I'm a Gage."

"That's the most ridiculous excuse I've ever heard," Anders scoffed. "We are people and so much more than our last names. Maybe Vincent and Valeria have it right. It's way past time we all get over a century-old feud that has nothing to do with any of us now."

"I'll admit, I'd never let a name stop me from loving somebody, but I can't be with you again, Anders. We had our one-night stand and now it's done."

He sighed and raked a hand through his hair. "For what it's worth, Frank was a stupid man to give you up."

"It was the best thing he could have done for me." She released her own deep sigh. "If you ever tell anyone about me breaking down, I'll have to shoot you."

He smiled at her. "Your secret is safe with me." His smile slowly faded. "Elle, you don't get your self-confidence from the people around you. You get it from within yourself. You have to believe that you're enough. You're beautiful and intelligent. You're great at your job, but unless you believe it you'll always have doubts about yourself."

"Thank you, Doctor, I'll be sure to put a check in the mail for this therapy session," she replied.

"No need to get snippy," he replied, and then grinned at her once again. "Are we having our first spat?"

"No, I'm too tired to spat, and sorry that I got snippy. It's been a long day and I'm completely exhausted." In truth she'd been tired for the past couple of days.

"Why don't I take Bonnie into my room for the night? That way you can get a good night's sleep without any interruptions and I can take care of her middle-of-the night feeding."

She hesitated for a moment. "Are you sure?" There was no question that the night feedings were beginning to take a toll on her. She had been functioning on far less sleep than she was used to.

"I'm positive. We should have been taking turns with her from the very beginning," he replied. "And don't worry about the dinner cleanup. I'll take care of that, too."

She looked at the baby and then back at him. "Okay, and thanks. I know it's really early, but I think I'm going to go on to bed right now."

"Sleep well," he replied.

"I'll do my best." She went into her bedroom and as she undressed she thought about everything that had transpired. It had been an evening of high emotion and secrets told, and she was utterly exhausted.

As she crawled into bed, Merlin flopped down on the floor next to her. Hopefully the night would bring no further drama and she really would sleep well and deep.

She had a feeling she wouldn't have blubbered so hard if she hadn't been so tired. But even so, the release of the tears had made her feel better than she had in years.

She felt amazingly clearheaded and she knew Anders had been right. Only when she really believed in herself would she know that she was enough for anyone.

The one thing that was certain was that making love again with Anders would have been a big mistake. The forced intimacy of their situation had made a physical relationship almost inevitable. She was certain that within a week or so, if nothing else happened here, she'd be pulled out and assigned to something else.

Making love again with Anders would also be a big mistake because at some point during her crying jag, she'd realized she was in love with him.

And she desperately didn't want to be.

* * *

Anders sat on horseback and stared out over the huge herd of cattle, but his mind was on Elle. It seemed his thoughts were always filled with her.

It had bothered him that she hadn't wanted to make love with him last night. It bothered him that he had no idea what her feelings were toward him.

With each day that passed he grew more and more crazy about her. As odd as it sounded, he'd been touched that she'd cried in front of him the night before. It had spoken of the deep level of trust she had with him. He seriously doubted that she ever showed such vulnerability with anyone else.

It had felt ridiculously good to talk about Rosalie and Brooke. It had been like lancing a wound he'd carried around with him for far too long. The relief had been instant.

He'd told her that the experience had made him unwilling to give his heart away again, but he'd been wrong. This morning he'd awakened to the epiphany that the answer to heartache was not to close yourself off, but rather to love deep and hard. No matter what the consequences, in the end love was worth it.

He'd had the happiness of believing he was Brooke's father for almost three wonderful weeks, and it was forever in his memory bank, but the following heartache shouldn't break him forever.

He wanted love in his life. He wanted a special woman to stand beside him through happiness and tears. And he believed he'd found that woman in Elle.

But at the moment he intended to keep his love for her to himself. She'd talked about two people being on the same page and he wasn't sure if the two of them were there yet.

Hopefully with another week or two, she'd fall in love with him. He intended to use that time to court her, to make her see that she was more than enough for him and that they belonged together forever.

It was almost time for him to return to the cabin and with this thought in mind, he rode to the edge of one of the pastures where he knew the South Dakota state flower bloomed wild at this time of year.

Sure enough when he arrived there, the ground was covered with the light blue, golden-centered pasque flowers. He dismounted and began to pick a bouquet to take back to the cabin.

He could have easily just driven into town and gone to the floral shop, but he wasn't sure it was open. The owner was dead and he knew the police were trying to figure out who had been sending Hayley flowers since Bo's murder.

Besides, he somehow believed that Elle would prefer the beautiful wildflowers he'd picked to any flowers he could just go into a store and buy.

Breakfast that morning had been a little awkward. She'd been a bit quiet and he suspected she was still embarrassed by her display of emotions the night before.

But she'd told him she'd slept wonderfully well and he'd felt bad that he'd put the entire nighttime duty of Bonnie on her the whole time she'd been here.

With a large handful of the pretty flowers, he got back on his horse and headed for home. The cabin had never felt like home as much as it did now with Elle in it.

He shook his head ruefully. He was turning into a lovesick fool and the strange thing was he didn't mind. He wanted his woman and he'd do whatever it took to gain her love.

Once again before he entered the back door he heard Elle's laughter. A glance through the window showed him that it wasn't Bonnie who was making her laugh. The baby was sleeping in her cradle on top of the kitchen table. Whoever she was on the phone with had evoked the laughter from her.

As he came in the door she turned to look at him and the flowers in his hand. "Oh, I have to go. Anders just got home. Okay, I'll talk to you soon."

She hung up and smiled at him. "Oh, they're lovely," she said.

"I thought you might enjoy them." He hung his

hat up on the hook and then reached out to give her the flowers.

"Wait, I need to find some kind of a vase."

"There should be one under the sink," he replied.

She bent over and looked. "Got it," she exclaimed in triumph and pulled out the tall glass vase. She filled it with water, set it in the center of the table and then took the flowers from him.

She looked lovely as usual. Clad in a pair of jeans that clung to her long legs and a pink T-shirt that hugged her breasts, she looked more like a model than a police officer.

He refused to believe that he'd never again kiss her with passion or feel those long legs wrapped with his. He refused to believe that he'd never make love with her again.

"Who was making you laugh on the phone?" he asked as she began to arrange the flowers. He wouldn't be surprised if she told him none of his business, because he knew he really had no right to ask her.

"Juliette Walsh," she replied. "She's a good friend of mine. Do you know her?"

He frowned thoughtfully. "The name sounds vaguely familiar."

"It should. She's a K9 cop who once dated your cousin Blake."

"That must have been before the time Blake left town," he replied.

"Yes, it was." She finished fussing with the flowers and stepped back to admire her own work.

"I'm not close to Blake, but I can tell you that I already like your friend Juliette."

She looked at him in confusion. "How can you tell me you like her when you don't even know her?"

"I like her because she made you laugh, and I definitely think you should do more of that."

She smiled. "I've done more laughing here with you and Bonnie than I've probably ever done in my life."

"Why is that?" he asked curiously.

Her eyes twinkled with a teasing light. "Probably because you're such a goofball."

He laughed in surprised delight. "I'll have you know that nobody in my entire life has ever had the audacity to call me a goofball."

"I call them like I see them, buster. I've caught you making those silly faces to get Bonnie to smile."

She was absolutely right. When Bonnie was awake and he had a moment alone with her, he became an utter fool. He baby-talked her and made all kinds of expressions to see if he could get her to smile…to laugh.

He looked at Bonnie now. "Ah, the princess is awake. It's time to make funny faces for her."

The smile fell from Elle's face and her dark eyes held his gaze soberly. "I know you want her to be yours, but I'm still desperately hoping she belongs to Demi and my brother." Sadness filled her eyes and it didn't take a rocket scientist to know she was thinking about her dead brother. "One of us is going to be bitterly disappointed."

"Then we just support each other no matter what happens," he said softly.

"I'm going to give Bonnie her tummy time," she said briskly, and picked up the cradle. It was obvious she wasn't going to let her emotions get the best of her today.

"And I'm going to take a quick shower and then fix dinner. How does a steak and baked potato sound?"

"That sounds perfect."

A half an hour later he was in the kitchen preparing the evening meal. Elle's voice drifted in from the living room, a soft, lovely melody that shot waves of enjoyment through him.

There was no question he'd gotten attached to Bonnie, but there was a part of him that wanted the baby to be Bo's so that Elle had a piece of her brother to hang on to. Only the DNA test would give them some answers and he hoped it came in sooner rather than later. It was definitely taking longer than he thought it would to get the results.

Forty-five minutes later they sat at the table enjoying the meal and a discussion about television shows. He was unsurprised to discover that she loved all the crime dramas while he preferred all the old Western movies and an occasional sitcom.

They were almost finished eating when her cell phone rang. "Excuse me a minute," she said as she grabbed the phone and got up from the table.

"Yes, Chief," she said as she left the kitchen and walked into the living room. Merlin trailed after her, her ever-present partner and companion.

Maybe she'd come back with some useful information. It was possible the DNA results had come in. Or maybe they caught the Groom Killer. That would be great news for the entire town.

"Everything all right?" he asked as she returned to the kitchen.

"Fine." She sat back down at the table. "That was Finn calling to tell me that if nothing else out of the ordinary happens out here within the next five days, then after that time I'm to leave this assignment."

Five days. He only had five more days of her staying with him. It was a woefully inadequate length of time. He wasn't near ready to tell her goodbye, but he also wasn't quite self-confident enough to ask her to stay.

Still, he knew with certainty that at some point

during the next five days he was going to put his heart on the line and pray that she didn't slice it in two by walking away from him.

Chapter 10

Five more days. The words thundered through Elle's head with an unwelcome rhythm as she went about her morning routine. She should be grateful to leave this babysitting assignment and work on something where she could really make a difference. But she wasn't.

Five more days. The words rang in her head like a death knell. She was supposed to be here as a police officer, but somehow in spending time in the cabin with Bonnie and Anders, she'd reclaimed herself as a woman.

She'd spent so much time trying to be tough, but here she'd rediscovered her softer side, her laughter, and she'd realized those things didn't make her weak at all.

Yes, she hated to leave here. This little cabin in the woods had felt like home. Having breakfast and dinner with Anders had felt so right. But she had to get all of that out of her head.

Her home was her apartment and it was time she got back to her real life. These days in the cabin had felt like a dream, but the dream was about to be over and it was time to get back to reality, and that meant life without Anders and Bonnie.

She stared at the flowers on the counter. He definitely didn't seem like the kind of man who would randomly pick flowers for his home. He'd picked those flowers for her. She wasn't sure why he had done such a thing, but she couldn't let it matter to her. She couldn't let *him* matter to her.

As if in protest of Elle's thoughts, Bonnie began to fuss. It was a little early for another feeding, so Elle gave her the pacifier and she immediately fell back asleep.

Elle got up from the sofa and wandered into the kitchen, deciding that it wasn't too early for her to eat lunch. She'd just finished a ham-and-cheese sandwich when Merlin alerted. She grabbed her gun and opened the door to see Carson.

"Elle, I swear I'm not here checking up on you," he said quickly.

She lowered her gun. "Then why are you here?"

"I thought I'd come by to see this baby who might belong to Bo and Demi."

"Well, if that's the case then you can come in." She gestured him inside.

"Hey, Merlin." He leaned over to greet the dog with a fast scrub of his fingers across Merlin's back. "Anders out on the ranch?"

"Yes, although I never know for sure when he'll get home." He followed her into the kitchen where Bonnie was in the cradle in the middle of the table.

Carson bent over and inspected her like he was looking at a curious crime scene. He straightened up and looked at Elle. "I don't know, to me she doesn't look like anyone. She just looks like a baby."

"But Demi has all that flaming red hair and Bonnie does have a bit of light red in her hair," Elle replied. She touched Bonnie's cheek. "It would be nice if she was Bo's." Grief pressed against her chest.

"I guess." Carson reached out for her hand. "Elle, I know you and Bo had words before his death, but I also know Bo wasn't the type of a guy to hold a grudge. You do know he loved you and he never doubted how much you loved him."

She sighed. "Intellectually I know that, but emotionally I'm just so sorry we had words at all."

Carson pulled her into a tight, big-brother hug. "You know he's up in heaven right now looking down and smiling at us. Hell, knowing Bo he's probably laughing at us all."

A small burst of laughter escaped her and she stepped out of his embrace. "You're probably right about that."

"I've got to get going, but I was interested to see the baby who might be a possible link to Demi. I've been hounding the lab for the DNA results on Bonnie and Anders. They're way behind but have promised to get them to us any day now."

Together they walked back to the front door. "Anything new on the case?" she asked.

His eyes darkened. "Nothing at all. I heard your duty here is just about over."

"Yeah, I've got five days left here. Since the big break-in nothing else has happened, so there's really no reason for me to stay on." She ignored the knot that wound tight in her chest at the thought of leaving.

"And you still don't have any idea what somebody was searching for?"

"Not a clue. According to Anders nothing was taken," she replied.

"You know there are many at the PD who still believe Anders might be hiding Demi someplace out here. They've given up on thinking Serena might be helping out Demi because of our relationship. I know Serena would never keep that kind of secret from me."

"And they should have the same respect for me—and therefore Anders. He's told everyone dozens of times that he isn't."

Carson's gaze held hers for a long moment. "Do you trust him?"

"I trust him with all my heart," she replied. "He wants Demi to be brought in as badly as the rest of us do. He's afraid for her."

"Lucas is damned and determined to bring her in." Carson opened the door.

She laughed, imagining their bounty hunter brother out there in the wilderness, tracking Demi, his biggest rival. "Lucas is always damned and determined when he's after somebody."

"I guess the next time I see you will be in the squad room." He stepped outside into the bright June sunshine.

"Five days and I'll be back in the action," she replied.

Minutes later she watched his car disappear from view and then she turned and went back into the house. Bonnie was ready for her bottle and as she fed the hungry baby, her thoughts returned to her conversation with Carson.

Did she trust Anders? She certainly hadn't when she'd first started staying here. But now she trusted him 100 percent. She wasn't sure when it had happened that all her doubts about him potentially hiding Demi had gone away, but they were gone. She also believed he knew nothing about the break-in or what somebody might have been looking for.

She'd just finished feeding Bonnie when Anders came home.

"You're home early," she said as he came through the back door. Dang, but the man seemed to get more handsome every time she saw him. His white T-shirt stretched tight over his broad shoulders and his worn jeans looked like they had been tailor-made for his long legs and slim hips.

"I got a hankering for chocolate cupcakes and decided to come in early and bake a batch for dessert tonight."

She stared at him wordlessly. One night when they'd been talking about food that they liked, she'd told him her favorite dessert was plain old chocolate cupcakes with chocolate frosting.

"What are you doing, Anders?" she asked uneasily. She put Bonnie back in her cradle.

He looked at her innocently. "What are you talking about?"

"What's with the flowers and the cupcakes?" Her heart beat an unsteady rhythm.

He shrugged. "I just want these last five days with you to be nice."

"The last five days that I'm here will be just fine without you going to any extra trouble," she replied. "You don't have to bake for me."

"Dammit, woman, let me make you cupcakes. Let me bring you flowers. You've been so good about taking care of Bonnie all this time. Let me do some nice things for you."

He swept his hat off his head and hung it up and then turned to look at her once again. "Now, if you don't mind, I have chef work to do."

"Then I'll just take Bonnie and get out of the chef's way," she replied. She carried the baby into the living room and spread down the quilt for some tummy time.

Gratitude. That explained the flowers. He was grateful to her for caring for Bonnie. Thank goodness she hadn't given him any indication of her depth of feeling for him. Thank goodness she hadn't told him she was in love with him.

She certainly didn't want to be. It wasn't time for

her to fall in love, especially with a man like Anders. He was a wealthy rancher who was bigger than life. Smart and so handsome, he deserved a better woman than her.

Even though she'd regained a lot of her self-confidence since being here with Anders, the debacle with Frank still haunted her. Even her brother Bo had told her she was too boring and a stick-in-the-mud. Of course, she had said some awful things to Bo during their fight.

Besides, she was focused on her job. It wasn't time for her to have it all…a husband…a family… and her work. She didn't even know why she was thinking about it. It wasn't like he'd told her he was in love with her.

He was just grateful.

When was the right time to tell a woman you loved her? Should he tell her when the scent of rich chocolate filled the cabin? Or should he wait until she was delving into one of the cupcakes?

Was tonight the right time or would tomorrow be better? As he waited for the treats to bake, he seasoned a couple of pork chops to go into the oven as soon as the cupcakes were finished.

He was suddenly nervous. He couldn't remember the last time he'd been so filled with anxiety. He wanted to tell her he was in love with her. He needed to speak the words out loud to her. But he was terrified of what her reaction would be.

What if he told her he loved her and she laughed at him? He instantly dismissed the idea. Elle would never laugh at him; that simply wasn't in her character. But she could look at him with that sober stare and tell him she wasn't in love with him.

Then they would have four more days in the cabin together. Things would be horribly awkward between them, but he was almost willing to accept that in order to speak his words of love to her tonight.

He knew the best time to tell her would be when she had one foot out the door. That way if she told him she wasn't interested, then she would leave and he wouldn't have to look at her, want her and love her for four more torturous days.

Be patient, he told himself as he pulled the cupcakes out of the oven. Wait until she's leaving and then tell her you want her to stay with you for the rest of your life. He had to be smart about this, and that seemed like the smartest choice he could make. Decision made, he began to relax. Tonight he just wanted them to have a good meal and enjoy each other's company. He might even point out how comfortable he was with her and how much he'd miss her when she was gone.

Once the cupcakes had cooled, he frosted them and placed them on a platter in the center of the table, and by that time the pork chops were ready.

He was particularly pleased with dinner. The pork chops were seasoned with an apple-flavored rub, the mashed potatoes had come out perfectly, and a salad rounded out the meal.

He went to the living room door and was about to tell her that dinner was ready, but the sight that greeted him stopped him. Elle was stretched out on her back on the floor. Bonnie was on her chest and both of them were sound asleep. Merlin was snuggled against Elle's side and his loud and even snores filled the room.

In that moment, a desire struck him so hard in the chest he couldn't breathe. God, he wanted this. He wanted Bonnie to be his daughter and he wanted Elle to be his wife. He even wanted the drooling dog to live with him forever.

He leaned against the doorjamb and continued to gaze at the sleeping trio, his heart huge in his chest. Bonnie was limp against Elle's chest as if she belonged there. Elle had one arm around the baby to keep her in place, but it was Elle's face he stared at.

Her features were all so relaxed and her lips

curved slightly upward as if her dreams were pleasant. He hoped her dreams were always good. More than anything he wanted to keep the three who slept on his grandmother's quilt safe from harm and here in his cabin forever.

Not making a sound, he returned to the kitchen and sank down at the table. Dinner would be late, but he didn't care. Elle obviously needed some extra sleep and he wasn't about to disturb her for a pork chop.

It was a little over an hour later when she and Merlin appeared in the doorway. "Oh my gosh, why didn't you wake me up?"

He smiled. "I figured you probably needed the extra sleep."

"I can't believe I did that," she replied. "I'm really not a nap kind of person."

"You weren't the only one who caught a nap." He looked pointedly at Merlin. "He was snoring so loud the neighbors called to complain."

"Ha ha, you're such a funny man," she replied drily.

"I assume Bonnie is still sleeping."

She nodded. "Something smells wonderful in here."

"That would be dinner. Are you hungry?"

"Starving," she replied.

"Then belly up to the bar and I'll serve the meal."

As she sat, he filled their plates and then carried them to the table. "It's going to be hard to eat the meal with those yummy-looking cupcakes staring me in the face, but the pork chop looks delicious, too."

The meal wasn't so delicious. The pork chops had been warmed for so long they'd become dry. The potatoes were too stiff and the salad was a bit limp.

"I'm sorry everything isn't better," he said when they'd been eating for a couple of minutes.

"Don't you dare apologize for a great meal. You couldn't know that I was going to fall asleep. Besides, I have a feeling on your worst day in the kitchen your food would still be great."

"I definitely had some pretty bad days in the kitchen when I first started cooking. When I lived in the big house all the meals were prepared for us by a variety of hired cooks. I never had to lift a finger to eat."

"That's the way I grew up, too," she replied. "But when I got out on my own I didn't teach myself to cook. Instead I taught myself what were the best frozen dinners I could zap in the microwave and eat."

She paused to take a drink of water and then continued, "Of course my hours working as an officer aren't always regular, especially now with the Groom Killer case. Everyone has been working a lot of overtime since the last murder."

"We are not going to talk about murder this evening," he said firmly. "Tonight we just focus on pleasant things."

"Sounds good to me," she replied with the smile that warmed his belly better than any expensive whiskey. "You know, if Bonnie is going to stay here it won't be too long before she's going to need a crib. She's growing like a weed and that cradle will only hold her for so long."

For the next few minutes they talked about Bonnie's growing needs. What they didn't discuss was how he would deal with a baby in the house if he was a single father. He didn't intend to be single.

"I'll bet you're going to be an overly protective father," she said with amusement sparking in her eyes. "I can just imagine Bonnie going out on her first date and you trailing behind them, hiding behind trees and darting into doorways so they don't see you."

"Nah, it isn't going to be like that," he replied. "I'm just going to make sure she doesn't date until she's thirty."

Elle laughed. "Good luck with that. What I'm now wondering about is, how long after dinner do I have to wait before having one of those scrumptious-looking cupcakes?"

He grinned at her. "Go for it." He picked up their empty dinner plates and carried them to the sink. He turned in time to see her with her eyes closed and a bit of cupcake in her mouth. Dark chocolate frosting clung to her upper lip, and his love for her buoyed up inside him.

"I'm in love with you, Elle." He blurted the words.

Her eyelids snapped open and she stared at him in obvious surprise. She slowly lowered the rest of the cupcake to the table and then picked up her napkin and wiped her mouth.

His heart beat unsteadily as he waited for her to say something…to say anything. There was no happy joy shining from her eyes, but a wild hope still filled him.

"I'm in love with you, Elle, and I want you here with me forever."

"Stop, Anders," she finally said.

"I can't stop," he replied. "I can't hold it in any longer."

"I still have four days left here and you're complicating things for both of us." She stared down at the table and her body had tensed as if she wanted nothing more than to run away from him.

"I'm not trying to complicate things," he protested. "I'm trying to make things wonderful. I'm in love with you, Elle."

"Stop saying that," she said, her voice verging on anger. "I was just supposed to be a one-night stand."

She tossed the napkin on the table and then stood. "I don't want to talk about this right now."

"Then when would be a good time?" The hope that he'd entertained slowly began to fizzle away. Surely if she felt the same way about him she would have jumped up and run into his arms. She would have told him she loved him, too. Instead she was trying to escape him.

"I would prefer we not discuss this again." She said the words firmly, but as her hand reached up to shove her hair away from her face, he noticed that her fingers trembled.

He took a couple of steps toward her. "Elle, I love you and I believe that you're in love with me."

She stared at him for a long moment and in the very depths of her beautiful brown eyes he believed he saw love. It was there only a moment and then gone as she broke eye contact with him.

"Elle, tell me that you love me, too. Tell me that you want a life with me," he said as he took another step toward her.

"I can't." Her voice held pain and still she stared down at the floor.

"Why can't you?"

She finally looked up at him and this time a touch of anger burned in her gaze. "I told you I wasn't looking for a relationship. I explained to you that right now I'm focusing on my career. Dammit, I made it clear what page I was on. Right now it's not time for love."

It was his turn to stare at her in surprise. "Elle, love doesn't know a timeline. You can't control who or when you love. It just happens. Besides, I would encourage you to continue to focus on your work. I know how important it is to you."

A mist of tears shone in her eyes. He didn't know what had caused them, but his first instinct was to draw her into his arms. No matter what was happening right now, he never wanted to see her cry. And the last thing he wanted to do was cause her any pain. He reached out for her, but she stepped back.

"Don't touch me, Anders. Please don't touch me." She wrapped her arms around herself. He dropped his hands back to his sides.

She sighed. "Anders, the truth is I'm just not in love with you."

The words seemed to echo in the cabin as the last of his hope blew away. Pain replaced the hope, a sharp, stabbing pain in his heart and through his very soul. "Well, then I guess that settles things," he said flatly.

"I'm so sorry, Anders," she said softly.

"Don't be. You can't help what your heart feels." He backed away from her and to the sink. "Why don't you finish your cupcake and I'll get the dinner dishes cleaned up."

"I'm really not hungry right now. If you don't mind, I'm just going to go into the living room and see to Bonnie."

He nodded. When she was gone he sank down at the table, his emotions too tightly wound in his chest for him to do anything at the moment.

How could he have been so wrong about her… about them? He'd been sure that she felt the same about him. He'd been so damned certain that she was in love with him.

He'd seen the joy that lit her eyes when he came home after working on the ranch. He wondered if she was even aware of how often she touched him… simple touches like a hand to his forearm, a brush across his shoulders. She'd acted like a woman in love…so what had happened?

And then he knew. She'd lied. When she'd told him she wasn't in love with him, it had been nothing more than a lie. Was she afraid to love him? Afraid that he would just be another Frank in her life? That he would somehow betray her? Surely she knew him better than that.

He thought of the tears she had shed, tears because she felt like she'd never been enough for anyone. Was it possible that was what was holding her back?

If that was the case then he had four days to convince her that she was more than enough for him. With this thought in mind he got up from the table and began to tackle the dishes, eager to get back into the living room with her.

Chapter 11

Elle got into bed and released an exhausted sigh. It had been the longest evening of her life. She'd played with Bonnie and made small talk with Anders.

Anders. Her heart cried out his name. The most difficult thing she'd ever done in her life was face him and declare that she didn't love him.

But she was doing what was best for both of them. She wasn't ready to have it all. She was terrified that she couldn't handle it.

She closed her eyes and tried to imagine what it would be like to have it all. Would he grow tired of her job? If they had children, would they suffer from a lack of a stay-at-home mother? It had to be possible to raise well-adjusted, well-loved children who had working parents. She knew women who had it all. But the real question was, could *she* do it?

No, it was better to walk away now than walk away months from now knowing that she'd failed.

Still, when he'd reached out for her, she'd known that if he touched her, if he drew her into an embrace, she would crumble. She had to remain strong enough to walk away.

However, as she once again closed her eyes, she thought about that moment when he'd first confessed his love for her. His eyes had been so blue and so filled with hope.

It had looked like love…but was it really? Whatever he felt toward her had to be tangled up with a large dose of gratitude. She'd been here day and night to take care of the baby he thought might be his. She couldn't help but think it was possible that his feelings for her might be confused.

There was no question they had been playing house and it had felt comfortable and good. He'd probably gotten caught up in a fairy tale of a family in his cabin in the woods.

But how could she dismiss his feelings of love when she shared them? Was she, too, caught up in the fairy tale? She knew she was in love with him, so why did she doubt that he really loved her?

She finally fell asleep and dreamed that the two of them were at sea. He was on a huge ocean ship and she was on a tiny raft that tossed and turned in windy, turbulent conditions. She clung tight to the bright orange raft, crying out as it nearly capsized.

"I'm coming," Anders yelled from on top of the ship. "Hang on, Elle."

She tried to shout back to him but the minute she opened her mouth a wave crashed over her and she coughed and choked on the salt water.

The ship horn blew, a loud forlorn sound that shot fear through her. Was the ship pulling away? Was Anders leaving her behind to the sharks and the sea?

The horn sounded again and suddenly she was awake. It took her a moment to realize the ship horn was actually Merlin's alert.

She fumbled for her gun on the nightstand, frantically wondering how long Merlin had been alerting. The sound of a commotion came from the living room. Adrenaline fired through her.

She flung open her bedroom door and stepped into the living room. In an instant her brain processed the scene. The overhead light was on and a big man in a ski mask stood next to the desk with a knife in his hand.

At his feet Anders was on the floor, bleeding from a head wound. Fear for him spiked inside her. Oh God, how badly was he hurt? Next to her she sensed all the muscles in Merlin bunching up for action.

"Where is it?" the man asked, his voice a low, rough growl. "Where is the bag?"

"What bag?" she asked in confusion as she kept her gun pointed directly at him. If he even inched toward Anders with the knife, she'd fire and ask questions later. Anders hadn't said a word, nor had he tried to get to his feet. That scared the hell out of her.

What also scared the hell out of her was that the man crouched so close to Anders she was afraid to shoot, fearing that she might harm Anders.

"The bag…the damned baby bag," he replied.

The baby bag? Why would he want that? She didn't stop to consider the answer. "Merlin…*aanval*," she said, using the word for attack. *"Aanval!"* As much as she hated putting Merlin at risk against a man with a knife, this situation was exactly what Merlin was trained for.

With a deep, menacing growl, the dog launched himself across the room toward the man. The intruder instantly turned and ran toward the door. He managed to get outside and slammed the door behind him before Merlin could take a bite out of him. Merlin growled and scratched at the door, eager to carry out her command to attack, despite the obstacle in front of him.

She told the dog to relax and then rushed to Anders's side. He sat up with a hand to the side of his head. "I'm all right," he said, and winced.

"You are not all right, you're bleeding," she replied worriedly. Fear tasted bitter in her mouth. "Did he stab you? Do you have any other wounds?" Oh God, how hurt was he?

"No, and no." He slowly got to his feet. "I heard him in here and when I confronted him he slammed me in the head with my desk lamp."

"Let's get that blood cleaned up," she said. "I'm calling for backup to check the area." She made the call and then with several commands she put Merlin on guard duty at the front door. She grabbed Anders's arm and led him into the bathroom.

He leaned against the sink as she got a washcloth out of the linen closet and held it beneath the running water. "Do you feel dizzy? Are you sick to your stomach?" she asked.

"No, nothing like that. My head hurts and I'm ticked off that he got the drop on me." He stood still as she began to gently clean off the wound.

It didn't appear to be too deep and it had already stopped bleeding. Thank God. She would have never forgiven herself if he had been seriously wounded or killed while she was on duty. Damn the dream that had made it difficult for her to recognize Merlin when he alerted the first time.

It didn't take long for her to clean it up and it was only then she became aware of Bonnie wailing in the bedroom.

"The baby bag. What would he want from a bag left on my porch filled with stuff to take care of a baby?" he asked.

"We're about to find out." She set the cloth on the sink and then together they left the bathroom and went into the bedroom where the yellow tote bag was on the floor next to the chair.

"You get her," she said. "All the commotion has her upset."

He picked up Bonnie and she grabbed the tote bag and emptied it out on the bed. The first thing she did was check the tote itself. She carefully felt for anything that might be hidden in the lining.

"Nothing," she said and set it aside. She eyed everything that was on the bed. Bonnie had quieted in Anders's arms and Elle focused solely on the items that had been in the bag when Bonnie was left on the doorstep.

She scanned the items…onesies and diapers, an unopened can of formula, the knit hats and baby powder. She stopped at the container.

Was it possible the baby powder was really co-caine? A sense of horror filled her. How many times had she sprinkled a little bit on Bonnie? She breathed a sigh of relief as she tasted it. Thank goodness it wasn't cocaine, but rather just plain old baby powder.

"I can't imagine what's going on," Anders said.

"Me, neither. But that man badly wanted this tote bag."

"He has to be the person who broke in and searched the place. I'm pretty sure he's the same man who was in the living room on the night that Bonnie was left here. Although he had on a ski mask both times, the body shape and size were the same."

"I agree," she replied. She picked up each little outfit and checked it, then set it aside. Something was here…but what? She picked up a plastic rattle and shook it. Was it possible something was inside it that shouldn't be?

She set it on the floor and smashed it with her foot. She had to hit it three times before it split in half, revealing several little bird-shaped pieces of plastic inside, but nothing more.

Bonnie had fallen back asleep and Anders put her in the cradle and joined Elle by the side of the bed. He grabbed one of the onesies and checked the material.

"It would be helpful if we knew exactly what we were looking for," he said.

"I know, but there has to be something here for that man to go to so much trouble to get it. Maybe he is the Groom Killer and Demi left clues to his identity somewhere in here."

She was frustrated that she'd let the man get away. She should have run to the front door and let Merlin loose, but she'd been so worried about Anders's condition. She'd wanted to check on Anders immediately.

In her mind a clock was ticking. Tick. Tick. Tick. There was no question that the man could return at any time and he'd probably have more than a knife in his hand.

He'd broken in the front door. The next time he could come through the back door or a window. Now that he knew about Merlin, with a single gunshot he could take that threat out of the equation.

Her heart squeezed tight at the very thought of losing Merlin. Her fingers worked faster, desperate to find whatever the man had wanted, the thing that she was certain he'd return for.

There were three little knit hats. Elle had put the yellow one on Bonnie when they'd gone outside, but she hadn't touched the pink or white one since Bonnie had been left with them. She picked up the pink one first and as her fingers ran around the edge she felt something that wasn't soft yarn but instead hard.

"Bingo," she said softly.

"Did you find something?" Anders asked.

"I think so." The hat had a hemmed brim and she ripped out the stitching to get to the small, hard object. When it finally came free she looked at Anders in stunned surprise.

"What in the hell?" He gazed at the thumb drive she held in her fingers.

"We need to get this to the police station as soon as possible."

"Before we do that, we both need to get dressed," he replied.

For the first time since Merlin had alerted and she'd stepped out of her bedroom, she realized she was still in her silk nightie and Anders was clad only in a pair of black boxers.

"Meet me in the living room as soon as possible," she said. "We need to get out of here before that man comes back, and I have no doubt that he'll be back. Here, take this." She shoved several diapers into the tote bag and handed it to him. "You might want to take a bottle with us."

As he left the room, she grabbed a clean uniform out of the closet and dressed as quickly as she could. The internal clock inside her continued to tick a menacing rhythm. The guy could burst into the house at any moment. They had to get out of here before that happened.

The thumb drive went into her pocket. A glance at the clock on the nightstand indicated that it was just after one. Finn wouldn't be at the station, but she wouldn't hand off the thumb drive to anyone but him.

She called him and updated him again on what was going on. "We're leaving Anders's place now to bring in the thumb drive."

"I'll meet you at the station," he replied. "I've got a couple of men on the way there to check out the area."

"Good. We're leaving now."

With the call completed, she picked up Bonnie and then walked into the living room where Anders awaited her. "You take her," she said, and held the baby out to him.

"We'll take my car," he replied. "The baby seat is already in it and that will save us some time."

"Don't step out of that door until I tell you to." She pulled her gun and motioned for him to stand just behind her. It was possible the man was just waiting for them to step out of the cabin. She didn't want them to be ambushed. She threw open the door and in a crouched position she stepped out on the porch.

She narrowed her eyes and scanned the darkness,

looking for danger lurking in the shadows. She saw nothing and Merlin didn't alert, but she remained in the crouch as she motioned for Anders to step outside.

She didn't relax until Bonnie was buckled into her car seat and Anders was in the driver seat. She finally slid into the passenger seat. "Go...go," she said.

Anders took off and as they gained a little distance from the cabin, she released a sigh of relief. "I was afraid before we could get out of there he'd come back and he might possibly bring friends with him."

"I thought the same thing," Anders replied. "I wonder what's on that thumb drive."

"I can't imagine. If the baby is Demi's then maybe it has clues as to who the real Groom Killer is. It's possible the Groom Killer was standing in your living room." She frowned thoughtfully. "I should have shot him. Instead of telling Merlin to attack him, I should have just shot the man, but he was so close to you. I was afraid of somehow shooting you."

"Don't beat yourself up over it. We have the thumb drive and hopefully before too long we'll know what's on it," he replied. "We'll be at the police station in fifteen minutes."

He pulled out of the Double C Ranch property and onto the two-lane road that would take them into town. Thankfully Bonnie was once again asleep with Merlin next to her in the back seat.

Fifteen minutes and it would all be over. She held the answer to the break-ins in her pocket. There would be no more reason to remain at the cabin. There would be no more reason to stay with Anders and Bonnie.

Two patrol cars passed them, heading onto the Double C property. "If that creep is still hanging around, they'll find him and hopefully get him under arrest," she said.

"And that would be a good thing," he replied. They drove in a tense silence for several minutes.

"Uh-oh, it looks like we have company," Anders said as he looked in the rearview mirror.

She turned around in her seat to see a vehicle approaching fast. "Maybe it has nothing to do with us." Even as she said the words, she doubted them.

She watched as the vehicle drew closer and closer. She could now see that it was a pickup truck. She hoped it was just going to pass them. She hoped that up until the time the truck slammed into the back of their car.

Chapter 12

"Dammit," Anders exclaimed as he stepped on the gas. He tightened his grip on the steering wheel. A glance in the rearview mirror let him know that despite his increase in speed he wasn't gaining any distance from the truck.

"Brace yourself, he's going to hit us again." He barely got the words out of his mouth when the impact occurred. Even though he thought he was prepared for it, the steering wheel spun and the car veered first to the right and then to the left before he managed to regain control.

Bonnie began to wail, a torturous sound in the

nightmare situation. Despite the coolness of the night a trickle of sweat worked down his back. The truck obviously had more horsepower than his car and the road was dark and narrow, making it even more dangerous to go too fast.

He glanced over at Elle. Lit by the dashboard illumination, her face was pale and her features were taut. She had to be afraid and he hated that.

He was supposed to protect those he loved and it didn't matter that Elle didn't love him back. It didn't matter whether Bonnie was his or not. Nothing mattered more than getting them to the police station where they would be safe.

The truck hit him again, this time spinning the car around by forty-five degrees. Elle screamed as he tried to correct. If he lost complete control they would wind up in a ditch or hitting one of the many trees that lined the street.

He took his foot off the gas and fought to gain control, his heart crashing against his ribs. He finally got the car straightened out and he once again stepped on the gas.

Elle rolled down her window and stuck her head out. "Come on, you bastard," she yelled as she pointed her gun behind them.

The truck came closer as if to meet her challenge.

She fired her gun at the truck. Once…twice and then a third time.

"Dammit, if I can just hit his windshield or blow out one of his tires then that might slow him down." She yelled to be heard over Bonnie's wails.

"We're only a mile or two from town. Surely he'll back off then," he replied.

But he didn't back off and the defensive driving Anders was doing made it near impossible for Elle to get off a shot that might count.

They reached the town proper and Anders ignored the speed limit. He ran red lights with the truck hot on their tail. It was only when Anders screeched to a halt in front of the police station that the truck sped on and quickly disappeared around a corner and out of sight.

"Do you really think he's gone?" Anders asked.

"He could have just turned the corner and gotten out of his truck. We can't be sure he doesn't have a gun. Just sit tight." She got out of the car and quickly came around to Anders's door, her gun leading the way.

He rolled down his window. "Get out and get Bonnie," she instructed. She moved aside so he could open his door. She didn't look at him, but rather kept her narrowed gaze shooting around the landscape.

It was at that moment he realized he trusted her completely, not just as the woman he loved, but also as a competent officer of the law. When he opened the back door Merlin jumped out and stood at Elle's side, a second sentry on duty.

He reached in and unfastened Bonnie from the car seat. "Shhh, it's all right," he said as he straightened with her and the tote bag in his arms.

"Get into the building as quickly as you can," Elle said.

He complied. He raced for the building with Elle just behind him. They flew through the front door where Finn was waiting for them.

"Problems?" he asked.

"You might say that," Elle replied and holstered her gun. "A truck chased us all the way here and slammed into our car over and over again. He was obviously trying to stop us from getting here."

Finn frowned. "I'll get some men to watch the street in front." He stepped away from them and got on his phone.

"Here it is," Elle said when he was finished. She reached into her pocket and withdrew the thumb drive.

Thankfully Bonnie had stopped crying, although she was awake and wide-eyed in Anders's arms.

"I called in Katie in case we need her," Finn said.

"Who is Katie?" Anders asked.

"Katie Parsons, tech whiz extraordinaire," Elle replied.

"She's waiting for us in her office," Finn replied. He turned and started down the hallway and Anders, Elle and Merlin followed.

They entered an office that had television screens and computer monitors on the wall. Behind the large desk sat an attractive young woman with shoulder-length dark hair sporting bright pink streaks.

"Hey, Katie," Elle greeted her. "Love the pink. Wasn't it blue last week?"

Katie grinned. "And next week who knows what it will be. Now, what do you have for me?" She looked at them eagerly.

Finn handed her the thumb drive. They all watched as she put it into her computer and the screen lit up with what looked like gobbledygook.

A fierce disappointment roared through Anders. Had they just nearly been killed for a thumb drive that was corrupted and of no use to anyone?

"It's encrypted?" Finn asked.

"Yes, but have no fear, Katie is here," she replied confidently. "And this encryption is an easy one to break. Just give me a couple of minutes."

While she worked, they told Finn about the evening's drama. "If Elle hadn't been there, I believe the intruder would have killed me to get to the baby bag," Anders said. "Elle saved my life." He looked at her with all his admiration.

Her cheeks dusted with color. "You would have managed to take care of things all by yourself. Besides, it wasn't me who made the bad guy turn and run, it was Merlin." She reached down to pat the dog's head.

"I'm just glad you all got here safely with whatever is on that thumb drive," Finn said.

"Dates," Katie said, drawing all their attention back to her computer screen. "It looks like it's dates of weapon shipments with the price next to each one."

"It's got to be about the Larson twins," Elle said, her features lit up with excitement.

"But we checked their warehouse on the night of the surveillance detail and there was nothing inside," Finn said.

"So that was a night a shipment didn't come in. I still believe it has something to do with those twins and their criminal activities," Elle replied.

"There's a name here, too," Katie said. "Donald Blakeman. The fool actually put his name on the file."

Anders frowned. "That name sounds really familiar to me. I think he might have worked for me for a couple of weeks late last year."

"Katie, pull up everything you can about the man. We'll be in my office. Bring whatever you find to me," Finn said. He motioned for the others to follow him.

Once inside Finn's office, he motioned them to the chairs that sat in front of his desk. "I didn't get a chance to let you know that the DNA results came in late this afternoon." He picked up an envelope from the desk and held it out to Anders.

For a long moment Anders merely stared at the envelope, afraid to look at it and afraid not to. He finally took the envelope from Finn, his heart suddenly pounding with an anxious rhythm. Inside was the answer as to whether Bonnie was his or not.

The warmth of her little body in his arms, the powder-sweet scent that wafted from her, shot an arrow straight to his heart. He wanted her to be his. Oh God, he wanted it so badly. Despite his desire to the contrary, the little girl had his heart.

Elle placed a hand on his arm as if she knew the tumultuous emotions that raced through him and wanted to support him no matter what.

Still he paused. He was scared to open it, yet excited at the same time. He didn't care who Bonnie's mother was, but he so desperately wanted to be her father.

The envelope burned in his fingers and he was acutely aware of both Finn and Elle waiting for him to open it.

He didn't look at either of them as he slowly slid a finger to unseal the envelope. Once again Elle reached out and lightly touched his arm.

He gave her a grateful smile and then opened the envelope.

His fingers trembled so hard for a moment it was difficult to read the contents. He scanned down the sheet to get to the probability issue. His heart crashed to the floor. Anders Colton had zero percent probability of being infant Bonnie's father.

Zero percent. There could be no mistake with zero percent. "She isn't mine," he managed to say despite the tight grief that pressed against his chest. He looked down into her sleeping face and his eyes misted.

"Oh Anders, I'm so sorry," Elle said, and squeezed his arm tightly. He looked at her and saw his pain reflected in the depths of her eyes. How could she profess not to love him when she gazed at him that way?

He tightened his arms around Bonnie. Now both the females who had been in his cabin, in the depths of his heart, would be gone. "So, what happens to her now?" he asked Finn, his voice tight with the grief that still swept through him.

"The odds just got better that she belongs to Demi," Finn said.

"And Bo." Anders looked at Elle. "I really hope she's Bo's baby." He meant it. He knew Elle would love to have a piece of her murdered brother in her life. Now that he knew for sure Bonnie wasn't his, he wanted her to be Demi and Bo's, for Elle's sake.

"What I'd like is to keep her at your place for a little while longer," Finn said. "And Elle, I'd like you to remain at Anders's place, too. I can't help but believe that if the baby is Demi's, Demi will be back. We ran an additional DNA test on the baby and DNA extracted from a toothbrush that belonged to Demi. We're still waiting for those results to come back."

"I can't imagine who else she would belong to," Anders said. "The note that was pinned to her said she was a Colton."

"What I can't figure out is how Demi got hold of that thumb drive that I'm sure relates to the Larson twins," Elle said.

Before she could say anything more, Katie appeared in the doorway, a sheath of papers in her hand. "Donald Blakeman is forty-two years old and lives at 1201 East Twelfth Street. He bought the house four months ago with cash and lists his job as an entrepreneur."

She handed them each a picture of him. "I also printed out a layout of his house."

Anders stared at the photo. Donald Blakeman looked like the unpleasant man he was. There was a cold flatness to his dark eyes and his mouth looked like it had never known a smile. "I don't know what he's doing now, but last year around Christmas time he worked for me and lived in the bunk barn."

"He doesn't look like an entrepreneur to me. He looks like a thug," Elle said. "I hope somebody can identify him as one of the Larson boys' thugs."

"He definitely fits the build of the man who hit me over the head," Anders said. He looked at Elle, who nodded in agreement.

Before anyone could say anything else Carson and an officer Anders didn't know flew into the room. "Sorry if we're late, Chief," Carson said.

"Actually, your timing is perfect," Finn replied.

"Why didn't you contact me?" Carson said to Elle. "Why didn't you call me the minute you were in trouble? I heard about your dangerous race to get here. Jeez, Elle, you could have been killed."

"I handled it," Elle replied with a hint of coolness in her voice.

"Carson, she handled it," Finn echoed firmly. Elle looked at Finn gratefully. He handed Carson the photo of Blakeman. "We need to get this man under arrest as soon as possible. He probably guesses we now have the evidence he was willing to kill for and that makes him a flight risk."

"Let me go with them," Elle said.

Although Anders wanted to protest, he kept his mouth shut. This was what Elle did. She had gotten him and Bonnie safely out of the cabin and to the police station and he knew she could handle whatever she needed to. Besides, it was bad enough that Carson had undermined her with his comments.

Finn looked at Elle thoughtfully. "I think your brother and Officer Jones can handle it."

"It wouldn't hurt to have me there, too." Elle held Finn's gaze and leaned forward in the chair. "Come on, Chief. I really want this. I've earned this."

Carson visibly stiffened, obviously not wanting Elle along, but not willing to say anything more.

"Okay, go," Finn replied. "All of you get out of here. Katie will fill you in on anything else you need to know."

"Elle, be safe," he said.

"Always," she replied with one of her smiles that warmed his heart. And then she was gone.

Anders stood, unsure what he was supposed to do. "Elle's patrol car is still at my cabin. Would it be a problem if I just hung around here until they get back?" he asked Finn.

"Not a problem at all," Finn replied, and also stood. "In fact, I'd prefer you stay here until Elle can go back to the cabin with you. Until Blakeman is in custody I don't know whether or not you might be in danger. We have no idea how crazy he is, and he might go after you for some sort of twisted revenge."

He motioned Anders out of his office. "You can

relax in the break room. Do you have everything you need for the baby?"

"Yeah, thank goodness we grabbed a bottle and a few diapers before we left," Anders replied.

"It was decided to leave Merlin here. Do you mind if he joins you? He's obviously comfortable with you and he'll just be sad if nobody is around him." Finn led him to a small room with a round table, a vending machine, a sink and microwave, and two cots.

"I'd love to have Merlin here with us," he replied.

Finn disappeared for a moment and then returned with the dog at his heels. Merlin walked over to Anders's side and sat.

"You should be fine here," Finn said.

"We will be, thanks," Anders replied, but it was a lie. He hated that Elle was without her partner, and he wouldn't be fine until she was back safe and sound.

Elle sat in the back seat of her brother's patrol car, adrenaline pumping through her. She wanted Blakeman under arrest so badly she could taste it.

Not only had he chased them through the night, but he'd also whacked Anders over the head. Anders could have been killed. They all could have been killed on the race to get to the station.

The bigger picture was that Blakeman could be the key to taking down the Larson twins' empire. If they could get him to roll over on them, then they could potentially have what they needed to put the two behind bars where they belonged.

Finn had managed to get them a search warrant and now Officer Roger Jones sat in the passenger seat using his utility flashlight to look at Blakeman's house plans.

"It's a typical ranch house with a front door and a back door," Roger said.

"He didn't display a firearm to us, but I imagine he has them in his house," Elle said. "And even though it's the middle of the night we know he's awake, because I'm certain he's the man who chased us to the station."

"Let's just hope he hasn't managed to get out of town yet," Carson replied.

"I'm sure he overestimated the time it would take us to read the thumb drive," Elle replied. "He didn't know for sure that we found it and just how smart our Katie is."

"There's no way we can go in quiet and slow on this," Roger said. "I think we need to go in hard and fast."

"I've got some flash-bangs in my trunk," Carson replied.

The flash-bang grenades blinded a person for

about five seconds. The loud noise disturbed the fluid in the ears, keeping the person unable to hear and with a loss of balance.

"I know where I'd like to lodge a flash-bang," Elle said drily. "I wouldn't mind if Blackman lit up from the inside out."

Carson bit back a small laugh. "I didn't know my sister could think such things." His laughter halted as they parked down the street from Blakeman's address.

"Okay, so here's the plan. Roger and I will breach the front door and throw in a flash-bang. After it's delivered, we'll rush inside. If he manages to get to his garage, we'll hear the door go up and can stop him there. Elle, I want you at the back door to make sure he doesn't escape that way."

She wanted to protest her brother's plan. She wanted to go in the front door, she wanted to prove herself once and for all, but she kept her mouth shut. She knew she was only here because of Finn's capitulation and was to play a supportive role for the other two more experienced officers. Part of being a good cop was being a team player.

They got out of the car and Carson opened his trunk to retrieve not only the flash-bangs, but also the tools they would need to breach the door. Finally he handed them each a set of ear protection that would protect them from the noise of the flash-bangs.

"Keep in mind, if he's home, it's possible he won't be alone," Elle warned them. "If he has anything to do with the Larson twins, then he probably has a lot of thug friends."

Carson nodded, a nearby streetlamp shining on his taut, serious features. "Okay, so we go in silent. We breach the front door and I throw in a flash-bang. Elle, when you see the flash, you'll know we're inside. Watch that back door closely because if there's a possibility for his escape, that's where he'll go." He looked at Elle and then at Roger. "Are we ready?"

They both nodded and then they were off, moving like silent shadows in the night. All the other houses on the street were shrouded in darkness, but when they grew closer to Blakeman's place, lights blazed out of his windows.

Her blood ran cold as she saw the pickup truck in the driveway…a pickup truck displaying a lot of front-end damage. It was definitely the truck that had rammed into them several times. So the bastard was home. He probably thought he had plenty of time to pack and get out of town before they could find what he'd wanted in that baby bag and decipher the code on the thumb drive.

When they reached the side of his house, Elle

went around to the back door and got into position. If Blakeman came out this door, she would do everything in her power to stop him.

In an instant the thought of Anders filled her head. His voice had cracked when he'd read the paternity results and her heart had nearly broken with his pain. It was surprising for her to realize that if given a real choice, she would have preferred that Bonnie be his rather than Bo's. That made two little girls he'd been cheated out of.

I know Anders, and when he loves, he loves hard. Valeria's words echoed in her mind. And Elle had walked away from his love.

She shook her head. She had no time for such thoughts. She had to stay solely focused on the task at hand. She couldn't allow herself to get distracted by Anders's profession of love for her.

She heard a *bang* and the splintering of wood, indicating Carson and Roger had successfully broken down the front door.

She turned her face from the window as a bright white light bathed the backyard. The *boom* that followed seemed to shake the very ground beneath her feet. Elle yanked off her ear protection.

"Red Ridge Police. Halt," Carson shouted from someplace inside the house.

Elle tensed. She stood right in front of the back

door, her gun steady in her hand. This time she wouldn't hesitate to shoot first and ask questions later. She should have done that after he'd attacked Anders.

"Blakeman, stop," Roger's voice rang out.

At that moment the back door flew open. Donald Blakeman stood before her, his eyes blazing with an angry desperation, a gun in his hand. "Stop or I'll shoot," she said.

In an instant his gaze shot around, as if looking for Merlin, and then he exploded out the door. Elle wanted to shoot him straight through his black heart, but she was aware that he was just a piece to a bigger puzzle. She didn't want him dead; dead men couldn't rat out their cohorts. When he turned, his gun pointed in her direction, she aimed at his leg and squeezed off a shot.

He howled and fell to the ground, the gun skittering beside him. Elle didn't hesitate; she ran toward him and kicked the weapon out of his reach before he could grab it.

Immediately Carson and Roger were at the back door. "Elle," Carson said in relief as Roger ran to Blakeman's side.

"Good work, sis." Carson threw an arm around her shoulder. "I'd take you as my backup partner anytime."

Those words warmed her heart as Blakeman was

loaded up into the back of an ambulance. Carson rode with him. She was called back into the station and Roger remained at the house, where he would be joined with other officers to process the scene.

When she reached the station Finn was waiting for her. He took her into his office, where she gave him a verbal report of what had occurred.

"This was your first time shooting a suspect. How do you feel?" Finn asked.

"I feel fine," she replied. "I did what I had to do. I just did my job."

Finn looked at her for a long moment and then nodded. "If you have any problems with it, you let me know. Now, get out of here and get back to Anders's cabin. Anders and the baby and Merlin are all in the break room waiting for you. I'm hoping we're on a little bit of a roll here and when Demi comes back for that baby you'll be able to arrest her."

She left his office and walked down the hallway to the break room door, which was closed. She opened it quietly and her heart expanded at the sight that greeted her.

Anders was asleep on one of the cots with Bonnie in his arms. Merlin lay on the floor next to them and his tail began to wag at the sight of her.

How was she supposed to continue living at the cabin with Anders after all that had happened between them? She supposed she could have argued with Finn and told him there was absolutely no danger posed to anyone and it was time for her to quit the assignment.

But Bonnie and Demi were the wild cards and Finn was right. There was still a possibility Demi would return for her baby. Elle was just going to have to suck it up and do her job.

For several long moments she remained just inside the door, staring at the sleeping man who had stolen her traitorous heart. She loved his strong jawline and the sensual lips that kissed her with such passion. Her fingers itched to caress his features, to memorize them for the time she had to really say goodbye to him.

She suddenly realized his eyes were open and he stared back at her. "I'm back," she said.

Anders sat up carefully so as not to disturb Bonnie. "Did you get him?"

"We did. He's going away for a very long time after he gets out of the hospital."

Anders raised an eyebrow. "The hospital?"

"Yeah, I had to shoot the bastard in the leg."

He grinned at her, that slow, sexy smile that always shot straight through her to the center of her heart. "Are you ready to go home?" she asked a bit curtly.

"We're all more than ready to get home."

As he drove them back to the cabin she told him about what had transpired at Blakeman's house. Dawn's light peeked over the horizon as they arrived back at the cabin.

"I'm glad you shot him," Anders said ten minutes later when they were in the living room. "This was my favorite desk lamp." He picked up the mangled light from the floor. "He needed to be shot for ruining it."

"Just thank goodness he didn't hit you any harder than he did," she replied.

Only now could she fully process the horror of that moment when she'd walked out of the bedroom and seen him covered in blood with a man wielding a knife standing over him.

What she wanted to do more than anything now was to stand in his arms, feel the warmth of his embrace and assure herself that he was really okay. He'd not only suffered a blow to the head, but also a blow to his heart in finding out Bonnie wasn't his. She'd seen the aching sadness that had radiated from his eyes when he'd read the DNA results.

"I need to get some sleep," she said. What she really needed was some distance from him right now. She'd be strong again after she got some rest, but at the moment she was tired and felt incredibly vulnerable.

"I'll keep Bonnie with me," he said. He smiled. "You worked all night and I didn't."

She didn't argue with him. Now that the drama was finally over, she was completely exhausted. "I'll see you in a couple of hours," she said, and then without waiting for a reply she went into her bedroom with Merlin following close behind.

Minutes later she was in bed with tears pressing close against her eyelids. Why did she feel like crying now? She'd performed in her job well and one big mystery had been solved. She should be celebrating.

But celebrating wasn't any fun all alone. At the end of a long day it was always great to come home to somebody who could share in both the celebrations and the disappointments.

Anders could be that man. This cabin could be her home. So why was she so afraid to reach out for that happiness? It was a question that haunted her until she fell asleep.

Chapter 13

It was just after noon when Elle came out of the bedroom. She was clad in her uniform and her face was utterly devoid of expression. "I got a call from Finn. There's a woman at the station claiming to be Bonnie's mother."

Anders pulled himself up from the floor where he had been playing with the little girl. "Who is it?"

"Finn didn't give me any further details, but I think it's safe to say it isn't Demi. I guess we need to pack up the tote bag."

A surge of unexpected grief shot through him. A shaky laugh escaped him. "Even knowing she isn't mine, the idea of giving her up to anyone still breaks my heart."

Elle's features softened. "I know, I feel the same way about her."

"I feel like there's about to be a death in the family and there's no way I can stop it." God, he couldn't believe how emotional he was being. The big, strong ranch foreman felt like crying over a little girl.

To his surprise Elle walked over to him and pulled him into a hug. He wrapped his arms around her and clung to her with a desperation he'd never known before. He wasn't just losing Bonnie, but with the baby gone he would also lose Elle. There would be no more time to convince her they belonged together.

He breathed in Elle's scent in an attempt to staunch the cold wind of despair that blew through him. His home had been filled with joy with Bonnie and Elle in it, and now they would be gone and he didn't know if he would ever know such happiness again.

He released her and stepped back, because holding her another minute was just too painful. "I'll go get the tote bag," he said. He went into his bedroom where he drew several deep breaths to get his emotions under control.

As he picked up the tote bag from the chair, questions roared through his head. Did he know Bonnie's mother? If he did, then why hadn't she knocked on the door and asked for his help? If he didn't know her then why had she chosen to leave her baby on his doorstep? What about the note that proclaimed her a Colton?

And how long would it take him to forget how much he loved Bonnie? How long before he forgot how much he loved Elle? He didn't have the answers and in any case he needed to pull himself together for the trip to the police station.

When he went back into the living room Bonnie was in her cradle and all the items that had come with her were neatly piled on the sofa.

He didn't look at Elle as he packed the things into the tote bag. "At least we'll finally have some answers," he said. For a long moment he gazed at Bonnie and she released a string of babble and then smiled. He looked away.

"We'll take my car," Elle said. "We can move the baby seat when we get outside."

"Are you afraid to drive with me after last night?" It was a feeble attempt at humor.

She smiled. "I can't think of anyone I'd rather have been at the wheel last night than you. You stayed calm and in control and that's the only thing that kept us on the road." Her smile faded. "We should get going."

She picked Bonnie up in her arms and it was at that moment he realized what this new twist meant for her. "Elle…if this woman at the police station is really her mother then that means…"

"That Bo isn't her father," she said.

"I'm so sorry. I really wanted that for you."

"It's all right. It just means this baby isn't Bo's, but someplace out there is Demi's baby and we know Bo is that baby's father. If fate puts that baby in my life somehow, someway, it would be wonderful. If fate isn't so kind, then I just have to be okay with that."

The inner strength that shone from her eyes awed him. He only hoped he could be as strong when it came time to hand Bonnie over to somebody else.

Minutes later they were in her patrol car and headed into town. "I'm sorry about your car," she said. "The back end of it is pretty smashed up."

"Thank God for insurance," he replied. "And thank goodness it was just my ranch car and not the fancy pickup truck I keep in the shed."

"At least it's beautiful day," she said.

A beautiful day for heartache, he thought. "I just can't imagine who the mother might be. The note said she was a Colton, but if she isn't mine and she isn't Demi's, then how can she be a Colton?"

"Do you have any cousins who were pregnant?"

"Not that I'm aware of, and in any case why would they leave her with me?"

"I guess we'll have some answers in a few minutes."

"I'm not handing her over to just anyone," he said. "What if the woman is some kind of kook who heard about Bonnie and just decided to claim her?"

"I'm sure Finn won't let that happen."

They fell silent for the rest of the ride. Anders stared out the passenger window and wondered when exactly he'd fallen in love with Bonnie. Was it the first time she'd smiled at him, or was it on that very first night when she'd cried and then had found comfort in his rocking arms?

It really didn't matter when it had happened. He just had to steel himself for her absence in his life. When they arrived at the police station and Elle had parked the car, he had her hold the little girl while he removed the car seat.

"We won't be needing this anymore and maybe the mother will be able to use it," he said.

They went straight to Finn's office where he was waiting for them. He rose from the desk as they entered. "I have the mother in the break room. Her name is Annie King."

Anders frowned. "That name sounds vaguely familiar."

"She was Donald Blakeman's girlfriend."

Memories clicked into place in Anders's head. She had lived with Donald in the bunk barn for the short period of time Donald had worked for him. Anders remembered her as a small, timid woman.

"I know you have a lot of questions for her and we're running a DNA test as we speak. I leaned on the lab and called in a few favors so I'm hoping to get the results within the next hour or so," Finn said.

"Then I guess it's time to talk to Annie," Elle said.

They all walked to the break room and the minute Elle walked in with the baby, the woman seated on the cot jumped up and began to cry.

"My baby, my sweet baby Angelina." She held out her arms to Elle. "Please, can I hold her?"

Elle hesitated a moment and then handed Bonnie to Annie. The petite strawberry blonde woman sat back on the cot. She smelled Bonnie's head and then stroked trembling fingers down Bonnie's cheek.

Elle and Anders sat at the small table and Finn excused himself and left the room. "Is it true?" Annie looked at Elle. "Is it true that you shot Donald?"

Elle nodded and her eyes turned wary. "It's true. I shot him in his leg."

"Thank you," Annie said fervently. "Is it also true that he's going to prison for a long time?"

"He's facing a lot of charges that will keep him locked up for a very long time," Elle replied.

"Good. He was an evil man. He beat me. He hurt me a lot, but I could never get the strength or the courage to leave him. Not until Angelina was born." She looked down at the baby who was asleep in her arms. "She gave me the strength I needed to get away."

"How and why did you end up at my place?" Anders asked.

"I don't have family in this area and Donald didn't let me have any friends. The day before he was going to pick me up at the hospital, I left. A kind nurse gave me some money to get a taxi and I had him drop us off at the Double C Ranch. I just needed time to figure out how I could get to my family in Montana. The hospital gave me extra diapers and formula and so I holed up in the old shed down by the stables."

She released a deep sigh and then continued, "I stayed well-hidden each time any police came to do a sweep of the area or any of the ranch hands were around, but it was difficult."

Once again she looked down at the baby and then back at Anders. "I tried to keep her with me and I'm ashamed to say I stole food from you, but after keeping her with me in the shed for ten days, I realized I needed help. She needed more than I could do for her. I realized I couldn't keep her with me any longer." Tears once again filled her eyes. "And that's when I left her on your doorstep. When I was at the ranch everyone spoke of how kind you were and I left that note on her hoping that would assure you'd take good care of her until I could come back for her."

Anders didn't need a DNA test to tell him she was Bonnie's mother. It all made sense now. His "Needy Thief" had been an abused mother trying to survive all on her own. Besides, her love for the baby was evident in the way she touched Bonnie, in the way she looked at her.

"What about my grandmother's quilt? Did you take that?" he asked.

She nodded her head. "It's in the shed. I didn't ruin it or anything like that. I just used it to cover us up at night when it was cold. I'm so sorry, Mr. Colton. I'm so very sorry."

"There's no reason to apologize for doing what you needed to do for your baby," he replied. Finn quietly reentered the room and stood silently next to the door.

"So, what are your plans now?" Elle asked.

"Since Donald is in jail now I can get a job and earn the money to get me to my sister's home." Once again tears glistened in her pale blue eyes. "I need to be with my family. We'll have love and support there."

"You aren't going to work a job here in Red

Ridge," Anders said. "I'll personally see to it that you get to your sister's home as soon as possible."

"Oh, Mr. Colton, I can't let you do that for me," Annie replied.

"I'm not doing it for you," he replied, the tight press of emotions back in his chest. "I'm doing it for Bon... Angelina. I'm crazy about that baby and I don't want you struggling to work a job and handing her off to babysitters. I'll pay for the transportation to a place where both of you will have support and love." Annie began to quietly weep.

"The test result is back," Finn said. "This woman is the baby's mother."

"Then we're done here," Anders said. He looked at Finn. "Could you see to her travel arrangements and let me know what the cost is?"

"Of course," Finn replied.

Anders and Elle stood. Anders walked over to Annie. "Could I hold her one last time?"

Annie stood and placed Bonnie in his awaiting arms. He knew he was torturing himself, but he wanted to smell her baby sweetness one last time. He needed to see her pretty little face once more and hold her against his chest.

She had brought such happiness, such joy into his life, but more than that she had given him a new wisdom about love. She had taught him about leaving old pains behind to keep the heart open to loving again.

He turned to Elle, to see if she wanted to say a personal goodbye, but she shook her head. "No, I'm good." But he saw the pain in her dark eyes and knew she was grieving the loss of Bonnie as well. In spite of their wishes to the contrary, Bonnie had gotten deep into their hearts.

He kissed Bonnie's little cheek and then handed her back to Annie. Suddenly his emotions were too big for this little room. He walked out into the hallway and fought against tears.

Jeez, he was a rough and tough cowboy. He could wrestle steers and ride broncos, but losing one itty-bitty little girl had brought him to his knees.

Elle came out of the room and placed a hand on his arm. She didn't say anything, but it was an offer of support that calmed the screaming grief inside him.

And now he had to prepare himself for saying goodbye to Elle, and that was going to be the most painful blow of all.

"I can't believe you didn't want to hold her one last time," Anders said to Elle when they were on their way back to the cabin.

"It would have been too painful," she replied. "It's

best when you're saying goodbye to somebody to just turn and leave without prolonging the agony."

And that's exactly what she intended to do with Anders. Before they had left the station Finn told her the case had been solved and he expected her at work the next morning for her usual shift.

She wanted to go inside the cabin, pack her bags and leave without any crazy emotions getting in the way. It was bad enough some of those crazy emotions were already working inside her.

"You know, I thought I loved my job because of the adrenaline rush of potential danger," she said thoughtfully. "I thought it was just about getting bad guys off the streets, but it's so much more than that. Last night we put away a bad guy, but more importantly we made it possible for an abused woman to live a better life. That's the real payoff. And what you did for Annie in paying her way to go to her sister's house was wonderfully generous."

She glanced over at him. He'd never looked as handsome as he did now just minutes before she told him goodbye. He'd never know how much he'd touched her heart when he told Annie he'd get her to her sister's home...to safety and security.

"I've got more money than I know what to do with. Hopefully with Annie going to her sister's place she can heal from whatever wounds Donald left behind and Bonnie—Angelina, I mean—will get the future she deserves."

"Even so, it was a really nice thing to do." She pulled up next to his car and they got out. Merlin bounded up to the front door as if he belonged inside.

"How about I put on a pot of coffee while you pack," Anders said as they entered the cabin. "Surely you have time to enjoy a cup of coffee before you take off."

"Okay," she agreed. This was going to be more difficult that she'd thought. She'd had it in her mind that she would pack quickly and leave before her brain could really process it.

She'd hoped not to feel anything when she left here. Her heart was already bruised by having to say goodbye to Bonnie and if she really thought about saying goodbye to Anders, she feared she'd completely break down.

She hurried into her bedroom and began shoving clothes into the duffel bag. He was just a one-night stand, nothing more. That's what she told herself as she folded up the sweatpants she'd worn on the night they'd made love.

He was a Colton and she was a Gage. For that reason alone they shouldn't be together. But hadn't two of her brothers and her sister shot that notion to high heaven? Carson, Vincent and Danica had fallen madly in love with Coltons. She smiled. Coltons and Gages weren't supposed to mix, but the new generation hadn't gotten the memo.

The scent of fresh-brewed coffee filled the air. She thought of all the mornings she'd awakened to that scent, all the mornings when she'd shared breakfast with him. And all those afternoons when she so looked forward to him returning to the cabin.

She steeled her heart and went into the bathroom to retrieve her toiletries. With everything packed up, she carried her duffel bag out of the bedroom and dropped it by the front door.

Anders was waiting for her in the kitchen. He sat at the table with Merlin at his feet. He stood as she entered the room. "Merlin and I were just having a nice conversation," he said. He gestured her to sit while he turned to the cabinet to pour the coffee.

She didn't sit. "Anders, I can't," she said as he turned back to face her with the two coffee cups in his hands.

He set the cups on the table. "You can't what?"

"I can't just sit here and have a goodbye cup of coffee with you. It would be like holding Bonnie one last time. It's just too painful."

He took a step toward her, his expression as serious as she'd ever seen it. "Why is it too painful?"

"It just is." She couldn't meet his gaze.

He took another step toward her. "I need to know why it's painful for you, Elle. If you don't have any feelings for me, then enjoying a last cup of coffee before you leave shouldn't be that difficult."

"But I do have feelings for you," she protested. "I care about you, Anders. I think you're a wonderful man."

"But you don't love me." His blue eyes held her gaze intently. "Tell me again that you don't love me, Elle."

It was as if he were sucking all the oxygen out of the room. Crazy, wild emotions pressed tight against her chest, making it difficult for her to draw a breath.

He took two more steps, bringing him so close to her she could smell the scent of him and see the bright blue irises of his eyes. She knew she needed to back away from him, but her legs refused to obey her faint mental command.

Before she saw it coming, he wrapped her in his arms and his lips crashed down on hers. The kiss tasted of something wild and wonderful, and she found herself responding with a desperate need of her own.

When the kiss ended, he dropped his arms to his sides, but didn't step away from her. "Tell me now, Elle. Tell me that you don't love me." His voice was low and filled with emotion.

It was finally she who stepped away. "Goodbye, Anders," she said, and then turned around and headed for the front door.

"You're a fool, Elle. Why can't you see we belong together?" he called after her, a touch of anger in his tone. "I would love you like no other man could ever love you. Why would you run away from that?"

She picked up her duffel bag and opened the door. "Let's go, Merlin." She needed to escape. Too much pain roared through her.

She loaded Merlin in the back seat and then got into the car. Thankfully, Anders hadn't chased her outside. She started the car but instead of putting it into gear and driving away, she remained there as tears blurred her vision.

What she'd had with Frank couldn't begin to compete with what she had with Anders. And the aching, stabbing pain that possessed her now was a pain she'd never, ever felt before.

She'd thought she could have a one-night stand with him and just walk away without her emotions involved. She'd been so wrong. She swiped at the tears with the back of her hand.

Merlin released a sad moan. He never liked it when she cried. She knew if she were on the floor he'd crawl right up in her lap and try to cheer her up.

She calmed down a bit and stared at the cabin.

A pain still hitched in her chest and with a sudden clarity she realized it was a self-inflicted wound.

Why was she leaving a man who had told her he'd love her like no other man ever would? Why was she running away from a man who had brought her such happiness?

She couldn't even blame it on his being a Colton and her being a Gage. Her own siblings had taken care of that. Anyway, she'd never care what his name was; she only cared what kind of a man he was.

He was handsome and a hard worker. He was kind and had a soft heart. He was also intelligent and funny and everything else she would ever want in a man.

So why was she running?

Was she enough for him? That was the question that kept her in the car, poised to drive away. She now knew she was good enough as a police officer.

And dammit, she was good enough to be the woman in Anders's life. She was good enough to be his wife and a cop. She could have it all…a husband, a career and children. So why on earth was she running away from love instead of toward it?

Because she was a stupid fool. She'd be a fool to run away from happiness. And her mama didn't raise no fool.

A burden suddenly lifted from her heart. The pain

fell away and she was left with only her love for Anders filling her heart, her very soul.

She shut off the car engine. "Merlin, I'm going to go get my man." Merlin barked as if in agreement.

She got out of the car and let Merlin out of the back seat. He beat her to the front door. She followed him through the living room and into the kitchen, where Anders sat at the kitchen table.

"Forget something?" he asked. His eyes looked so sad.

"Yes, I forgot to tell you that I'll love you like no other woman will ever love you," she replied.

Her body nearly vibrated from the emotions that raced through her. "Anders, I don't want to leave. I want to stay here with you forever."

His eyes filled with a love so great it washed over her like a warm summer breeze. He got to his feet. "Are you sure, Elle?" he asked softly.

"I've never been so sure of anything in my entire life, and if you don't come around that table and take me in your arms, I'm going to have to shoot you."

He laughed, that rich, deep laughter she loved to hear. He hurried toward her and when he reached her, he pulled her into an embrace that nearly stole her breath away.

"I love you, Elle. I'll spend the rest of my life making you happy." His gaze bored into hers.

"And I love you, Anders, and I'll spend the rest of my life making you happy," she replied.

His lips took hers in a kiss that tasted of love and commitment, of tenderness and desire. When the kiss ended she placed her hands on either side of his face.

"I know that with your love and support I can have it all. I can have my life here with you, and my career, and eventually I can give you a baby girl that nobody will be able to take away from you."

He covered her hands with his and smiled. "A little boy might be nice, too."

"Yes, a little boy might be nice," she said with a laugh. "But we already have a little boy." She looked down at Merlin, who was dancing around their feet. She gazed back up at the man who held her heart. "We're going to be so happy, Anders."

"As long as you're in my life, I'm a happy man." He gazed at her for a long moment. "What made you decide to come back inside?"

She dropped her hands to her sides and his went to her waist. "I realized I loved you more than I feared my own inadequacies." She raised her chin. "I am enough. I deserve you and love and happiness."

"You deserve all the happiness in the world." He lowered his lips to hers once again and this time his lips tasted of not just love, but also of future and forever.

Epilogue

Elle walked down the hall toward the locker rooms with a spring in her step and Merlin at her side. The Groom Killer was still a mystery, Demi Colton continued to be on the run, and the Larson twins persisted with their suspected illegal activity. But none of that could stop the happiness that soared through her knowing that within a half an hour or so she'd be home with Anders.

It had been five days since she'd gone back into that cabin to claim her man, and those days and nights had been more than wonderful. She was certain she was where she was supposed to be, in that cabin and with Anders Colton.

She entered the locker room to find Juliette Walsh there as well. "Hey, I was looking for you earlier," she said to her friend and fellow officer.

"I've been wanting to catch up with you, too. I've heard the craziest rumors about you...like you've fallen in love with Anders Colton and you're moving in with him."

"Not a rumor," Elle replied with a smile. "It's all true."

Juliette grinned. "You go, girl." She sat on the bench in front of the lockers. "I also heard about your harrowing ride here with a thumb drive that might bring down the Larson twins."

"One can only hope. Did you also hear that I'm going to start cross-training Merlin in the art of tactical detection? If he'd had that training then he would have been able to sniff out the thumb drive sooner than all the time it took for us to discover it."

"Merlin will do great at the new training," Juliette replied. "He's such a smart dog, aren't you, boy?" Merlin ran to her and Elle laughed as he presented his backside to Juliette, obviously looking for a good back rub.

Juliette leaned over and stroked down Merlin's back while Elle opened her locker to retrieve the lunch box that was inside. "So, why were you looking for me?" she asked.

"I heard a rumor, too." Elle closed her locker door and turned to face Juliette.

"What kind of a rumor?" Juliette straightened.

"There are whispers that Blake Colton is coming back to town."

All the color left Juliette's face. "How many whispers?" she asked in a faint voice.

"Enough to believe it's probably true. I just wanted to give you a heads-up." Elle looked at her sympathetically. She knew the secret of Juliette's child, but nobody else did. "What are you going to do?"

"I don't know, but thanks for the heads-up." Juliette stood. "I need to get home."

"I'll see you tomorrow," Elle said.

Minutes later Elle and Merlin were in her car and headed home. Home…to a cozy cabin in the woods. Home…to the man who owned her heart.

When she finally pulled up in front of the cabin, Anders sat on the front porch waiting for her. His black cowboy hat sat at a cocky angle but his smile wasn't as bright as usual.

Was something wrong? Had he changed his mind about her? About them? She and Merlin got out of the car. Merlin raced ahead of her and sat, his butt wiggling as he waited for Anders's hello.

"Hey, boy." Anders scratched the happy dog behind his ears and then stood. "And how was your day?" he asked Elle.

"It was good. What about yours?"

"It was all right." He opened the door and they all went inside. "I've got a big glass of iced tea ready for you in the kitchen."

"Sounds great." She followed him in and sat down at the table, still disturbed by the way he was acting. He hadn't really looked at her and he hadn't kissed her hello like usual.

He remained standing. "Do you want a little snack before dinner? I can get out some crackers and cheese."

"No, I'm good. Anders, is something wrong?" Had he decided he didn't want her anymore? Was he trying to find the words to let her down easy?

"Yes, something is wrong," he said, and frowned. Her stomach clenched. "I've racked my brain all day to figure out a clever way to say what I need to ask you."

Her mouth dried. "Wha-what do you need to ask me?"

He walked closer to her and pulled a small velvet box from his pocket. He then dropped to one knee and held her gaze with his. "Elle, will you marry me?" He opened the box to reveal a beautiful diamond ring. It wasn't the shine of the ring that held her attention, rather it was the shine of love that flowed from his eyes.

She jumped up out of her chair, her heart exploding with joy. "Yes…oh yes, I'll marry you, Anders."

He got to his feet and then slid the ring onto her trembling finger. "I know you can't wear this in public until the Groom Killer is caught since that'll put me on the hit list. But *we* know we're engaged. And I can't wait to pair this ring with a wedding band. I promise to love you forever, Elle."

"And you know what happens if you break that promise?" she asked.

He laughed. "I believe I do know what will happen. You'll shoot me."

She smiled at him. "I can't wait for you to kiss me," she replied.

His eyes sparkled. "My pleasure," he said, and then covered her mouth with his.

The cowboy and the cop, she thought as his lips plied hers with heat. A Colton and a Gage. Name and position didn't matter; together they had magic, and she knew with certainty that the magic would continue throughout the rest of their lives.

* * * * *

Look out for COLTON'S CINDERELLA BRIDE
by Lisa Childs,
the next installment of the
COLTONS OF RED RIDGE *miniseries,*
available in July 2018!

And don't miss the previous
COLTONS OF RED RIDGE *stories,*
all available now from
Harlequin Romantic Suspense!

THE COLTON COWBOY
by Carla Cassidy
COLTON AND THE SINGLE MOM
by Jane Godman
COLTON K-9 COP BODYGUARD
by Lara Lacombe
COLTON'S DEADLY ENGAGEMENT
by Addison Fox
COLTON BABY RESCUE
by Marie Ferrarella

*If you enjoyed this intriguing tale,
don't miss the next chapter of the*
COLTONS OF RED RIDGE *series:*
COLTON'S CINDERELLA BRIDE *by Lisa Childs.*

*When billionaire Blake Colton returns home to
Red Ridge, he finds the woman who's haunted his
dreams. But beautiful K-9 cop Juliette Walsh has a
secret of her own: a little girl who's a Colton!*

Turn the page to get a glimpse of
COLTON'S CINDERELLA BRIDE.

Chapter 1

Everything happens for a reason...

Mama had told Juliette that so many times over the years and so often during the long months of her terminal illness. Not wanting to argue with or upset an invalid, Juliette had just nodded as if she'd agreed with her. But she hadn't really. She had seen no reason for Mama getting sick and dying, no reason for her having to work two jobs to pay off Mama's medical bills and her own community college tuition.

But as she stared up at the little blond-haired angel sitting atop the playground slide, her heart swelled with love, and she knew Mama had been right. Everything happened for a reason, and Pandora was that reason.

Her daughter was Juliette's reason for everything that had happened in the past and for everything that she did in the present.

"Is it too high?" she called up to the little girl, who'd convinced Juliette that since turning four, she was old enough to go down the big kid slide. She was small for her age, though, and looked so tiny sitting up so high that a twinge of panic struck Juliette's heart.

Maybe she was just uneasy because it looked as though it might start storming at any moment. The afternoon sky had turned dark, making it look more like dusk than five thirty. Since July in Red Ridge, South Dakota, was usually hot and dry, rain would be a welcome relief—as long as it came without lightning and thunder, which always scared Pandora.

Juliette probably shouldn't have stopped at the park that apparently everyone else had deserted for fear of that impending storm. But when she'd finished her shift as a Red Ridge K-9 officer and picked up her daughter from day care, the little girl had been so excited to stop and try the slide that she hadn't been able to refuse.

"Come on, honey," she encouraged Pandora as she pushed back a strand of her own blond hair that had slipped free of her ponytail. "I'm right here. I'll catch you when you reach the bottom." She wouldn't let her fall onto the wood chips at the foot of the slide.

"I'm not scared, Mommy," Pandora assured. "It's super cool up here. I can see all around…" She trailed off as she stared into the distance. Maybe she could see the storm moving in on them.

As if she sensed it, too, Sasha—Juliette's K-9 partner—leaped up from the grass on which she'd been snoozing. Her nose in the air, the beagle strained against her leash that Juliette had tethered around a light pole. Sniffing the air, she emitted a low growl.

Despite the heat, a chill passed through Juliette. Sasha had been trained for narcotics detection. But what was she detecting and from where? Nobody else was in the park right now. Maybe the scent of drugs had carried on the wind from someplace else, someplace nearby.

"Mommy!" Pandora called out, drawing Juliette's attention back to where she was now half standing, precariously, at the top of the slide.

"Honey, sit down," Juliette said, her heart thumping hard with fear.

Pandora ignored her as she pointed across the park. "Why did that man shoot that lady with the purple hair?"

Juliette gasped. "What?"

Pandora pointed again, and her tiny hand shook. "Over there, Mommy. The lady fell down in the parking lot and she's not getting back up."

Like her daughter, Juliette was quite small, too, so she couldn't see beyond the trees and playground equipment to where her daughter gestured. She hurried toward the slide and vaulted up the steps to the top. Then she looked in the direction Pandora was staring, and she sucked in a sharp breath. About two hundred feet away, in the parking lot behind the playground area, a woman lay on the ground, a red stain spreading across her white shirt while something red pooled on the asphalt beneath her.

"Oh, no…" Juliette murmured. She needed to get to the woman, needed to get her help…but before she could reach for her cell to call for it, a car door slammed and an engine revved. That car headed over the grass, coming across the playground.

The shooter must have noticed Pandora watching him and knew she'd witnessed him shooting—maybe killing—someone.

Juliette's heart pounded as fear overwhelmed her. She wrapped her arms around Pandora and propelled them both down the slide. Ordinarily her daughter would have squealed in glee but now she trembled with the same fear that gripped Juliette.

The car's engine revved again as it jumped the

curb and careened toward them. Juliette drew her gun from her holster as she gently pushed Pandora into the tunnel beneath the slide. The side of thick plastic tunnel faced the car, which had braked to an abrupt stop. A door creaked open.

Juliette raised her finger to her lips, gesturing at Pandora to stay quiet. The little girl stared up at her, her green eyes wide with fear. But she nodded.

Sasha was not quiet. She barked and growled, straining against her leash. Instinctively she knew Juliette and Pandora were in danger. But with the man between them now, Juliette could not release her partner to help. And maybe that was a good thing. She had no doubt that Sasha would put her own life in danger for hers and especially for Pandora's.

So would Juliette.

Crouched on the other side of the tunnel so he wouldn't see her, Juliette studied the man who'd stepped out of the sedan. He'd pulled the hood of his light jacket up over his head, and despite the overcast sky, he wore sunglasses. He was trying hard to disguise himself. But was it already too late? Had Pandora seen him without the hood and the glasses?

Who was he?

A killer.

She had no doubt that the young woman he'd shot was bleeding out in the parking lot. Frustration and guilt churned inside her, but she couldn't call for help now and alert him to where she'd hidden her daughter. If not for Pandora, the cop part of Juliette would have been trying to take him down—even without backup. But because Pandora was in danger, the mother part of her overruled the cop.

Especially since he was heading straight toward the slide. But Pandora was no longer perched atop it. So he looked around, and he tensed as he noticed the tunnel beneath it. He raised the gun he held at his side, pointing the long barrel toward that tunnel.

Toward Juliette's daughter...

Her heart pounding so hard it felt as if it might burst out of her chest, she raised her gun and shouted, "Police. Drop your weapon! You're under arrest!"

But instead he swung the gun toward her, and his glasses slid down his nose, revealing eyes so dark and so cold that a shiver passed through Juliette.

He shook his head and yelled, "Give me the damn kid!"

And she knew—Pandora had seen him without the hat, without the glasses. Then the wind kicked up again and blew his hood back and Juliette saw his dark curly hair. And something pinged in her mind. He looked familiar to her, but she wasn't sure where she'd seen him before.

"Put down the gun!" she yelled back at him.

But he moved his finger toward his trigger, so she squeezed hers. When the bullet struck his shoulder, his face contorted into a grimace of pain. He cursed—loudly.

"Stop!" she yelled. "Drop the gun!"

But despite his wounded shoulder, he held tightly to his weapon. Before she could fire again, he turned and ran back toward his car. Over his shoulder, he called out, "That kid is dead and so are you, lady cop!"

Juliette started after him. But a scream drew her attention. And a little voice called out urgently, "Mommy!"

The car peeled out of the lot, tires squealing against the asphalt. Juliette stared after it, trying to read the license plate number, but it was smeared with mud. From where? It had been so dry.

He'd planned to obscure that plate. He'd planned to kill that woman.

Now he planned to kill her and Pandora. She moved toward the end of the tunnel and leaned over to peer inside at her daughter. "Sweetheart, are you okay?"

The little girl's head bobbed up and down in a jerky nod. "Are you dead, Mommy?"

A twinge struck Juliette's heart. "No, I'm fine, honey." But that woman was not. She pulled out her cellphone and punched 911. After identifying herself as a police officer, she ordered an ambulance for the shooting victim, an APB on the killer's car and her K-9 team to help.

But she knew they would arrive too late. She doubted that woman could be saved, and she was worried that the killer might not be caught. At least not until he killed again...

And he'd made it clear who his next targets would be. Her and her daughter...

Pandora began to cry, her soft voice rising and cracking with hysteria as her tiny body shook inside the tunnel. Juliette's legs began to shake, too, then gave out so that she dropped to her knees. She crawled inside the small space with her daughter and pulled her tightly into her arms.

Pandora was Juliette's life. She could not lose her. She had to do whatever necessary to protect her.

What the hell am I doing back here?

There was nothing in Red Ridge for Blake Colton. He'd built his life in London and Hong Kong and Singapore—because his life was his business. And those were the cities in which he'd built Blake Colton International into the multibillion-dollar operation that it was.

That was probably why Patience had called him— because of his money—since he and his sister had never been close. He wasn't close to any of his other sisters, either, or to his father or mother. Maybe that was partially his fault, though, because he'd left home so young and had been gone so long now. But Patience hadn't called to see how he was doing; she'd called to ask him to help.

He didn't know how he could provide the kind of help his family needed, though. In addition to their father's business problems, she'd told him about a murderer on the loose. A murderer everyone believed to be a Colton, too; this one was a cousin, so not as distantly related as the other killer Coltons.

Blake pulled his rental vehicle into an empty parking spot outside the long one-story brick building on Main Street: the Red Ridge Police Department. Maybe his cousin Finn, who was the police chief, could explain to him just what the hell was really going on in Red Ridge.

But only Blake could answer the question of what had compelled him to hop on his private plane and head back to Red Ridge. And he had no damn idea…

With a sigh, he pushed open the driver's door and stepped out. The sky was dark with the threat of a storm that hadn't come. Blake felt the weight of those clouds hanging over him like guilt.

He knew what Patience wanted—what she expected him to do. Bail out their father so that their sister Layla wasn't forced to marry some old billionaire to save Colton Energy. How like their father to care more about his company than his kids...

That was the Fenwick Colton Blake knew and had spent most of his life resenting. But he could understand his father a little better now. He didn't have any kids, but his company was like his child. If he withdrew the kind of money required to save Colton Energy, he could cripple his own business and put thousands out of work.

He couldn't do that—not for his father and not even for Layla. There had to be another way. Finn probably wouldn't have any answers to that, but he would know all there was to know about this crazy Groom Killer and if Layla could be in any danger herself because of her engagement.

With a rumble of thunder sounding ominously in the distance, Blake hurried toward the doors of the police department. He didn't want to get caught in a deluge. A woman rushed toward the building, as well. She had one arm wrapped around a child on her hip, her other arm extended with the leash she held of the beagle rushing ahead of her. He stepped forward and reached around her to open the door and, as he did, he caught a familiar scent.

He hadn't smelled it in years. Nearly five years...

But he'd never forgotten the sweet fragrance and the woman who'd worn it. It hadn't been perfume, though. She'd admitted it had been her shampoo, so it had been light, smelling like rain and honeysuckle.

The scent wafted from the woman in front of him, from her hair that was the same pale shade of the long hair of the woman who'd haunted him the past five years. But it couldn't be her...

He'd looked for her—after that night—and hadn't been able to find her anywhere. She must have checked out of the hotel and left town.

She certainly hadn't been a Red Ridge police officer like this woman was. She wore the distinctive uniform of a K-9 cop and carried the leash of her partner. But when she turned back toward him, her gaze caught his and held. And he recognized those beautiful blue eyes...

Remembered her staring up at him as he'd lowered his head to kiss her...

But no, it could not be her. Being back in Red Ridge, staying at the Colton Plaza Hotel, had brought up so many memories of her, of that night, that he was starting to imagine her everywhere.

He'd found her easily enough. But he couldn't take out her or her daughter here—outside the damn Red Ridge police department. Hell, after that bitch had shot him, he could barely raise his arm.

Blood still trickled from the wound, soaking into

his already saturated sleeve. He needed medical attention. But he'd have to find it somewhere other than a hospital or doctor's office. RRPD would have someone watching those places, waiting for him.

Damn the timing…

The park had looked deserted. He hadn't noticed anyone else around—until he'd heard the dog bark. Then he'd seen the little girl—but not before she had watched him fire those shots into that thieving dealer's chest. Did she understand what she'd witnessed?

She was old enough that she probably did. And because he hadn't known anyone else was around, he hadn't had his hood up or glasses on then. So she would be able to identify and testify against him. And so would her damn cop mama.

But that wasn't going to happen.

She and her mother were not going to live long enough to bring him down.

Don't miss
COLTON'S CINDERELLA BRIDE
by Lisa Childs,
coming July 2018,
available wherever
Harlequin Romantic Suspense books
and ebooks are sold.
www.Harlequin.com

COMING NEXT MONTH FROM

⬦ HARLEQUIN®
™

ROMANTIC suspense

Available July 3, 2018

#1999 COLTON'S CINDERELLA BRIDE
The Coltons of Red Ridge • by Lisa Childs

Juliette Walsh is a K9 cop and single mom determined to protect her daughter—be it from the murderer hoping to silence her or devastatingly attractive Blake Colton, the powerful father who could take her little girl away.

#2000 CAVANAUGH'S SECRET DELIVERY
Top Secret Deliveries • by Marie Ferrarella

After helping a stranger deliver her baby, Dugan Cavanaugh never expected to see Toni O'Keefe again. But when the Aurora PD gets involved in taking down a drug cartel, the only journalist who can get Dugan the answers he needs is none other than Toni herself!

#2001 AGENT BODYGUARD
To Protect and Serve • by Karen Anders

The last time NCIS agent Austin Beck saw Jenna Webb, he was a marine guard for the US Embassy and she was the ambassador's wife. Six years and one divorce later, Austin is investigating her cousin's murder. Jenna's safety has to be his number-one priority, no matter the strong, tempting attraction between them.

#2002 BRAVING THE HEAT
Escape Club Heroes • by Regan Black

When a mysogynistic lawsuit turns deadly, firefighter Kenzie Hughes finds refuge with family friend Stephen Galway. He's been living in self-imposed exile since his fiancée's death, but braving the heat with Kenzie might be just what this loner needs...

YOU CAN FIND MORE INFORMATION ON UPCOMING HARLEQUIN® TITLES, FREE EXCERPTS AND MORE AT WWW.HARLEQUIN.COM.

HRSCNM0618

Get 4 FREE REWARDS!

We'll send you 2 FREE Books <u>plus</u> 2 FREE Mystery Gifts.

Harlequin® Romantic Suspense books feature heart-racing sensuality and the promise of a sweeping romance set against the backdrop of suspense.

FREE Value Over **$20**

YES! Please send me 2 FREE Harlequin® Romantic Suspense novels and my 2 FREE gifts (gifts are worth about $10 retail). After receiving them, if I don't wish to receive any more books, I can return the shipping statement marked "cancel." If I don't cancel, I will receive 4 brand-new novels every month and be billed just $4.99 per book in the U.S. or $5.74 per book in Canada. That's a savings of at least 12% off the cover price! It's quite a bargain! Shipping and handling is just 50¢ per book in the U.S. and 75¢ per book in Canada*. I understand that accepting the 2 free books and gifts places me under no obligation to buy anything. I can always return a shipment and cancel at any time. The free books and gifts are mine to keep no matter what I decide.

240/340 HDN GMYZ

Name (please print)

Address   Apt. #

City   State/Province   Zip/Postal Code

Mail to the **Reader Service:**
IN U.S.A.: P.O. Box 1341, Buffalo, NY 14240-8531
IN CANADA: P.O. Box 603, Fort Erie, Ontario L2A 5X3

Want to try two free books from another series! Call 1-800-873-8635 or visit www.ReaderService.com.

---

*Terms and prices subject to change without notice. Prices do not include applicable taxes. Sales tax applicable in N.Y. Canadian residents will be charged applicable taxes. Offer not valid in Quebec. This offer is limited to one order per household. Books received may not be as shown. Not valid for current subscribers to Harlequin® Romantic Suspense books. All orders subject to approval. Credit or debit balances in a customer's account(s) may be offset by any other outstanding balance owed by or to the customer. Please allow 4 to 6 weeks for delivery. Offer available while quantities last.

Your Privacy—The Reader Service is committed to protecting your privacy. Our Privacy Policy is available online at www.ReaderService.com or upon request from the Reader Service. We make a portion of our mailing list available to reputable third parties that offer products we believe may interest you. If you prefer that we not exchange your name with third parties, or if you wish to clarify or modify your communication preferences, please visit us at www.ReaderService.com/consumerschoice or write to us at Reader Service Preference Service, P.O. Box 9062, Buffalo, NY 14240-9062. Include your complete name and address.

HRS18

"If I had someone to come home to, I might be more inclined not to burn the midnight oil."

The sound of Austin's voice and her desire for the same thing dropped on her like a ton of bricks. She glanced at him, but he was polishing off his Danish and didn't look at her. She couldn't read too much into those words. He was just talking.

"Jenna, I think we need to talk about this thing between us."

She set her empty cup on the tray with a thump. She stared at him for a moment. "I know. But I don't want to pick it apart, Austin. I feel something for you and you feel something for me."

"It's not that simple. I'm working on a case that directly involves your family member, we have a past and if my boss finds out I'm sleeping with you... Jesus." He ran his hand through his hair.

"We won't tell her, Austin. It's our business. Sure, we have a past, and we have some things we need to work through and figure out, but I want to do that. You have a life in San Diego and I have one in DC. We have limited time together—do we have to be rational and serious?"

His expression changing again, he reached down and cupped her jaw, running his thumb along her bottom lip. His eyes were dark and shadowed, but she could see the hunger in them. "I'm a realist," he said, his voice gruff. He caressed her mouth again. "I understand what you want to do, but we'll have to face whatever comes. I just don't want to be blindsided, and I don't want to freaking take advantage of you."

She couldn't help but smile through this serious conversation. "Were you there this morning when I seduced you?"

He released a breath on a half laugh. "Right, and, lady, you did a thorough job of it." He caressed her cheek with his thumb. "I'm serious about this. I don't want to hurt you, and I'm not keen on getting hurt."

"I don't want that, either. But can't we just enjoy this for as long as we can? Save the big decisions for later?"

He closed his eyes and pulled her close. She slid her arm around his waist, and her eyes burned as he caught her up in a fierce hold, his face turned against hers. "All right. I'm apparently weak when it comes to you. I can't resist this...or you," he whispered.

She wanted time with him to discover exactly what had driven them apart six years ago. But a little voice whispered in her head, *You're afraid*, as the wind whipped up into a frenzy and blew hard and hot against the complex. She shivered and he drew the covers up over her shoulders.

Or maybe it was because she might discover something she couldn't live without.

Don't miss
AGENT BODYGUARD by Karen Anders,
available July 2018 wherever
Harlequin® Romantic Suspense books and ebooks are sold.

www.Harlequin.com

Need an adrenaline rush from nail-biting tales
(and irresistible males)?

Check out **Harlequin® Intrigue®**
and **Harlequin® Romantic Suspense** books!

New books available every month!

CONNECT WITH US AT:

Harlequin.com/Community

 Facebook.com/HarlequinBooks

Twitter.com/HarlequinBooks

Instagram.com/HarlequinBooks

Pinterest.com/HarlequinBooks

ReaderService.com

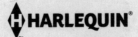

**ROMANCE WHEN
YOU NEED IT**

SGENRE2017

LOVE
Harlequin
romance?

Join our Harlequin community to share your thoughts and connect with other romance readers!

Be the first to find out about promotions, news, and exclusive content!

Sign up for the Harlequin e-newsletter and download a free book from any series at

www.TryHarlequin.com

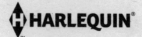